William Walters

Life and Labours of Robert Moffat, D. D., Missionary in South Africa

With Additional Chapters on Christian Missions in Africa and Throughout...

William Walters

Life and Labours of Robert Moffat, D. D., Missionary in South Africa
With Additional Chapters on Christian Missions in Africa and Throughout...

ISBN/EAN: 9783744757317

Printed in Europe, USA, Canada, Australia, Japan

Cover: Foto ©Raphael Reischuk / pixelio.de

More available books at **www.hansebooks.com**

OF

ROBERT MOFFAT, D.D.,

MISSIONARY IN SOUTH AFRICA,

WITH

ADDITIONAL CHAPTERS ON CHRISTIAN MISSIONS IN
AFRICA AND THROUGHOUT THE WORLD.

BY

REV. WILLIAM WALTERS.

———•———

NEW YORK:

ROBERT CARTER & BROTHERS,

530 BROADWAY.

Preface.

CHRISTIAN Foreign Missions, on the scale and in the manner in which they are now carried forward by the Church of Christ, are characteristic of the nineteenth century. Among the men sent out to preach the Gospel to the heathen are some of the greatest and best of the age, and some of the most eminent benefactors of the race. A true missionary is one of the world's highest nobles. The Rev. Griffith John, who has been for above a quarter of a century teaching Christianity in China, said the other day: "I look upon the missionary work as the noblest work under heaven; and I look upon the position of the missionary, though he be the humblest, as the highest and noblest in the world." That is a correct estimate of missionary work and character.

Robert Moffat, whose life has been sketched in the following pages, occupies a place in the front rank of the missionary band. His history is a marvellous illustration of the grandeur and power of goodness, and his labours are full of proof of the saving efficacy and civilising effects of the Gospel of Jesus Christ. He still lives among us, having retired from his more active toils to enjoy in his old days the happy recollections of his past useful life, and to look forward with all the pleasures of a "good hope" to his heavenly reward.

It has been thought well to add two chapters—one on African Missions generally, and another on missions throughout the world—as calculated to increase the usefulness of the book and promote the cause to which Dr. Moffat has devoted his life.

The writer is indebted to many sources for the varied information he has been enabled to collect and present in this volume. While gratefully acknowledging his obligations to all, he would make special mention of "Missionary Labours and Scenes in South Africa," by Robert Moffat; "Ten Years North of the Orange River," by Rev. John Mackenzie; and the "Printed Proceedings of the General Conference on Foreign Missions," held in London in October 1878.

WILLIAM WALTERS.

TYNEMOUTH, *March 1882.*

CONTENTS.

CHAPTER I.

PAGE

CHAPTER II.

CHAPTER III.

CHAPTER IV.

CHAPTER V.

CHAPTER VI.

CHAPTER XVI.

CHAPTER XVII.

CHAPTER XVIII.

CHAPTER XIX.

CHAPTER XX.

CHAPTER XXI.

CHAPTER XXII.

CHAPTER XXIII.

CHAPTER XXIV.

CHAPTER XXV.

CHAPTER XXVI.

CHAPTER XXVII.

CHAPTER XXVIII.

LIFE OF ROBERT MOFFAT, D.D.

CHAPTER I.

FIRST CHRISTIAN MISSIONS TO SOUTH AFRICA.

IN presenting our readers with a narrative of the life and labours of ROBERT MOFFAT, the "Apostle of South Africa," it may be well to devote one or two chapters to some notice of missionary labours in that part of the world prior to his time.

The honour of sending forth the first Christian missionary to South Africa belongs to the Dutch nation. In 1652 the Cape of Good Hope, which was discovered and doubled by Bartholomew Diaz, a Portuguese navigator, as early as 1486, was taken possession of by Holland, and became a Dutch colony. The whole of the district, afterwards designated the colony proper, was inhabited by Hottentots, a degraded, despised, and oppressed race. Some Christian people in Amsterdam hearing of their sad condition were moved with compassion towards them, and resolved to make an effort to promote their present and eternal welfare by providing them with the Gospel. They accordingly applied to the Moravian Church to send out a missionary to the Cape, that he might instruct the natives in the Christian religion.

One George Schmidt, a native of Germany, a man of zeal and courage, offered himself for this service, and in 1736 left Europe for Africa. The following year he arrived at the Cape, and ultimately fixed his residence at a desert place on Sergeant's River, about one hundred and twenty miles east of Cape Town, known by the name of Bavian's Kloof, or the Baboon's Glen—a name which was afterwards changed to Gnadenthal, or the Vale of Grace. Here he assembled many of the people, and began a school, which soon numbered fifty children. He also preached the glad tidings of salvation through Jesus Christ ; and though he could only address these Hottentots through the medium of an interpreter, the blessing of God so rested on his labours that in a short time some of his hearers were led to a saving knowledge of the Gospel, and became true Christians. At the same time the general native population regarded him with reverence and affection. The mission appeared likely to prove very prosperous, and was shewing signs of great encouragement, when, in 1743, circumstances compelled Schmidt to return to Europe.

This enforced abandonment of the work was extremely unfortunate. The enemies of religious instruction, both in the mother-country and the colony, exerted themselves to prevent his resumption of it, and their unhallowed efforts were but too successful. The Dutch East India Company, who exercised authority in the colony, actuated by representations that to instruct the Hottentots would be injurious to colonial interests, refused to sanction the missionary's return to his field of labour. The Church of Holland was in this matter unfaithful to her Lord, and failed in the discharge of her solemn duty, in spite of the earnest representations and entreaties of a faithful few within her pale. The successful opposition to the missionary's departure again for Africa, and resumption of his work there, was all the more distressing to those who sympathised with his noble efforts, because of the intelligence which was received of the anxiety with which the Hottentots awaited his return. Patiently they assembled from time to time to edify one another by reading the word of God, and by praying that their eyes might once more see their teacher. Their desires and prayers, however, were in vain. Every attempt to resume the mission was for the time fruitless.

At length, almost half a century after Schmidt's labours, three other missionaries—Marsveldt, Schwinn, and Küchnel—were allowed to sail for the Cape. They arrived toward the end of November 1792, and were well received. The place indicated to them as the most eligible for a settlement was the very spot which Schmidt had occupied. Accordingly they hastened thither. On their arrival they found part of the walls of his house still standing, and also several fruit-trees planted by him in his garden; among them was a large pear tree, under whose shade they held their meetings for worship until their new dwelling was completed. At a short distance from the remains of the missionary's house other ruined walls marked the site of the humble cottages which his affectionate hearers once inhabited. Among the people who came to visit them was an old woman, who, though about seventy years of age, seemed to have a tolerable recollection of her former pastor, and shewed them a Dutch New Testament which he had given her, and which, from its worn condition, appeared to have been in constant use. She had preserved it as a precious treasure, and, although feeble and bending under the weight of years, she expressed her great joy at their arrival to renew the work which had been abandoned so long. This old disciple spent her last years in peace at the Moravian station, and amidst many bodily sufferings maintained the character of a true child of God.   She died in January 1800, being, as was thought, nearly a hundred years old.

The Hottentots who had any recollection of Schmidt and his labours, or who had heard of them from others, soon gathered around his successors.   A school was opened shortly after their settlement, in which both adults and children received instruction.   Their attendance was most regular, and they manifested an eager desire for learning.   In the first year seven of them professed Christianity.   Many and severe were the trials and distresses of the missionaries; and they were often threatened by their enemies with the destruction of their goods and with death.   But God had them in his safe keeping, so that no harm befel them.   The new converts, too, had to encounter much opposition from the Dutch colonists, and even from some of the officials at Cape Town.   The following incident is worthy of preservation, and cannot fail to be read with interest.   One of the converts, finding that his master wished to prevent his going to the meetings conducted by the missionaries, said to him, "If you will answer for my soul then I will stay." The words arrested the master's attention and pierced his conscience.   "I cannot answer," he replied, "for my own soul, much less for that of another;" and forthwith he granted the servant full permission to go.   In spite of all opposition the work was attended with such success that, in 1799, out of about twelve hundred residents at the settlement of Bavian's Kloof, upwards of three hundred were members of the congregation.   The blessed effects of the Gospel were seen not only in the spiritual change of the people, but also in the general and very marked improvement of their temporal condition.

In March 1799, another devoted band of Christian missionaries, sent out under the auspices of the London

Missionary Society, landed at Cape Town. The chief of these was the Rev. Dr. Vanderkemp, a native of Holland—a man of distinguished talents and attainments, great courage and decision of character, considerable experience, and heroic self-sacrifice. Having cast his eye over the condition of the Hottentots, he concluded that there was scarcely any possibility of making progress among a people so proscribed by Government, and at the mercy of their white neighbours, on whom they could not look without indignation, as any other human beings would have done under similar circumstances; he consequently very naturally directed his steps to those who were yet free from these unjustifiable restrictions. Instead, therefore, of settling amongst the Hottentots, Vanderkemp determined to go and preach to the Caffres. In a few months after his arrival he left Cape Town for Caffraria, the chosen scene of his labours. The country through which he and Mr. Edmonds, his companion, travelled was thinly populated, and they experienced many narrow escapes from wild beasts, as well as from Hottentots and Bushmen, of character still more ferocious. They were, however, kindly treated by the colonists through whose farms they passed, and who embraced every opportunity of hearing them preach. After a journey of about eight weeks they reached the borders of Caffraria, and sent an embassy to Gaika, the king of the country, who invited them to settle in his territories. When, however, they arrived at his residence, and explained their object to him, he informed them that they had come at an unfortunate time, for disturbances had broken out between the colonists and some of his people, which might expose them to danger.

The truth of the matter was, that a deadly strife had long existed, and was now bitterly raging, between the Caffres and the colonial farmers. The former were continually making depredations on the farms of the latter, whom they regarded as intruders, and stealing their cattle; while the latter naturally resisted these raids, and fought for the preservation of their property. It should be stated that the native chiefs affirmed that they were prompted to their conduct by the example set first, and on a larger scale, by the colonists. Such being the state of affairs, Gaika and his people regarded their new visitors as spies, who had come to try to secure their cattle, and probably get possession of their country. The missionaries found their residence among the people full of inconvenience and peril, and not likely to be productive of much good. Mr. Edmonds soon left, and afterwards proceeded to the East Indies. After remaining a few months longer, Vanderkemp also retired from the country, and settled down to labour among the Hottentots. He wrought hard among these people for upwards of ten years, not only imparting religious instruction and seeking their salvation, but endeavouring, by practical sympathy with them in their oppression, by publicly exposing their wrongs and pleading on their behalf, to lighten their temporal lot. Not content with this sphere of self-sacrifice and toil, he had long contemplated a mission to Madagascar; and though he was advanced in years, his soul burned with youthful ardour to enter on that difficult and dangerous undertaking. It was in his heart, but God had ordered otherwise. After a few days' illness he died, in the midst of the Hottentot people, December 15th, 1811. His last words were—" All is well."

Speaking of Vanderkemp's character, Dr. Moffat bears this noble testimony :—" He was a man of exalted genius and learning. He had mingled with courtiers. He had been an inmate of the universities of Leyden and Edinburgh. He had obtained plaudits for his remarkable progress in literature, in philosophy, divinity, physic, and the military art. He was not only a profound student in ancient languages, but in all the modern European tongues, even to that of the Highlanders of Scotland, and had distinguished himself in the armies of his earthly sovereign, in connection with which he rose to be captain of horse and lieutenant of dragoon guards. Yet this man, constrained by the love of Christ, could cheerfully lay aside all his honours, mingle with savages, bear their sneers and contumely, condescend to serve the meanest of his troublesome guests—take the axe, the sickle, the spade, and the mattock—lie down on the place where dogs repose, and spend nights with his couch drenched with rain, the cold wind bringing his fragile house about his ears. Though annoyed by the nightly visits of hungry hyenas, sometimes destroying his sheep and travelling appurtenances, and even seizing the leg of beef at his tent door; though compelled to wander about in quest of lost cattle, and exposed to the perplexing and humbling caprice of those whose characters were stains on human nature—whisperings occasionally reaching his ears that murderous plans were in progress for his destruction— he calmly proceeded with his benevolent efforts, and to secure his object would stoop with the meekness of wisdom to please and propitiate the rude and wayward children of the desert whom he sought to bless. He came from a university to stoop to teach the alphabet to the poor native Hottentot and Caffre—from the society of nobles to associate with beings of the lowest grade in the scale of humanity— from stately mansions to the filthy hovel of the greasy African—from the army to instruct the fierce savage the tactics of a heavenly warfare under the banner of the Prince of Peace—from the study of physic to become the guide to the balm in Gilead, and the physician there—and finally, from a life of earthly honour and ease, to be exposed to perils of waters, of robbers, of his own countrymen, of the heathen, in the city, in the wilderness." "He was little," says another in fewer words, yet not less expressive and true, "behind the chiefest apostles of our Lord."

CHAPTER II.

MOFFAT'S IMMEDIATE PREDECESSORS.

WE have already spoken of Dr. Vanderkemp and his work, but some mention should be made of the labours of others no less devoted, though perhaps not so distinguished—men whose witness is in Heaven and whose record is on high. While Dr. Vanderkemp and Mr. Edmonds proceeded to Caffraria, three of their companions, Messrs. Kicherer, Kramer, and Edwards, directed their way to the Zak River, between four and five hundred miles northeast of Cape Town. Here they laboured with untiring diligence and zeal among the Bushmen, a degraded race. It is scarcely possible to find a more wretched people among all the tribes of the earth. "With the exception of the Troglodytes, a people said by Pliny to exist in the interior of Northern Africa, no tribe or people are surely more brutish, ignorant, and miserable than the Bushmen of the interior of Southern Africa. They have neither house nor shed, neither flocks nor herds. Their most delightful home is afar in the desert, the unfrequented mountain pass, or the secluded recesses of a cave or ravine. They remove from place to place, as convenience or necessity requires. The man takes his spear, and suspends his bow and quiver on his shoulders; while the women, in addition to the burden of a helpless infant, frequently carries a mat, an earthen pot, a number of ostrich egg-shells, and a few ragged skins, bundled on her head or shoulder. Accustomed to a migratory life, and entirely dependent on the chase for a precarious subsistence, they have contracted habits which could scarcely be credited of human beings. Hunger compels them to feed on everything edible—Ixias, wild garlic, mysembryanthemums, the core of aloes, gum of acacias, and several other plants and berries, some of which are extremely unwholesome, constitute their fruits of the field; whilst almost every kind of living creature is eagerly devoured—lizards, locusts, and grasshoppers not excepted. The poisonous as well as innoxious serpents they roast and eat. They cut off the head of the former, which they dissect, and carefully extract the bags, or reservoirs of poison, which communicate with the fangs of the upper jaw. They mingle it with the milky juice of the euphorbia, or with that of a poisonous bulb. After simmering for some time on a slow fire it acquires the consistency of wax, with which they ‚cover the points of their arrows."

To the above description, supplied by Moffat, we may add the further testimony of Mr. Kicherer, whose opportunities, while living among them, of becoming acquainted with their condition were most ample. "Their manner of life is extremely wretched and disgusting. They delight to besmear their bodies with the fat of animals, mingled with ochre, and sometimes with grime. They are utter strangers to cleanliness, as they never wash their bodies, but suffer the dirt to accumulate, so that it will hang a considerable length from their elbows. Their huts are formed by digging a hole in the earth about three feet deep, and then making a roof of reeds, which is, however, insufficient to keep off the rains. Here they lie close together, like pigs in a sty. They are extremely lazy, so that nothing will rouse them to action but excessive hunger. They will continue several days together without food rather than be at the pains of procuring it. When compelled to sally forth for prey, they are dexterous at destroying the various beasts which abound in the country ; and they can run almost as well as a horse. They are total strangers to domestic happiness. The men have several wives, but conjugal affection is little known. They take no great care of their children, and never correct them except in a fit of rage, when they almost kill them by severe usage. In a quarrel between father and mother, or the several wives of a husband, the defeated party wreaks his or her vengeance on the child of the conqueror, which in general loses its life."

The labour of the missionaries among these people was beset by many difficulties and discouragements ; and though some were enlightened, and gave evidence of conversion to God, the mission as a whole proved a failure, and the station was at length given up. Mr. Kicherer having visited Europe, found things on his return in a declining state ; and despairing of resuscitating them, he entered the Dutch church, leaving the station in charge of two brethren. The men to whose care it was entrusted, though distinguished by exemplary patience under great privations and hardships, were at length compelled, in 1806, to retire from the post. On the day of their departure one of them thus writes :— "This day we leave Zak River, the place which has cost us so many sighs, tears, and drops of sweat ; that place in which we have laboured so many days and nights for the salvation of immortal souls ; the place which, probably before long, will become a heap of ruins."

Not altogether disheartened by the small success among the Bushmen at Zak River, the friends of missions made other efforts to benefit this degraded tribe. In 1814 Messrs. Smith and Corner established a mission at Toornberg, south of the Great River. About five hundred Bushmen took up their abode with these brethren, and for a time things looked bright and encouraging. The people however became suspicious of their teachers. There was strife between the Bushmen and the farmers ;- and though the missionaries endeavoured to be just and impartial in all their conduct, they were regarded by many of the Bushmen as agents employed by the farmers to carry out their purposes and plans. Consequently, while a Christian church was formed and Christian civilisation began to dawn, yet the early promise of success was not fulfilled in the results. Another mission, begun among the Bushmen at Hephzibah, passed through a similar experience. It was extremely difficult for the missionaries to keep themselves clear of the disputes between the aborigines and the colonists, and the evils to which their position exposed them soon proved the means of obstructing their labours and blighting all their hopes of usefulness. At length the Cape authorities issued an order requiring all the missionaries to retire within the borders of the colony, and thus evangelising labours among these wild people ceased.

Though Zak River, and the other stations formed specially for the benefit of the Bushmen, did not fulfil the desires and expectations of their promoters, yet they served to point the way and become a stepping-stone to other fields which have since yielded an abundant harvest. It was by means of the mission to the Bushmen and Hottentots of Zak River that the Namaquas, Corannas, Griquas, and Bechuanas became known to the Christian world.

As early as 1801 a Mr. Anderson, who had lately arrived at the Zak, set off for the Orange River, to make known the Gospel in that district. He had to encounter many difficulties, but succeeded in forming the settlement of Griqua Town, together with a number of smaller stations near at hand, in all of which he introduced a knowledge of agriculture, and established order and obedience to authority.

When the Rev. John Campbell visited this station in 1813 he found upwards of two thousand six hundred Griquas and Corannas living near, some of whom were members of the church.

In October 1804, two brothers, Messrs. Christian and Abraham Albrecht, and others, were sent out by the Netherland Missionary Society from Holland to South Africa, and settled in Namaqua Land. The country is described as most destitute and miserable. Moffat says that when he journeyed thither, several years after, he asked a person whom he met on the road, and who had spent years in the country, what was its character and appearance. "Sir," the man replied, "you will find plenty of sand and stones, a thinly scattered population, always suffering from want of water, on plains and hills, roasted like a burnt loaf under the scorching rays of a cloudless sun." The truth of this description was soon proved. The inhabitants of the district were a tribe or tribes of Hottentots, distinguished by all the characteristics of that nation, which includes Hottentots, Corannas, Namaquas, and Bushmen. In their native state they were deeply sunk in ignorance, and were disgusting in their appearance and manners; but their intercourse with such European sailors as had visited them from the western coast, and with other white men professedly Christian, had tended to degrade them lower still. They regarded white men with savage disgust. When Moffat asked one of them why he had never visited the missionary station, his reply was: "I have been taught from my infancy to look upon hat-men (hat-wearers) as the robbers and murderers of the Namaquas. Our friends and parents have been robbed of their cattle, and shot by the hat-wearers."

The devotion of the Albrechts and their companions to the welfare of these people involved much self-sacrifice, toil, and suffering. Those whom they sought to benefit were, moreover, suspicious of their real motives, and utterly unable to appreciate their philanthropic and Christian zeal. The government authorities at the Cape, instead of affording them hearty encouragement, fettered them with needless and annoying restrictions. Nevertheless, some blessing rested on their efforts. They soon had a considerable number of the natives under their care, whose temporal condition was much improved, and not a few, it is hoped, were converted to God.

In February 1815, four other missionaries were sent by the London Missionary Society from England to South Africa. The Rev. John Campbell, who had gone out to visit the stations and report on them and on the prospects of missionary work generally in that part of the world, had represented Lattakoo as a proper place for a station. The new comers, after making two unsuccessful attempts to settle at that town, found the king resolutely opposed to the religious instruction of his people; but at length, after learning that various articles would be sent for the use of himself and his subjects, he mitigated his opposition. They were allowed to build at a new town, about three days' journey from Lattakoo, a commodious place of worship, capable of holding four hundred persons, and a long row of houses, provided with excellent gardens. With the assistance of the Hottentots attached to their service they dug a canal three miles long, by which the whole water of the neighbouring river could be brought into their extensive fields. Still they found the bigoted adherence of the natives to their ancient customs a most powerful barrier in the way both of their civilisation and conversion to Christianity. After all, the seed of Divine truth was not sown by these faithful men in vain. The way was being prepared for that eminent and successful toiler in the same field of whose life and work we begin a record in the next chapter.

CHAPTER III.

SCOTLAND has given to the Church of Christ some of her best men—men who have fought with distinguished bravery in the foremost ranks of the soldiers of the Cross. Of this number Robert Moffat is one. He was born at Ormiston, near Haddington, in Haddingtonshire or East Lothian, in 1795. The county is distinguished for many things. Here are two battle-fields—Dunbar, where Cromwell defeated the Covenanting army in 1650, and Prestonpans, where the Pretender defeated the Royal troops in 1745. It has long enjoyed, in a special degree, high agricultural fame. It produces from year to year abundant crops of the best turnips and potatoes, rape and clover, and wheat. It has also given birth to some eminent men; not the least eminent is the veteran missionary who is the hero of our pages.

Though Ormiston was his birthplace, his youthful years were for the most part spent at Carron Shore, near the great Carron Ironworks, about three miles to the east of Falkirk. Here his father held an appointment in the Customs. The boy was only about twelve years of age when a ship's captain, who was a friend of his father, endeavoured to persuade him to become a sailor, and for this purpose induced him to try a taste of sea-life in a coasting vessel. The first trial however was sufficient. A seafaring occupation was not to the lad's mind, and he returned to school. When the time came for him to leave school, he felt and expressed a strong desire to study botany and horticulture; and that his desire might be gratified, and that he might be trained for some useful calling in life, he was apprenticed as a "Scotch gardener." Some time after this his father was removed from Carron to Inverkeithing, in the county of Fife; and he, going with the family, took service in the Earl of Moray's gardens near that town. After remaining at this post a year he crossed the Tweed (like so many of his calling, for "Scotch gardeners" are to be found in every county of England and Wales), having accepted an invitation to a situation in Cheshire. In this manner God was ordering the plan of his life. He was preparing the way for the circumstances which were to rule the whole current of future years, and He was preparing the man for some of the peculiarities of his life-long work. Moffat filled this 'Cheshire situation with credit to himself and satisfaction to his employers for nearly three years.

The parents of the Scotch youth feared God. The father was such a man as Robert Burns has immortalised in his "Cottar's Saturday Night;" and his consistent example produced on his son its natural impression and result. It was the mother, however, who took the most pains in imparting instruction to the lad of a positively religious nature. Like the mother of Timothy, and tens of thousands of Christian mothers since her day, this excellent woman had set her heart upon his knowing from a child the Holy Scriptures, believing that they were able to make him wise unto salvation, through faith which is in Christ Jesus. She used to talk to him about the progress of the Gospel; and as the labours and hardships of the Moravian Brethren in

Greenland were at that time exciting much interest, she endeavoured to inform the child's mind and fire his heart with the story of their adventurous mission.   When he was about to leave Scotland for Cheshire, she was filled with the deepest concern for his spiritual welfare.   She thought of him, removed from the religious restraints and influences of his pious home, exposed perhaps to many temptations; and having in her mind the truth of the Psalmist's words—it may be the very words themselves—" Wherewithal shall a young man cleanse his way? by taking heed thereto according to Thy word," she earnestly besought him to promise her, before going, that he would read the Bible morning and evening every day.   The request he felt to be one of great importance.   Conscious of his own weakness, and feeling, probably, a boyish disinclination to commit himself to such a course of daily action, he parried the question. At the last moment she pressed his hand, and looking him full in the face, imploringly said—" Robert, you *will* promise me to read the Bible, more particularly the New Testament, and most especially the Gospels—those are the words of Christ Himself, and there you cannot possibly go astray." It was the hour when all his nature was dissolved in filial affection, and he found it impossible to refuse a request thus made by one whom he so dearly loved.   " Yes, mother," he replied, " I make you the promise."   He knew, as he afterwards said when relating the circumstance, that the promise, once made, must be kept; and keep it he did, with sacred honour,—not reluctantly, but with a glad heart.

It was while he was in Cheshire the circumstances occurred which led to his consecration to the missionary cause.   One calm summer's evening he was walking in an abstracted, meditative mood from High Leigh into Warrington, when, just as he had crossed the bridge, a placard caught his eye.   He had never seen one of the kind before. Two lines (it may have been partly from the size of the type) especially arrested his attention; they were "London Missionary Society," and "Rev. William Roby of Manchester." These two lines changed, and henceforth dominated, his whole life. He could not move from the spot or withdraw his eyes from the placard. Passers-by may have thought that he was some ignorant youth thirsting for knowledge, and striving, by the aid of these large letters, to learn to read. He saw that the bill was out of date, the meeting announced having been already held, and that therefore he could receive no instruction or influence from its proceedings. But thoughts had been awakened in his mind that could no longer sleep, and he had already started on a new career. The sight of the placard alone had, to use his own expression, "made him another man;" and between the few hours of his coming to Warrington and returning to Leigh, "an entire revolution had taken place in his views and prospects." The stories his mother had told him concerning the Moravian missionaries, amid the snows and ice of Greenland, were recalled to his memory. He was fired with a noble resolve to emulate their example, and become a messenger of salvation to some benighted part of the world. "A flattering and lucrative prospect, far beyond what such a youth as he could expect," lay before him, but immediately it lost all its attractions. All at once it dwindled into nothingness and vanished out of sight. It was totally eclipsed by the bright prospect of service among the perishing heathen. So thoroughly had the missionary spirit possessed him, that it ruled all his thought and feeling, speech and action. Friends who had both the power and will to serve him, who were ready to further his temporal interests, when they heard him talk about renouncing every prospect in this country, and going to spend his life among savage tribes, said "his brains were turned." "And so they were," he said, "but the right way."

We cannot think of Moffat's decision for a missionary life without reflecting how little we know of the result of our most ordinary conduct.   Sometimes those actions which seem to us the least noteworthy are most fruitful, and live with mightiest power.   When the mother of Moses placed him in a cradle on the banks of the Nile, she could have had no thought of the consequences that would accrue. When Ruth went up with Naomi from Moab to Bethlehem, she never dreamt of the subsequent events by which she was to become ancestress of David, and so of "David's greater son."   Our Lord's disciples little imagined that when they asked Him to teach them to pray, they were providing in form, as well as in substance, for the liturgy of the church through all time.   When Mary anointed our Lord, she had no idea that it would be told for a memorial of her wheresoever the Gospel should be preached, and would become the inspiration and the measure of devotion to His cause.   So, when the Warrington billsticker posted that placard announcing Mr. Roby's visit on behalf of the mission cause, he never thought that it would be a chief agency in sending out to Africa an angel of mercy, whose long residence among its heathen tribes would be one of its greatest and most lasting blessings.   Yet so it was.   He who worketh all things according to the counsel of His own will wrought in this fashion, so ordering His providence, and so influencing His servant's heart.

Other steps led on.   Though he was a stranger to Mr. Roby, and only a youth, he resolved to go to Manchester, seek him out, and tell him all that was in his heart. Arriving in Manchester, he found the minister's house, and with some trepidation and distrust knocked at the door. He was admitted, and the interview served to strengthen his purpose and scatter his fears to the winds.   He sums up all that took place in these few but expressive words:— "He received me with great kindness, listened to my simple tale, took me by the hand, and told me to be of good courage."

The next stage was reached when Robert Moffat, acting under Mr. Roby's advice, offered himself to the Directors of the London Missionary Society. From that point the purposes and plans of Providence ripened fast. After hearing all that the youth had to say, and such opinions of others as were offered in his favour, they declared their satisfaction. The question now came—a most proper question under such circumstances—"Have you acquainted your parents with your purpose?" At this question trembling and faintness seized him, for he had not spoken to them on the matter, and he was afraid they might withhold their consent. Here again his fears were set at rest, and his way made plain. Feeling the claims of God upon themselves, and appreciating the spirit and motives of their son, they replied, when he laid the matter before them—"We have thought of your proposal to become a missionary; we have prayed over it, and we cannot withhold you from so good a work." Thus they surrendered their son to Him who is worthy to receive our best gifts, whose love to us is so great, especially His love in our redemption by Jesus Christ, that we may well say :—

> " Were the whole realm of nature mine,
>   That were a present far too small,
>   Love so amazing, so divine,
>   Demands my soul, my life, my all."

CHAPTER IV.

ALL the preliminary examinations and inquiries having proved satisfactory, Robert Moffat was accepted by the Directors of the London Missionary Society for service in Africa. He was only twenty years of age—a mere stripling—but he was a mature man in self-possession and in Christian faith; and these are the main qualities required in missionary enterprise.

Early in October 1816, he was publicly designated in Surrey Chapel, London, to his work. The meeting at which this was done was one of deep and unusual interest. Nine young men were on that occasion ordained as missionaries. Four of the nine were set apart for the South Sea Islands; the remaining five were appointed to South Africa. Without under-estimating the work or usefulness of any of these honoured men, we cannot help remarking that one in each of these divisions has proved pre-eminently a great man—John Williams, "The Apostle of Polynesia and the Martyr of Erromanga," and Robert Moffat. In the preface to his well-known volume, "Missionary Labours and Scenes in South Africa," Moffat makes this brief allusion to the meeting:—"Of those who began at the same period with himself the career of missionary toil, the greater number have sunk into the grave, and not a few of those who followed long after have also been gathered to their fathers. He is especially reminded of one, much honoured and endeared, whose tragical death, of all others, has most affected him. John Williams and he were accepted by the Directors at the same time, and designated to the work of God, at Surrey Chapel, on the same occasion."

On the last day of October 1816, Moffat sailed for the Cape of Good Hope, and in due time reached the place of his destination. Like the pioneers of Protestant missions in India, he was tried by a discouraging reception; but he was not to be turned aside by the first wind of opposition. He had devoted himself to the cause without wavering, and he entered on his arduous work with self-reliant hope. His first battle was not with the heathen, however, but with the British governor, who was loath to give his sanction to missionaries proceeding outside the Cape Colony, as it was feared that, through want of discretion, they would get the 'tribes of the interior into misunderstandings and broils. He was as firm in his representations and applications as the governor was in his refusals, and patiently waited his time. The post of resident with one of the Caffre chiefs was offered to him, where, in the discharge of his duties, he might have acted as Government agent and as Christian instructor at the same time; but he declined to be fettered, as he felt he must be in such a position, and sought the untrammelled liberty of a missionary of the Cross.

The missionary's time of waiting was not wasted. While he was thus detained in suspense within the colonial territory, he took up his abode with a pious Hollander, who taught him the Dutch language. By this means, on leaving his friend's hospitable roof, he was qualified to preach to the Boers, and to as many of their native servants as had acquired a smattering of this imported tongue.   So he made the best use of his time and opportunities.

At length he was permitted to go up the country.   On his journey he sometimes encountered rather rough treatment.   On the whole, however, he was well received. Many years afterwards, writing with the experience of this up-country journey in mind, he says:—"The Dutch farmers, notwithstanding all that has been said against them by some travellers, are, as a people, exceedingly hospitable and kind to strangers.   Exceptions there are, but few, and perhaps more rare than in any other country under the sun."   On one occasion, while thus going out into the wilderness, he begged of one of these men a night's lodging. The burly farmer roared out his denial like an enraged lion, and the denial itself was less dreadful to the young stranger than the stern and rough tones in which it was conveyed. Nevertheless, he retained his self-possession and common-sense.   His request, negatived by the husband, he made to the wife, and she, having the heart of a woman and a mother, gave the homeless stranger a very different reception.   Cheerfully she offered board and lodging; but she was anxious to know whither he was bound, and what was his errand.   When he told her that he was bound for Orange River, to teach the rude tribes of that country the way of salvation, she exclaimed with astonishment and unbelief—"What! to Namaqua Land, that hot and barbarous region; and will the people there listen to the Gospel, do you think, or understand it if they do?"   The good woman then added that she would be very glad if he would preach in the evening to the family.   The evening came, and arrangements were made for the service.   The Boer had a hundred Hottentots in his employ, but these did not at first appear.   Looking down the long barn in which the meeting was to be held, the young missionary could only see, beside the master of the house and his *frau*, three boys and two girls. "May none of your servants come in?" he said to the master. "Eh!" roared the man; "Hottentots! Are you come to preach to Hottentots? Go to the mountains and preach to the baboons; or, if you like, I'll fetch my dogs, and you may preach to them!" The reply suggested to the quick-witted preacher his text. He had intended taking the question, "How shall we escape if we neglect so great salvation?" but taking the word out of his gruff entertainer's lips, he read as his text, "Truth, Lord; yet *the* dogs eat of the crumbs which fall from their master's table." Again and again was the text repeated with emphasis, and every fresh repetition seemed to drive the nail further into the man's conscience. At last he cried, "No more of that. Wait a moment, and I'll bring you all the Hottentots in the place." He was as good as his word. Soon the barn was crowded, the sermon was preached, and the service gave evident satisfaction to all. After the people had dispersed, the farmer, in much subdued and more pleasant tones, said to Moffat, "Who hardened your hammer to deal my head such a blow? I'll never ,object to the preaching of the Gospel to Hottentots again."

As Moffat was on his way to the Orange River, the nearer he approached the boundaries of the colony the more did the farmers seek to terrify him with their predictions as to the unfavourable reception he would get. Africaner, the powerful chief, who had made his name a terror by his maraudings and murders, was especially represented as a man to be feared. On all hands the young missionary was warned against approaching him. Referring to the dread expressed, he says :—"One said he (Africaner) would set me up as a mark for his boys to shoot at; and another, that he would strip off my skin and make a drum of it to dance to; another most consoling prediction was, that he would make a drinking-cup of my skull. I believe they were serious, and especially a kind motherly lady, who, wiping the tear from her eye, bade me farewell, saying, 'Had you been an old man it would have been nothing, for you would soon have died, whether or no; but you are young, and going to become a prey to that monster.'"

In spite of these prophecies of evil Moffat went on—over desert plains, where sometimes the oxen would sink down in the sand from sheer fatigue, and where the want of water was a terrible infliction; and over rocky mountains, where the exposure to the scorching heat of the hot season was like to induce fever every moment. The following description of passages in the journey is from his own hand:—"The task of driving the loose cattle was not an easy one, for frequently the oxen would take one course, the sheep another, and the horses a third. It required no little perseverance as well as courage, when sometimes the hyena would approach with his unearthly howl, and set the poor timid sheep to their heels; and the missionary, dreading the loss of his mutton, in his haste gets his legs lacerated by one bush, and his face scratched by another, now tumbles prostrate over an ant-hill, and then headlong into the large hole of a wild boar. He frequently arrives at the halting-place long after the waggons, when the keen eye of the native waggon-driver surveys the cattle, and announces to the breathless and thirsty missionary that he has lost some of his charge. He sits down by the fire, which is always behind a bush, if such is to be found, tells his exploits, looks at his wounds, and so ends his day's labours with a sound sleep. Next morning he gets up early to seek the strayed, and if it happen to be a sheep he is almost sure to find only the bones, the hyena having made a repast on the rest. We had troubles of another kind, and such as we did not expect in so dry and thirsty a land. Rain had fallen some time previous in the neighbourhood of Kamies Berg; the loose soil, abounding in limy particles, had become so saturated that frequently, as the oxen and waggons went along the road, they would suddenly sink into a mire, from which they were extricated with difficulty, being obliged to unload the waggons and drag them out backwards."

He describes in another place how they went through a comparatively trackless desert:—" Having travelled nearly the whole night through deep sand, the oxen began to lie down in the yoke from fatigue, obliging us to halt before reaching water. The next day we pursued our course, and on arriving at the place where we had hoped to find water we were disappointed. As it appeared evident that if we continued the same route we must perish from thirst, at the suggestion of my guide we turned northward, over a dreary, trackless, sandy waste, without one green blade of grass, and scarcely a bush on which the wearied eye could rest. Becoming dark, the oxen unable to proceed, ourselves exhausted with dreadful thirst and fatigue, we stretched our wearied limbs on sand still warm from the noontide heat, being the hot season of the year. Thirst aroused us at an early hour, and finding the oxen incapable of moving the waggon one inch, we took a spade and, with the oxen, proceeded to a hollow in a neighbouring mountain. There we laboured for a long time digging an immense hole in the sand, whence we obtained a scanty supply, exactly resembling the old bilge-water of a ship, but which was drunk with an avidity which no pen can describe. Hours were occupied in incessant labour to obtain a sufficiency for the oxen, which, by the time all had partaken, were ready for a second draught; while some, from the depth of the hole and the loose sand, got scarcely any. We filled the small vessels which we had brought, and returned to the waggon over a plain glowing with a meridian sun: the sand being so hot it was distressingly painful to walk. The oxen ran frantic till they came to a place indurated with little sand. Here they stood together to cool their burning hoofs in the shade of their own bodies, those on the outside always trying to get into the centre. Three days I remained with my waggon-driver on this burning plain, with scarcely a breath of wind, and what there was felt as if coming from the mouth of an oven. We had only tufts of dry grass to make a small fire, or rather flame, and little was needful, for we had scarcely any food to prepare. We saw no human being, although we had an extensive prospect; not a single antelope or beast of prey made its appearance, but in the dead of the night we sometimes heard the distant roar of the lion on the mountain, where we had to go twice a-day for our nauseous but grateful beverage."

As the missionary came near the end of his journey fresh difficulties presented themselves. The river had to be crossed, and this was how it was done :—"The waggon and its contents were swam over piecemeal on a fragile raft of dry willow logs, about six feet long, and from four to six inches in diameter, fastened together with the inner bark of the mimosas, which stud the banks of the river, which is at this place five hundred yards wide, rocky, with a rapid current. The rafts are carried a great distance down by the stream, taken to pieces every time of crossing, each man swimming back with a log. When, after some days' labour, all was conveyed to the opposite shore, the last raft was prepared for me, on which I was requested to place myself and hold fast. I confess, though a swimmer, I did not like the voyage, independently of not wishing to give them the trouble of another laborious crossing. I withdrew along the woody bank, and plunged into the river, leaving my clothes to be conveyed over. As soon as they saw me approaching the middle of the current, terrified lest evil should befall me, some of the most expert swimmers plunged in, and laboured hard to overtake me, but in vain; and when I reached the northern bank an individual came up to me, almost out of breath, and asked, 'Were you born in the great sea water?'" After the whole party had safely crossed, great pressure was brought to bear on the missionary to induce him to settle at a station called Warm Bath. The native teacher there and his people beset the waggon, reasoning, pleading, and praying that he would go with them. The women came like a regiment, and declared that if he left them he must take the waggon over their bodies, for they would lie down before the wheels. It was in vain he pleaded the necessity of proceeding first to Africaner, to whom specially he had been sent. At last a party of Africaner's people, with three of his brethren, having heard of Moffat's arrival, were seen approaching in the distance. This ended the painful scene; for, awed by their presence, Magerman, the teacher, and his people retired in grief and tears.

CHAPTER V.

RESIDENCE AT AFRICANER'S KRAAL.

THE post of duty which Moffat was appointed to occupy was on the north-west border of the colony, beyond the Orange River, where a Hottentot family, known as the Africaners, had gathered a body of marauders about them and fixed their abode. Their chief, the eldest of the brothers, had, from his shrewdness and prowess, obtained the reins of the government of his tribe at an early age. He was now outlawed from the colony for the cold-blooded murder of a farmer named Pienaar, who was shot down in the presence of his wife and family. Commandos had gone out against him; rewards were offered for his capture, but he defied the Colonial Government and the farmers, and dared them to approach his territories. Their efforts to take him only roused himself and his followers to further outrages on the scattered residents of the border, until the name of Africaner became a terror throughout the Namaqua Land frontier.

On the 26th of January 1818 Moffat reached Africaner's kraal. His reception was not cordial. The chief kept him waiting for an hour before he came to welcome him. At length he made his appearance, but his manner was cool and reserved. After the customary salutation, he asked if Moffat was the missionary sent out from England. On receiving an affirmative reply, he expressed his pleasure, and said that he hoped himself and his people might long enjoy the missionary's residence in their country. He then ordered a number of women to build a house for the new visitor. Immediately they formed a circle, fixed a number of long slender poles, tied them down in a hemispheric form, covered them with native mats, and had the house finished and ready for habitation in less than an hour. For nearly six months Moffat lived in this hut. It was frequently shaken and loosened by storms, and needed repairs. At the best it was an uncomfortable dwelling-place. He thus describes it:—"When the sun shone, it was unbearably hot; when the rain fell, I came in for a share of it; when the wind blew, I had frequently to decamp to escape the dust; and in addition to these little inconveniences, any hungry cur of a dog that wished a night's lodgings would force itself through the frail wall, and not unfrequently deprive me of my anticipated meal for the coming day; and I have more than once found a serpent coiled up in a corner. Nor were these all the contingencies of such a dwelling, for as the cattle belonging to the village had no fold, but strolled about, I have been compelled to start up from a sound sleep, and try to defend myself and my dwelling from being crushed to pieces by the rage of two bulls, which had met to fight a nocturnal duel."

During the stillness of the first night's repose in this new habitation the young missionary reviewed his past history; he thought of the home and friends he had left, perhaps for ever; he reflected that the vast ocean rolled between them and the present dreary land to which he had come; he thought of the goodness and grace of God towards him in bygone years; and again and again he involuntarily said or sung the grateful lines of Robinson :—

> "Here I raise my Ebenezer,
> Hither by Thy help I'm come."

An unpleasant feeling, of the existence of which Moffat had no previous knowledge, existed between Mr. Ebner the missionary whom he had joined, and who had resided at the station some time, and the people. This hostility culminated in a quarrel with one of Africaner's brothers, and in Mr. Ebner's determination to leave the place for Warm Bath, where the chief Bondlezwarts had invited him to labour. Ebner's departure left Moffat alone with a people suspicious in the extreme, and jealous of their rights, which they had obtained by hard and bloody conflict. He felt his isolated condition keenly. "I had no friend or brother," he writes, "with whom I could participate in the communion of saints,—none to whom I could look for counsel and advice; a barren country; a small salary of £25 per annum; no grain, and consequently no bread, and no prospect of getting any, from the want of water to cultivate the ground; and destitute of all means of sending to the colony."

But this servant of God knew the secret of strength and peace. Mark his testimony :—"These circumstances led to great searchings of heart, to see if I had hitherto arrived at doing and suffering the will of Him in whose service I had embarked. Satisfied that I had not run unsent, and having in the intricate and sometimes obscure course I had come heard the still small voice saying, 'This is the way, walk ye in it,' I was wont to pour out my soul among the granite rocks surrounding this station, now in sorrow and then in joy; and more than once I took my violin (once belonging to Christian Albrecht), and reclining on one of the huge masses, have, in the stillness of the evening, played and sung the well-known hymn, a favourite with my mother :—

> 'Awake, my soul, in joyful lays,
> To sing the great Redeemer's praise,'" &c.

Apart from his confidence in God, Moffat's natural qualities fitted him in the highest degree for the perilous and difficult service in which he was now engaged. He displayed in a remarkable manner promptitude, shrewdness, firmness, and tact. If you study the portraits of him as he looked when he was in the maturity and fulness of his strength, you see in his eye and in his whole bearing that he was born to manage men. Had he continued in his secular calling he would no doubt have been a most successful man of business. The grace of God consecrated his natural faculties, and so he became an able and a successful missionary.

His fitness for the work which he had undertaken was thoroughly tested at the very outset; but his wisdom was equal to every emergency, and his chivalrous devotion rose as hardships and difficulties increased. In spite of the barrenness of the country, the want of water, the thinness of the population, the dangers that surrounded him, he began his work. He established stated services for worship and instruction, which, according to the missionary custom of that period, were public worship morning and evening, and school for three or four hours during the day. He travelled among the surrounding villages, speaking to the people about Christ and His great salvation, wherever and whenever an opportunity offered. His food was milk and flesh; living for weeks together on one, and then on the other, and then for a while on both, often having recourse to a "fasting girdle."

The chief Africaner himself was one of Moffat's most regular and attentive hearers. Already he had manifested some interest in religion, hence the missionary's visit to his kraal. There had been, however, much vacillation in his conduct, and for some time past he had been in a doubtful state. Now he attended the services with regularity, and the rise of to-morrow's sun might have been as well doubted as his attendance on the appointed means of grace. One of his brothers, who was a terror to most of his neighbours, and a fearful example of wickedness, became also a greatly altered man, and a steady and unwavering friend to the missionary. He was the only person of importance who had two wives, and resisted all persuasion to give either of them up, though he admitted that a man with two wives was not to be envied. "He is often in an uproar," he added, "and when they quarrel he does not know whose part to take." Two other brothers were zealous assistants in the mission work of the station, and truly Christian men.

So Moffat laboured for years. Often it seemed to him as if he was beating the air, and his soul was heavy and sank within him. It was well that he had outward as well as inward resources. He could put his hand to anything; this helped him to pass away many hours in a pleasant and useful manner that otherwise would have proved very long and wearisome. It also secured him respect from the Namaqua men more than his learning. "My dear old mother," he tells us himself, "to keep me out of mischief in the long winter evenings, taught me to knit and sew. When I would tell her I meant to be a man, she would say, 'Lad, ye dinna ken whaur your lot may be cast.' She was right, for I have often had occasion to use the needle since." He was not seldom in sore straits for food, but he only found more time for prayer. He travelled, and taught, and preached without faltering, and after many days the blessing came.

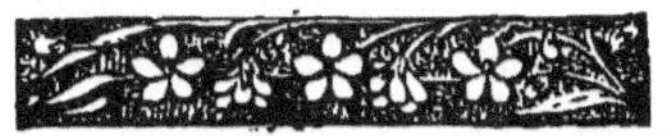

CHAPTER VI.

TRAVELLING IN THE INTERIOR.

AFTER some stay at Africaner's station Moffat discovered that the general character of the place and the condition of the people were such that he never could make it a permanent residence. Having come to this conclusion, he resolved on a journey of exploration in a northerly direction, that he might examine a country near Damara Land, which was said to abound with fountains of water. But how was such a resolution to be carried into effect? He had only one waggon, and that was in a broken-down state. There were neither carpenters nor smiths on the station to repair the vehicle; and the unfordableness of the Orange River at the time, and the ricketty condition of the waggon, rendered it impossible to convey it to Pella, where it might have been repaired.

There was only one course, and that was for the missionary to try and repair it himself. He had seen the smiths at work in their shops at Cape Town, and had picked up a few lessons, which he now brought to bear upon the necessities of the case. His first effort to weld some iron was unsuccessful, owing to the imperfection of the native bellows employed; but setting his wits to work, he soon made improvements in the instrument, and had all the people around him to witness the success of his operations. Finishing what was necessary for the waggon, he then repaired the gun-locks, which were as essential for the comfort and success of the journey as the waggon. Everything being in readiness, he started with an exploring party of thirty men. Although at first the formidable appearance of so large a party was not to Moffat's mind, yet he afterwards found that it was none too large. Africaner had suggested that a large party would have the tendency of preventing any attack, and in this it turned out he was perfectly right.

The following specimen of African travel will be interesting to our readers :—"The country over which we passed was sterile in the extreme, sandy from the abundance of granite. Ironstone was also to be found, and occasionally indications of copper. Slaty formations were also to be met with, and much quartz, filling up large fissures occasioned by former convulsions, and the hills in some places presenting a mass of confusion ; the strata bending and dipping from the perpendicular to the horizontal, and in others extending in a straight line from one hill to another. Native iron, in a very pure state, is procured in these regions ; and from the account given by the natives, I should suppose some of it is meteoric. The plains are invariably sandy, and there are even hills of pure sand. I also found near some of the mountains large pieces of trees in a fossil state. Zebras abounded, and wild asses, though less numerous than the former. Giraffes were frequently met with, sometimes thirty or forty together. Elks, koodoos, and the smaller species of antelopes were also in great numbers. The rhinoceros (the kenengyane, or black chukwm of the Bechuanas) is also to be found, but scarce. Buffaloes had nearly disappeared, at least in the region I visited. We had a tolerable supply, chiefly of the flesh of zebras and giraffes ; the latter, when fat, was preferred, though nothing came amiss to hungry travellers. When one of the larger animals was shot, we generally remained a day to cut the meat up into thin pieces, which, spread on the bushes, soon dried. The best parts were always eaten first; and when pressed with hunger, recourse was had to the leaner portions, which had been stowed away in the waggon; and to make it palatable (for it much resembles a piece of sole leather) it was necessary to put it under the hot ashes, and then beat it between two stones till the fibres were loosened; and then it required very hard chewing: and many. a time have I risen from a meal with my jaw-bone so sore I felt no inclination to speak. Meat prepared in this way, or fresh, with a draught of water, was our usual fare. I had a small quantity of coffee with me, which, as long as it lasted, I found very refreshing. Some may think that this mode of life was a great sacrifice, but habit makes it much less so than they suppose. It is true I did feel it a sacrifice to have nothing at all to eat, and to bind the stomach with a thong to prevent the gnawing of hunger, and, under these circumstances, to break the bread of eternal life to the perishing heathen. Water was in general very scarce; sometimes in small pools, stagnant, and with a green froth; and more than once we had to dispute with lions the possession of a pool. One day our guide (for it was a country without roads) led us towards a ravine which presented an animated appearance, the sides of the hills being covered with a lovely green, but on our reaching them, scarcely anything was to be seen but a species of euphorbia, useless either to man or beast, and through which we with difficulty made our way. Being hot, and the oxen worn out, we halted; and some of the men having been successful in finding honey in the fissures of the rocks, we ate with no little relish, thinking ourselves fortunate, for food was scarce. Shortly after, an individual complained that his throat was becoming very hot; then a second, then a third,

till all who had eaten felt as though their throats were on
fire.   A native coming up, and seeing our hands and faces
besmeared with honey, with the greatest simplicity said :
' You had better not eat the honey of this vale ; do you not
see the poison bushes (euphorbia), from the flowers of which
the bees extract the honey and the poison too ?'   Every one
had recourse to the little water that remained in the vessels,
for the inward heat was terrible ; and the water, instead of
allaying, only increased the pain.   No serious consequences
followed, but it was several days before we got rid of a most
unpleasant sensation in the head as well as the throat."

On their journey the party occasionally came to a Namaqua village : in such cases they always halted for a day or
two, so that the people might hear the Gospel of salvation.
They continued their journey till they reached some of the
branches of the Fish River, where they were brought to a
stand.   The inhabitants of the district were suspicious of
their visit, and it was not quite certain whether they would
flee or endeavour to oppose their progress.   Probably if the
travelling party had been smaller the latter course would
have been adopted.   Notwithstanding their suspicions, they
listened with great attention to the Gospel message.   Here
they met a native sorcerer, who, the previous night, had
made the people believe that he had entered into a lion
which had been killing their cattle.   Moffat coaxed him
into conversation by giving him a piece of tobacco, but he
declined to suffer his powers to be tested, adding that
Moffat was a white sorcerer himself, from the strange
doctrines he taught.

At Africaner's suggestion, the party, instead of proceeding
further, determined to return.   The report received of the
country further north was not encouraging, and there was
some risk of resistance, and consequently the shedding of
blood.   On their homeward route they halted at a spot
where a strange scene once occurred, and which was described

AN INCIDENT IN THE LIFE OF PARK

by an individual who witnessed it when a boy. Moffat thus refers to it:—"Near a very small fountain, which was shewn to me, stood a camel-thorn-tree *(Acacia Giraffe).* It was a stiff tree, about twelve feet high, with a flat, bushy top. Many years before, the relater, then a boy, was returning to his village, and having turned aside to the fountain for a drink, lay down on the bank and fell asleep. Being awoke by the piercing rays of the sun, he saw, through the bush behind which he lay, a giraffe browsing at ease on the tender shoots of the tree, and to his horror a lion, creeping like a cat only a dozen yards from him, preparing to pounce on his prey. The lion eyed the giraffe for a few moments, his body gave a shake, and he bounded into the air to seize the head of the animal, which instantly turned his stately neck, and the lion missing his grasp, fell on his back in the centre of the mass of thorns, like spikes, and the giraffe bounded over the plain. The boy instantly followed the example, expecting, as a matter of course, that the enraged lion would soon find his way to the earth. Some time afterwards the people of the village, who seldom visited that spot, saw the eagles hovering in the air, and as it is almost always a certain sign that the lion has killed game or some animal is lying dead, they went to the place and sought in vain, till, coming under the lee of the tree, their olfactory nerves directed them to where the lion lay dead in his thorny bed. I still found some of his bones under the tree, and hair on its branches, to convince me of what I scarcely could have credited. The lion will sometimes manage to mount the back of a giraffe, and, fixing his sharp claws into each shoulder, gnaw away till he reaches the vertebræ of the neck, when both fall; and oftimes the lion is lamed for his trouble. If the giraffe happens to be very strong, he succeeds in bringing his rider to the ground. Among those that we shot on our journey, the healed wounds of the lion's claws on the shoulder, and marks of his teeth on the back of the neck, gave us ocular demonstration that two of them had carried the monarch of the forest on their backs, and yet came off triumphant."

They endeavoured to return by a shorter route farther to the east, but nearly paid heavily for their haste, for they found themselves in a plain of deep sand, and thought at one time they would have to abandon their waggon. Every one went in search of water, but none could be found ; and though they met with some water-melons, they were bitter as gall. When at length a number of them found water and drank some, their thirst became excessive. The whole party hastened to the river, and a most exciting scene ensued. All the people, without exception, rushed down the bank ; some kept their feet, others rolled, and some tumbled headlong into the muddy pool, or deep bed at the top of the river. It was well that the water was warmed by the scorching rays of the sun ; for instances have been known of thirsty travellers drinking largely in their heated state, and dying at once with their faces in the water. This journey to the north and back decided Moffat to remain for the present at Africaner's station.

He now resumed on a larger scale his itinerating expeditions. Riding on the back of an ox with horns was both awkward and dangerous. Cases have occurred of persons so riding having been thrown forward on the horns and killed. Yet this was at times the only mode of travel. These preaching journeys were often full of privations as well as dangers. Owing to the migratory habits of the people in search of water and grass, they could not always be found. Starting in the morning, having breakfasted on a good draught of milk, he and his interpreter would travel slowly all day, and in the evening reach their proposed destination, to find the natives all removed, having left nothing but empty huts. The only living creatures to be seen would be some vultures or crows perched on a bush or rock, picking up bits of skin

and other refuse.   Hungry and thirsty they would lie down
to rest, not seldom disturbed by visits from hyenas, jackals,
and sometimes the lion himself.   The first concern the next
morning would be to find water; if successful, they would
breakfast on a draught, and again set off on their lonely
course, going slowly, not to lose the spoor, or track, and
thankful if at last they succeeded in finding the wanderers.

Frequently, after a long and hot day's ride, they would
reach a village in the evening, and after taking a drink of
sweet milk, gather young and old in a nook, that the
missionary might address them on the nature and importance
of salvation.   When the service was over, he would take
another draught of milk, renew his conversation with the
people, and then lie down on a mat to rest for the night.
Sometimes a kind and thoughtful housewife would hang a
wooden vessel filled with milk on a forked stick near his head,
that he might, if necessary, drink through the night.   Once
he slept on the ground near the hut of the principal man in
the village.   In the night he heard something moving about
outside the thorn fence, and in the morning he said to
the man, "It looks as if some of your cattle have broken
loose."   "Oh," he replied, "a lion has been;" adding, "A
few nights ago he sprang over on to the very spot on which
you have been lying, and seized a goat and carried it off.
Here are some of the mats we tore from the house and
burned to frighten him away."   When Moffat asked him
how he could think of choosing that spot for him to sleep
on, he exclaimed, "Oh, the lion would not have had the
impudence to jump over on you!"

CHAPTER VII.

AS we have seen, Moffat and his party were often exposed to danger from lions, which from the scarcity of water frequented the pools or fountains. One night they were encamped at a small pool, when, just as they had closed their evening worship, they heard the terrific roar of a lion. The oxen, which were quietly chewing their cud, rushed about in terror, trampled down the fires, knocked down the men, and left them prostrated in a cloud of dust and sand. Hats and hymn-books, Bibles and guns, were all scattered in wild confusion. Providentially the forest king did not make his appearance, and no great harm was done.

Going on one occasion through a valley, they came to a spot where the lion appeared to have been taking leaping exercise. Presently they met a native who had been an eye-witness of what had transpired. A large lion had crept towards a short black stump, very like a man; when about a dozen yards off he bounded on his imagined prey, but fell a foot or two short. For a time he lay steadfastly eyeing his supposed meal, then arose, smelt it, and returned to the spot whence he had taken his leap. The first leap was followed by four others in succession, till at last he placed his paw on the object. Discovering his mistake, he turned away in disappointment and disgust. Moffat relates another lion scene witnessed by Africaner. A troop of zebras were passing round a rock when a lion attempted to leap on the large stallion, which always brings up the rear, but missed his mark. After repeated attempts, and ultimate failure, two more lions came up, and the whole party seemed to enter on a serious consultation. After they had indulged in an interchange of roars, the first lion led the other two twice round the rock, and closed the conference by making a final grand leap, as if to shew what could and must be done. After this the trio departed, and were seen no more. At that time an encounter of some sort with a lion was one of the most common adventures in South African travelling. One night about a dozen hunters were sleeping around a fire, within a circle of bushes; as soon as the blaze of the fire was out a lion sprang in upon them, seized one by his shoulder, and conveyed him to some distance. The others, aroused by the noise, fired in the direction of the retreating lion and hit him. In the act of roaring he let the man drop, who immediately bolted in among his companions. Moffat afterwards saw the marks of the lion's teeth in the man's shoulder.

We cannot resist the temptation to add another scene of African life:—"A man belonging to Mr. Schmelen's congregation at Bethany, returning homewards from a visit to his friends, took a circuitous course in order to pass a small fountain, or rather pool, where he hoped to kill an antelope to carry home to his family. The sun had risen to some height by the time he reached the spot, and seeing no game, he laid his gun down on a shelving low rock, the back part of which was covered over with a species of dwarf thornbushes. He went to the water, took a hearty drink, and returned to the rock, smoked his pipe, and being a little tired, fell asleep. In a short time the heat reflected from the rock awoke him, and opening his eyes, he saw a large lion crouching before him, with its eyes glaring in his face, and within little more than a yard of his feet. He sat motionless for a few minutes, till he had recovered his presence of mind, then eyeing his gun, moved his hand slowly towards it.. The lion seeing him, raised its head, and gave a tremendous roar; he made another and another attempt, but the gun being far beyond his reach he gave it up, as the lion seemed well aware of his object, and was enraged whenever he attempted to move his hand. His situation now became painful in the extreme; the rock on which he sat became so hot that he could scarcely bear his naked feet to touch it, and kept moving them, alternately placing one above the other. The day passed, and the night also, but the lion never moved from the spot; the sun rose again, and its intense heat soon rendered his feet past feeling. At noon the lion rose and walked to the water, only a few yards distant, looking behind as it went, lest the man should move, and seeing him stretch out his hand to take his gun, turned in a rage, and was on the point of springing upon him. The animal went to the water, drank, and returning, lay down again at the edge of the rock. Another night passed : the man, in describing it, said he knew not whether he slept, but if he did, it must have been with his eyes open, for he always saw the lion at his feet. Next day, in the forenoon, the animal went again to the water, and while there he listened to some noise apparently from an opposite quarter, and disappeared in the bushes. The man now made another effort, and seized his gun; but on attempting to rise, he fell, his ankles being without power. With his gun in his hand he crept towards the water and drank, but looking at his feet he saw, as he expressed it, his 'toes roasted,' and the skin torn off with the grass. There he sat a few moments

THE ABANDONED MOTHER — AN INCIDENT IN THE LIFE OF MOFFAT

expecting the lion's return, when he was resolved to send the contents of the gun through its head ; but as it did not appear, tying his gun to his back, the poor man made the best of his way on his hands and knees to the nearest path, hoping some solitary individual might pass. He could go no further, when, providentially, a person came up who took him to a place of safety, from whence he obtained help, though he lost his toes and was a cripple for life."

The missionary tells a heart-rending story of the way in which aged parents are sometimes abandoned by their own children. During one of his journeys, he was so sleepless one night through thirst that he rose very early in the morning, and set off with a companion in search of water. After walking a great distance, they saw smoke curling up among the bushes. The sight quickened their steps, as they expected now to be able to quench their thirst. Approaching the bushes, they were startled to see by footprints on the sand that lions had been there only a short time before. Still the thirst for water, and the hope of obtaining it, overcame their fear, and they hurried on. Reaching the spot whence the smoke ascended, they beheld an object of heart-rending distress. Crouching on the ground before the fire was an old woman, with her head leaning on her knees. She was terrified at their presence, and tried to rise, but, trembling with weakness, fell to the ground. After her fears had been overcome by the kindness of her visitors, she told them that four days ago her children, three sons and two daughters, had gone away and left her there to die. When asked why they had abandoned her, she replied, spreading out her hands, "I am old, you see, and I am no longer able to serve them. When they kill game, I am too feeble to help in carrying home the flesh ; I am not able to gather wood to make fire ; and I cannot carry their children on my back as I used to do." Though the missionary's tongue was cleaving to the roof of his mouth for want of water, yet the sight of the old woman forsaken by her children to die, and her touching story, made his eyes fountains of tears. They would have taken her with them, but she was so terrified at the proposal that death seemed imminent. They collected wood, therefore, to replenish the fire, gave her some dried meat, some tobacco, a knife, and other necessaries, and telling her to keep up a good fire, left, promising to return. On the way back, true to his word, Moffat went to the spot, but the old woman was nowhere to be seen. Months afterwards he heard that her sons having heard of his visit, feared that he was a great chief who would come and punish them for their cruelty, and so fetched her away, and took her once more to their home.

Moffat's general mode of living in Namaqua Land was very plain ; there was, as we have remarked already, little variety in his food. He had neither bread nor vegetables. A friend once sent him, from Pella, a bag containing a few pounds of salt ; but when he came to use some he could scarcely tell whether there was most sand or salt, and having become accustomed to do without it, he hung it upon a nail, where it remained untouched. Sometimes, after the morning service, he would shoulder his gun, and go to the plain or the mountain in search of something to eat. His raiment was as scanty as his food was plain. The clothes he carried from England soon wore out. There were no laundrymaids there, nor anything like ironing or mangling. The old woman who washed his linen, sometimes with soap, oftener without, used to make one shirt into a bag and put the others in it. When he was a youth at home, his mother once shewed him how to smooth a shirt by folding it properly, and pounding it with a piece of wood. Wanting a nice shirt on one occasion, he folded it up, placed it on a block of fine granite, and with a mallet of wood hammered lustily. When he had finished he found the shirt riddled with holes, some large enough to receive the point of his finger. Thus, like the first preachers of the Gospel, he was in much patience, in necessities, in labours, in watchings, in fastings; yet with Paul he could say, "I have learned in whatsoever state I am therein to be content. I know how to be abased, and I know also how to abound; in everything and in all things have I learned the secret both to be filled and to be hungry, both to abound and to be in want."

CHAPTER VIII.

THOUGH Moffat still continued to labour in Namaqua Land, it was felt that another attempt should be made to find a more convenient spot for the mission. Africaner was as anxious to leave as Moffat, and he urged a visit of inspection to the Griqua country, to which he and his people had been invited by the Griqua chiefs. Accordingly Moffat, with two of Africaner's brothers, his son, and a guide, undertook the journey. Their course lay chiefly on the north side of the Orange River. They found few villages on their way, and these were small, with a scanty population. They suffered much from hunger and thirst. Sometimes they were compelled to scramble over the rocks, where baboons were numerous and impudent; at other times they had to cross the river. On reaching the Falls, the river presented the appearance of a plain, miles in breadth, entirely covered with mimosa trees, among which the many branches of the river run, and then tumble over the precipices, raising clouds of mist. Here Moffat learnt something of the habits of African crows. He was reclining on a rock one day, when he noticed a crow rise from the earth, carrying something dangling in its talons. On directing his companions to the sight, they said, "It is only a crow with a tortoise—you will see it fall presently;" and down it fell. The crow descended, and up went the tortoise again to a still greater height, from which it dropped, and the crow instantly followed. On hastening to the spot they found the crow feasting on the mangled tortoise; and looking around the flat rock, they saw the place covered with the shells of victims that had been slain in the same manner. The natives said the kites killed the tortoises after the same fashion.

"The windings of the river sometimes flowed through immense chasms, overhung with stupendous precipices, and then like a translucent lake, with the beautiful towering mimosas and willows reflected from its bosom, and a rich variety of birds, of fine plumage, though without a song; wild geese, ducks, snipes, flamingoes, in perfect security feeding on the banks, beneath the green shade, or basking in the sun's rays on the verdant islands, far from the fowler's snare. The swallows also, mounting aloft, or skimming the surface of the mirror stream; while the ravens, with their hoarse note, might be seen seeking their daily food among the watery tribe, or cawing on the bending tops of the weeping-willows. Flocks of guinea-fowl would occasionally add to the varied scene, with their shrill cry and whirling flight from the open plain to the umbrage of sloping bank, where they pass the night amidst the branches of the tall acacias. But here, too, the curse reigns; for the kites and hawks might be seen hovering in the air, watching the motions of the creatures beneath, and ready to dart down with the fleetness of an arrow on a duckling straying from its parent, or on a bird or a hare moving too far from the shelter of a bush or tree. The fox might also be seen stealing slowly along from the desert waste to slake his thirst in the refreshing stream, and seek for some unfortunate brood which might fall within his reach, and the cobra and green-serpent ascending the trees to suck the eggs or to devour the young birds; while the feathered tribe, uniting against the common enemy, gather around and rend the air with their screams. The African tiger, too, comes in for a share of the feathered spoil. With his sharp claws he ascends the trees in the dead of night, and seizes the guinea-fowls on their aerial roost. The hyena, also, here seeks his spoil, and gorges some strayed kid, or pursues the troop for the new-fallen antelope or foal; and to fill up the picture, the lion may be heard in the distance roaring for his prey."

As they journeyed on they fell in with various kinds of persons, and their reception changed according to the character of the people whom they met. When they came upon any among whom missionaries had sojourned they at once felt at home, and were treated with kindness. At other times the people would neither give them meat nor drink.

This journey was full of adventure. On one occasion Moffat experienced a marvellous escape from death through drinking poisoned water. After a long ride under a burning sun, they came one afternoon to a little pool branching off from the river, and being thirsty he dismounted, and lay down to drink. Immediately he felt a strange taste in his mouth, and looking at the water, and the bush fence round it, suspected it was poisoned for the purpose of killing any game who might come there to drink. At that moment a Bushman from a village near by came running in breathless haste, and took him by the hand, as if to prevent him from approaching the water, and talking in a very excited manner, though they could not understand a single word. When Moffat made signs that he had drank, the poor man seemed for a moment struck dumb, and then hastened back to the village. Moffat and his party followed. The poor Bushmen looked on the poisoned man with great compassion;

but when they found that though shewing symptoms of the effects of the poison, yet he did not die, they grew frantic with joy—the women striking their elbows against their naked sides. Soon after they gave the travellers some meat of zebras which had died the previous day from drinking this poisoned water; and the missionary says that having fasted all day he enjoyed a steak of the black-looking flesh with its yellow fat.

The dangers of the journey were many and great. One evening they had scarcely ended their worship before retiring to rest, when the howls of the hyena and the jabbering of the jackal announced that these were to be their companions for the night. To these sounds were added a blowing and snorting chorus from the hippopotami on the river. When a little while after the dismal notes of the hooting owl were heard also, one of the men remarked, "We want only the lion's roar to complete the music of the desert."

At times they were reduced almost to starvation. One evening, after two days' fasting, they reached a bushless plain, and made a fire. The terrific roar of a lion soon startled them, and as it was again and again repeated, kept them in a state of terror. They resumed their journey in haste, and at last escaped the danger, and halted to rest. "The last sound we heard to soothe us," says Moffat, "was the distant roar of the lion, but we were too much exhausted to feel anything like fear. Sleep came to our relief, and it seemed made up of scenes the most lovely, forming a glowing contrast to our real situation. I felt as if engaged, during my short repose, in roving among ambrosial bowers of paradisaical delight, hearing sounds of music as if from angels' harps: it was the night wind falling on my ears from the neighbouring hill. I seemed to pass from stream to stream, in which I bathed and slaked my thirst at many a crystal fount flowing from golden mountains enriched with living green. These Elysian pleasures continued till morning dawn, when we awoke speechless with thirst, our eyes inflamed, and our whole frames burning like a coal. We were, however, somewhat less fatigued, but wanted water, and had recourse to another pipe before we could articulate a word." He went in search of water, but could find none. Happening to cough, he was instantly surrounded by almost a hundred baboons, some of them very large. They grunted, grinned, and sprang from rock to rock, protruding their mouths, and drawing back the skin of their foreheads, threatening an instant attack. Though he had his gun with him he dared not fire, for if he had wounded one of them, he would have been skinned in five minutes. After a time they halted and appeared to hold a noisy council, and the traveller passed on unharmed.

It was on this journey that Moffat first saw the *mirage*. Still searching for water, they were driving slowly and silently over the burning plain when this strange phenomenon tantalised them with exhibitions of pictures of lakes and pools studded with lovely islets, and magnificent trees on their banks. Some seemed to be mercantile harbours, with jetties, coves, and moving rafts and oars. Sometimes the heat was so intense that they thrust their heads into old ant-hills excavated by the ant-eater, that they might have something solid between their heated brains and the fierce rays of the sun. The crown of the head felt as if covered with live coal, and their minds began to wander. At length they came to water. Not daring to drink at once, they rested for a while under a bush to cool. When they ventured to drink, although the pool was moving with animalculæ, muddy, and nauseous with filth, it furnished a reviving draught. That night they reached their journey's end. At a late hour they arrived at the house of Mr. Anderson, one of the missionaries at Griqua Town. Moffat entered the door haggard and speechless, covered with perspiration and dust, but at once procured, by signs, a draught of water. Afterwards he was refreshed with a cup of coffee and some food, which he had not tasted for three days.

Moffat found the society of the missionaries and their wives at Griqua Town most refreshing. The crowded and attentive congregation, and the work of education in the daily school, soon caused him to forget all the inconveniences and hardships of the journey, and he found unspeakable joy in preaching to the Griquas the glad tidings of redemption. From Griqua Town he went on to Lattakoo, about a hundred miles to the north, on the Kuruman River. Here he received a hearty welcome from the missionaries at the station, and stopped some days. At this place he first saw, in any numbers, the Bechuanas, but little thought, as he addressed them on the great salvation, that this part of the continent was to be the scene of his future labours.

The time came for the party to return to Namaqua Land, and the return journey had its adventures as well as the journey out. They were overtaken by a thunderstorm and torrents of rain, till they were drenched to the skin. The biscuit that had been given them at Griqua Town was completely destroyed by the wet. They could light no fires. At nights they were nearly frozen with cold, and they were almost scorched during the day. They were "in fastings oft." God, however, watched over them, and sometimes interposed remarkably on their behalf. One incident may be given in proof. "We had passed the night without food, and after a long day's ride the sun was descending on us, with little prospect of meeting with anything to assuage the pains of hunger, when, as we were descending from the high ground, weak and weary, we saw at a great distance, on the opposite ridge, a line of dust approaching with the fleetness of the ostrich. It proved to be a spring-buck, closely pursued by a wild dog, which must have brought it many miles, for it was seized within two hundred yards of the spot where we stood and instantly despatched. We of course thankfully took possession of his prize, the right to which the wild dog seemed much inclined to dispute with us. I proposed to leave half of it for the pursuer. 'No,' said one of my men, 'he is not so hungry as we are, or he would not run so fast.'"

The night before reaching Africaner's station they had a narrow escape from a hippopotamus. They were crossing the river at a narrow part when the animal came furiously up the stream, snorting so loud as to be echoed back from the neighbouring rocks. It was with the utmost difficulty they succeeded in making their escape. These animals are timid enough in their undisturbed lakes and pools, but when they have been hunted from year to year they become dangerous.

On their arrival home they were welcomed with joy by Africaner, before whom they laid an account of their expedition. The whole of their researches and proceedings gave him the fullest satisfaction; and it was thought best to defer for a season his removal to Griqua Town. Before we proceed further, it is important that we should give something more than a passing notice to the remarkable career of Africaner, inasmuch as he offers one of the noblest illustrations of the triumphs of the Gospel in this or any other age. The next chapter will therefore be devoted to a sketch of his life and character.

CHAPTER IX.

HISTORY AND CHARACTER OF AFRICANER.

" AFRICANER and his father once roamed over their native hills and dales within one hundred miles of Cape Town, pastured their own flocks, killed their own game, drank of their own streams, and mingled the music of their heathen songs with the winds which burst over the Witsemberg and Winterhock mountains, once the strongholds of his clan." Gradually the Dutch settlers encroached upon their lands, and they were driven farther and farther away from the home of their forefathers, until at length Africaner and his diminished clan became the servants of one of these settlers. In a quarrel which afterwards arose between them, the Hottentot clan murdered the farmer and his family, and Africaner, outlawed from the colony, fled with them to the Orange River. Here he became a terror, not only to the colony on the south, but also to the tribes on the north. His name carried dismay even to the solitary wastes of the desert. When the missionaries Albrecht and their companions settled at Warm Bath station, they were about one hundred miles west of the neighbourhood of Africaner. That desperado and part of his people occasionally attended their instructions, and they visited his place in return. Even at this time he listened with attention, and he used afterwards to refer to it as the period when he saw "men as trees walking."

When the Rev. John Campbell first visited Africa to examine into the state of the missionary cause there, he found in every village through which he passed the terror of Africaner's name. Feeling how important it was that such a man should be won to Christ, Mr. Campbell wrote him a kind conciliatory letter, and forwarded it by a trusty messenger. To this letter Africaner sent a favourable reply, and the result of the correspondence was a promise to send out a missionary to Africaner's own station. Hence when the directors of the London Missionary Society sent Robert Moffat out to South Africa, this was his destination.

Africaner may be regarded as the first convert of the mission. During the nine years of Moffat's hard labours in Namaqua Land, he seemed to himself often as if beating the air or talking to the deaf, but the gain of this one man was a great success. Africaner was no ordinary character, and his mind, once aroused by the quickening influence of the Spirit of God, knew no rest till it found peace in the love of God as revealed in Jesus Christ. His attention to the means of grace was most exemplary. He was not a very fluent reader, but the New Testament became his constant companion. He might be seen under the shadow of a great rock, nearly all day, eagerly perusing the pages of Divine inspiration; or he would sit in his hut, unconscious of the affairs of the family around or the entrance of a stranger, with his eye gazing on the blessed Book, and his mind absorbed in spiritual and Divine things. Often, too, at night, he would sit on a great stone at the door of the missionary's dwelling conversing till the dawn of the next day on creation, Providence, redemption, and the heavenly world.

On these occasions he would repeat to his friend and teacher, generally in the very words of Scripture, such passages as he could not fully comprehend, and ask their meaning. He loved to *search* the Scriptures. He had no commentary except the living voice of the missionary. He had not even the help afforded by marginal references; but he soon discovered the importance of consulting parallel passages, and having an excellent memory, he was able readily to find them. He studied the volume of Nature as well as that of revelation. He would regard the starry heavens with the deepest interest and the works of God around him. Sometimes, after Moffat had been explaining to him the wonders of creation, he would rub his hands on his head and say, "I have heard enough; I feel as if my head was too small, and as if it would swell with these great subjects."

Speaking of his character, Moffat says:—"During the whole period I lived there I do not remember having occasion to be grieved with him, or to complain of any part of his conduct; his very faults seemed to lean to virtue's side. One day, when seated together, I happened in absence of mind to be gazing steadfastly on him. It arrested his attention, and he modestly inquired the cause. I replied, 'I was trying to picture to myself your carrying fire and sword through the country, and I could not think how eyes like yours could smile at human woe.' He answered not, but shed a flood of tears. It may be emphatically said of Africaner that 'he wept with those that wept,' for wherever he heard of a case of distress thither his sympathies were directed; and notwithstanding all his spoils of former years, he had little to spare, but he was ever on the alert to stretch out a helping hand to the widow and fatherless. At an early period I also became an object of his charity, for, finding out that I sometimes sat down to a scanty meal, he presented me with two cows, which, though in that country giving little milk, often saved me many a hungry night to which I was exposed. He was a man of peace; and though I could not expound to him that the 'sword of the magistrate' implied that he was calmly to sit at home and see Bushmen or marauders carry off his cattle and slay his servants, yet so fully did he understand and appreciate the principles of the Gospel of Peace, that nothing could grieve him more than to hear of individuals or villages contending with one another. He who was formerly like a firebrand, spreading discord, enmity, and war among the neighbouring tribes, would now make any sacrifice to prevent anything like a collision between two contending parties; and when he might have raised his arm, and dared them to lift a spear or draw a bow, he would stand in the attitude of a suppliant and entreat them to be reconciled to each other; and pointing to his past life, add, 'What have I now of all the battles I have fought and all the cattle I took but shame and remorse?'"

Africaner's love for Moffat was sincere and lasting, and he experienced many proofs of it. During a season of sickness—a severe attack of bilious fever—which in the course of a few days induced delirium, opening his eyes in the first lucid moments he saw Africaner sitting before his couch gazing on him with eyes full of sympathy and tenderness. He nursed him throughout the season, and when he saw him fully restored his joy was unbounded.

The outlawed robber chieftain now yielded himself entirely to the instruction and guidance of his Christian teacher; and when, after some time, circumstances required Moffat to visit Cape Town, and he desired Africaner to accompany him, the chief expressed his readiness to do so. At first, when the proposal was made to him, he looked at his friend with a searching glance, and gravely asked if he were in earnest. "I had thought you loved me," he said, "and do you advise me to go to the Government to be hung up as a spectacle of public justice?" And putting his hand to his head, he asked, "Do you not know that I am an outlaw, and that a thousand rix-dollars have been offered for this poor head?" When Moffat assured him that he need not fear any evil consequences—that the results would be satisfactory to himself and to the Governor of the Cape, he said, "Well, I shall deliberate, and commit" (or, as he used the word according to the Dutch translation) "roll my way upon the Lord; I know He will not leave me."

When they started for Cape Town nearly all the inhabitants accompanied them half a day's journey to the Orange River, and there they parted amid the shedding of tears on both sides. When they reached Pella the scene was most affecting. Men met who had not seen each other since they had met in mutual combat for each other's destruction—met now as brethren in Christ, and talked of Him who had subdued both by His love. After spending some pleasant days here they set off to pass through the territories of the farmers to Cape Town.

Their appearance in the colony surprised all. "Some of the worthy people on the borders of the colony congratulated me," says Mr. Moffat, "on returning alive, having often heard, as they said, that I had been long ago murdered by Africaner. Much wonder was expressed at my narrow escape from such a monster of cruelty, the report having been spread that Mr. Ebner had but just escaped with the skin of his teeth. While some would scarcely credit my identity, my testimony as to the entire reformation of Africaner's character and his conversion was discarded as the effusion of a frenzied brain. It sometimes afforded no little entertainment to Africaner and the Namaquas to hear a farmer denounce this supposed irreclaimable savage. There were only a few, however, who were sceptical on this subject. At one farm a novel scene exhibited the state of feeling respecting Africaner and myself, and likewise dis-

played the power of Divine grace under peculiar circumstances.   It was necessary, from the scarcity of water, to
call at such places as lay in our road.   The farmer referred
to was a good man in the best sense of the word, and he
and his wife had both shewn me kindness on my way to
Namaqua Land.   On approaching the house, which was on
an eminence, I directed my men to take the waggon to the
valley below, while I walked towards the house.   The
farmer, seeing a stranger, came slowly down the descent to
meet me.   When within a few yards I addressed him in
the usual way, and, stretching out my hand, expressed my
pleasure at seeing him again.   He put his hand behind him,
and asked me rather wildly who I was.   I replied that I
was Moffat, expressing my wonder that he should have
forgotten me.   'Moffat!' he rejoined in a faltering voice;
'it is your ghost!' and moved backward.   'I am no ghost,'
I replied.   'Don't come near me!' he exclaimed; 'you
have long been murdered by Africaner.'   'But I *am* no
ghost,' I said, feeling my hands as if to convince him, and
myself too, of my materiality, but his alarm only increased.
'Everybody says you were murdered; and a man told me
he had seen your bones;' and he continued to gaze at me,
to the no small astonishment of the goodwife and children
who were standing at the door, as also to that of my people,
who were looking on from the waggon below.   At length
he extended his trembling hand, saying, 'When did you
rise from the dead?'   As he feared my presence would
alarm his wife, we bent our steps towards the waggon, and
Africaner was the subject of our conversation.   I gave him
in a few words my views of his present character, saying,
'He is now a truly good man;' to which he replied, 'I can
believe almost anything you say, but *that* I cannot credit;
there are seven wonders in the world—that would be
the eighth.'   I appealed to the displays of Divine grace in
a Paul, a Manasseh, and referred to his own experience.

He replied, *these* were another description of men, but that Africaner was one of the accursed sons of Ham, enumerating some of the atrocities of which he had been guilty. By this time we were standing near to Africaner, on whose countenance sat a smile, for he well knew the prejudices of some of the farmers. The farmer closed the conversation by saying, with much earnestness, 'Well, if what you assert be true respecting that man, I have only one wish, and that is to see him before I die; and when you return, as sure as the sun is over our heads, I will go with you to see him, though he killed my own uncle.' I was not before aware of this fact, and now felt some hesitation whether to discover to him the object of his wonder; but knowing the sincerity of the farmer and the goodness of his disposition, I said, 'This, then, is Africaner!' He started back, looking intensely at the man, as if he had just dropped from the clouds. 'Are you Africaner?' he exclaimed. The chief arose, doffed his old hat, and making a polite bow, answered, 'I am.' The farmer seemed thunderstruck; but when, by a few questions, he had assured himself of the fact that the former bugbear of the border stood before him, now meek and lamb-like in his whole deportment, he lifted up his eyes and exclaimed, 'O God, what a miracle of Thy power! what cannot Thy grace accomplish!' The kind farmer, and his no less hospitable wife, now abundantly supplied our wants; but we hastened our departure, lest the intelligence might get abroad that Africaner was with me, and bring unpleasant visitors."

The arrival of Moffat and Africaner at Cape Town gave satisfaction to all parties. Lord Charles Somerset, the Governor, as a testimony of his good feeling, presented Africaner with an excellent waggon. Mr. Campbell and Dr. Philip, who had just arrived at the Cape from England for the purpose of examining into the state of the African missions, rejoiced to see before them such a trophy of Divine grace. Africaner's appearance excited much interest among the people of Cape Town generally. They were struck with his mildness and gentleness of disposition, and with his piety and accurate knowledge of the Bible. His New Testament was an interesting object of attention, it was so completely thumbed and worn by use.

When Moffat went with Africaner to Cape Town, it was his full intention to return with him to his station, but this was not to be, for it was the wish of Mr. Campbell and Dr. Philip that the tried missionary should accompany them in their visits to the several stations, and eventually be appointed to mission work among the Bechuanas. Much to Africaner's regret, though with his full consent, he was thus separated from his old friend, and went home alone. About a year afterwards they met once more. On this occasion they parted with some hope that again they might see each other on earth ; but no—it was the last farewell ; for scarcely two years had elapsed when Africaner was called to enter into the joy of his Lord. His death was calm and peaceful. The Rev. J. Archbell, Wesleyan missionary, in a letter to Dr. Philip, thus describes the closing scene of the life of this remarkable man :—" Africaner was a man of sound judgment, and of undaunted courage ; and although he himself was one of the first and severest persecutors of the Christian cause, he would, had he lived, have spilled his blood, if necessary, for his missionary. When he found his end approaching, he called all his people together, after the example of Joshua, and gave them directions as to their future conduct. 'We are not,' said he, 'what we were, *savages*, but men professing to be taught according to the Gospel. Let us then do accordingly. Live peaceably with all men, if possible ; and if impossible, consult those who are placed over you before you engage in anything. Remain together as you have done since I knew you. Then, when the directors think fit to send you a missionary, you may be ready to receive him. Behave to any teacher you may have sent as one sent of God, as I have great hope that God will bless you in this respect when I am gone to Heaven. I feel that I love God, and that he has done much for me of which I am totally unworthy. My former life is stained with blood, but Jesus Christ has pardoned me, and I am going to Heaven. Oh, beware of falling into the same evils into which I have led you frequently; but seek God, and He will be found of you to direct you."

CHAPTER X.

THE BECHUANA MISSION.

THE first visit Mr. Moffat paid to Cape Town, after his residence at the Orange River, was most important, regarded in the light of his future career. Here, and now, he was united in marriage to the partner and sharer of his toils and labours, Miss Smith, to whom he had been long previously engaged, and who had arrived from England. She was his loving and faithful companion for upwards of fifty years of his life in Africa, and returned home with him to England at the close of his missionary work. After a short illness, ending in bronchitis, she died in peace on 10th January 1871. Their English loneliness on Africa's soil made the wife as essential to the husband's usefulness as the husband was essential to the wife's safety. They were thoroughly one in thought, feeling, purpose, and aim. She always studied her husband's comfort, never hindered him in his work, but did what she could at all times to keep him up to it. The following brief but faithful sketch of her character is from the *Missionary Chronicle* of February 1871 :—" Mrs. Moffat arrived in Cape Town, and was married to the Rev. Robert Moffat in 1819 ; and henceforth, for fifty-one years, she was a sharer of all the toil, the sorrow, and the joy of her devoted husband. Her object was to live for him, that he might be wholly free to live for the tribes around. None looked upon the dark races with a more compassionate eye—none more tenderly yearned over them in their ignorance, or more truly longed for the day of their redemption. During the last few weeks of her life, night and day, her soul was full of the thought that a new edition of the whole Bechuana Bible is to be printed in London; and she contemplated with intense satisfaction the prospect of its wide circulation among the tribes who seemed to have wakened up anew to appreciate it. The loss to Mr. Moffat of one who was his beloved companion, not only for so many years, but in circumstances which made them all-in-all to each other, is unspeakably great."

Another important event, growing out of Moffat's visit to Cape Town, was his appointment to the Bechuana mission. Apart from the regret of leaving Africaner and the Namaqua congregation, this new field of labour was a very inviting one to the young missionary, whose fitness and zeal in the apostolic work had been increased by experience. The station he was appointed to occupy was one of the foremost posts on heathen soil, and beyond it were regions thickly populated by races who had never seen the face of a white man, and to whom Christianity and its attendant blessings were as yet unknown. Twenty years before this an attempt had been made by the Dutch Missionary Society in Cape Town among the Bechuanas. The two men who were sent to them not being able to accomplish anything as missionaries, turned their attention to trading. In 1805, Dr. Lichtenstein visited the Bechuanas, and after him Burchell and others. In 1816, two missionaries were sent out by the London Missionary Society, at the request of the chief Mothibi; but when the chief and his people found they came empty-handed, and had nothing to trade or barter, they declined to receive them, and actually re-yoked their waggons and ordered them away. In 1821, Mr. and Mrs. Moffat settled among them under more auspicious circumstances, and such blessed results, as these pages will presently shew.

For some years Mr. Hamilton shared with them, at Lattakoo or Lithako, the labours and anxieties of this frontier station. Their difficulties were increased by the unsettled condition of the country. There was no peace in the land. Cattle-lifting expeditions were constantly on the move, and in these engagements the Bechuanas were not always the victors. They had no religious system, no idea of a Creator, no belief in the immortality of the soul—nothing which might form a groundwork for conveying to them instruction in spiritual things. "They looked on the sun with the eyes of an ox." For a bit of tobacco, or some small equivalent, the missionary might gain their attention for a little time, but his efforts to convey to them the idea of a Creator and of a Saviour appeared as futile as to convert a granite rock into arable land.

The following description of the people is from the pen of Mr. Cumming, who describes them as he saw them :— "As I had now reached the southern border of that vast tract of Southern Africa inhabited by the numerous tribes of the Bechuanas, it will be necessary, before proceeding further, to give a sketch of their manners and customs. They are a lively and intelligent race of people, and remarkable for their goodhumour; they are well-formed, if not starved in infancy. They possess pleasing features, and very fine eyes and teeth ; their hair is short and woolly ; the colour of their complexion is of a light copper. The various tribes live in kraals or villages of various sizes, along with their respective chiefs. Their wigwams are built in a circular form, and thatched with long grass ; the floor and wall, inside and out, are plastered with a compound of clay and cow-dung. The entrances are about three feet high and two feet broad. Each wigwam is surrounded by a hedge of wicker-work, while one grand hedge of wait-a-bit thorns surrounds the entire kraal, protecting the inmates from lions and other animals.

"The dress of the men consists of a *kaross*, which hangs gracefully from their shoulders, and another garment called *tsecha*, which encircles their loins, and is likewise made of skin. On their feet they wear a simple sandal, formed of the skin of the buffalo or camelopard. On their legs and arms they carry ornaments of brass and copper, of different patterns, which are manufactured by themselves. The men also wear a few ornaments of beads round their necks and on their arms. Around their necks, besides beads, they carry a variety of other appendages, the majority of which are believed to possess a powerful charm to preserve them from evil. One of these is a small hollow bone, through which they blow when in peril; another is a set of dice formed of ivory, which they rattle in their hands and cast on the ground, to ascertain if they are to be lucky in any enterprise in which they may be about to engage; also a host of bits of root and bark which are medicinal. From their necks also depend gourd snuff-boxes, made of an 'exceedingly diminutive species of pumpkin, trained to grow in a bottle-like shape.

"They never move without their arms, which consist of a shield, a bundle of assagais, a battle-axe, and a knobkerry. The shields are formed of the hide of the buffalo or camelopard; their shape among some tribes are oval, among others round. The assagai is a sort of light spear or javelin, having a wooden shaft about six feet in length attached to it. Some of these are formed solely for throwing, and a skilful warrior will send one through a man's body at one hundred yards. Another variety of assagai is formed solely for stabbing. The blades of these are stouter, and the shafts shorter and thicker, than the other variety. They are found mostly among the tribes very far in the interior. Their battle-axes are elegantly formed, consisting of a triangular-shaped blade fastened in a handle formed of the horn of the rhinoceros. The men employ their time in war and hunting, and in dressing the skins of wild animals.

"The dress of the women consists of a kaross, depending from the shoulder, and a short kilt, formed of the skin of the pallah or some other antelope. Around their necks, arms, waists, and ankles they wear large and cumbrous coils of beads of a variety of colours, tastefully arranged in different patterns. The women chiefly employ their time in cultivating their fields and gardens, in which they rear corn, pumpkins, and water-melons, and likewise in harvesting their crops and grinding their corn. Both men and women go bare-headed; they anoint their heads with *sebilo*, a shining composition, being a mixture of fat and a grey sparkling ore, having the appearance of mica. Some of the tribes besmear their bodies with a mixture of fat and red clay, imparting to them the appearance of Red Indians. Most of the tribes possess cattle; these are attended to and milked solely by the men, a woman never being allowed to set foot within the cattle-kraal. Polygamy is allowed, and any man may keep as many wives as he pleases; the wife, however, has in the first instance to be purchased. Among tribes possessed of cattle the price of a wife is ten head of cattle; but among the poorer tribes a wife may be obtained for a few spades with which they cultivate their fields. These spades, which are manufactured by themselves, are fastened in the end of a long shaft, and are used as our labourers use the hoe. Rows of women may be seen digging together in the fields, singing songs, to which they keep time with their spades."

Mr. Thompson, in his "Travels," correctly remarks that, "like most barbarians, their political wisdom consists in

NATIVES FISHING ON THE NYASSA

duplicity and petty cunning; and their ordinary wars were merely predatory incursions upon their weaker neighbours, for the purpose of carrying off cattle, with as little exposure as possible of their own lives. Their expeditions against the Bushmen were peculiarly vindictive, and conducted with all the insidiousness and murderous ferocity, without the heroic intrepidity, of American or New Zealand savages." Falsehood, revenge, robbery, and murder were among their chief characteristics, and in all of which they were adepts.

The Bechuanas were as tenacious of their customs as the Hindoos of caste. "Their youth, for instance," says Moffat, "would forfeit anything rather than go uncircumcised. This national ceremony is performed from the age of eight to fourteen, and even to manhood, though the children born previous to their parents being initiated cannot be heirs to regal power. There is much feasting and dancing on the occasion, and every heart is elated at these festivities. The females also have their *boyali* at the same age, in which they are under the tuition of matrons, and initiated into all the duties of wives, in which it merits notice that passive obedience is especially inculcated."

After these tedious ceremonies are over the youth appears lubricated, assuming the character and wearing the dress of a man, while he is considered able to bear the shield and wield the javelin. The girls also, when they have gone the round of weeks of drilling, dancing, singing, and listening to the precepts of the grave old women, have a piece of iron rather hot put into their hands, which they must hold fast for a time, though painful, to shew that their hands are hard and strong for labour. They are then anointed, and having put on the usual female dress, the lower part of their hair is shaven off, and the upper part profusely bedaubed with a paste of butter and *sebilo*—black shining ochre. Raised thus from comparative infancy to what they consider womanhood, they view themselves with as much complacency as if they were enrobed in the attire of the daughters of an eastern potentate. They have reached nearly to a climax in their life, for they expect soon to be married, and to be a mother they consider the chief end of a woman's existence.

These ceremonies were prodigious barriers to the Gospel. Polygamy was another obstacle, and the Bechuanas, jealous of any diminution in their self-indulgence by being deprived of the services of their wives, looked with an extremely suspicious eye on any innovation on this ancient custom. While going to war, hunting, watching the cattle, milking the cows, and preparing the furs and skins for mantles, was the work of the men, the women had by far the heavier task of agriculture, building the houses, fencing, bringing firewood, and heavier than all, nature's charge, the rearing of a family. The greater part of the year they are constantly employed ; and during the season of picking and sowing their gardens their task is galling, living on a coarse, scanty fare, and frequently having a babe fastened to their backs while thus cultivating the ground.

The men, for obvious reasons, found it convenient to have a number of such vassals rather than only one, while the woman would be perfectly amazed at one's ignorance were she to be told that she would be much happier in a single state or widowhood than being the mere concubine and drudge of a haughty husband, who spent the greater part of his life in lounging in the shade, while she was compelled, for his comfort as well as her own, to labour under the rays of an almost vertical sun, in a hot and withering climate. Their houses, which require considerable ingenuity as well as hard labour, are entirely the work of the women, who are extremely thankful to carry home even the heavier timbers, if their husbands will take their axes and fell them in the thicket, which may be many miles distant. The centre of the conical roof will in many houses be eighteen feet high, and it requires no little scrambling, in the absence of ladders, for females to climb to such a height, but the men pass and repass, and look on with the most perfect indifference; while it never enters their heads that their wife, their daughter, or their mother may fall and break a leg or neck. These houses, though temporary, and requiring great labour to keep them constantly in repair, are nevertheless very well adapted to the climate. They admit little light, which is not desirable in a hot country, and among millions of house-flies; but during the winter season they are uncomfortably airy and cold.

For more than five years these people continued callous and indifferent to all instruction, unless it were followed by some immediate temporal benefit. Notwithstanding their many discouragements, the mission party perseveringly went on with their work. They had to build their own dwellings and enclose their gardens and folds. The site of the station was a light sandy soil, where no kind of vegetables would grow without constant irrigation; it was necessary, therefore, to make water-furrows, leading from the Kuruman River, to water their grain and vegetables. When their crops came to perfection, or before, they were often stolen by the natives. Standing in the sawpit, labouring at the anvil, treading clay for making bricks, preaching to the motley few who attended their place of worship—such were the duties of each returning day. When the evening came, it was often the burden of conversation that their utensils and tools had been taken, or their water-furrows destroyed. More than once, on returning from preaching, they found a stone left in the pot instead of the meat they had placed there, and on which they had hoped to dine. Their mortifications, losses, and disappointments were endless. Still, they encouraged themselves in the Lord their God. Though cast down there was no yielding to despair. They knew they were at the post of duty, and that fidelity was required of them. They knew that though they were not responsible for success, yet they were responsible for faithfulness. They knew that if they persevered in their labours, sooner or later they should witness success. They remembered the words of their Lord, and rejoiced in them :—" All authority hath been given unto me in heaven and on earth. Go ye therefore, and make disciples of all the nations, baptizing them into the name of the Father and of the Son and of the Holy Ghost; teaching them to observe all things whatsoever I commanded you ; and lo, I am with you alway, even unto the end of the world."

CHAPTER XI.

TO add to all their other trials, a rain-maker, imported from a distant tribe, brought upon them the reproaches and hostility of the people. The country had long suffered from a severe drought; the heavens were as brass; scarcely a cloud had been seen for months; the land was barren; cattle were dying rapidly; and many of the people, emaciated almost to skeletons, were living on reptiles and roots. In Southern Africa, the people at such a time resort to rain-makers for help. Mr. Kay very properly calls these men "the missionaries inveterate enemies;" and says that they uniformly oppose, to the utmost of their power, the introduction of the Gospel among their countrymen. Like the *angekoks* of the Greenlanders, the *pawaws* of the Indians, and the *greegrees* of Western Africa, they are amongst the strongest pillars of Satan's kingdom. Their influence over the minds of the people is greater than even that of the chief or king, who is obliged to yield to their commands. The Bechuanas held a council, and passed resolutions to send for a rain-maker of renown from the Bahurutsi tribe, two hundred miles north-east of the Kuruman station. The ambassadors who were sent to

request his presence and help, promised that if he would
return with them and cause the needed rain to fall, he
should receive rewards beyond all calculation.   One day,
after the return of the messengers was overdue, and the
people were waiting in anxious expectation, a sudden shout
was raised, and the whole town was .in motion.   The rain-
maker was at hand.   Every voice was elevated to the
highest pitch in exclamations of joy.   All at once the
clouds began to gather, the lightnings darted, the thunders
roared in awful grandeur, and a few heavy drops of rain
fell.   The deluded people were frantic with excitement;
and as the impostor proclaimed aloud that that year the
women would have to cultivate their gardens on the hills,
because the valleys would be deluged, the shoutings of joy
baffled all description.   After the noise and tumult had
somewhat subsided, a few of the multitude waited on the
missionaries, and treated them and their doctrines with
derision.   One asked, with a sneer, "Where is your God?
Have you not seen our Morimo?   Have you not beheld
him cast from his arm his fiery spears, and heard his voice
in the clouds?   You talk of Jehovah, and Jesus; what can
they do?"   Referring to this interview, Moffat observes:
"Never in my life do I remember a text being brought
home with such power as the words of the Psalmist—'Be
still, and know that I am God; I will be exalted among
the heathen.'"

Just then there was every probability of the darkness
which had gathered around the missionaries becoming darker
still.   The rain-maker boasted of his powers, and told the
most wonderful tales of his control over the elements on
former occasions and among other tribes.   But all too soon
the clouds in Bechuana vanished again; no shower followed
the first few drops; the burning sun once more parched the
earth, and all creatures that had life seemed as if they
must soon die.   The clouds were obstinate, and the showers

of rain more obstinate still ; the rain-maker called them, but they would not come.   Various obstacles were suggested as being in the way, and various remedies thought of.   The women were required to gather certain roots and herbs, that when the moon was new, and afterwards full, he might kindle fires with them on the hills.   There was smoke, but no rain.   A baboon was to be brought to him, without a blemish, and that had never lost a hair ; the baboon was brought, but no rain came.   A lion's heart was needed, for the clouds required strong medicine ; the lion's heart was procured, but no rain.   A tree that had been struck with lightning was cut down and burned to ashes, yet no rain fell.   All the men of the town were sprinkled with a zebra's tail that had been dipped in water, with which had been mixed an infusion of certain bulbs, still no rain.   At last the people grew impatient ; and then it appeared that the man had been privately attributing his failure to the presence of the missionaries.

The people now poured forth their curses on Messrs. Hamilton and Moffat as the cause of all their sorrows. They said the bell that was rung for public worship frightened the clouds ; blame was cast upon their prayers. "Don't you," said a chief angrily, "bow down in your houses, and pray and talk to something bad in the ground?" For a fortnight the rain-maker kept himself secluded ; at the close of that period he publicly proclaimed that he had discovered the cause of the drought.   "Do you not see," he exclaimed, "when clouds come over us, that Hamilton and Moffat look at them?"   This question receiving a hearty and unanimous affirmation, he added that their white faces frightened the clouds away, and that no rain need be expected so long as they were in the country. Shortly after, Moffat learnt that the unfortunate man was to be speared on account of his failures, and pleaded hard, and at last successfully, for the preservation of his life.

Mothibi, the chief, conducted him over the plain towards the Matluarin River, and sent him to his own land.

Though the rain-maker was removed, and therefore one great danger taken away, yet a public opinion had been created opposed to the continued residence of the missionaries in the country. As they proceeded with their work their prospects became worse and worse. They were suspected of befriending the Bushmen, because they condemned the Bechuana system of vengeance and extirpation practised against them; they were told to go to certain professors of religion whose conduct out there had been inconsistent with their profession, and make them good before attempting to reform the Bechuanas; and they were still accused of being the cause of all the drought. At length the hostility towards them grew to such a height that they were informed they must immediately leave the country, and that measures of a violent nature would be resorted to if they disobeyed.

One day, about noon, a chief and a dozen of his men came and seated themselves under the shadow of a large tree near Moffat's house. A secret council had been held in the field, under pretence of a hunt, and the present party was a deputation to apprise the missionaries of the result. They stood patiently to hear the message. The chief quivered his spear in his right hand, and rising, confronted Moffat. Mild though he was, Moffat was in courage and nerve a match for the sternest and bravest of men. Before the deputed chief and his twelve attendants he fearlessly held his own—weak in himself, but strong in the Lord. There, too, stood his intrepid wife, an infant in her arms. With a steadfast gaze the tall missionary looked the spear-bearing chief straight in the eyes, while he listened to the declaration that it was the determination of the chiefs of the people that he and his companions should leave the country. Then came the brave reply:—"We have indeed felt most reluctant to leave, and are now more than ever resolved to abide by our post. We pity you, for you know not what you do. We have suffered, it is true; and He whose servants we are has directed us in His Word, 'When they persecute you in one city, flee ye to another;' but although we have suffered, we do not consider all that has been done to us by the people amounts to persecution; we are prepared to expect it from such as know no better. If you are resolved to rid yourselves of us, you must resort to stronger measures, for our hearts are with you. You may shed our blood or burn us out. We know you will not touch our wives and children. Then shall they who sent us know, and God, who sees and hears what we do, shall know, that we have been persecuted indeed." When Moffat had finished speaking, the chief looked at his companions, remarking to them, with a significant shake of the head, "These men must have ten lives, when they are so fearless of death; there must be something in immortality." The meeting broke up, the deputation leaving to inform those who had sent them that these were impracticable men.

The missionaries were devoutly thankful that this interview closed so favourably. They were also thankful that there was no public prohibition issued against attendance on Divine worship; a few therefore generally came. A large majority had never entered the chapel, being threatened by their superiors if they did; and others would not for their lives have set a foot within the threshold. No further threats were made against life; and presently circumstances occurred which, threatening the Bechuanas and the missionaries with common danger, tended to establish more friendly relations between them, and led to results most favourable to the mission.

CHAPTER XII.

INVASION BY THE MANTATEES.

FOR a year or more alarming rumours came from all quarters of the advance from the interior of an invincible army, numerous as the locusts, carrying with them everywhere death and desolation. Some of the reports were of the wildest character. It was said that the head of this mighty army was a woman, that she nourished it with her own milk, and sent out hornets before its march. Mr. Moffat had long felt a desire to visit Makaba, the chief of the Bauangketsi, a powerful tribe situated upwards of two hundred miles north-east of Lithako. He was anxious to become better acquainted with the surrounding tribes—with their localities, habits, and language. He thought, too, that he might do something to promote friendliness between them, and so prepare the way for the wider spread of the Gospel. About this time, receiving an ivitation from Makaba, the path of duty was plain; but Mothibi and his people were against the step. So strong was Mothibi's opposition that on the day of departure, finding he could not prevail by argument, he positively forbade those under his control to accompany the party. Moffat, feeling no inclination to abandon his

purpose, started with such men as he had. He had not
proceeded far when he ascertained that the invading force
was near at hand ; that they were known as Mantatees, a
section of the Basuto race, who, having been driven from
their own country by the Zulus, had fallen back upon
weaker tribes, and gathering strength with each successive
victory, were now advancing upon Lithako.

Respecting the real name of the Mantatees there is some
difference of opinion. Stockenstrom, who was familiar with
many of the tribe, says that the word *Mantatee* signifies
"invader," or "marauder," in the Bechuana language, and
that the tribe universally disclaimed it. They are described
as a tall, robust people, in features resembling the Bechuanas.
Moffat, speaking from personal observation, says :—"This
barbarous horde appeared, when all collected in one body,
extremely numerous, amounting at the very lowest compu-
tation to about forty thousand souls. The men were tall
and muscular, and their bodies being smeared over with a
mixture of charcoal and grease, they appeared as black as
pitch. Their natural colour is scarcely a shade darker than
that of the Bechuanas, whom in features they also nearly
resemble. Their language appears to be merely a dialect of
the Bechuana tongue. Their dress consisted in general of
prepared or tanned skins, hanging loose over their shoulders.
Some of the chiefs had karosses of a superior description,
and not a few wore very long loose shawls of cotton cloth ;
' but most of the women were almost destitute of clothing,
having for the greater part only a small piece of skin suspended from their loins to cover their nakedness. The men,
during the engagement, having thrown off their mantles,
were entirely naked, excepting this piece of skin tied about
their loins. Their ornaments were plumes of black ostrich
feathers on their heads, large copper rings, sometimes six or
eight in number, round their necks, with numerous rings of
the same metal on their arms and legs, and rings or large

plates hanging from their ears. Their weapons were spears or assagais, battle-axes, and clubs; and many of them had a weapon of a very peculiar construction, being an iron blade of a circular shape, with a cutting sabre-edge, fastened on a stick with a heavy knobbed head, and used both as a missile and in close combat. They had also large shields of bullock's hide, which, like those of the Caffres, covered almost the whole body." Referring to another attack the Mantatees made on their neighbours, he says:—"Their appearance was extremely fierce and savage, and their attitude very menacing. It was evident that they were reluctant to depart, which was a convincing proof that a night attack was premeditated; and when it was growing dark they compelled us to retreat, till a few shots were fired into the air, when they again fled, and we pursued, hoping to increase their flight. We overtook one, whom we surrounded for the purpose of informing him who we were, and that we had no intention of doing them harm. He stood with his shield and war-axe in his left hand, and a spear in his right, raised as if in the act of hurling it. I confess I never saw anything so fiend-like as that man, and concluded that, if he was a specimen of his tribe, all hope had fled for the Baralongs. His body lubricated with grease and charcoal; a large round cockade of black ostrich feathers on his head; his eyes glaring with rage; while his open mouth, displaying his white teeth, poured forth the most opprobrious epithets and obscene curses, threatening to give our flesh to the hyenas and our eyes to the crows, as he made a run first at one of us and then at another. One of the men, in order to frighten him, fired a ball directly over his head, when he fell, and the horsemen rushed forward to seize him before he rose, but he was too expert, and made us quickly turn away in no little confusion; and had it not been for the fear of losing his spear, it would certainly have been plunged into one of our number. It was now becoming too dark to make any further attempts, and we let him go, and turned in the direction of the waggons, which were about seven miles distant."

As soon as Mr. Moffat was assured of the near approach of the Mantatees, he hastened back to apprise the Bechuanas of the impending danger; and apprehending from their weakness and cowardice they would easily fall a prey to the enemy, determined to go on to Griqua Town to secure assistance. This bold and judicious action saved from destruction the chief and people, who a little while before had sought to drive their best earthly friends from the country. The Griquas formed a strong commando, and joining with the Bechuanas, advanced against the invading army. A terrible battle ensued, and after a long and sometimes doubtful struggle, and great loss of life on the side of the invaders, they were put to flight. As fighting was not Moffat's province, he avoided discharging a single shot, though at the request of the chiefs he remained with the commando as the only means of safety. As soon as the enemy had fled, the Bechuanas began to plunder and despatch the wounded men, and to butcher the women and children with their spears and war-axes.

The compassion of the missionary was stirred by the heartrending scenes he was compelled to witness, and his influence was exerted to prevent these acts of cruelty. By galloping in among them, he deterred many of the Bechuanas from their barbarous purpose. It was distressing to see mothers and infants rolled in blood, and the living babe in the arms of a dead mother. The women, seeing that through Moffat's influence mercy was shewn them, instead of fleeing, generally sat down, and baring their bosoms, exclaimed, "I am a woman, I am a woman!" The men, struggling with death, would raise themselves from the ground and discharge their arrows at any within their reach, and several times the missionary narrowly escaped their spears and war-axes while he was busy in rescuing the women and children.

Reviewing these events, Dr. Philip judiciously and devoutly observes :—"We cannot help noticing with gratitude the hand of God in all the circumstances connected with the deliverance of our missionary friends and the people of Lithako. Had Mr. Moffat not undertaken the journey he proposed, he might have remained ignorant of the approach of the enemy; or had he gone forward on his journey without hearing of them, as he might have done in that country, Lithako must have fallen, and he himself and the mission families might have been involved in the same destruction ; and had he been spared to return from his visit to Makaba, one cannot contemplate him, even in imagination, standing on the ruins of Lithako and treading on the ashes of his murdered wife and children, without shuddering with horror! But the circumstances which indicate an invisible arm in the preservation of our friends do not stop here. Had he delayed his journey, or had he deferred calling in the Griquas, whatever escape might have been provided for him and our other missionary friends, Mothibi and his people would have been ruined. The influence of the missionaries upon them would in all probability have been lost, and their circumstances might have been rendered so desperate as to preclude all hope of being of any service to them in future."

The circumstances connected with the invasion of the Mantatees made a marked impression upon the chief Mothibi and his people in favour of the missionaries, whose self-sacrificing conduct they could not but feel and acknowledge. They wondered that they remained in the country when they might have escaped to the Colony with comparatively little loss of property, and they did not hesitate to express their wonder with evident admiration. Advantage was taken of this state of things to obtain a new site for the mission, the place which they occupied being in many respects unsuitable. Owing to the succession of dry seasons, there was every prospect, from the diminution of the fountain that supplied them with water, of its becoming still more trying. A place eight miles distant, and about three miles below the Kuruman fountain, was examined, and appeared from the locality to be a more eligible spot than any other. The Kuruman fountain issues, full and flowing, from caverns in a little hill, composed of the blue and grey limestone, mixed with flint. Its noble stream, though pure and wholesome, is rather calcareous. Its source must be at a very great distance, for the rains falling on the hills and plains for forty miles round, in any one year, could not supply such a stream even for a month. Indeed, throughout this limestone basin fountains are very precarious; even the Kuruman does not send forth its former torrents, and like many other African streams, it is largest at its source, and, partly by evaporation and partly by absorption, is completely lost about ten miles to the northwest.

While arrangements were pending for removing to Kuruman, Mr. Moffat, taking with him the chief's son and one of the principal men, paid a visit to Cape Town. It was hoped that the visit would make a favourable impression on the young prince and his companion, and convince them, and through them their people, that the missionaries had friends, and were not obliged to live among the Bechuanas because they could not live anywhere else. They were delighted with their reception at Cape Town, and with everything they saw. It was with great difficulty they were prevailed upon to go on board one of the ships in the bay. The size of the hull and the height of the masts astounded them. When they saw a boy mount the rigging and go to the masthead, they thought he was an ape. When they entered the cabin, and looked down into the hold, they thought the ship was resting on the bottom of the ocean. "Do these water-houses," said they, "unyoke like waggon-oxen every night?" "Do they graze in the sea to keep them alive?" When asked what they thought of a ship in full sail that was approaching the roads, they replied, "We have no thoughts here; we hope to think again when we get on shore." This visit to the Cape gave great satisfaction to all parties. Having completed the business for which it had been made, Moffat prepared to return; and after enduring for two months the tedium and monotony of an African journey, reached the station in May 1824. The original engagement for the land on which to establish their new station was ratified, and forthwith they proceeded to settle themselves at Kuruman.

CHAPTER XIII.

MOFFAT'S VISIT TO THE CHIEF MAKABA.

SOON after the removal to the Kuruman, Mr. Moffat fulfilled a promise he had made to visit Makaba, king of the Bauangketsi. As he and his party proceeded on their journey they travelled over a country of limestone, covered with the hookthorn acacia in some places; in others. adorned with trees and shrubs of various kinds, and alive with an abundance of game. The principal part of the game obtained by the natives they caught in pitfalls. Some of the holes were sixteen feet deep, where even the tall giraffe and ponderous rhinoceros were entrapped. Some of them were formed like a funnel, others were an oblong square, with sharp stakes fastened in the bottom; the earth taken out was generally scattered, and the opening covered over with sticks and grass.

The latter part of the journey was through pleasant scenery, and as they approached the Molapo River, on the distant horizon hills in the Bauangketsi country were seen, apparently covered with timber, indicating a fertile region. When they reached Pitsan, the principal town of the Barolong tribe, Tauane, the chief, tried to dissuade Moffat from visiting Makaba. Pitsan contained upwards of twenty thousand people, all of whom had congregated there after the attack of the Mantatees. As the party remained there over the Sabbath the missionary held Divine service, and conversed with the principal men on the subject of a missionary settling among them.

Outside Makaba's town they were met by messengers whom he had sent out to welcome them, and who said the chief had not slept for joy because of their approach. As they reached the top of the hill, at the foot of which lay the capital of the Bauangketsi, and looked to the north, they were surprised at the immense number of towns which lay scattered in the valleys. Makaba, standing at the door of one of his houses, welcomed them on their approach, and provided them with refreshment. About sunset he sent one of his wives to deliver a sack full of thick milk; and next morning he sent for slaughter three oxen, and in the course of the day boiled corn, pottage, and beer. Moffat repeatedly endeavoured to interest the chief in mission work, and offered to send a missionary to labour among his people; to which he replied, that he hoped in future no grass would be allowed to grow on the road between the Kuruman and his country, and that men of peace should live in every nation to keep up friendly intercourse. But his ideas concerning the benefit to be derived from the residence of a missionary were very vague, and he resolutely refrained from conversing on religious subjects. Sometimes, when the missionary had been trying to arrest his attention by repeating something striking in the works of God, or in the life of the Saviour, he would interrupt by asking a question as distant as the antipodes from the subject.

The time for Mr. Moffat's return to Kuruman was approaching, and he felt miserable at the prospect of leaving without the satisfaction of having told Makaba what was the only object of a missionary, especially as he had professed his wish to have one. He therefore determined to pay him a formal visit for this purpose. One Sabbath morning, after prayer, taking some of his company with him, they went into the town, and found the chief seated amidst a large number of his principal men, all engaged either preparing skins, cutting them, sewing mantles, or telling news. Arrived in the presence of the great man, surrounded by his nobles and counsellors, he said he had come to tell him good tidings. The chief's countenance lighted up in the expectation of hearing about some subject or other congenial to his savage disposition; but when he found that the tidings were only about God and Christ and salvation, he resumed his knife and jackal's skin, and began to hum a native air.

Though, however, Makaba was inattentive, one of his nobles appeared struck with the character of the Lord Jesus Christ, and especially with the account of His miracles; and on hearing that He had raised the dead, exclaimed, "What an excellent doctor He must have been!" This led to some further talk as to His power in the resurrection of the dead at the last day. The ear of Makaba was opened, and in a quick and astonished tone, he exclaimed, "What! what are these words about? The dead, shall they arise?" "Yes, all the dead shall arise." "Will my father arise?" "Yes, your father will arise." "Will all the slain in battle arise?" "Yes." "And will all that have been killed and devoured by lions, tigers, hyenas, and crocodiles again revive?" "Yes, and come to judgment." "And will those whose bodies have been left to waste and wither on the desert plains and be scattered to the winds, again arise?" he asked, with a kind of triumph. "Yes," was the reply; "not one will be left behind." Looking then at Moffat for a few moments with a searching gaze, he turned to his people, and exclaimed, "Hark, ye wise men, whoever is among you, did you ever hear such news as this? This is strange and unheard of news indeed!" Then addressing himself to the missionary, he said, "Father, I love you much. Your visit and your presence have made my heart as white as milk. The words of your mouth are sweet as honey, but the words of a resurrection are too great to be heard. I do not wish to hear again about the dead rising. The dead cannot arise! The dead must not arise!" "Why?" was the inquiry. "Why must not one speak of a resurrection?" Raising and uncovering his arm, and shaking his hand as if quivering a spear, he solemnly answered, "I have slain my thousands, and shall they arise?" The dawning of the light of revelation upon his dark mind awoke his slumbering conscience, and remorse and fear began to torment him for the countless deeds of rapine and murder which had marked his past career.

The parting between the missionary and the mighty chief was satisfactory and pleasant on both sides. The man against whom Moffat had been warned as a dangerous enemy, in whose hands his life would not be safe, he found a most agreeable and hospitable host. On his return, however, Moffat nearly fell into the hands of the marauding Mantatees, as they surged onward in their devastating course among the tribes of the interior. For several days the lives of himself and his companions were endangered; but God was his merciful and strong refuge, and he thankfully bent his course at last to his home. During this time Mrs. Moffat, left alone at the station, was exposed to the most distressing suspense.

About this period a party of marauders from the Orange River collected in the Long Mountains, some forty miles west of the station, attacked several villages along the Kuruman River, and were preparing to attack the mission premises. This, of course, excited in Mrs. Moffat's mind much alarm. She knew their desperate character, and feared they might be tempted to attack the house for the sake of the ammunition they might get there. One evening the servant came in wringing her hands, and in great distress said the Mantatees were on their way to the Kuruman. This was no pleasant news to one who, with two babes, had no means of escape. A message was sent to Mothibi, the chief, who said the news was too true, but he thought there was no danger till the morning. The noble woman commended herself and her little ones to the care of God, and lay down to sleep. At midnight she was awoke by a loud rapping at the door; Mothibi had come to announce the dreaded intelligence that the Mantatees were approaching. The sound of alarm and uproar was raised in every part of the town; preparations were made for a hasty flight; warriors were assembling; each succeeding messenger brought fresh alarms: but about noon the next day it was ascertained that the dreaded invaders had directed their course away from the Kuruman.

This glad intelligence scattered all gloomy fears, and filled every heart with joy; but the news that made the people generally so glad produced in Mrs. Moffat the greatest terror, as the conviction flashed across her mind that if the Mantatees were on the march to the Barolongs as reported, nothing less than a miracle could save her husband from destruction, as he would be returning through that region at that time. Though the people saw the danger, and sympathised with her in her fears and distress, no one could be persuaded to go in search. The very idea of her husband's falling in with such a horde of savages was almost unendurable, and for three weeks she was in a state of the extremest mental agony. Nothing but incessant prayer sustained her. During this period continual reports came to hand that Moffat had been killed. One man had seen a piece of the waggon; another had found a part of his saddle; and some had picked up portions of his linen stained with blood. At last two or three men were prevailed on to go and ascertain

the facts, and they started on their expedition on the morning of the very day on which Moffat made his appearance.
Thus, though there had been abundant cause for alarm, and
for the exercise of prayer and trust in God, yet through His
gracious providence their fears were turned to rejoicings
and songs of praise.

CHAPTER XIV.

MOFFAT'S position during the first years of his life at Kuruman was a difficult one in many ways. He shall state some of the trials himself:—"Some of our newly-arrived assistants, finding themselves in a country where the restraints of law were unknown, and not being under the influence of religion, would not submit to the privations which we patiently endured, but murmured exceedingly. Armed robbers were continually making inroads, threatening death and extirpation. We were compelled to work daily at every species of labour, most of which was very heavy, under a burning sun and in a dry climate, where only one shower had fallen during the preceding twelve months. These are only imperfect samples of our engagements for several years at the new station, while at the same time the language, which was entirely oral, had to be acquired. A spelling-book, catechism, and small portions of scripture were prepared, and even sent to the Cape to be printed, in 1825; but, as if our measure of disappointment was not full, they were by some mistake sent to England, and before they could possibly return to our station we might have had several improved editions."

The missionary had long felt that the acquisition of the language was an object of the first importance. At Lithako the circumstances were most unfavourable, as there was neither place nor time for study, and no interpreter worthy the name. "Mary," said Moffat one day to his wife, "this is hard work." "It is hard work, my love," she said; "but take courage, our lives shall be given us for a prey." "But think, my dear," he replied, "how long we have been preaching to this people, and no fruits yet appear." The wise woman, it is said, rejoined after this manner:—"The gospel has not yet been preached to them in their own tongue wherein they were born. They have heard only through interpreters, and interpreters who have themselves no just understanding or real love of the truth. We must not expect the blessing till you are able, from your own lips and in their own language, to convey it through their ears into their hearts." "From that hour," said Mr. Moffat, in relating the conversation, "I gave myself with untiring diligence to the acquisition of the language."

At first only a few words were collected, and these were very incorrect, owing to the ignorance of the interpreter. It was something like groping in the dark, and many ludicrous blunders were made. The native wags took pleasure, when giving him sentences and forms of speech, in leading him into all sorts of egregious mistakes and blunders. Though, however, he had to pay in this coin for his credulity, he learned something. Perseverance was ultimately crowned with success. Of that success we shall presently have to record a series of signal illustrations and proofs. The printing-press of Kuruman has been one of the greatest blessings to South Africa; but the history of its operations require a chapter to itself.

For several years the region had suffered from great drought; but in 1826 it was blessed with plentiful rains, and the earth grew verdant, and gave promise of plenty. Soon, however, the hopes of abundance were cut off by swarms of locusts which infested every part of the country, and devoured every kind of vegetation. Moffat's description of them is most graphic, and though lengthy, cannot well be abridged :—"They might be seen passing over like an immense cloud, extending from the earth to a considerable height, producing with their wings a great noise. They always proceed nearly in the direction of the wind, those in advance descending to eat anything they light upon, and rising in the rear as the cloud advances. 'They have no king, but they go forth, all of them, by bands,' and are gathered together in one place in the evening, where they rest, and from their immense numbers they weigh down the shrubs, and lie at times one on the other to the depth of several inches. In the morning when the sun begins to diffuse warmth, they take wing, leaving a large extent without one vestige of verdure ; even the plants and shrubs are barked. Wherever they halt for the night or alight during the day, they become a prey to other animals, and are eaten not only by beasts of prey but by all kinds of game, serpents, lizards, and frogs. When passing through the air, kites, vultures, crows, and particularly the locust bird, as it is called, may be seen devouring them. When a swarm alights on gardens, or even fields, the crop for one season is destroyed. I have observed a field of young maize devoured in the space of two hours. They eat not only tobacco and everything vegetable, but also flannel and linen. The natives embrace every opportunity of gathering them, which can be done during the night. Whenever the cloud alights at a place not very distant from a town, the inhabitants turn out with sacks, and often with pack-oxen gather loads, and return the next day with millions. It has happened that, in gathering them, individuals have been bitten by serpents ; and on one occasion a woman had been travelling several miles with a large bundle of locusts on her head, when a serpent, which had been put into the sack with them, found its way out. The woman supposing it to be a thong dangling about her shoulders, laid hold of it with her hand, and feeling that it was alive, instantly precipitated both to the ground and fled. The locusts are prepared for eating by simple boiling, or rather steaming, as they are put into a large pot with a little water, and covered closely up ; after boiling for a short time they are taken out and spread on mats in the sun to dry, when they are winnowed, something like corn, to clear them of their legs and wings ; and when perfectly dry, are put into sacks, or laid upon the house floor in a heap. The natives eat them whole, adding a little salt when they can obtain it ; or they pound them in a wooden mortar, and when they have reduced them to something like meal, they mix them with a little water and make a kind of cold stir-about.

" When locusts abound, the natives become quite fat, and would even reward any old lady who said that she had coaxed them to alight within reach of the inhabitants. They are, on the whole, not bad food, and when hunger has made them palatable, are eaten as a matter of course. When well fed they are almost as good as shrimps. There is a species not eatable, with reddish wings, larger than those described, and which, though less numerous, are more destructive. The exploits of these armies, fearful as they are, bear no comparison to the devastation they make before they are able to fly, in which state they are called ' boyane.' They receive a new name in every stage of their growth, till they reach maturity, when they are called ' letsie.' They never emerge from the sand where they were deposited as eggs till rain has fallen to raise grass for the young progeny. In their course, from which nothing can divert them, they appear like a dark red stream, extending often more than a mile broad, and from their incessant hopping, the dust appears as if alive. Nothing but a broad and rapid torrent could arrest their progress, and that only by drowning them; and if one reached the opposite shore, it would keep the original direction. A small rivulet avails nothing, as they swim dexterously. A line of fire is no barrier, as they leap into it till it is extinguished, and the others walk over the dead. Walls and houses form no impediment; they climb the very chimneys, either obliquely or straight over such obstacles, just as their instinct leads them. All other earthly powers, from the fiercest lion to a marshalled army, are nothing compared with these diminutive insects. The course they have followed is stripped of every leaf or blade of verdure. It is enough to make the inhabitants of a village turn pale to hear that they are coming in a straight line to their gardens. When a country is not extensive, and is bounded by the sea, the scourge is soon over, the winds carrying them away like clouds to the watery waste, where they alight to rise no more. Thus the immense flights which pass to the south and east rarely return, but fresh supplies are always pouring down from the north."

In the same year Moffat paid a visit to the Barolongs, near the Malapo, that he might devote himself more closely to the study of the language. His journey lay over a wild and dreary country, and thinly inhabited. One night they came across no fewer than six full-grown lions and a cub, and knew not how soon any one of them, fearless of the travellers' small fire, might rush in among them; but the lions were apparently as distrustful of them as they were of the lions. The few natives that he fell in with furnished the saddest proofs of ignorance and depravity. The description he gave of the character of God, and the sinful and ruined condition of men only amused them, and drew forth expressions of pity that he should talk such foolishness. At two of the villages of the Barolongs he spent ten weeks studying the language. The people were kind, and his blunders in conversation gave rise to many bursts of laughter. No one would correct a word or sentence till he or she had mimicked the original so effectually as to give great merriment to others. Every opportunity was embraced to try to instruct them, but all the preaching and talking seemed like casting seed on the wayside or the rock. Their highest happiness consisted in having an abundance of meat. The missionary found the place not very favourable to study, after all, and he prepared to return. Before leaving he received a visit from Sebegne, the son of Makaba, who was now king of the Bauangketsi, in the stead of his late father. He desired Moffat to go and live with him and his people, and when informed that this was not possible, at least at present, he said at parting, "Well, then, trust me as you trusted my father."

The Sabbath before Moffat left he gathered the Barolongs together and preached his last discourse to them, exhorting them to forsake their sins and believe in Jesus Christ the Saviour. Having reached his home at Kuruman, he could not but feel grateful for the comforts that surrounded him there, and the progress he had been able to make in the language. One of the difficulties of a missionary residence in the country at that time was the uncertainty of communication. It was not easy to convey letters, owing to a dangerous desert path, and the tribes living in constant suspicion of each other. Often ambassadors never returned, and trading parties were entirely cut off. Postmen and carriers were not easily found, though they were safe if known to belong to the missionaries. More than once Moffat found it difficult to convince a messenger that the letter would not say a word to him on the road, and part of a journal and a letter to Mrs. Moffat were thrown away from this superstitious fear.

About the year 1828 our missionary began to see some

fruit of his labours at Kuruman. The prospect, which had hitherto been so dark that there was some talk on the part of the Directors in London of abandoning the station as hopeless, began to brighten. Some thousands of the natives had gathered near them on the opposite side of the valley, and would collect in different parts of the town for instruction. They manifested a greater desire to attend to the Gospel, and though there was nothing like true conversion, there were indications of coming blessing—enough to excite thanksgiving and hope. Aid in the erection of a church and school-house was voluntarily and cheerfully given. Great improvements appeared in the social habits of the people. Their greasy skins were covered with decent raiment. During public worship those who were present behaved with greater propriety and decorum. The arts of civilized life were to some extent studied and became better known. Some who had years before regarded a waggon as a "walking-house," and gazed at it with wonder, now learned to make one. As they stood around the forge while Moffat blew the bellows, or smote the iron on the anvil, his long black beard tied in a knot at the back of his neck to escape the sparks, they learned something of the usefulness and pleasure and dignity of labour. As they assembled at the doorway of the room where a printing-press had been put up, they stared with astonishment at the process by which sheets of white paper, after disappearing for a moment, came again to view covered with letters, conveying to them in their own language the word of God.

At last the set time to favour Zion had come. "The moral wilderness," says Moffat, "was now about to blossom. Sable cheeks bedewed with tears attracted our observation. To see females weep was nothing extraordinary; it was, according to Bechuana notions, their province, and theirs alone. Men would not weep. After having by the rite of circumcision become men, they scorned to shed a tear. In family or national afflictions it was the woman's work to weep and wail, the man's to sit in sullen silence, often brooding deeds of revenge and death. The simple Gospel now melted their flinty hearts, and eyes now wept which never before shed the tear of hallowed sorrow. Notwithstanding our earnest desires and fervent prayers, we were taken by surprise. We had so long been accustomed to indifference that we felt unprepared to look on a scene which perfectly overwhelmed our minds."

The formation of the first native church in Kuruman took place in 1829, in the presence of strangers from all parts of the region around. The whole of the first service was conducted in the language of the country. Hymns and prayers, lessons and sermon, were all in Sechuana; the preparatory examination of candidates for membership had been of course in the same tongue, with one exception, where the person examined was questioned in Dutch, she being more conversant with that language. We may imagine the feelings of the missionaries on that memorable occasion. The time had come on which all their energies had been fixed, for which they had fervently and without ceasing prayed; the time when they should see a church gathered from among a people who had so long boasted that they would never worship and confess Jesus as their Lord. Now again, as often before in the history of the people of God, was fulfilled the words of the psalmist, "He that goeth forth and weepeth, bearing precious seed, shall doubtless come again with rejoicing, bringing his sheaves with him."

CHAPTER XV.

THE Kuruman Station was commenced in 1824. A tract of about two miles of the country was bought by the missionaries from Mothibe, and paid for with articles which Mr. Moffat had brought from Cape Town. Here were raised ultimately a large and substantial church and some good dwelling-houses, all of stone. The station was laid out by Mr. Moffat, who to his services as land-surveyor and architect added, with equal diligence, the humbler but no less necessary and arduous callings of quarrier of stones and hewer of timber. The Kuruman station became one of those marks in a country which testify to the skill and power of the founders, and to the beneficial influences of Christianity.

From a succession of travellers we obtain three or four charming pictures of the station, as it has appeared at different periods and impressed different men. In 1834, Dr. Andrew Smith, at the head of an exploring party sent out to obtain a knowledge of the geography, the inhabitants, and the products of the country, paid the missionaries a visit. He was much gratified with all he saw and heard; but found Moffat prostrated by fever—the effects of over-

work at translation and printing in the hot season of the
year. The missionary, as soon as he recovered, consented to
guide this expedition to the dominions of Moselekatze, whom
he had previously visited himself. Dr. Smith, in his published report, gives an interesting account of their friendly
reception by the Matabele king, and testifies that "nothing
could exceed the respect shown by him for Mr. Moffat, a
circumstance which was exceedingly pleasing to me,
inasmuch as I knew it was most abundantly merited."

David Livingstone first visited Kuruman in 1840. After
speaking of his arrival at the Cape from England, he
says :—"I shortly afterwards went to Algoa Bay, and soon
proceeded inland to the Kuruman mission-station, in the
Bechuana country. This station is about seven hundred
miles from Cape Town, and had been established many
years before by Messrs. Hamilton and Moffat. The mission-
houses and church are built of stone. The gardens, irrigated
by a rivulet, are well stocked with fruit-trees and vines, and
yield European vegetables and grain readily. The pleasant-
ness of the place is enhanced by the contrast it presents to the
surrounding scenery, and the fact that it owes all its beauty
to the manual labour of the missionaries. Externally it
presents a picture of civilised comfort to the adjacent tribes ;
and the printing-press, worked by the original founders of
the mission and several younger men who have entered into
their labours, gradually diffuses the light of Christianity
through the neighbouring region. This oasis became doubly
interesting to me, from something like a practical exposition
of the text, Mark x. 29 ; for after nearly four years of
African life as a bachelor, I screwed up courage to put a
question beneath one of the fruit-trees, the result of which
was that, in 1844, I became united in marriage to Mr.
Moffat's eldest daughter Mary. Having been born in the
country, and being expert in household matters, she was
always the best spoke in the wheel at home ; and when I

took her with me on two occasions to Lake Ngami, and far beyond, she endured more than some who have written large books of travels."

In another passage connected with the life at Kuruman he says:—"In consequence of droughts at our station further inward, we were mainly dependent for supplies of food on Kuruman, and were often indebted to the fruit-trees there, and to Mrs. Moffat's kind foresight for the continuance of good health.

"A native smith taught me to weld iron; and having acquired some further information in this art as well as in carpentering and gardening from Mr. Moffat, I was becoming handy at most mechanical employments in addition to medicine and preaching. My wife could make candles, soap, and clothes; and thus we had nearly attained to the indispensable accomplishments of a missionary family in Central Africa — the husband to be a jack-of-all-trades *without* doors, and the wife a maid-of-all-work *within*."

In 1849 the Rev. J. J. Freeman visited Africa, and on arriving at Kuruman received a cordial welcome from Mr. and Mrs. Moffat. The village assumed in his sight a pretty and pleasing appearance, especially the mission premises, with the walled gardens opposite, forming a street wide and long. The gardens were well stocked with fruit and vegetables, requiring much water, but it was easily obtained from the fountain. On the Sunday morning the chapel bell rang for early service. Breakfasting at seven, all were ready for the schools at half-past eight. The infants were taught by Miss Moffat in their school-house; more advanced classes were grouped in the open air or collected in the adjacent buildings. The work of separate teaching was over by ten, when young and old assembled in the chapel for public worship. The large and lofty building was comfortably filled with men, women, and children, for the most part decently dressed. The day passed in a succession of services similar to those of the morning. Monday came, and Mr. Freeman inspected Mr. Moffat's printing-office and bindery. Although till that time the whole burden of these establishments had rested on one pair of shoulders, yet they were as orderly, if not as complete, as if they had been in the neighbourhood of Paternoster Row. Mr. Freeman, who had been sent out to inspect the stations of the London Missionary Society and report on their condition, returned to England with a deep impression of the value of the station as on the high road to the interior, and as a union and centre of influence to all around.

Mr. James Chapman, the African traveller, visited Kuruman in 1854, and thus describes what he saw :—"Next day I rode over to Kuruman, where I found my friend Mr. Thompson, who afterwards travelled in company with us. Here I was introduced to the worthy missionaries, Messrs. Moffat and Ashton, and their families, the memory of whose uniform kindness I shall ever cherish. Milk, new bread, and fresh butter, we were never in want of while near these good people, and of grapes, apples, peaches, and all other products of the garden, there was never any lack at our waggons. Every one is struck with the beauty of Kuruman, although the site cannot boast of any natural charms. All we see is the result of well-directed labour. A street of about a quarter of a mile in length is lined on one side by the missionary gardens, enclosed with substantial walls, and teeming with fruit and vegetables of every description. A row of spreading willows is nourished by a fine watercourse, pouring a copious stream at their roots for nearly a mile, and beyond the gardens flows to the eastward the river Kuruman, between tall reeds, with flights of water-fowl splashing on its surface. The river issues a few miles south from a grotto said to be one hundred yards long, and very spacious, the habitation of innumerable bats, owls, and serpents of a large size. Stalactites of various shapes and figures are to be found in this grotto. I have seen some beautiful specimens adorning mantel-pieces. One party discovered in the roof of this grotto portions of a human skeleton perfectly petrified, and a part of which was broken off.

"On the opposite side of the street, and facing the row of gardens, the willows, and the stream, is a spacious chapel, calculated to hold more than five hundred people. It is built of stone, with a missionary dwelling-house on either side of it, and a trader's dwelling-house and store at the western end. All these, as well as the smaller but neat dwellings of the Bechuanas, built in the European style, and in good taste, have shady syringa trees planted in the front. At the back of the missionary premises there are store and school-rooms, workshops, &c., with a smithy in front. Behind the chapel is a printing-office, in which native compositors were setting type for the new editions of Mr. Moffat's bible. Thousands of Sechuana books have been as well printed and as neatly bound in this establishment, under the superintendence of Mr. Ashton, as they could be in England. The natives here are the most enlightened and civilised I have seen, the greater portion wearing clothes, and being able to read and write. It was pleasant on Sunday to see them neatly and cleanly clad going to church three times a day. In their tillage they are also making rapid progress, and having adopted European practices, instead of the hoe they use the plough."

The visit of Livingstone to this country in 1856, and the publication of his South African researches, greatly revived missionary interest as to that part of the world. One result was, that several young men offered themselves for work in that part of the mission field. Among the number was the Rev. John Mackenzie, who reached the Cape in July 1858. Some years afterwards he published a most interesting and valuable record of his first ten years labours, entitled,

"Ten years north of the Orange River," in which he sketches with a facile pen his views and impressions of the head-quarters of Moffat's operations. In a few months after their arrival in Africa, he and Mr. Price his companion, both of whom were on their way to the Makololo, called at Kuruman, and thus he writes of it :—"It was late on Monday night before we reached Kuruman ; but we were delighted with the appearance of the country in the bright moonlight—the thorn-trees on both sides of the road near Kuruman remind-ing us of the grounds of a country house in England. On approaching the station we found everything in profoundest stillness ; the little village was asleep. Our knocking, how· ever, soon roused Mr. Moffat, who gave his unexpected visitors a joyous welcome to his South African home, which was repeated by his family, and in the morning by Mr. Ashton, his colleague. I found that most of the people living at Kuruman have considerable knowledge of agricul-ture and the ordinary management of a garden. The hoe has largely given place to the plough, and in such cases the work of the garden ceases to belong to the women, and is performed by the men. Here are the best kept native gardens in Bechuana land ; but even here the straight line in fence and furrow is not always what it ought to be."

Speaking of the more strictly religious aspect of the place, Mr. Mackenzie goes on to say :—"If you wish to see Kuruman to advantage, you must come to church on Sunday morning. I do not mean to the prayer-meeting at sunrise, but during the hour before service, when the people assemble in groups outside the church in the grateful shade of the syringa trees. Some read the scriptures ; others are going over the spelling-book ; acquaintances are greeting each other ; while occasional strangers from the interior stand in the background in their karosses, and gaze with mute wonder on the scene. Inside the church and school-room the children are singing hymns and listening to the instructions of their teachers. You see many people who are respectably dressed. Most of the men belonging to the station wear European clothing; the trousers, however, are frequently of skin, tanned and made by themselves. The Bechuanas are skilful in patching; and one sees coats and gowns of many colours, and wide-awake hats so operated upon that you cannot well describe either their shape or colour. Most of the women wear a handkerchief (or two) tied tightly round the head; and it is counted rather elegant to have one coloured, while the other is black silk. Ladies' hats were patronised by a few; and there seemed to be a division of opinion as to whether the hat ought to be worn on the bare head, or over a handkerchief rather ingeniously folded so as to imitate long hair in a net. Shoes are now neatly made, somewhat after the fashion of brogues in Scotland; but stockings are regarded as equally superfluous with gloves. You observe that a good many have brought with them a pretty large bag, while some also carry a chair on their shoulder. The bag contains the Sechuana Bible, which is in three volumes, and the hymn-book, which, here as elsewhere, is a great favourite. The chairs are brought chiefly by the aristocracy of the village, the reason being, as you see on entering the church, that the congregation sit on benches or forms without backs, which is not the most comfortable position to hear a sermon. The bell rings for service, and the people hasten into the church. The mothers who have little children remain on forms near the door, so that in case of a squall they can readily make their exit.

"The minister of the day ascends the pulpit; and as the London Missionary Society is a very broad institution, and takes no notice whatever of clerical dress and appointments, black cloth seldom extended further than the coat; while pulpit-gowns and bands, and even white neckties, were nowhere; and it was not unusual for one of the ministers to make his appearance in smoking-cap and wrought slippers!

The cap was off in church, and the slippers were not seen in the pulpit, and when both were seen outside, instead of shocking any of the congregation, they seemed to be much admired. The singing at Kuruman in 1859 was equalled only by that of a Dutch frontier congregation. The latter would bear off the palm on account of the strength of the voices and lungs of the Dutch people. But at Kuruman a great improvement took place in the singing in a very short time. Lessons in church psalmody were given by the Misses Moffat, assisted by an excellent harmonium kindly sent out for the use of the station by some Christian ladies in London. Many of the Bechuanas showed themselves possessed of a fine musical ear.

" The service now proceeds with the reading and exposition of scripture, succeeded by solemn prayer. A sermon or lecture follows, in which the preacher strives to introduce some incident in the sacred narrative — some parable or doctrine, so as to impress its lesson on the minds of his audience. In 1859 there were three such services at Kuruman on the Sunday. In the course of the week there is one public evening service conducted by one of the missionaries, and another entirely in the hands of the natives."

It is impossible for any candid person to read these several testimonies (not all of them from missionaries, or even men unduly prejudiced in favour of missionary operations) without acknowledging the power and value of the gospel of Christ; and the ability, integrity, and self-sacrificing zeal of those who had gone with their lives in their hands to preach it to these heathen tribes. There are people who make it their business to misrepresent and slander Christian missionaries, and speak of them as indolent and self-seeking men. Let such people hear the testimony of Mr. Chapman, whose description of Kuruman has been already given. He spent fifteen years in South Africa hunting and trading, and saw a great deal of missionary life and labour; and, as an impartial observer, bears this honourable testimony:—"The lot of a missionary in Africa is a hard one; his life is one of trial and self-denial. Deprived, often for months together, of the common necessaries of life, cut off from society, from friends and relations, with the prospect of never seeing them more, it is cruel that they should be looked upon with suspicion by those whom they have come to benefit, and be despised and slandered by their own countrymen. That a missionary trades in this country is only because he is compelled to do so to obtain the supplies necessary for the wants of his family. You never hear of missionaries exporting cattle, ivory, or any other commodity. They trade for cattle with merchandise, because money is neither known or esteemed. Could the missionary send to the butcher and the baker every day, and buy his few pounds of meat or bread, he would not be compelled to purchase the cattle from the natives. He is compelled to keep a small number of cattle, and slaughter the increase; and if his wife wants a little milk for her young children, they must have several cows to furnish the supply, as a dozen Damara cows give scarcely as much milk as one European. If God blesses this little flock with a healthy increase, they are pointed out by the jealous and selfish white man as the profits of trade. I have seen a great deal of missionary life, and have every reason to sympathise with them. Their labours are difficult, their trials many, their earthly reward a bare subsistence. I believe that the real causes of dislike to the missionaries in South Africa are the avarice of trade and jealousy of the influence they possess, and the check they are upon those who would like to exercise an arbitrary and unjust authority over the natives. I could say a great deal more on this subject; but the missionaries are a class of men, generally speaking, so irreproachable, that the scandals of the unprincipled cannot affect them with well-thinking men, nor do their characters require any further defence by me."

As to the success of missionary labours in Kuruman and the regions around, Dr. Livingstone thus gives us his own honest and intelligent impressions, and the sensible and discriminative judgment of one of the native chieftains:— "Many hundreds of both Griquas and Bechuanas have become Christians, and partly civilised, through the teaching of English missionaries.   My first impression was that the accounts of the effect which the gospel had had upon them were too highly coloured.   When, however, I passed on to true heathens in countries beyond the sphere of missionary influence, I came to the conclusion that the change produced was unquestionably great.   It is a proof of the success of the Bechuana Mission, that when we came back from the interior we always felt on reaching Kuruman that we had returned to civilised life.   On asking an intelligent chief what he thought of the converts, he replied : 'You white men have no idea how wicked we are ; we know each other better than you.   Some feign belief to ingratiate themselves with the missionaries ; some profess Christianity because they like the new system, which gives so much more importance to the poor, and desire that the old system may pass away; and the rest—a pretty large number— profess, because they are really true believers.'   This account is very nearly correct."

CHAPTER XVI.

MOSELEKATSE AND THE MATABELE.

THE Christian influence of Moffat and his fellow-labourers was not confined to Kuruman and its immediate neighbourhood. Tidings concerning their character and doings had been conveyed to some of the more interior tribes. Their amazing skill, their fearlessness and bravery, their purity of living, their kindness and compassion, all were reported—in some cases by those who had themselves seen them, in other cases only from hearsay.

Among those who heard the news was Moselekatse, king of the Matabele, whom Moffat calls "this Napoleon of the desert." This chief was a man of a bold and intrepid character, and had been a marauder from his youth. For years his career was an interminable catalogue of crimes. There was scarcely a spot over extensive regions that did not bear the marks of his deadly ire. His native cunning, and his knowledge of human nature, enabled him to triumph over the minds of his people, and made them regard him as an invincible sovereign. Those who resisted him he butchered. "He trained the captured youth in his own tactics, so that the majority of his army were foreigners;

but his chiefs and nobles gloried in their descent from the Zulu dynasty. He had carried his arms far into the tropics, where, however, he had more than once met his equal; and on one occasion, of six hundred warriors only a handful returned, who were doomed to be sacrificed, merely because they had not conquered or fallen with their companions." He numbered his warriors by thousands, and governed with a most despotic rule, owning no law but his own capricious will. The country under his sway was that now known as the Transvaal.

This man was curious to know something more of the white men whose fame had reached him; and so, in 1829, he sent two of his chief men, in the company of some returning traders, to visit these teachers at Kuruman, and make themselves more particularly acquainted with their manners and instructions. The missionaries, of course, received them with courtesy and kindness, and shewed them every mark of attention, exhibiting everything that was likely to interest, and specially endeavouring to explain and impress on their minds the great truths of the Gospel. The men were savages, yet a natural politeness and dignity marked their whole behaviour, and shewed that they were persons of rank in their own country. The houses and gardens, the water-ditch conveying water for irrigation from the river, and the smith's forge, especially excited their wonder and admiration, which they expressed in the most respectful manner. "You are men," said they, "we are but children; Moselekatse must be taught all these things."

When standing in the hall of Moffat's house looking at the furniture, so strange in their eyes, Mrs. Moffat handed one of them a looking-glass. He looked intently on his reflected countenance, and never having seen such a thing before, supposed it was that of one of his attendants on the other side. Abruptly putting his hand behind it, he bade him begone; but looking again at the same face he cautiously turned it. Seeing nothing, he returned the glass with great gravity, observing at the same time that he could not trust it. Nothing, however, in all they saw seemed to interest them so much as the public worship in the chapel. The sight of men like themselves meeting together with such decorum, mothers hushing their babes, the elder children sitting still and silent, was a novel scene. When the missionary ascended the pulpit, they listened to the singing and prayer, the reading and address, with astonishment and reverence; though, from their ignorance of the Sechuana language, they could not fully understand. They asked many questions as to the nature of the service, and were greatly surprised to find that the hymns were not war-songs, expressive of the wild reveries which the associations of music alone brought to their minds.

Moselekatse's ambassadors had intended to visit the colony, that they might see the white man's country; but this was found inconvenient, and involved considerable difficulty as to how they were to return in safety. The question of their departure to their own land now occasioned perplexity. Reports were in circulation that some of the Bechuana tribes, through whom they would have to pass on their homeward way, were meditating their destruction; and the missionaries had reason to fear that the reports were true. They therefore wished their visitors had not come to their station, because they could not pretend to defend them by physical force; and they could not help trembling at the possible consequences of their being attacked and murdered on the road.

After much thought and prayer, Moffat resolved that he would himself undertake to conduct them through the several tribes from whom danger was anticipated, going with them as far as the Bahurutsi country, from which they could proceed without danger to their own land and people. The undertaking was attended with considerable risk ; all through the hundreds of miles that lay before them dangers were to be apprehended both from wild beasts and wild men. But that gracious Providence which watched over the missionary and directed his steps on this remarkable journey preserved him from all harm, and, with the influence of his own good name, secured him kindness and a hearty welcome from the sons of the desert.

As they went along in some parts, like the mariner on the ocean, they saw the expanse around them bounded only by the horizon. Here and there were clumps of mimosas and grass, like tall wheat, waving in the breeze. All kinds of game roamed at large. Occasionally some of the solitary inhabitants who lived only on roots and the chase intercepted their path, and begged a little tobacco, and sometimes passed the night where they encamped. On retiring to rest one night a lion passed near the waggons, occasionally giving a roar, which died away on the extended plain, and was responded to by another in the distance. Directing the attention of these homeless wanderers to the sound, Moffat asked if they thought there was danger ; they immediately turned their ears as to a voice with which they were familiar, and after listening for a moment or two replied, " There is no danger ; he has eaten, and is going to sleep." They were right, and the travellers slept also. Being asked in the morning how they knew the lions were going to sleep, they replied, "We live with them ; they are our companions."

Approaching Moselekatse's country the face of nature changed, and the scenery was quite different from what they had passed through. It was now mountainous and wooded to the summits ; evergreens adorned the valleys, in which numerous streams of excellent water flowed through many a winding course. "I was charmed exceedingly," says Moffat, "and was often reminded of Scotia's hills and dales. As it was a rainy season, everything was fresh; the clumps of trees that studded the plains being covered with rich and living verdure. But these rocks and vales and picturesque scenes were often vocal with the lion's roar. It was a country once covered with a dense population. On the sides of the hills and Kashan mountains were towns in ruins, where thousands once made the country alive, amidst fruitful vales now covered with luxuriant grass, inhabited by game. The extirpating invasions of the Mantatees and Matabele had left to beasts of prey the undisputed right of these lovely woodland glens. The lion, which had revelled on human flesh, as if conscious that there was none to oppose, roamed at large, a terror to the traveller, who often heard with dismay his nightly roaring echoed back by the surrounding hills. We were mercifully preserved during the nights, though our slumbers were often interrupted by his fearful howlings. We had frequently to take our guns and precede the waggon, as the oxen sometimes took fright at the sudden rush of a rhinoceros or buffalo from a thicket. More than one instance occurred when a rhinoceros being aroused from its slumbers by the crack of the whips, the oxen would scamper off like race-horses, when destruction of gear and some part of the waggon was the result. As there was no road, we were frequently under the necessity of taking very circuitous routes to find a passage through deep ravines; and we were often obliged to employ picks, spades, and hatchets to clear our way. When we bivouacked for the night, a plain was generally selected, that we might be the better able to defend ourselves; and when firewood was plentiful, we made a number of fires at a distance around the waggons. But when it rained, our situation was pitiful indeed; and we only wished it to rain so hard that the lion might not like to leave his lair."

When they came to the outposts of the Matabele, they

halted by a fine rivulet; and a scene presented itself such as Moffat had not before witnessed. "My attention," he observes, "was arrested by a beautiful and gigantic tree standing in a defile leading into an extensive and woody ravine, between a high range of mountains. Seeing some individuals employed on the ground under its shade, and the conical points of what looked like houses in miniature protruding through its evergreen foliage, I proceeded thither, and found that the tree was inhabited by several families of Bakones, the aborigines of the country. I ascended by the notched trunk, and found to my amazement no less than seventeen of these aerial abodes, and three others unfinished. On reaching the topmost hut, about thirty feet from the ground, I entered and sat down. Its only furniture was the hay which covered the floor, a spear, a spoon, and a bowl full of locusts. Not having eaten anything that day, and from the novelty of my situation not wishing to return immediately to the waggons, I asked a woman who sat at the door with a babe at her breast permission to eat. This she granted with pleasure, and soon brought me more in a powdered state. Several more females came from the neighbouring roosts, stepping from branch to branch, to see the stranger, who was to them as great a curiosity as the tree was to him. I then visited the different abodes, which were on several principal branches. The structure of these houses was very simple. An oblong scaffold, about seven feet wide, is formed of straight sticks; on one end of this platform a small cone is formed also of straight sticks, and thatched with grass. A person can nearly stand upright in it: the diameter of the floor is about six feet. The house stands on the end of the oblong, so as to leave a little square space before the door. On the day previous I had passed several villages, some containing forty houses, all built on poles, about seven or eight feet from the ground, in the form of a circle; the ascent and descent is by a knotty branch of

TYPES OF VARIOUS AFRICAN TRIBES

a tree placed in front of the house. In the centre of the circle there is always a heap of the bones of game they have killed. Such are the domiciles of the impoverished thousands of the aborigines of the country, who having been scattered and peeled by Moselekatse, had neither herd nor stall, but subsisted on locusts, roots, and the chase. They adopted this mode of architecture to escape the lions which abounded in the country. During the day the families descended to the shade beneath to dress their daily food. When the inhabitants increased, they supported the augmented weight on the branches by upright sticks; but when lightened of their load, they removed these for firewood."

Having accompanied his charge nearly to the borders of their own country, Moffat, as they could now proceed without danger, desired to leave them and return to his work at Kuruman. The ambassadors, however, pleaded with him to proceed to the end of the journey. They said that as he had shewn them so much kindness, and proved himself such a true friend, he must go and experience the kindness and friendship of their king. Besides, Moselekatse, they said, would kill them if they suffered their guardian to return without having seen him. "Yonder," said they, pointing to the mountains in the distance, "dwells the great Moselekatse, and how shall we approach his presence if you are not with us? If you love us still, save us, for when we shall have told our news, he will ask why our conduct gave you pain to cause your return; and before the sun sets on the day we see his face, we shall be ordered out for execution, because you are not with us. Look at me and my companion, and tell us, if you can, that you will not go, for we had better die here than in the sight of our own people." This appeal overruled all Moffat's objections, and he resolved to accompany them to their king.

The nearer they approached the king's residence the more striking and numerous were the evidences of his despotic and destructive power. Ruined villages, heaps of stones and rubbish mingled with human skulls, told their sad tale. It was clear that not long ago thousands of people had dwelt in the beautiful and charming region through which the travellers were passing. But the extirpating invasions of the Matabele had swept them all away. It was evident, too, that the ambassadors wished to preserve silence on this state of things, and took care to be always present if possible when any of the aborigines appeared. One of their three servants belonged to the Bakones, and was a native of the country. He would sometimes whisper of the times of war and devastation. He would describe the Bakones and the Bahurutsi as being once numerous as the locusts, rich in cattle, and maintaining a large trade with the distant tribes of the north. His stories of the carrying away of cattle and other possessions, the butchering of the inhabitants, and the wasting of towns and villages by fire, were heartrending. The commandos of Chaka, the Zulu tyrant, had made frightful havoc, but it was as nothing to the final overthrow of the aboriginal tribes by Moselekatse.

One Sabbath morning Moffat ascended a hill to command the prospect around, when his Bakone companion suddenly appeared. He had come to converse with his white friend. Seeing before them a large extent of level ground covered with ruins, the missionary asked what had become of the inhabitants. The man had just sat down, but he immediately arose, and stretching forth his arm in the direction of the ruins, said, "I, even I, beheld it!" He paused a moment, as if in thought, and then continued: "There lived the great chief of multitudes. He reigned among them like a king. He was the chief of the blue-coloured cattle. They were numerous as the dense mist on the mountain brow; his flocks covered the plain. He thought the number of his warriors would awe his enemies. His people boasted in their spears, and laughed at the cowardice of such as had fled from their towns. 'I shall slay them, and hang up their shields on my hill. Our race is a race of warriors. Who ever subdued our fathers? they were mighty in combat. We still possess the spoils of ancient times. Have not our dogs eaten the shields of their nobles? The vultures shall devour the slain of our enemies.' Thus they sang and thus they danced, till they beheld on yonder heights the approaching foe. The noise of their song was hushed in night, and their hearts were filled with dismay. They saw the clouds ascend from the plains. It was the smoke of burning towns. The confusion of a whirlwind was in the heart of the great chief of the blue-coloured cattle. This shout was raised, 'They are friends,' but they shouted again, 'They are foes,' till their near approach proclaimed them Matabele. The men seized their arms, and rushed out as if to chase the antelope. The onset was as the voice of lightning, and their spears as the shaking of a forest in the autumn storm. The Matabele lions raised the shout of death, and flew upon their victims. It was the shout of victory. Their hissing and hollow groans told their progress among the dead. A few moments laid hundreds on the ground. The clash of shields was the signal of triumph. Our people fled with their cattle to the top of yonder mount. The Matabele entered the town with the roar of the lion; they pillaged and fired the houses, speared the mothers, and cast their infants to the flames. The sun went down. The victors emerged from the smoking plain, and pursued their course, surrounding the base of yonder hill. They slaughtered cattle, they danced and sang till the dawn of day, they ascended and killed till their hands were weary of the spear." Then stooping to the ground on which he stood, the narrator took up a little dust in his hand; blowing it off, and holding out his naked hand, he added, "That is all that remains of the great chief of the blue-coloured cattle!" Moffat found from other aborigines that this outburst of native poetic eloquence was no fabled song, but merely a compendious sketch of the fearful catastrophe which had overwhelmed those unhappy tribes.

Nothing could exceed the heartiness of Moffat's reception by the Matabele king. It took place in a large cattle-fold, which was lined by a thousand warriors wearing kilts of ape-skins, their legs and arms adorned with the hair and tails of oxen, and their heads with feathers. Motionless as statues they stood behind their shields, which reached to their chins. After some minutes of profound silence they began a grand war song, when out marched the barbarian monarch, followed by a number of men bearing baskets and bowls filled with food, which were placed at the missionary's feet. The king then shook hands with his visitor, and invited him to partake; and in reply to his expressed desire that a spot outside the town might be appointed for encampment, said, "The land is before you ; you are come to your son ; you must sleep where you please." As the waggons approached, he grasped the missionary's hand with awe, and then drew back in doubt as to whether or not they were living creatures. When the oxen were unyoked he ventured, still holding fast by Moffat's arm, to examine the "moving houses." The wheels especially excited his wonder ; the greatest mystery of all being how the large band of iron surrounding the felloes of the wheel came to be in one piece, without either end or joint. One of the ambassadors whose visit to Kuruman had made him wiser than his royal master, took hold of Moffat's hand and said, "My eyes saw that very hand cut these bars of iron, take a piece off one end and then join them as you now see them." When the welded part was shewn to the monarch, he said to the ambassador "Does he give medicine to the iron?" "No," was the reply ; "nothing is used but fire, a hammer, and a chisel."

Anxious to exhibit himself and his nation to the best

advantage, he on one occasion assembled his warriors to the number of ten thousand from their various villages, so that they might engage in a sham fight and a war dance. Moffat took advantage of the exhibition to shew him the evils of war, especially such unprovoked and cruel wars as he had promoted; and caused no little astonishment by the expression of his sentiments and his lack of interest in the military display. Moselekatse had not been accustomed to be spoken to after the fashion in which he was now addressed; but the missionary who now spoke to him in the name of the God of Peace was one who never feared the face of any man, and who flinched not from upholding the standard of the Gospel even in the strongest holds of heathenism.

Man of blood as the barbarian king was, and indifferent as he shewed himself to the message of salvation, he nevertheless took kindly to Moffat, and was grateful for the way in which the ambassadors had been treated. One day, placing his hand on the missionary's shoulder, he said, "Father! you have made my heart white as milk. I cease not to wonder at the love of a stranger; you never saw me before, but you love me more than my own people: you fed me when I was hungry, you clothed me when I was naked, you carried me in your bosom, and your arm shielded me from my enemies." When the missionary replied that he was unconscious of having rendered him such service, he pointed to the two ambassadors who were standing near, and said, "These are great men. When I sent them from my presence to see the land of the white man, I sent my ears, my eyes, my mouth. What they heard I heard; what they saw I saw; and when they spoke, it was Moselekatse who spoke. You fed them and clothed them; and when they were to be slain you were their shield. You did it unto me; you did it unto Moselekatse, the son of Machobane!"

CHAPTER XVII.

VARIED EXPERIENCES.

ON Moffat's return home the Matabele king accompanied him for two or three days, travelling for the first time in an African waggon. Advantage was taken to renew entreaties that he would abstain from war; and as he professed a desire that missionaries should be sent to reside with him, a promise was given that such should be the case. The two friends then parted, to meet, however, again in coming days. After an absence of two months, Moffat reached Kuruman, and found all well, and the Divine blessing resting still on the work of the mission.

Shortly after, Mr. and Mrs. Moffat went with their children, by way of Algoa Bay, to Cape Town. On intimating to the people before leaving that he meant to collect money in the colony towards their new place of worship, a number of them readily came forward and begged to contribute their mite. Some subscribed oxen, some goats, a few gave money, and a number engaged to work. This was very cheering to the missionary's heart. Arriving at Graham's Town, he left his family there while he went to visit several of the mission stations in Caffre Land, and then some of those within the colony. Ultimately they all reached Cape Town in October 1830. Here he toiled at arduous printing engagements. These labours were scarcely finished before a severe attack of bilious fever came on, occasioned by over exertion in the hottest season of the year; and he was brought so low that when they started on their homeward journey he had to be carried on a mattress on board ship. A voyage of fourteen days in rough weather to Algoa Bay proved, however, most beneficial; and by June 1831 they found themselves once more at the Kuruman.

They returned to the station bearing many precious treasures,—an edition of the Gospel of Luke and a hymn-book in the native language, a printing-press, type, paper, ink, contributions for the new chapel, and a box of materials for clothing, for the encouragement of such as were making efforts to clothe themselves. A sewing-school was established and carried on, to the great comfort and improvement of the natives. But this season of pleasure had also its alloy, for the small-pox entered the country and swept away many of the inhabitants, and amongst them one of the missionary's own children.

Above all, the favour and blessing of God were seen in the real conversions which took place at this time. Considerable accessions were made to the number of believers. Strangers from distant tribes were received into the church. There are two illustrations of the power of Divine grace furnished by Moffat himself that carry with them their own praise. "Mamonyatsi, one of these, some years after died in the faith. She was a Matabele captive, and had accompanied me from the interior, remaining some time in the service of Mrs. M., and early displaying a readiness to learn to read, with much quickness of understanding. From the time of her being united with the church till the day of her death she was a living epistle of the power of the Gospel. Once while visiting the sick, as I entered her premises, I found her sitting weeping, with a portion of the word of God in her hand. Addressing her, I said : ' My child, what is the cause of your sorrow ? Is the baby still unwell ?' 'No,' she replied, 'my baby is well.' 'Your mother-in-law ?' I inquired. 'No, no,' she said, ' it is my own dear mother who bore me.' Here she again gave vent to her grief, and holding out the Gospel of Luke, in a hand wet with tears, she said, ' My mother will never see this word, she will never hear this good news !' She wept again and again, and said, ' Oh my mother and my friends ! They live in heathen darkness; and shall they die without seeing the light which has shone on me, and without tasting that love which I have tasted ?' Raising her eyes to heaven, she sighed a prayer, and I heard the words again, ' My mother, my mother !' This was the expression of the affection of one of Africa's sable daughters, whose heart had been taught to mourn over the ignorance of a far-distant mother. Shortly after this evidence of divine love in her soul I was called upon to watch her dying pillow, and descended with her to Jordan's bank. She feared no rolling billow. She looked on the babe to which she had but lately given birth, and commended it to the care of her God and Saviour. The last words I heard from her faltering lips were, ' My mother !' "

The other is the case of an aged blind woman, who from the time of her conversion till her death, a period of several years, continued to adorn her profession by a consistent walk and conversation. " A few days before her death she wished her children to be gathered together in her presence, desiring to speak to them before she left them. They surrounded her bed, and when informed that all were present, she addressed them : ' My children, I wish you to know that I am to be separated from you, but you must not on that account be sorrowful. Do not murmur at the thought of my decease. The Lord has spared me not a few days, He has taken care of me many years, and has ever been merciful to me; I have wanted no good thing. I know Him to whom I have trusted the salvation of my soul. My hope is fixed on Jesus Christ, who has died for my sins, and lives to intercede. I shall soon die and be at rest; but my wish is that you will attend to these my words. My children, hold fast your faith in Christ. Trust in Him, love Him, and let not the world turn you away from Him; and however you may be reviled and troubled in the world, hold very fast the word of God, and faint not in persevering prayer. My last word is, strive to live together in peace. Avoid disputes. Follow peace with all, and especially among yourselves. Love each other, comfort each other, assist and take care of each other in the Lord.' After this charge to her children she said but little. Her last words were spoken some hours before her death, when a church member, ever in attendance at sick beds, called upon her. She heard his voice, and said, 'Yes, I know thee, Mogami, my brother in the Lord. I am going, but thou wilt remain. Hold fast the word of God. Turn not from His ways. And take a message to thy wife, my sister in the Lord, that she must use all diligence to ensure eternal life.'"

Moffat's visit to Moselekatse and the reports of traders who had arrived from the north excited considerable interest in Cape Town, and led to the sending out of the exploring expedition under Dr. Andrew Smith to which we have already alluded. At the earnest request of Dr. Smith, who, as we have seen, called at Kuruman on his way out, Moffat consented to accompany the expedition; thus he visited the Matabele king a second time. While the members of the exploring party roamed over the country acquainting themselves with its natural productions, the missionary remained with the king endeavouring to lead him to Christ, pleading for the poor and oppressed, and urging upon him the exercise of mercy and compassion.

Before returning to Kuruman he was gladdened by the king's consent to the establishment of a mission among his people.

Towards the close of 1836 Mr. Moffat left home, at the repeated request of the people in the towns on the Kolong River to pay them a visit. Pursuing his course, he met large and attentive congregations. The demands for spelling-books were beyond what he could supply. Proceeding on, he reached at last the distant and isolated village of Mosheu, a Coranna chief. His acquaintance with this man began in 1834, when an entire stranger, with two or three attendants riding on oxen, he stopped at the missionary's door. He was clean and well-dressed, looked mild and pleasant, and asked where he might lodge. He was pointed to an outhouse, to which he went, and where he and his companions slept. He had brought his own supplies of food with him, which in the case of visitors was most unusual. When asked the object of his visit, he replied that he had come to see the white man. After remaining two days, he left, apparently much pleased with his visit. On leaving, he said to Moffat while holding his hand, "I came to see you ; my visit has given me pleasure, and now I return home."

After some time Mosheu appeared at Kuruman again with a large retinue, consisting of wives and other relations, servants and oxen. The missionary's words about the love of God in Jesus Christ spoken during the former visit had taken such hold of him, that now he came back to ask what he and his friends must do to be saved. Having remained for some time to hear the gospel of salvation and learn the truth more perfectly, they all took their departure ; not, however, till a promise had been given by Moffat in response to their earnest request to visit their village at the earliest opportunity.

In fulfilment of this promise Moffat now travelled to Mosheu's village. The journey had been long and wearisome, and at its termination he was so wearied that he longed for quiet and repose. Rest, however, was out of the question. No sooner did he approach the village than old and young came flocking around to welcome him; and five hundred people were in a few minutes holding out their hands to shake his, crowding forward, and pressing upon one another in their eagerness. It was twelve o'clock that night before they were satisfied and he was able to lie down in his waggon to sleep. Next morning by early dawn they were around the waggon again, all waiting for him to preach to them. He heard their eager clamorous voices while dressing himself, and as soon as he appeared, messengers ran to tell those who had not come to the waggon that he was up. Without waiting to take his breakfast, he at once began to preach to the crowd, and spoke to them for an hour on the words, "God so loved the world that He gave His only-begotten Son, that whosoever believeth in Him should not perish but have everlasting life." They listened with the utmost attention. The cattle wandered away unheeded. Women who had been milking stood with their vessels of milk in their hands all the time; and some strangers who came up with bows and spears laid down their weapons and listened also.

The preacher at the close of the service, and while the people were dispersing, went to a neighbouring pool to refresh himself with a wash, and then returned to his waggon to breakfast. What was his surprise to find the people assembled again, and to learn that they wanted another sermon at once. Pleading hunger, he begged them to wait for half-an-hour. Hearing this, one of the chief women hastened to her hut, and returning with a wooden bowl filled with sour milk, said with a smile, "There, drink away; drink much, and you will be able to speak long." Cheerfully accepting this hasty African breakfast, the preacher resumed his station, and delivered a second discourse to, if possible, a still more attentive congregation. As soon as this second sermon was finished the people divided into groups to talk over what had been said. One young man who had a good memory and power of mimicry, and who had attended to all that had fallen from the preacher's lips, repeated, with all the preacher's movements, the whole of the sermon to a crowd of listeners.

Two sermons were not enough to satisfy these hungry souls. After the cows had been milked in the evening, when the sun went down, they came once more to the waggon. There, while the clear silvery moon shone on the scene, they listened again to God's message of love; and long after the service was ended they lingered about asking questions and talking over what they had heard. Next morning tempestuous weather prevented preaching out of doors, so the missionary spent the day talking with them in their huts and trying to teach them to read. Towards evening the wind subsided, and there was preaching again; but at bed-time all the people wanted another lesson in reading. Two or three young men who had already learned to read had accompanied Moffat from Kuruman. A few spelling-books and sheets of letters were in the waggon, and soon the Kuruman readers were each surrounded by a circle of scholars calling out "A, B, C." It was moonlight, and the letters were small, so that all could not see them clearly; but all were able to shout "A, B, C." One of the young men from Kuruman had told them that in the schools there the children *sang* their alphabet. Although it was growing late they began to cry out, "Oh teach us the A, B, C with music!" The lesson was therefore sung to "Auld Lang Syne." The people picked it up very quickly, and were so pleased with their new acquirements that it was between two and three o'clock in the morning before they allowed their teachers to leave them. When Mr. Moffat lay down to sleep the people were still singing "A, B, C" to "Auld Lang Syne," and when morning dawned the women went to milk the cows and the boys to tend the calves still humming "A, B, C" to "Auld Lang Syne."

When the time came for Moffat's return the whole population of the village accompanied him to a considerable distance, and then stood gazing after him till his waggon was out of sight. Often after this Moshew and his people made visits to Kuruman. It was an interesting spectacle to see forty or fifty men, women, and children traversing the plain all mounted on oxen, accompanied by a number of milch cows, that they might not be burdensome either to the missionaries or the Kuruman people. Their object was to obtain instruction; and they would remain for several weeks at a time diligently attending to all the opportunities afforded.

With one incident illustrative of the power of Christian principle in this people, and the influence of their manifestation of it on their enemies, we close this chapter. One Sabbath morning they were assembled in the centre of the village to hold their early prayer-meeting. While at worship a band of marauders made their appearance. Mosheu arose, and begged the people to sit still and trust in God, while he went to meet the strangers. To his question what they wanted, the reply was, "Your cattle; and it is at your peril you raise a weapon to resist." "There are my cattle," replied the chief, and then retired and resumed his position in the meeting. A hymn was sung, a chapter read, and then all kneeled in prayer to God, who alone could save them in the day of trouble. The sight was too sacred and solemn to be gazed on by such a band of ruffians, and they all withdrew from the place without touching a single article belonging to the people.

CHAPTER XVIII.

TRANSLATIONS AND THE PRINTING-PRESS.

FOR a long time after he began his work in Africa Moffat had to carry it on through the medium of interpreters. But these were sometimes incompetent men. As in the days of Job and in the land of Uz, an interpreter to any good purpose was barely one among a thousand. One day addressing an audience, the missionary said : "The salvation of the soul is a great and important subject." In conveying the statement to the people the interpreter told them that the salvation of the soul was a very great "sack." He found at last that he must fling his interpreters away, for they could neither understand themselves nor make others understand. "A missionary who commences giving *direct* instruction to the natives, though far from competent in the language, is proceeding on safer ground than if he were employing an interpreter who is not proficient in both languages, and has not a tolerable understanding of the doctrines of the Gospel." Even though an interpreter be ever so competent, it is well to try to dispense with his services as soon as possible.

We have seen how Moffat set about learning the Sechuana tongue. It was no easy task. The difficulties of mastering the language were increased by the variety of its dialects. In the towns its purity and harmony are preserved by means of their "pitchos" or public meetings, at which it is best spoken, and of their festivals and ceremonials, as well as of their songs and their social intercourse. "But with the isolated villages of the desert," as Moffat remarks in a passage to which Max Muller refers in his *Lectures on Language*, "it is far otherwise. They have no such meetings, no festivals, no cattle, nor any kind of manufactures to keep their energies alive; riches they have none, their sole care being to keep body and soul together. To accomplish this is with them their 'chief end.' They are compelled to traverse the wilds often to a great distance from their native village. On such occasions fathers and mothers, and all who can bear a burden, often set out for weeks at a time, and leave their children to the care of two or more infirm old people. The infant progeny, some of whom are beginning to lisp, while others can just master a whole sentence, and those still further advanced, romping and playing together through the live-long day, the children of nature become habituated to a language of their own. The more voluble condescend to the less precocious, and thus from this infant Babel proceeds a dialect composed of a host of mongrel words and phrases joined together without rule, and in the course of a generation the entire character of the language is changed."

Having acquired the language, Moffat felt that the time had now come to enlist the services of the press as an auxiliary to the living voice, without which there could be no great or permanent success. He translated the Assembly's Catechism, and put it to press. He also composed, printed, and put into use a collection of hymns for public worship; and it is one of his many titles to grateful remembrance that he wrote the first hymn ever penned in the native language, and became in fact the poet of the

Bechuana sanctuary. But one great need pressed on Moffat's mind—the natives had not the Bible in their own tongue. He saw that it was essential to the prosperity of the great work in which he was engaged that the whole of the Scriptures should be translated into the Sechuana language, which, with certain modifications, is the language of the interior of Africa. He doubted his own powers, fancying that his early education had not been such as to qualify him for the undertaking, and therefore appealed to the Society in England to send out some one specially to engage in it.

The circulation of the Scriptures in Africa was taken up by the British and Foreign Bible Society shortly after its formation. Dr. Carlyle, Professor of Arabic at Cambridge, issued a prospectus in 1803 for printing an edition of the Bible in that language. Mungo Park and others encouraged the experiment, inasmuch as they thought Arabic was widely understood. The death of Dr. Carlyle caused a delay, but the enterprise was taken up by his successor and by the Oxford Professor of Arabic, who, together with Barrington, Bishop of Durham, and Porteous, Bishop of London, brought the matter before the Bible Society. "It would," said the latter prelate, " do great credit to the society, and might be of infinite service in sowing the seeds of Christianity over the whole continent of Africa." Three hundred copies were printed from the text of the Polyglot. To the accuracy of that text, however, Dr. Adam Clarke demurred, as did other Arabic scholars, of whom Henry Martyn was one. The expediency of translating the Scriptures into the native tongue seems to have been first suggested by Dr. Philip. "The discoveries daily making," he remarked, "lead to a supposition that all the languages spoken, from the Keiskamma to the Arabian Gulf, and from the mouth of the Zambezi to that of the Congo, are derived from the same parent stock, and are so nearly allied to each other as to furnish great facilities for the translation and general circulation of the Scriptures." A translation of the New Testament was undertaken in the Namaqua language, and the four Gospels were printed at Cape Town. It was the first book ever printed in that language. Meanwhile no help came to Moffat, and the necessity for the work becoming more and more pressing, he resolved to enter upon it himself. For many years he applied every spare moment to translating; the intervals between preaching and teaching, ploughing, working at the forge or at the printing-press, were devoted to it, so that he became almost a stranger in his own family.

In the year 1832 Moffat completed a translation into Sechuana of the Gospel according to Luke. Even at Cape Town printing at that time of day was in its infancy. Sir Lowry Cole, the Governor, kindly permitted the missionary to use the official press. But who was to supply him with compositors? There was nothing for it but that the translator must be his own compositor; and, joined by his colleague, he set in type and struck off, under the superintendence of the official printer, both his translation of Luke's Gospel and his own hymns. He then returned in triumph to his station, carrying with him the books, the press which had been presented to him by Dr. Philip, and the other articles of which we have previously spoken.

Four years after he writes of one of his missionary visits thus :—" On this station, as well as at other places I lately visited in the course of my itinerating journey, I was delighted to hear that the attention of the people was first aroused to a sense of the importance of divine truth and a concern for their souls by hearing that Gospel (Luke's) read in their own language. I have frequently listened with surprise to hear how minutely some who were unable to read could repeat the story of the woman who was a sinner, the parables of the great supper, the prodigal son, and the rich man and Lazarus, and date their change of views to these simple but all-important truths delivered by the great Master Teacher."

In a subsequent letter written to the British and Foreign Bible Society in 1838, he says : " Within the last twelve months we have had the inexpressible joy of receiving seventy-one adults (some aged) into the church.   The natives on all sides are learning to read.   Though there must be about four thousand spelling-books in circulation, the demand for them is increasing.   Many are able to read well. Lately we increased the hymns to one hundred, and printed two thousand copies, and also two thousand copies of the large spelling-book, both of which were greatly wanted ; very few copies remain of the Gospel of Luke.   Some people who live two hundred miles beyond us are learning to read, and some can read tolerably well."

By 1840 Mr. Moffat had completed the translation of the entire New Testament, and became anxious about the printing of it.   The press at his station was not equal to the undertaking ; he therefore proposed at first having it done at the Cape, and two hundred and fifty reams of paper were voted by the Bible Society for the printing of four thousand copies.   When, however, he reached the Cape, it was thought desirable that the work should be executed in this country, and that he should come over here for the purpose of superintending it.   On his arrival he found himself much assisted by the counsels and help of the Society's valuable editorial superintendent, the Rev. Joseph Jowett.   An edition of the Psalms was added to that of the New Testament.

Supplies of the Sechuana Testament and Psalms were soon sent out to Africa, and when they reached their destination spread joy among the sons of the desert.   One of the missionaries on the spot thus wrote on their arrival : " It is with great pleasure I can now inform you that the

five hundred copies of the Sechuana New Testament con-
signed to the Rev. D. Livingstone were brought to this
station by him in safety and good order. Immediately on
the boxes being taken down from the waggon a distribution
was made, by assigning fifty, sixty, or eighty copies to the
other stations where there are Bechuana readers. When
it became known that the 'books' had arrived, great
satisfaction was evinced by the natives, and applications for
copies were made with urgency, some offering payment,
others promising to do so when able at some future time.
Some who were not well able to read, and others resolving
to learn to read, applied also for copies."

Mr. Moffat quitted England in 1843 to resume his missionary labours among the Bechuana tribes, and took with
him two thousand Testaments and Psalms in the Sechuana
language. During his stay in this country six thousand copies
were printed in London under his superintendence. It is
an interesting circumstance that to convey this boon was the
first of an unparalleled series of benefits conferred upon the
continent of Africa by Moffat's son-in-law and the renowned
missionary traveller David Livingstone. On Moffat's
return to his station at Kuruman with Messrs. Livingstone,
Ross, Inglis, and Ashton, to reinforce the mission, the work
was prosecuted with renewed vigour and marked success.
Urged by the younger men, Moffat applied himself to the
translation of the Old Testament. It was, as we shall see,
a labour of years; but he continued steadily at it as he had
leisure, daily and nightly also, without intermission, until
it was completed.

We can only note briefly the successive stages of the
work. In 1848 the books of Proverbs and Ecclesiastes
had been finished and Isaiah begun. In 1851 Mr. Hughes
of Griqua Town, writing to the Bible Society in London
concerning Mr. Moffat's several translations, says: "The
last work is one lately published, containing the books of

Proverbs, Ecclesiastes, and Isaiah, of which about two hundred copies may be in circulation at the present time. The whole of the Old Testament, however, has been translated, and may be expected ere long to be printed in the Sechuana language. Some thousands of Bechuanas' hearts will leap with joy to see the happy day; God speed it!" The *rough draft* of the whole Old Testament was completed, but much revision was still needed. The work of translating, revising, and printing still went on. Joshua succeeded to the Pentateuch, and Samuel to Joshua; and in 1853 the Second Book of Kings was nearly ready for press.

From a communication of the translator's own pen in 1854 we learn that he was still engaged in making the version as perfect as he could. "The longer I live," he writes, "the more powerfully is my mind impressed with the duty of every missionary making way for the Bible by getting the people, such as are in this country, taught to read. 'Nothing like the Bible,' says the new convert, burning with his first love, and 'Nothing but the Bible,' responds the venerable Christian, bowing down like the full grain ready to be gathered. It has been frequently remarked that as the children of God advance in old age they stick closer and closer to the Bible, and the Bible only; and who can wonder, who knows its value, or rather, that it cannot be valued? The first volume of the Old Testament is nearly completed. Little more than half of the Second Book of Kings remains to be printed; and if the covers arrive by the time the remaining sheets are being printed off, all will be in season, and they will soon be in the hands of the natives. Many are the inquiries made as to when it will be finished, and many wonder why it cannot be done with greater expedition. They know the pen and the press can be made to go pretty fast, but it will be some time before they are convinced that too much time and pains cannot be taken to ensure correctness in a book which is in Sechuana phraseology, 'Molome oa Jehova,'—the mouth of Jehovah."

Moffat was now approaching the completion of his translation labours. Jeremiah was in the press, Ezekiel far advanced, Daniel and the remainder ready for the compositor, and then the Old Testament would be finished. "A couple of months," he wrote to a friend, "will finish Ezekiel; a load will then be removed from off my mind—a load with respect to which I have often felt as if it would crush me, yet have so often felt as though my very existence depended upon the prosecution of this work. I have felt, in short, as if I must die if I dropped it, or at least be miserable to the end of my days did I not enlist all the time, research, and perseverance at my command in its accomplishment. In fine, I have found it to be an awful work to translate the Book of God; and perhaps this has given to my heart the habit of sometimes beating like the strokes of a hammer. After getting the brain refreshed, I shall hasten to a revision of the New Testament—a comparatively easy work."

At length the long labour of years came to an end, and the last verse of the Old Testament was translated into the Sechuana tongue. Moffat thus describes his emotions at this time :—"I could hardly believe that I was in the world, so difficult was it for me to realise the fact that my work of so many years was completed. Whether it was from weakness or overstrained mental exertion I cannot tell, but a feeling came over me as if I should die, and I felt perfectly resigned. To overcome this I went back again to my manuscript still to be printed, read it over and re-examined it, till at length I got back again to my right mind. This was the most remarkable time of my life, a period I shall never forget. My feelings found vent by my falling upon my knees and thanking God for His grace and goodness in giving me strength to accomplish my task."

Before we pass away from this story of translation, we shall here give the views of an eminent authority on the value of the work.   In 1852, when Dr. Livingstone was on his travels, he called at Kuruman, and found Moffat busy at his loved employ.   He says: "During the period of my visit at Kuruman, Mr. Moffat, who has been a missionary in Africa upwards of forty years, was engaged in carrying the Bible in the language of the Bechuanas through the press at his station.   As he was the first to reduce their speech, which is called Sechuana, to a written form, and has had his attention directed to the study for thirty years, he may be supposed to be better adapted for the task than any other man living.   The comprehensive meaning of the terms in this tongue may be inferred from the fact that there are fewer words in the Pentateuch in Mr. Moffat's translation than in the Greek Septuagint, and far less than in our English version.   It is fortunate that the task has been completed before the language became adulterated with half-uttered foreign words, and while those who have heard the eloquence of the native assemblies are still living.   The young who are brought up in our schools know less of the tongue than the missionaries.   The Sechuana vocabulary is extraordinarily copious.   Mr. Moffat never spends a week at his work without discovering new words.   It would be no cause for congratulation if the Bechuana Bible was likely to meet the fate of Elliot's Chocktaw version, in which we have God's word in a language which no tongue can articulate and no mortal can understand.   A better destiny seems in store for Mr. Moffat's labours, for the Sechuana has been introduced into the new country beyond Lake Ngami, where it is the court language, and will carry a stranger through a district larger than France."

Upon Moffat God has conferred the unspeakable honour of giving the Bible to South and Central Africa.   He has done for the tribes of this vast region of the earth what

Morrison has done for the natives of China, Carey and Marshman for the races of India, and other missionaries for the peoples of other lands,—placed in their hand the word of God in their own tongue. He did the work we may say single-handed. It has been remarked by some one that "no evidence can be produced that the whole of the Scriptures was by any person rendered into Saxon. Even Wickliffe had the help of many predecessors; much more Coverdale. Bede was translating the Gospel of John at the time of his decease. But Robert Moffat, who began with the Gospel of Luke, has lived to translate the whole Bible into the barbarous dialect of South Africa." It is true that his colleague Mr. Ashton rendered him invaluable help for many years, still the work in a peculiar and emphatic sense is his own. Carefully as it has been done, it may not be free from minor mistakes. Even in this present century we are revising the authorised version of the English Bible. The infallible book is liable to the errors of fallible men. Still competent authorities assure us of the excellency of the Sechuana version, and among the peoples of South Africa who read and value the Bible it is held in the highest estimation.

In the execution of this work Moffat has bestowed on Africa a priceless boon. It is the source of all other benefits—the spring whence flow the precious streams of liberty, knowledge, social and domestic blessedness, enlightened commerce, and all that contributes to personal and national good. The natives themselves testify to the value of the Bible and to the benefits it has conferred on South Africa. Here is the evidence of a Christian Hottentot at a public meeting of the London Missionary Society convened in London :—"I wish to tell you," said he, "what the Bible has done for Africa. What would have become of the Hottentot nation and every black man in South Africa had you kept the word of God to yourselves? When you received the word of God, you thought of other nations who had not that word. When the Bible came amongst us we were naked; we lived in caves and on the tops of the mountains; we had no clothes, we painted our bodies with red paint. At first we were surprised to hear the truths of the Bible. The Bible charmed us out of the caves and from the tops of the mountains. The Bible made us throw away all our old customs and practices, and we lived among civilized men. We are tame men now. Now we know there is a God; now we know we are accountable creatures before God. But what was our state before the Bible came? We knew none of these things. We knew nothing about heaven. We knew not who made heaven and earth. The Bible is the only light for every man that dwells on the face of the earth. I thank God in the name of every Hottentot—of all the Hottentots in South Africa—that I have seen the face of Englishmen.

"I have been looking whether a Hottentot found his way to this meeting, but I have looked in vain; I am the only one. I have travelled with the missionaries in taking the Bible to the Bushmen and other nations. Where the word of God has been preached, the Bushman has thrown away his bow and arrows. I have accompanied the Bible to the Caffre nation, and when the Bible spoke the Caffre threw away his shield and all his vain customs. I went to Lattakoo, and they threw away all their evil works; they threw away their assagais, and became the children of God. The only way to reconcile man to man is to instruct man in the truths of the Bible. I say again the Bible is the light; and where the Bible comes the minds of men are enlightened. Where the Bible is not, there is nothing but darkness; it is dangerous in fact to travel through such a nation. Where the Bible is not, man does not hesitate to kill his fellow; he never even repents afterwards of having committed murder. I thank you to-day; I do nothing but thank you to-day. Are there any of the old Englishmen here who sent out the word of God? I give them my thanks; if there are not I give it to their children."

On the occasion of his first visit to England, when as yet the people had only the Gospel of Luke in their hands, Moffat addressing a meeting in London said: "I have known individuals to come hundreds of miles to obtain copies of St. Luke. Yes, they have come, and driven sheep before them to obtain these copies. They did not intend to beg them, but to buy them. And could you have beheld with what gratitude and feeling they received these portions of God's word, you would be animated more and more to go on in the blessed work of preparing the word of God for these dark benighted nations. I have known families travel fifty or sixty miles with their babes on their shoulders to come and ask for the word of God. And why? Because they had acquired, at a distance, the knowledge of reading, and they had a feeling that they ought to buy this word, not to beg it. And I have seen them receive portions of St. Luke, and weep over them, and grasp them to their bosoms, and shed tears of thankfulness, till I have said to more than one, 'You will spoil your books with your tears.'"

In the same speech he tells how a man seeing a number of people reading the Gospel of Luke, said to them: "What things are these that you are turning over and over? What in the world is this that I see among the people? Is it food?" "No," they replied, "it is the word of God." "Does it speak?" he asked. "Yes," said they, "it speaks to the heart." He asked a chief to unravel this mystery to him; when the chief told him that this was God's Book, and that it turned people upside down and made them new. "Do they eat the books?" said the astonished man. "They eat them with the soul," said the chief, "not with the mouth."

"Once," he said, "an individual came to me to speak about his soul. I asked him how he became acquainted with the gospel. He said, 'I was on a journey and I sat down to rest myself by the side of a shepherd, who was talking to something I could not understand. I asked what he was doing, and he said he was reading. I inquired what the book was, and desired him to explain it to me. He said it was the word of God, and was given to us to make our dark hearts light, to turn our foolishness into wisdom, and to tell us that after we have lived well here we shall go to another world hereafter.' This man came to me to learn to read, and returned home with the Gospel of Luke. In one of my journeys in a village I met a young man and a number of women ; he was exhorting them to be faithful and zealous, and diligent in reading the Scriptures. He said to me, ' I would like to ask you one question, and it is one that has made us talk a great deal. But you have so much wisdom that I am ashamed to ask you.' 'What is it,' said I. At last he said, 'Did those holy men who wrote the word of God know that there were Bechuanas in the world ?' My reply was, that certainly the word of God was intended for all men. 'But what is your opinion ?' said I. He said, 'I think they did, because the word of God describes every sin the wicked Bechuanas have in their hearts. You know that they are the most wicked people in the world, and it is all described in that book ; so that those who are unconverted do not like to hear us read, because they say that we are turning their hearts inside out.'"

Moffat finishes his marvellous record of missionary labour in South Africa during the earlier years of his residence there with the following striking illustration of the value of the Bible, and with it we close this chapter :—"The vast importance," he says, "of having the Scriptures in the language of the natives will be seen when we look on the scattered towns and hamlets which stud the interior, over which one language, with slight variations, is spoken as far as the Equator. When taught to read they have in their hands the means not only of recovering them from their natural darkness, but of keeping the lamp of life burning even amidst comparatively desert gloom. In one of my early journeys with some of my companions we came to a heathen village on the banks of the Orange River, between Namaqua Land and the Griqua country. We had travelled far and were hungry, thirsty, and fatigued. From the fear of being exposed to lions we preferred remaining at the village to proceeding during the night. The people at the village rather roughly directed us to halt at a distance. We asked water, but they would not supply it. I offered the three or four buttons that still remained on my jacket for a little milk; this also was refused. We had the prospect of another hungry night at a distance from water, though within sight of the river. We found it difficult to reconcile ourselves to our lot, for in addition to repeated rebuffs, the manner of the villagers excited suspicion. When twilight drew on, a woman approached from the height beyond which the village lay. She bore on her head a bundle of wood, and had a vessel of milk in her hand. The latter, without opening her lips, she handed to us, laid down the wood, and returned to the village. A second time she approached with a cooking vessel on her head and a leg of mutton in one hand and water in the other. She sat down without saying a word, prepared the fire and put on the meat. We asked her again and again who she was. She remained silent till affectionately entreated to give us a reason for such unlooked for kindness to strangers. The solitary tear stole down her sable cheek, when she replied, 'I love Him whose servant you are, and surely it is my duty to give you a cup of cold water in His name. My heart is full, therefore I cannot speak the joy I feel to see you in this out-of-the-world place.' On learning a little of her history, and that she was a solitary

light burning in a dark place, I asked her how she kept up
the life of God in her soul in the entire absence of the
communion of saints.   She drew from her bosom a copy of
the Dutch New Testament, which she had received from Mr.
Helm when in his school some years previous, before she had
been compelled by her connections to retire to her present
seclusion.   'This,' she said, 'is the fountain whence I drink;
this is the oil which makes my lamp burn.'   I looked on the
precious relic, printed by the British and Foreign Bible
Society, and the reader may conceive how I felt, and my
believing companions with me, when we met with this
disciple, and mingled our sympathies and prayers together
at the throne of our heavenly Father."

CHAPTER XIX.

FOR the long space of twenty-three years Moffat continued his arduous labours in South Africa without once returning home to see his friends or recruit his strength. At length an occasion arose which made it desirable that he should come to this country and make some little stay. He had completed his translation of the New Testament and the Psalms into Sechuana, and was anxious to have it printed and put into circulation as soon as possible. After arrangements had been made for doing the printing at the Cape, it was thought, on reflection, better for him to bring the manuscript to this country and have it printed in London, where he might have the aid of the Rev. Joseph Jowett, the Bible Society's editorial superintendent, with other advantages not to be commanded at Cape Town. Accordingly, in 1840, he and his excellent and devoted wife left for a season their work in Africa, and appeared in England among their Christian friends.

While part of his time was occupied in superintending his translation in its progress through the press, he was busy in preparing his useful and interesting volume, "Missionary Labours and Scenes in South Africa,"—a work which had a large circulation in its original form, and the cheap edition of which has multiplied to thirty thousand copies. No work on modern missions has been read with greater eagerness and delight, or done more to deepen and extend the interest of the Christian church in missionary operations.

Moffat's services, too, were enlisted by the London Missionary Society, the British and Foreign Bible Society, and other institutions, to advocate their claims at public meetings throughout the country. His speeches were full of striking facts, narratives of personal adventure, earnest and exciting appeals. His visits were welcomed everywhere, and produced the most favourable results. The then Marquis of Bristol, after hearing his account at a public meeting of the progress of the Gospel in South Africa, turned to him and said, "I must see you again; this is grand." Speaking of his oratorical power, the late Dr. John Campbell, who often heard him, and who was a most competent judge, says :—"Mr. Moffat eminently possesses the poet's eye; he sees everything through the medium of the imagination, and Genius stands by ready to robe his perceptions in the most beautiful attire. The sovereignty of his spirit is immediately confessed by his hearers; and in spite of a very defective manner, and a most barbarous elocution, made up of the worst Scottish dialect disguised in divers African intonations, he reigns supreme in every audience, whether metropolitan or provincial." There are persons still living who can well remember the fascination which his speeches and addresses exercised upon all who heard them. The thrilling narratives, the tender feeling, the poetic tone, always attracted and deeply impressed the lovers of missions.

Missionary meetings were very different gatherings forty years ago from what they are now. Now, as a rule, they are very indifferently attended, and too often those who address them are anything but instructive or interesting. There is as much sympathy as ever with missionary operations, but it does not shew itself at missionary meetings. Forty years ago they were the best attended, the most enthusiastic, and the most profitable Christian seasons of the church. Many a youth was constrained by what he heard on such occasions to yield himself to Christ, and many a Christian youth was led to engage in active service in the Lord's work either at home or abroad. Moffat's deputation addresses were eminently blessed in producing these results. One of. his speeches in Scotland was the means of inducing William Ross to enlist for missionary services in Africa, where he proved himself for upwards of twenty years a most earnest and useful labourer. Mr. Ross as a youth followed the plough in the Carse of Gowrie, and afterwards served an apprenticeship as a house-carpenter. He went to St. Andrews' University and passed a regular course there, went through his theological curriculum in Edinburgh, became a licentiate of one of the Presbyterian Churches in Scotland, and then, moved by the earnest and eloquent appeals of Moffat, went out to Africa, and from 1842 to 1863, when he died, laboured unweariedly among the Bechuanas.

Moffat possessed the rare faculty of speaking with effect to children. Many persons who address children think that to secure the attention of their audience it is necessary to be childish. Others again shoot far above the heads of the little ones; not half they say is understood. There is no subject about which men more miscalculate their gifts than that of addressing children. Moffat could speak as effectively to an audience of children as to an audience of adults. The Rev. Samuel Goodall, late of Durham, says he heard him on one occasion address a large congregation of Sunday school children in the north for an hour and a half, and hold them in fixed attention throughout the whole of the time. This was the case all over the country. At juvenile missionary meetings he was a king. The result was that the Sunday schools and the youthful part of the Christian congregations of that day were thoroughly impregnated with a missionary spirit, and a powerful impetus was given to the missionary cause.

In the beginning of 1843 Mr. Moffat and his wife sailed again for Africa. The home visit had been very refreshing to his own heart, and had proved a rich blessing to the British churches. The awakened interest in the condition of the heathen abroad had not only given fresh life to foreign missionary effort, it was attended by increased concern and more earnest endeavour for the conversion of sinners at home. The African missionary was now known by name throughout Christendom, and henceforth the eyes of all the churches were directed to his distant station. On his return to Kuruman, accompanied by three or four new helpers to reinforce the mission, the work was prosecuted with renewed vigour and marked success. It was then, urged by Livingstone and his other coadjutors, he applied himself to the translation of the Old Testament. It was a labour of years, as we have seen, but he went on with it as he had leisure daily and nightly without intermission.

The year 1846 was a year fraught with much encouragement. Nearly fifty members were added to the church of which Moffat was pastor, and at the out-stations the blessing of God was vouchsafed to the simple efforts of the native assistants. In all its departments the mission was advancing, and, in the peaceful death of the chief Matebe, Moffat had witnessed a conspicuous proof of the Gospel over barbarian minds. The following year, on the contrary, was one of peculiar trouble and anxiety. From long and severe drought the crops had almost wholly failed, and distress and dismay were general. While, however, this disaster hindered the work of grace in the individual heart, the preparatory work of instruction knew no intermission. " As some portions of the Sechuana Scriptures were passed through the mission press, others were being rendered into that language by the indefatigable leader of the missionary host. While the father was producing ten thousand copies of the erudite Assembly's Catechism in the rudest of tongues, and while the Proverbs of Solomon, simultaneously with the Pilgrim of Bunyan, were issuing in the speech of the Bechuanas from the same press, the daughter in her infant school was preparing the babes and sucklings of the tribe to appreciate and enjoy them. From year to year the work of Christian education proceeded, not indeed at those large and rapid strides to which older races are accustomed, yet with a sure though gradual advance. Few years passed without some additions to the church. These it is evident might easily have been more frequent and more numerous, but for the conscientious care judiciously taken to guard against the premature entrance of imperfectly converted or slenderly informed candidates."

It was found necessary now and again to exercise extreme discipline upon great or persisting offenders; still, those who were cut off from church communion were neither forgotten nor neglected, and the missionary frequently had the joy of readmitting the penitent to Christian fellowship. The year 1851 was a year of excessive and protracted drought. For nine months there was no moisture; and, except upon spots watered by artificial means, the country was without harvest, without grass, and without milk. Like Elijah of old, Moffat carried the matter to God in persevering prayer, and at length there came an abundance of rain. The year 1852 was one of mingled encouragement and trial. Some of the church members brought dishonour on their Christian profession, and grieved their pastor's heart; yet as many as seven native evangelists had by this time gone forth from Kuruman, and were labouring in different districts with encouraging success.

By the death of Mr. Hamilton, Moffat lost a faithful colleague, with whom he had been united in labour for thirty-four years.   In Mr. Ashton, however, the missionary had received a most vigorous, active, and able helper. While the country beyond was greatly disturbed by the marauding attacks of the Boers, Kuruman was mercifully exempt from their rude and robber-like incursions.   "The state of the mother and daughter churches grew more encouraging, the minds of the people were better informed, their grounds were being brought under more careful cultivation, and not a few made a livelihood out of the produce of their gardens, besides the purchase of tools and clothes. Beyond Kuruman, necessity, the mother of invention, had stimulated the native mind; and in imitation of their more advanced countrymen the outlying people began to work the fountains and lead out the waters.   Indicative of a true and therefore lasting civilization, the greater permanence of the new state of things, and the more settled ways of the people, were almost uniformly found in connection with the power of reading with ease, and the capability of conducting religious services."   Moffat sighed for more conversions among the people, but rejoiced in the fact that the new habits of life were taking firmer hold upon them, and that the example set by their moral and intellectual leaders were conducting them up the path of true progress.

CHAPTER XX.

IN 1840 David Livingstone landed at Cape Town, having been sent out by the London Missionary Society to join the missionary staff in South Africa. In accordance with his instructions, after a brief stay at the Cape he proceeded to Kuruman, with the view of establishing a mission station still further to the north, where ground had not yet been broken. At Kuruman he found Moffat and his coadjutors hard at work, and remained with them a few months familiarising himself with their mode of operations, making himself acquainted with the Bechuana people—Sechele, chief of the Bakwena, one of their tribes, being favourable to his projects.

Sechele was a remarkable man, as had also been his father and grandfather before him; the latter was a great traveller, and the first who had ever told his people of the existence of a race of white men. During his father's life the two distinguished travellers, Dr. Cowan and Captain Donovan, lost their lives in his territory, and were supposed to have been murdered by the Bakwena, until Livingstone learned from Sechele that they had died from fever in descending the river Limpopo, after they had been hospitably

entertained by his father and his people.   The father of
Sechele was murdered when he was a boy, and a usurper
proclaimed himself the head of the tribe.   The friends of
the children applied to Sebituane, chief of the Makololo, to
reinstate them, which he successfully accomplished.

Livingstone settled as a missionary among the Bakwena
at Kolobeng, and the first time he held a public religious
service with them Sechele listened with much attention.
Receiving permission to ask questions regarding what he
had heard, he inquired if the missionary's forefathers knew
of a future judgment, and on receiving an affirmative
answer, he said, "You startle me; these words make all
my bones to shake; I have no more strength in me.   But
my forefathers were living at the same time yours were,
and how is it they did not send to tell them about these
things?   They all passed away into darkness without
knowing whither they were going."

So eager was Sechele to learn to read that he learnt the
alphabet the first day of Livingstone's settlement with him.
After he was able to read, nothing gave him greater
pleasure than to read the Bible.   Isaiah was his favourite
book, and he would frequently say, "He was a fine man,
that Isaiah; he knew how to speak."   At his own request
Livingstone held family worship in his hut, in the hope
that it might induce his people to embrace Christianity.
Speaking of the influence of the example of a chief in all
other things, he said bitterly, "I love the Word of God,
and not one of my brethren will join me."   He frequently
remarked, with reference to the difficulties in the way of an
open profession of Christianity, especially as regarded the
number of his wives, the putting away of all of whom, save
one, would get him into trouble with their relatives, "Oh, I
wish you had come to this country before I became entangled
in the meshes of our customs."   When at length he determined on publicly uniting himself with the Christian church,

he sent all his superfluous wives to their parents, with all the goods and chattels they had been in the habit of using, intimating that he found no fault with them, but must follow the will of God. Crowds attended to witness his baptism, many of them shedding tears of sorrow over what they termed the weakness of their chief in forsaking the ways of his forefathers.

After remaining some years at Kolobeng with Sechele and his tribe, Livingstone began his great journeys of discovery. When the chief found that the missionary was resolved to leave him, he determined to send his five eldest children to the Kuruman station, that Mr. and Mrs. Moffat might educate them on Christian principles. The mothers and other relations of the children strongly objected to this course, and did what they could to prevent them from going; but sorry as their father himself was to part with them, as he believed it was for their good, he sent them away. Although no previous intimation had been given of their coming, they found at the mission station a hearty welcome. While the children were thus safe among Christian friends, the father was in danger and trouble. The Boers had already broken up and sacked several mission stations, conquering the tribes which gave them shelter, and carrying away men and women as slaves. But Livingstone and the Bakwena escaped until he was absent on his first journey to Lake Ngami, when four hundred armed Boers attacked Sechele, slaughtered a considerable number of adults, and carried away over two hundred children as captives, among whom were two of Sechele's own little ones. The Bakwena defended themselves bravely until nightfall, killing eight of the Boers, when they retreated to the mountains. Under the pretext that Livingstone had taught them to defend themselves, and was consequently responsible for the slaughter of their fellows, the Boers plundered his house, destroyed his books and stock of medicines, and carried off his furniture and clothing, and large quantities of stores left by English gentlemen, who had gone northwards to hunt; and sold them to pay the expenses of their lawless raid.

Sechele had now no home. He sent tidings of the attack to Moffat at Kuruman by his wife Masabele. She had been hidden in the cleft of a rock over which a number of Boers were firing. Her infant (whom she now carried to Kuruman) began to cry, and terrified lest this should attract the attention of the men, the muzzles of whose guns appeared at every discharge over her head, she took off her armlets as playthings to quiet the child. The letter which her husband sent by her to Moffat tells its own tale. The following is as nearly as possible a literal translation :—

"Friend of my heart's love, and of all the confidence of my heart, I am undone by the Boers, who attacked me, though I had no guilt with them. They demanded that I should be in their kingdom, and I refused; they demanded that I should prevent the English and Griquas from passing (northwards). I replied : 'These are my friends, and I can prevent no one (of them). They came on Saturday, and I besought them not to fight on Sunday, and they assented. They began on Monday morning at twilight, and fired with all their might, and burned the town with fire and scattered us. They killed sixty of my people, and captured women and children and men, and the mother of Baleriling (a former wife of Sechele) they also took prisoner. They took all the cattle and all the goods of the Bakwena, and the house of Livingstone they plundered, taking away all his goods. The number of waggons they had was eighty-five, and a cannon ; and when they had stolen my own waggon, and that of Macabe, then the number of their waggons (counting the cannon as one) was eighty-eight. All the goods of the hunters (certain English gentlemen hunting and exploring in the north) were burned in the town, and of the Boers were killed twenty-eight. Yes, my beloved friends, now my wife goes to see the children, and Kobus Hae will carry her to you.—I am, SECHELE, the son of Mochoasele."

Having sent his wife with the above letter to Moffat, Sechele set out for the Cape, purposing to visit England and lay his case before the Queen. He resolved to tell her of the unjust and cruel conduct of the Boers, and ask her to make them give up the prisoners they had carried away; but when he reached Cape Town and saw the sea, and learnt its extent and the cost of his intended voyage, he was constrained to relinquish his purpose and return home. His people recovered from their alarm and rebuilt their ruined town, and Sechele became a more powerful chief than before.

When Moffat some time after left Kuruman to take letters and other things that Livingstone, who was then on his travels, might need to Linyanti, he called at Kolobeng to see Sechele. The chief was very pleased to see his old friend. When he heard the waggons were approaching he went out, accompanied by his wife and children, to receive his visitors. Moffat and his friend accompanied him home. There was a verandah outside the front of his house, and behind were courts and sheds, in which corn, pumpkins, dried water-melons, and other fruits of the earth were stored. The house was large and convenient, and partitioned so as to make a sitting-room on one side and a bed-room on the other. The floor was hard and clean. Guns, bullet-pouches, and powder-horns hung on the walls. In the sitting-room were chairs and a table, and at a fire the maids were cooking. Clean scoured bowls were placed on the table, and the contents of the pot on the fire soon poured into them. Clean spoons were handed to Moffat and his two companions, Messrs. Edwards and Chapman, with the help of which they quickly consumed their porridge. The chief and his wife and children were all neatly dressed, and had a most respectable appearance.

As the sun sank in the west a bell was rung to call the people to school. The missionary, anxious to see in what condition the school was, how many availed themselves of its advantages, and what they were learning, went with the chief to the school-house. The appearance of the place was not clean and orderly; the attendance was scanty. A hymn was sung, when the teacher read a chapter from the New Testament, Moffat's translation of course; another hymn was sung, and then began a reading lesson. There appeared a general neglect of learning.

The next day Moffat had a long talk of the highest importance with Sechele about his own spiritual state, the moral condition of the family, and the aspect of the community generally. The elder children wished to return to heathenism, although they had been under Christian influences in the missionary's family at Kuruman, and had seen its superiority over the religion of their ancestors. This was a great grief to their father, who desired that Moffat would point out to them their folly and wickedness, and endeavour to lead them back into the right way. Having finished his visit to his friend, and encouraged him to persevere in the faith and practice of the gospel, and having done what he could to establish the wavering children, and save them from relapsing into heathenism, Moffat with his party proceeded on their journey.

It is interesting to see, in connection with the foregoing record, Mr Mackenzie's account of Sechele when he visited him at Liteyana in 1860:—"Two days after our departure from Kanye we reached Liteyana, which was then the residence of the Bakwena tribe under the chief Sechele. Our reception here was gratifying; the chief himself made his appearance at the waggon, and politely greeting us in English fashion, offered us also the African welcome of an ox for slaughter, which was accordingly shot on the spot. Sechele was the finest specimen of the Bechuanas which I had yet seen, being tall and well made, with a good head, an open countenance, and unusually large eyes. His dress was somewhat singular. At one time he appeared in a suit of tiger-skin clothes made in European fashion. On another broiling day he was dressed in an immense Mackintosh overcoat, with huge water-boots. After a youth of romantic adventure and great hardship, Sechele found himself at the head of the Bakwena, then considerably reduced owing to recent wars and dissensions. In 1842 he was first visited by Dr. Livingstone, who was to exercise so much influence over his mind. The doctor afterwards resided with the Bakwena, and Sechele gave himself to instruction, and proved himself an apt scholar. I should say there is no native in Bechuana land better acquainted with the Bible than Sechele. I have heard Dutchmen describe with amazement his readiness in finding texts in both Old and New Testaments, but especially the former.

"After some three years' probation Dr. Livingstone admitted Sechele into the church by baptism. So long as the encouraging and stimulating influence of his teacher was near to him, this chief's conduct would seem to have been all that could be desired; but this consistency was not kept up after the Dutchmen had attacked his town, and he was left alone to pursue his own course amid the querulous taunts of his own people. He was well-nigh alone in his tribe in his profession of Christianity; and many of his people refused to see more in it than a vain desire to make himself a 'white man.' Then the rain-making and other customs were still carried on in the town, and at the expense of a younger brother of the chief called Khosilintsi. But if this person paid for the rain, and otherwise performed the 'orthodox' customs every year, he would, in point of fact, be the preserver of the town, and its virtual head in the

11

public estimation. I believe Sechele's first compromise of principle was an interference to arrest what he supposed would lead to the total subversion of his power. He resolved himself to send for rain-makers, and pay them out of his own cattle. At first this compromise was secret and unacknowledged, but it became gradually known in the country that 'Sechele was now making rain.' By and by the secrecy was thrown aside, and he openly assisted in the performance of heathen ceremonies.

"But it must be borne in mind that all this time this singular man was most exact in the observance of private and family prayers, and stood up regularly every Sunday to preach to the Bakwena. His position seemed to be one which he has not been by any means the first to occupy—that Christianity might be engrafted upon heathen customs, and that the two would go together. For instance, he himself would go with the people in their rain-making ceremonies, but he would not neglect at the same time to pray to God. He would use charms and incantations, washings and purifyings according to the old rule, and yet profess faith in Him whose blood cleanseth from all sin. The Bible, in short, did not require him to give up the customs of his ancestors although it required him to believe in the Lord Jesus Christ. He could be an orthodox Bechuana and a good Christian at the same time. This was a position which he took up, and the tenor of many of his discourses. I have spent many of the hours of night with this clever chief in the earnest discussion of these points. When one after another his arguments failed him, he has said to me, 'You have conquered : your idea of the Christian life is the right one, but was I not alone? What is one man against all the Bakwena?' 'How hard it is for us all, Sechele, and for me as well as for you, to believe that God with us is greater than all who can be against us!' 'Munare' (Sir), he replied with feeling, 'not hard for you—you are a missionary; your faith is great; but hard for me, who am chief of a heathen town.'"

At the time of Mr. Mackenzie's visit, Liteyana was under the care of missionaries belonging to the Hanoverian Society. These German missionaries were active, devoted men. "Besides attending to the acquisition of the language, they had built a dwelling-house for themselves and another for the chief. The latter was neatly finished, and Sechele, who had been to Cape Town and had seen the interior of many English homes, was very careful in keeping everything in order. Masabele, his wife, was well dressed, and if not quite abreast of her husband as to politeness, was very kind, and interested herself much in making inquiries about our relatives in England. We were introduced to Sechele's family, some of whom had been to Kuruman, and had resided for a time in Mr. Moffat's house. Like the chief himself, these young people were kind, intelligent, and pleasant, but entirely lacking in decided views or strong preference as to religion. Compromise seemed the motto of all."

CHAPTER XXI.

SECOND AND THIRD VISITS TO MOSELEKATSE.

OFFAT'S close and continued application to his task of translating the Scriptures into the Sechuana tongue interfered so seriously with his health that by the time he had completed the Second Book of Kings he was almost incapacitated to proceed. He felt himself that he needed some relaxation and change, and the Directors of the London Missionary Society, afraid he was killing himself with overwork, urged him either to revisit England or take a holiday at some of the seaports of the colony. With his characteristic devotion to duty he declined these invitations to what he considered ease and idleness, and determined to go and see his old acquaintance Moselekatse, who was known to occupy the country to the north of the River Limpopo, and try the effects of change of air there. At the same time he resolved to convey letters and supplies to Livingstone, who was now exploring unknown regions, and engaged in his memorable journey across the African continent. If he returned safely from the West Coast, it was desirable that supplies should reach him at Linyanti, and Moffat hoped to get Moselekatse to aid him in forwarding them.

Two travellers—Mr. Chapman, whose name has been mentioned before, and a Mr. Edwards—were proceeding northwards, in May 1854, on a hunting and trading expedition, and Moffat joined them. Mr. Chapman thus refers to the circumstance: "At Kuruman we found Mr. Moffat in rather indifferent health, suffering from a peculiar affection of the head, brought on by close application to his laborious studies in translating the Bible. On learning that Moselekatse's was our destination he determined to accompany us. He had previously decided on accepting an invitation which that chieftain had given him, but until our arrival had given up the idea of going this year." They left Kuruman on the 22nd of May, and travelling by easy stages reached Sekome's Town on the 19th of June. Here Messrs. Edwards and Chapman changed their original purpose, and resolved to part company, one to go in a north-west direction, the other to pursue a north-easterly course to the country of Moselekatse. Having determined on this plan, they drew lots for the choice, and it fell to Mr. Edwards to visit the Matabele chief. On the 21st, Edwards accompanied by Moffat started for their destination.

There was no road or track to guide them, and they had to have recourse to their compass in threading their way through the prairies of long grass, through dense forests, and across rocky ravines and hills. At length they met with some natives who were subject to the Matabele king, and whom they sent forward as messengers to the nearest village to announce that Moffat (or Moshete, as they pronounced it) of Kuruman was seeking Moselekatse. Although those who heard the message had never seen Moffat before, they were familiar with the name, and assured him that the king had long been inquiring after him, and would receive him with delight. A week afterwards they reached his royal residence. Nearly twenty years had passed since the barbarian monarch and the missionary had before met. The travellers were not greeted with the martial display which took place on the occasion of Moffat's first visit; still the welcome was hearty, and the scene impressive.

Moffat's narrative of the entire visit is most graphic and interesting :—" When we at last reached Mattokottoko, we found him sick, and with difficulty brought to the porch leading to his residence. I saw his condition, and while with one hand he eagerly grasped mine, he appeared deeply affected, and drew his mantle over his face with the other, unwilling, I suppose, that his vassals, who sat in silence at a distance, should see the hero of a hundred battles weep, even though it were for joy. After becoming composed, he gave full expression to the joy he felt on seeing me once more. Pointing to his feet, he said, 'I am very sick, but your God has sent you to heal me.' Though we had passed several of his towns, and had been two weeks conversant with his people, no one dared to whisper, 'Moselekatse is sick.' The fact was too sacred to be pronounced by vulgar lips. Though he had not been out of his house for some time before, he sat the livelong day (for it was yet early when we arrived) looking at us getting everything ready for the Sabbath. And a season of rest was indeed most acceptable, after a most harassing month's journey from the Bamanquato, during which we were very often obliged to use our axes from the time of unyoking till halting for the night, cutting our way through thickets.

"As Moselekatse very naturally felt anxious to be restored to health, I engaged to prepare for him suitable medicine, provided he would, like myself, drink no beer, and eat only the kind of food I prescribed. To this he most willingly assented. The means used were, by God's blessing, successful, and in a couple of weeks he was on his feet again, to his great joy and that of his people. There I remained for more than four weeks, having daily intercourse with the great chief, whose kindness was unbounded. But he would not listen to my plan of going to Sekeletue's country in search of Livingstone. He started objections, and raised every bugbear he could think of. Though he had been at war with Sebetoane, the father of Sekeletue, he had no idea that they would do me harm, but the deadly miasma of the country beyond he thought a sufficient reason for my not attempting the journey. I assured him that nothing of that kind should deter me from undertaking it.

"During the time already elapsed, although I was not idle, I could not prevail on Moselekatse to allow me to proclaim to him and his people the truths of the Gospel. As he could refuse me nothing that I thought proper to ask, he would give evasive answers, and endeavour to assure me that he believed the word of God was good for him, but at the same time hinting that his nobles and warriors might not like it from the principles of peace it inculcated. But I was aware that they were really desirous of hearing those principles inculcated which they knew had had a salutary influence on the mind of their master ever since my last visit, more than twenty years before. Though at that time I was barely able to reach his understanding, my strong remonstrances with him to modify the severity of his government had produced so thorough a change in his views, that the cruel and revolting forms of execution were nearly obsolete, while a sense of the value of human life and the guilt of shedding human blood characterised his measures to an extent his subjects had never before witnessed.

"They knew nothing about the nature or requirements of the Divine word; for to harbour the idea that there was a God greater than Moselekatse would be viewed as the veriest madness, and expose any one to the danger of being hanged. His people, though nearly all youths and children when I last visited him, knew that their yoke had been made lighter in consequence of some influence or charm which I had infused into the heart of their monarch, and hence the general joy my visit imparted to all ranks. It was difficult to account for his reluctance to allow me to preach to his people, except it was from the impression that the exhibition of the character of the Divine Being—life, death, and immortality—would repress the martial spirit of his warriors, whose highest happiness was to fight for or die for Moselekatse, the son of Machobane. His hand, like that of Ishmael, was against every man, and every man's hand against him, and to his soldiers (and every man of the Matabele is a soldier ready to grasp the weapon at a moment's notice) he looked for the defence and security of his kingdom. It was natural for me to feel melancholy, situated as I was, surrounded with multitudes of savages who loved me, and yet I could not instruct them. I tried at times to look morose, while he would try in vain to make me smile. I used to say pleasantly that if he would not hear of my Lord and Master he should not have me, neither would I receive the shadow of a present from him, but that I should one of these mornings shoulder my gun and march off to Sekelete's country. I cannot now describe the process by which I at last overcame his objections. The incident was unexpected and interesting. He gave full permission for me to preach to him and his warriors the Gospel of salvation.

" Daily, at a minute's warning, they were assembled before me, and nearer to him, who sat at my left hand, than they dared to approach on any other occasion. Never in my life did I witness such riveted attention whilst I, amid the stillness of the grave, published to them the Word of God. The people of Moselekatse exhibit characteristics of intelligence far above the neighbouring tribes. Numbers were arriving daily at headquarters, and returning to the different towns of his vast dominions to bring news and convey orders and instructions, so that what was preached in the presence of Moselekatse was conveyed to the extreme ends of his territories; some who heard it at second-hand published to others at a distance the strange news that had been brought to the ears of the Matabele. I felt that my prayers had been answered, and that I had obtained my heart's desire. After concluding the first day's service I turned to Moselekatse, and laying my hand on his shoulder, said, 'You have now made me happy; I want nothing else that you can give; I shall sigh no more.' 'How,' he asked, 'can you sigh when I and my kingdom are at your disposal? You must preach daily, and receive my presents also.'"

This visit had extended over a month, but as Moffat wanted to forward Livingstone the letters and supplies, he was now wishing to be gone. The king put every possible obstacle in his way, but found him so resolved that the only resource was to go with him, as he did not wish to be separated from his friend "Moshete." Accordingly, on the day that Moffat started Moselekatse appeared, and without any ceremony or asking any permission, told his men to help him into the missionary's waggon. The king's own new waggon followed, but he preferred the missionary's, and made himself quite at home, taking possession even of the bed. Among his walking attendants were many of his principal men, twenty women carrying large calabashes of beer on their heads, and others carrying karosses and food. The want of roads made the travelling very unpleasant to the king; he could walk but little, and as the waggon jolted and tilted over the uneven ground he was unmercifully tumbled about and bruised.

At last the travelling was brought to a sudden stop. Some men who had been sent forward to find water returned with the intelligence that it would take the oxen four days to reach the next supply of water, and that it was in a part of the country infested with the tsétse. Moffat told the king that if he would allow him to take some of the Matabele to help to carry the things, he would walk to Linyanti with them. "If you go," said Moselekatse, "I will go too. I cannot walk; more men must go, and they shall carry me, that I may remain with you." "Well," said Moffat, "if you will give me enough men to carry all Livingstone's goods to Linyanti, I and my men will return with you."

To the arrangement thus proposed the king at length agreed. A selection of the men best acquainted with the country was made, who were repeatedly instructed what they would have to do. Placing the bags, parcels, and boxes on their heads and shoulders, with shields and spears in their hands, they marched off on their journey through, perhaps, as wild and desolate a region as can well be found —through forests, over mountains and morasses—to the country of those who were their enemies. They performed their duty faithfully, leaving the goods on an island near the Zambesi Falls, where the Makololo took charge of them, and where Livingstone found them nearly a year afterwards.

While Moffat remained with the king waiting the return of the messengers to Linyanti, he preached several times. The king always listened, but nothing seemed to make much impression on him. Towards the end of October, the men having come back from Linyanti, the missionary took his leave. The king pressed him to prolong his stay, pleading that he had not seen enough of him, and that he had not yet shown him sufficient kindness. "Kindness!" replied Moffat, "you have overwhelmed me with kindness, and I shall now return with a heart overflowing with thanks." Leaving him a supply of suitable medicines to keep his system in tolerable order, and admonishing him to give up beer-drinking, and to receive any Christian teacher who might come as he had received him, the missionary took his departure.

Moselekatse himself went with the waggons for some distance, and then with great reluctance said "Good-bye." He took Mr. Moffat's hand at parting, and said with emphasis, "May God take care of you on the road, and bring you safe to Kuruman and Ma-Mary (Mrs. Moffat). Tell her how glad I have been to see you." Just at the last moment Moffat became very unwell. This caused the king great distress. He ordered an escort of men to go with him for the first hundred and fifty miles; and six of them had to go on until they could return and say that "Moshete" was quite well again.

We get one solitary peep of the missionary on his homeward journey in Mr. Chapman's "Travels." Giving an account of his return from the north-west, he says:—"I remained at Lupèpè until the 12th of November, taking very successful lessons from the Bushmen in honey-hunting and stalking game. When nearly giving up all hope of meeting my friends, Moffat and Edwards, I received a letter from the latter informing me of their arrival at Sekome's Town. Upon this I immediately saddled horses and rode to meet them. On arriving at Sekome's I found Mr. Moffat, with a patriarchal white beard, working hard at a new axle for his waggon. On the 15th of November we took rather a melancholy leave of Mr. Moffat, who immediately trekked southward for Kuruman, while on the following day we steered back into the wilds, not well knowing our own destination." By this journey Moffat's health was much improved, his intercourse and friendship with the people of the interior were cemented and extended, and he looked forward with hopeful assurance to the early extension of Christianity to these distant regions.

The visit of Livingstone to England in 1856, after his memorable walk from Loando to Quillemane—from the shores of the Atlantic to those of the Indian Ocean—gave a fresh impetus to the cause of Foreign Missions in this country. The great object he aimed to enforce upon the public mind was the elevation of the natives of Africa ; to him " the end of the geographical feat was the beginning of the missionary enterprise." The London Missionary Society redoubled their generous exertions, and resolved to extend their labours by establishing missions among the Matabele and the Makololo. Moffat, in his home at Kuruman, received the news with great gladness. He was asked whether he could go to Moselekatse with any missionaries who might be sent out to settle in his country, and stay a few months until they were fairly established. Moffat replied that he was sure, if the king was still alive, he would gladly welcome missionaries to live in his country ; and although he was now advanced in years, he set out at once, with all the ardour of youth, for the Matabele country, in order to obtain Moselekatse's consent to the settlement of the missionaries among his people.

Moffat felt the paramount necessity of giving to the proposed mission the full weight of his influence and authority, in order to secure for the new teachers the confidence both of the king and of his people. At the same time he endeavoured to make careful provision for the future aid and comfort of those brethren who would thus constitute the advanced outpost of Christianity beyond the limits of civilised communication in that distant region. " There is one thing," he writes to the directors, " which I think ought not to be lost sight of ; that is, an intermediate station as a connecting link between this and Moselekatse, for seven hundred miles is a long stretch in an ox waggon. This station ought also to be sufficiently strong to allow one missionary to itinerate on a large scale ; that is, so as to enable him to go and remain two months at one, and then at another, or more interior station."

As Moffat again approached the Matabele territory, he was gratified to learn that both the king and the people waited with joyful anticipation to see him. His previous visits, especially the last, had been of great service to the Matabele ; they had themselves heard what the missionary had taught, and his teaching had made the king more lenient and forgiving, and had influenced him to modify his severe measures. The only wish now was that Moffat might not relax in his counsels, and that the king might become a still better ruler.

Moselekatse extended to his visitor a cordial and unreserved welcome, and once more the voice of the Christian teacher was heard pleading with the monarch on behalf of the captive and the oppressed. ˋOwing to illness, the king was unable to appear much in public, but in his own residence he held long and frequent converse with his old friend and counsellor. At an early interview Moffat made known the special object of his visit, and told the king that the Christians in England, having heard of his willingness to be instructed, had resolved to send him two teachers. The king at once replied, "You must come too. How shall I get on with people I do not know if you are not with me?" Then, snapping his fingers, "By all means—by all means," he said, "bring teachers; you are wise—you are able to judge what is good for me and my people better than I am. The land is yours, you must do for it what you think is good." He was told that nothing was required but a place where there was a command of water, where the missionaries could live and teach the people ; that they would not look to him for food, but would plant, sow, and purchase what they might require. To this the king assented ; and though the subject was frequently referred to on subsequent occasions, he in no case deviated from his first assent. While Moffat thus obtained the king's consent to receive the missionaries, he took care at the same time to make him fully understand the nature of their duties—that he was not to expect that they would ever become traders, but that he would have to look for foreign supplies to those other persons who made it their business to traffic in the country.

A striking proof of Moffat's influence over the Matabele king occurred at this time, in the deliverance, at his intercession, of a princely captive then in his power. Macheng, the captive, was a young man of about twenty-six years of age, the son of the former king of the Bamanguatos, who was killed in an engagement while Macheng was yet a child. During his minority the boy was under the care of the chief Sechele. While Sechele was absent on a foray some of the Matabele fell upon his undefended town and carried away many captives, among whom was the young prince, then only ten years of age. He had continued a captive for sixteen years, and but for Moffat's interference would in all probability have remained so to the end of his days. When entreated by the missionary for his release, the king said that it was contrary to the custom of the Matabele to return a royal prisoner to his people, but after a long conversation he finally placed the young man at Moffat's disposal. Straightway Macheng was called. The king, sitting in his arm-chair, said: "Macheng, man of Moffat, go with your father. We have arranged respecting you. Moffat will take you back to Sechele. That is my wish as well as his, that you should be in the first instance restored to the chief from whom you were taken in war. When captured you were a child; I have reared you to be a man." Tones so sweet had never before fallen upon the captive's ear. The attendants praised the greatness and goodness of their king; while, as Moffat left the royal presence to return to his waggon, the shout was raised, "There goes Macheng; Moffat is taking Macheng to his people."

The impression which this liberation of Macheng produced on the surrounding tribes was marvellous. When Moffat arrived with his charge at Sechele's town, he with the other chiefs of his tribe met them, and forming a procession marched before them to a sort of natural amphitheatre, which was crowded with at least ten thousand people, all dressed out in their various equipments of war. After Sechele had stood up and commanded silence, he introduced the business of the meeting.

One speaker after another followed, expressing in the most enthusiastic language their delight at the return of Macheng from captivity. "Ye tribes, ye children of the ancients," said one of them, "this day is a day of marvel. That which awakes my heart to wonder is to see the Spirit's work. My thoughts within me begin to move. Verily the things I have seen and the words I have heard assume stability. When I first heard the word of God I began to ask, Are these things true? Now the confusion of my thoughts and of my soul is unravelled. Now I begin to perceive that those who preach are verily true. If Moffat were not of God he would not have espoused the cause of Sechele in receiving his words and delivering Macheng from the dwelling-place of the beasts of prey to which we Bechuanas dared not approach. There are who contend that there is nothing in religion. Let such to-day throw away their unbelief. If Moffat were not such a man he would not have done what he has done, in bringing him who was lost—him who was dead—from the strong bondage of the mighty. Moselekatse is a lion; he conquered nations, he robbed the strong ones, he bereaved mothers, he took away the son of Khari. We talk of love. What is love? We hear of the love of God. Is it not through the love of God that Macheng is among us to-day? A stranger, one of a nation—who of you knows its distance from us?—he makes himself one of us, enters the lion's abode, and brings out to us our own blood."

One of the Matabele who accompanied Moffat and the prince, and in whose charge Macheng had been placed during his captivity, then addressed the meeting in a most touching speech. At its close, looking around on the silent multitude, he asked rather sternly, "Ye tribes, why did ye covet my child?" and then turning to the missionary with softened tone, "Why did you, Moffat, prevail with the son of Machobane to make me childless? I shall return to the desert and weep. He is gone from me, but I shall never forget that I am the father of the son of Khari, who is now the son of Moffat." He concluded his pathetic address with some remarks in praise of Moselekatse. The whole scene produced a thrilling effect; and the minds of the assembly which had been taken by surprise by the presence of the dreaded Matabele among them were in raptures at hearing such expressions of kindly feeling from those who, though distant, had been till then a terror by night and day. Such a demonstration had never before been made in the country, and could not readily be forgotten.

CHAPTER XXII.

ON returning from his third visit to Moselekatse, Moffat went to Cape Town, and met Livingstone (whom he had not seen for six years), then on his way to the Zambesi to prosecute his geographical search, and to choose a site for the ill-fated University Mission in the Shire Valley. A few months afterwards, in July 1858, he had the pleasure of welcoming his own son, John Moffat, who with Messrs. Price, Thomas, Sykes, and Mackenzie, had arrived from England to labour among the Matabele and Makololo Mr. Mackenzie thus refers to Moffat's welcome :—" Kind friends who were expecting us speedily boarded our vessel, and gave us a very hearty welcome to Africa. One of the first of these was the Rev. Robert Moffat, and we were delighted to meet a missionary whose writings and whose life had been familiar to us from childhood. Nor were we alone in these feelings. 'Please to introduce me to Mr. Moffat,' said a fellow-passenger to me— a young officer proceeding to join his regiment. 'My mother would be so pleased to hear that I had met him ! '" Here also Moffat received the hearty co-operation of Sir George Grey, Her Majesty's High Commissioner, who warmly encouraged the proposed plans for extending Christianity and commerce to the interior tribes, and who arranged with him for establishing a postal communication with the Zambesi *viâ* Kuruman. Having completed all the preparations which human foresight could devise for the success of the enterprise, he started off with the mission party for their destination. At Kuruman they divided— one branch going to the Makololo, the other, under Moffat, to the Matabele.

We give the account of the reception and first experiences of the Matabele party supplied by Mr. Mackenzie :—" The missionaries destined to preach the gospel among the Mata- bele arrived at the headquarters of Moselekatse on the 28th October 1859. As pneumonia, a deadly and infectious disease, had broken out among their cattle, as soon as they reached the borders of Moselekatse's country they sent forward a messenger to beg the use of the chief's draught oxen, in order that they might be able to keep their own outside the country until the disease should disappear from among them. They dreaded the consequence of associating their arrival in the country with the coming of a disease which had produced such ravages wherever it hitherto had appeared. At first the chief invited them to come on, with the assurance that no one would blame them even if the disease did break out; but afterwards, on a second messenger being despatched to him, he took the warning, and expressed his thanks to the missionaries for their interest in his pros- perity, and promised to send them assistance.

"Instead of oxen, however, to pull the waggons, he sent men, who took to their tasks cheerfully, but after all were not able to compensate for the absence of the steady and patient oxen. The party certainly presented a novel ap- pearance, with Matabele soldiers in the place of oxen, and the sides of the waggon covered with shields and spears. Having also the nightly noise of the men at their camp-fires close to the waggons, and witnessing daily the slaughtering and eating of the cattle with which the chief kept his soldiers supplied, the young missionaries and their wives became somewhat accustomed to the Matabele before they reached their destination. At length the chief was pleased to accede to the request of the missionaries, and sent his draught oxen to relieve the soldiers and bring forward the waggons to his encampment.

"During the first two months after the arrival of the mission party in the Matabele country their position was a very unpleasant and trying one. After the first civilities were over, the manner of both chief and people completely changed. Confidence and regard gave place to distrust and unconcealed aversion. One morning, about three weeks after their arrival, the missionaries observed an unusual stir about the chief's quarters. He was leaving for another locality—the waggons were already moving; and yet the guests had received no intimation or explanation from Moselekatse. Having no oxen in the country, they were of course fixtures where they stood. Mr. Moffat resolved to ascertain the meaning of this movement, and followed the receding party for some distance for that purpose. But as soon as he approached the chief's waggon, he was turned back by the attendants of Moselekatse. The old attachment between the chief and his friend was for a time entirely inoperative.

"As to the young missionaries, their first impressions of Moselekatse were very unfavourable. They were disappointed at the manner of their reception. Instead of generosity, or even friendliness, they met with excessive selfishness, meanness, and duplicity. Instead of their imaginary 'noble savage,' they found a greedy, unreasonable, cunning old man. But they had to content themselves with the exercise of patience, a virtue which is needed everywhere, but nowhere more than in the establishment of a new mission in Southern Africa.   Insulting messages were now sent to them from the chief.   They were told that they were spies, and had come to find out the resources of the Matabele country; they must pay the chief for his assistance in pulling their waggons during the latter part of their journey; one waggon-load of goods must be given to him at once, etc.   For about two months the mission party were virtually prisoners; they were forbidden to leave the waggons or to kill game, and the Matabele were commanded not to sell them food, or even milk for their coffee.   They asked permission to purchase cows; the chief replied he had ivory but no cows for sale, and he wished in return guns and ammunition.   Determined not to compromise their character at the very outset, the missionaries refused to purchase a single pound of ivory.   They explained that other men would come to trade with him; they had come to teach him and his people."

The chief reasons for this disaffection are easily given. When Moselekatse engaged to receive the missionaries, he took the precaution to send messengers to the chief of the country in which the Kuruman station is situated to inquire into the whole scope, bearing, and results of mission work. He had heard Moffat's case; he would now hear the chief's view of the matter in whose country he had so long lived and laboured.   The report sent back by the messengers was not favourable.   The missionaries were blamed for the complications of the natives with the Boers; the missionaries, it was said, had been the means of bringing the Boers into the country.   The opinion, therefore, was that if they were allowed to settle and build among the Matabele, other white men would come and in the end take the land.   Hence the opposition on the part of the people.   The opinion does not seem to have been shared by Moselekatse, but he had his own grievance.   Moffat's visit had been so pleasant to him, and so profitable also, that he thought the residence of

Moffat's son in the country could not fail to be of advantage. He did not see that a mere visitor might render services and bestow favours which could not be expected from a person coming to reside in the country for the purpose of carrying on regular missionary work. The king had one view of the matter, the missionaries another. The king determined to employ the missionaries for his advantage. In spite of all that was said to explain the object of the mission, he insisted that they should begin a trade in ivory, and offered to load up their waggon at once, so that one of their number might go to the Colony and return with such articles as the chief desired. The missionaries would not comply. It was this battle that was fought out during the period of suspense at the beginning of the Matabele mission. Moselekatse's theory of a missionary must perish, and he must receive him on the sole ground of a teacher of the Word of God. In the end, and by a faithful resistance to the king's proposals, the missionaries triumphed.

After the struggle had gone on for about two months, the chief informed Moffat and his friends that if the situation pleased them they could have the fountain and valley of Inyate, to be occupied and cultivated according to their own ideas. Thus they were happily extricated from their difficulties, and their hearts were filled with gratitude to that God who had so far changed the king's mind and given them acceptance in his sight as teachers of His Word. Mr. Moffat, upon whom, as the founder of the mission and the leader of the expedition, a double responsibility and anxiety rested, felt his mind relieved of a heavy burden. He reflected with joy on the fact that the Gospel was extending— extending through his agency, and that the kind of life he had been living for years at Kuruman was to be reproduced among the Matabele by his son.

The missionaries now requested that interpreters might be provided, from whom they might learn the language, and through whose help they might preach to the people. The king promised to furnish them, but put off from time to time the fulfilment of his promise. Some months passed away before the interpreters were produced and the missionaries were able to commence preaching. At first the king was always present at public worship, and shewed his knowledge at once of Sechuana and the doctrines of the Bible, as Moffat had previously taught him, by occasionally interrupting the interpreter, and helping him to the right word. He did not hesitate, if he disapproved of what was said, to contradict the speaker openly, and was known even to exclaim, "That's a lie!" As he found, however, that his disapprobation did not change the character of the preaching, he at last gave up attending public worship, though his outward friendliness to the missionaries continued the same as ever.

After a year's residence in the country, permission was obtained to preach in other towns and villages as well as at Inyate, and they began to visit regularly the three nearest. By this time Mr. Thomas, who had obtained this liberty for himself and his colleagues, was able to address the people in their own language. The missionaries continued steadily and quietly to pursue their work. After some years Mr. John Moffat was removed to Kuruman, to assist and afterwards succeed his venerable father in the charge of that station. The death of Moselekatse, which took place in 1868, was felt to be a crisis in the history of the tribe and the mission; but in all the discussions and difficulties with reference to his successor, the influence and presence of the missionaries were recognised by all parties. The despotism of Matabele rule does not yet permit any one in that country to own any other god than the chief. The late war in the Transvaal entirely stopped for a time all communication with the missionaries in the Matabele country and their friends in this land, but a letter not

long ago received has been a ray of light shooting out of
thick darkness. There, whence Mr. Thomson wrote in
1874 that after fourteen years of labour there did not seem
to be a single man or woman who could be called a Christian,
the Rev. W. Sykes, who was one of the party that established the mission, finds unmistakable evidences of stirrings
of heart, and tells of several who have come under the
power of the Gospel, though they dare not openly confess
the change.

While Moffat had conducted his band of missionaries in
safety to their destination, a most terrible calamity had
overtaken the other missionary party, which, under the
guidance of Mr. Helmore, had proceeded to the Makololo,
north of the Zambesi river. It was in July 1859 that Mr.
and Mrs. Helmore, and Mr. and Mrs. Price, set out from
Kuruman for the country of the Makololo. Mr. Mackenzie
remained behind with his wife, who was ill, intending to
follow as soon as she was better. The melancholy fate of the
party will long be remembered as one of the most sad and
touching stories of missionary disaster. The difficulties and
dangers attendant on their journey to Linyanti were such
as nothing but the noblest Christian principle would have
induced them to encounter or enabled them to surmount.

During the months Mr. Mackenzie remained behind at
Kuruman he devoted himself to the study of Sechuana,
giving his spare time to the study of medicine. In May
1860 he started in the wake of Messrs. Helmore and Price,
with supplies which a native had failed to take on, as he
had agreed to. When he reached Shoshong, which is one
of the largest Bechuana towns, and where afterwards he
resided and laboured for some years, he met Mr. Moffat,
who was on his way to Kuruman from Moselekatse's
country. From him Mr Mackenzie learnt that the mission
to the Matabele had been established at Inyate, and that
the missionaries were already preaching through an in-

terpreter. Mr. Moffat was also the bearer of a message from Moselekatse to Sekhome, chief of the Shoshong, which he now delivered. It was to the effect that he might "sleep," as Moselekatse had now no intention of going to war with any one. He had promised Moffat, in 1854, that he would avoid everything like aggressive war, and now announced his intention to adhere to that promise. Subsequent events abundantly proved that there was little truth or sincerity in the message of the Zulu despot. During the stay at Shoshong, Moffat discoursed to the people with great solemnity on death, judgment, and the world to come— themes seldom present to the heathen mind.

After parting with Moffat at Shoshong, Mr. and Mrs. Mackenzie commenced the most difficult part of their journey, and travelled through a country most monotonous and uninteresting. The hollows which contain pools of water were dried up, and along the river-bed there was not a drop of water. No living creature was to be seen for miles. It was a region of emptiness. When they had gone forward through the desert, so as to get news of Mr. Helmore's party, they found that they had suffered much from want of water in passing through it. At Lotlakane they came upon the first traces of their predecessors. The Bushmen living there pointed out where the waggons had stood, and described the sufferings the party had endured from thirst. In a letter from which the following extracts are taken, Mrs. Helmore gives her own account of them :-- "The last stage of our journey has been, without exception, the most trying time of travelling I have experienced in Africa. We are now within the tropics, and on a journey we are more exposed than in a house ; the heat during the day is intense, 102° in the shade, and often affects me with faintness and giddiness ; but the early mornings are still pleasantly cool. We may expect rain this month, and are longing for it, as those only can long who have travelled through a dry and parched wilderness where no water is. Our poor oxen were at one time four, and another five, days without drink. It was quite painful to see how tame they were rendered by thirst; they crowded round the waggons, licking the water casks, and putting their noses down to the dishes and basins, and then looked up to our faces, as if asking for water. We suffered very much ourselves from thirst, being obliged to economise the little we had in our vessels, not knowing when we should get more. We had guides, but they either could not or would not give us any information.

"Tuesday, the 6th inst., was one of the most trying days I ever passed. About sunrise the poor oxen which had been painfully dragging the heavy waggons through the deep sand during the night, stopping now and then to draw breath, gave signs of giving up altogether. We had not gone as many miles as we had travelled hours. My husband now resolved to remain behind with one waggon and a single man while I and the children and the rest of the people went forward with all the oxen, thinking that we should certainly reach water by night. We had had a very scanty supply the day before; the men had not tasted drink since breakfast until late in the evening. We divided a bottleful among four of them. There now remained five bottles of water; I gave my husband three, and reserved two for the children, expecting that we should get water first. It was a sorrowful parting, for we were all faint from thirst, and of course eating was out the question; we were afraid even to do anything lest exercise should aggravate our thirst. After dragging slowly on for four hours, the heat obliged us to stop.

"The poor children continually asked for water. I put them off as long as I could, and when they could be denied no longer, doled the precious fluid out a spoonful at a time to each of them. Poor Selina and Henry cried bitterly,

Willie bore up manfully, but his sunken eyes shewed how much he suffered. Occasionally I observed a convulsive twitching of his features, shewing what an effort he was making to restrain his feelings. As for dear Lizzie, she did not utter a word of complaint, nor even asked for water, but lay all the day on the ground perfectly quiet, her lips being parched and blackened. About sunset we made another attempt, and got on about five miles. The people then proposed going on with the oxen in search of water, promising to return with a supply to the waggon, but I urged their resting a little and then making another attempt, that we might possibly get near enough to walk on to it. They yielded, tied up the poor oxen to prevent their wandering, and lay down to sleep, having tasted neither food nor drink all day.

"None of us could eat. I gave the children a little dried fruit, slightly acid, in the middle of the day, but thirst took away all desire to eat. Once in the course of the afternoon dear Willie, after a desperate effort not to cry, suddenly asked me if he might go and drain the bottles. Of course I consented, and presently he called out to me with much eagerness that he had found some. Poor little fellow! it must have been little indeed, for his sister Selina had drained them already. Soon after he called out that he had found another bottle of water. You can imagine the disappointment when I told him it was cocoa-nut oil melted by the heat. But this is a digression; I must go back to our outspanning about nine P.M. The water was long since gone, and as a last resource just before dark I divided among the children half a teacupful of wine and water which I had been reserving in case I should feel faint. They were revived by it, and said how nice it was, though it scarcely allayed their thirst. Henry at length cried himself to sleep, and the rest were dozing feverishly.

"It was a beautiful moonlight night, but the air hot and

sultry. I sat in front of the waggon unable to sleep, hoping that water might arrive before the children awoke on another day. About half-past ten I saw some persons approaching; they proved to be two Bakalahari bringing a tin canteen half-full of water, and a note from Mrs. Price saying, that having heard of the trouble we were in from the man whom we had sent forward, and being themselves not very far from the water, they had sent us all they had. The sound of water soon roused the children, who had tried in vain to sleep, and I shall not soon forget the rush they made to get a drink. There was not much, but enough for the present. I gave each of the children and men a cupful, and then drank myself. It was the first liquid that had entered my lips for twenty-four hours, and I had eaten nothing. The Bakalahari passed on after depositing the precious treasure, saying that though they had brought me water they had none for themselves. They were merely passing travellers; I almost thought they were angels sent from heaven. All now slept comfortably except myself; my mind had been too much excited for sleep. And now a fresh disturbance arose—the poor oxen had smelt the water, and became very troublesome, the loose cattle crowding about the waggon, licking and snuffing and pushing their noses towards me, as if begging for water.

"At two o'clock I roused the men, telling them that if we were to make another attempt to reach water no time was to be lost. They were tired and faint, and very unwilling to move, but at last they got up and began to unloose the oxen and drive them off without the waggon. I remonstrated, but in vain; they had lost all spirit,—'Lipelu li shule,' as the Bechuanas say. I was obliged to let them go, but they assured me I should have water sent on as quickly as possible, and the cattle should be brought back again after they had drank. They knew no more than I did the distance to the water.

"When they left us I felt anxious at the thought of perhaps spending another day like the past, but they had not been gone more than half-an-hour when I saw in the bright moonlight a figure at a distance coming along the road. At first I could not make it out, it looked so tall, but on coming nearer who should it prove to be but my servant-girl Kionecoe, eighteen years of age, carrying on her head an immense calabash of water! On hearing of our distress she volunteered to assist us. She had walked four hours. Another servant had set out with her, but as he had driven the sheep the day before a great distance without either food or water, he became so exhausted that he lay down under a bush to rest, and on the girl came alone, in the dead of night, in a strange country infested with lions, bearing her precious burden. Oh, how grateful I felt to her! Surely *woman* is the same all the world over! She had only lived with me since June, was but an indifferent servant, and had never shewn any particular attachment to the children, but this kind act revealed her heart, and seemed to draw us more closely together, for her conduct since then has been excellent. I made a bed for her beside me in the forepart of the waggon, and the children having slaked their thirst with the deliciously cool water, we all slept till six o'clock. I made coffee, and offered some to Kionecoe and her companion, who had now come up. At first they declined it, saying the water was for me and the children.

"I had now the happiness of seeing the children enjoy a meal of tea and biscuits; and then once more filling up my two bottles, I sent the calabash with the remainder of its contents to my husband, who by this time stood greatly in need of it. The distance was about twelve miles. I afterwards found that we were about the same from the water. About noon a horseman rode up, leading a second horse with two water-casks, and a tin canteen on his back. This was a supply for your brother, sent by our kind fellow-travellers, Captain and Mrs. Thompson, who had heard of our distresses from the Prices. While we were preparing the coffee, up came a pack-ox sent by Mr. Price, with two water-casks for me, and soon after some Bakalahari arrived with a calabash, so we had now an abundant supply, and my heart overflowed with gratitude to our Father in heaven, who had watched over me and mine as over Hagar of old, and sent us relief."

For more than a week every drop of water they used had to be walked for about thirty-five miles. One afternoon, when the thermometer was standing at 107° in the shade, Mrs. Helmore was saving just one spoonful of water for each of the dear children the next morning. Mr. Helmore was away searching for water; and when he returned next morning with the precious fluid, it was found that he had walked fully forty miles.

At length, after enduring innumerable difficulties and privations for seven months, they reached Linyanti, the residence of the Makololo chief, Sekeletu. Here Livingstone was to have met them and introduce them to the chief, but nothing had been seen or heard of him. The place was unhealthy; but Sekeletu refused to allow them to remove elsewhere, or even to point out a healthy place where they could settle down and wait Livingstone's arrival, and proposed that they should live with him. Of necessity they accepted the proposition, and forthwith began to build temporary houses. Bitter sorrows now filled their cup. There in Linyanti, among the dank weeds and oozy mud of the river's banks, and the thick overgrown swamps around, the enemy was lurking. The pestilence that walketh in darkness was upon them before they knew of its approach. They were overcome by it before they were aware. Mr. and Mrs. Helmore, the four little children, and all the servants, were in a few days lying on their beds unable to rise, delirious and restless, or quite unconscious.

Mr. and Mrs. Price also were very ill and their infant babe.

The first to die was little Henry Helmore; two days after the infant child of Mr. Price was laid by his side. Four days from that Selina Helmore was cut off, and on the following day Mrs. Helmore fell asleep in Jesus. Within six weeks of his wife's death Mr. Helmore also breathed his last, and the lonely mission was deprived of its veteran leader. It was a forlorn little company that Mr. Helmore left behind. There were his two orphan children, Mrs. Price, who in consequence of her illness had lost the use of her feet, and Mr Price, weak and ill and overpowered with grief. From this scene of pestilence and death the solitary missionary and his devoted wife prepared to depart, as the only means of saving their own lives and the lives of the little orphans entrusted to their care.

Up to that time the Makololo had not much interfered with them, though they did not seem to care whether the missionaries lived or died. But now they saw Mr. Price preparing to depart, they began to steal their property; even the clothes Mr. Price had been wearing during the day were stolen at night from the foot of the bed. When he was on the point of starting, Sekeletu came, and without any ceremony took possession of Mr. Helmore's new waggon, and a quantity of other goods, with all the guns and ammunition; and finally a messenger came from the chief making yet more extravagant demands before he would allow the missionary to leave. Mr. Price told him that if he did not let him go soon they would have to bury him beside the others, to which they simply replied that he might as well die there as anywhere else.

At length, after much entreaty, a few things were allowed for the journey. "Already," writes Mr. Price, "they had taken all my bed-clothing, with the exception of what was just sufficient for one bed. But before my oxen could cross the Chobe I had to deliver up one blanket. Every grain of corn which I had for food for the men they had taken, and I did not get even a goat for slaughter on the road. These were my prospects for a journey of upwards of a thousand miles to Kuruman."

The missionary's cup of affliction was not yet full. Just as he and his wife were beginning to breathe again after their heavy trials, and to look forward to further service for Christ, the message came to call the brave woman to her rest and reward. "My dear wife," writes her sorrowing husband, "had been for a long time utterly helpless, but we all thought she was getting better. In the morning early I found her breathing very hard. She went to sleep that night, alas! to wake no more. I spoke to her and tried to wake her, but it was too late. I watched her all the morning. She became worse and worse, and a little after mid-day her spirit took its flight to God who gave it. I buried her the same evening under a tree—the only tree on the immense plain of the Mahabe. This is indeed a heavy stroke, but God is my refuge and strength, a very present help in trouble.'"

Mr. Mackenzie met Mr. Price as he was leaving Linyanti, and having heard the sad story of all his sufferings and trials, resolved to return with him. At Shoshong, which they reached on the 1st of December 1860, and where they remained two months, they were agreeably surprised to meet their veteran friend Moffat, who was on his way to search for them and bring them relief. The news of the calamity at Linyanti had reached Kuruman through a native hunter who had visited the Victoria Falls. Mr. Moffat had communicated the sad intelligence to friends in Cape Town, where a public subscription was set on foot to send relief to the surviving members of a mission, all the members of which had but a short time before left that town in good health and spirits. Moffat, whose Kuruman home since 1855 was, to use his own words, "more like the lodge of a wayfaring man than a permanent abode," had cheerfully volunteered to act as agent for those kind friends at the Cape; and he was, in a peculiar sense, now the "messenger of the churches" to their suffering brethren.

Mr. and Mrs. Mackenzie and Mr. Price, with the two orphan children of Mr. Helmore, reached Kuruman in February. The calamity that overtook the mission at Linyanti resulted from the fact that Mr. Helmore the leader and the party entrusted to his care, instead of being allowed to remove to a salubrious locality, were compelled to remain amidst swamps teeming with pestilence and death. Soon after this the Makololo tribe were utterly destroyed; and in Bechuana Land, and especially among the heathen community in the northern part, the feeling is very general that their destruction so soon after their inhospitable and perfidious conduct towards the missionaries is to be traced to the justice and righteous judgment of God. Even some of the Christians say when any one counsels injury to the missionaries,—"Let the missionary alone; the Makololo injured the missionaries, and where are the Makololo?"

CHAPTER XXIII.

CHANGES AT KURUMAN.

MOFFAT remained for some months with the missionary party at Inyate; indeed it was absolutely necessary that he should. Had it not been for his influence over Moselekatse and his wonderful tact and management, the probability is that the expedition would have failed of its object and the mission not have been established at all. He continued therefore for a time assisting in the necessary negotiations with the king and preaching to the people. The king wished him to remain altogether, but that was out of the question: his family, his work, his companions in labour, his converts—all were waiting and longing for his return. When the king found he could not prevail on his friend to stay with him, he begged him at least to accept a handsome present of ivory; this Moffat resolutely refused, as he had on all former occasions.

Having returned in safety to Kuruman, the missionary resumed his home work. Henceforth Kuruman was with him chiefly a centre for many and varied journeys to points of usefulness and interest. The station was kept in peace, notwithstanding the disturbances produced in other places by the threats and actual molestations of the Boers. In all

13

his dealings with the Boers Moffat's conduct was marked by the utmost prudence;—he was conciliatory, yet firm. He took care never to endanger the interests of the natives, and yet he acted justly towards their enemies. There were times when he felt called upon to maintain his freedom of action and his just rights. In 1859 he received a letter, signed by two officers of the Government of the Transvaal Republic, warning him not to proceed to the establishment of missions in the interior until he had received the sanction of the President of the Republic. As both the Matabele and the Makololo countries were far beyond the territories of the Transvaal, and the road thither did not lead through any part of the Republic, he regarded this as an unreasonable demand with which he could not comply.

Mr. Moffat's station was not exempt from the visitations of drought; the consequence was that many of the people had to go for a livelihood to the hunting-grounds, and others had to betake themselves to the adjoining settlements in search of remunerative employment. These were seasons of anxiety both to missionary and people. There were times, however, when their hearts were made glad by witnessing success in all departments of church life and work; especially was this the case when Moffat's own two daughters gave themselves first of all to the Lord and then to His people. The year 1862 was a year of severe and unusual trial, for in addition to drought and its dreadful effects there was the prevalence of infectious disease. Measles and smallpox broke out and spread among the people at Kuruman and in the districts around, but they must all have felt the value of medical resources, and of the benefit of civilised habits, when they saw how much less severe and less fatal these diseases were among the converts at the mission station than among their less favoured neighbours. The next year the drought continued, and was aggravated by an intense heat. There was a famine in the land.

Wholesome food became so scarce that the starving population were compelled to wander through the wilderness in quest of supplies, and were glad to devour whatever they could find growing there; as the result, many fell sick, and some died. Just as this plague of famine was at its worst, God graciously sent a plentiful and continuous rain, and turned the distress of the people into general rejoicing.

The year 1863 saw great domestic sorrow in Moffat's household. News came of the death of Mrs. Livingstone, their eldest daughter. She had joined her husband, who was at the time at Shupanga. During the unhealthy season several of his party suffered from fever, and about the middle of April 1862 Mrs. Livingstone was prostrated by that disease, and notwithstanding that she received every attention which affection and skill could render, she died on the 27th of that month, and was buried on the following day under the shadow of a giant baobab-tree—the Rev. James Stewart, who had shortly before come out to inquire into the practicability of establishing a mission in connection with the Free Church of Scotland, reading the burial service. Shortly after Mr. and Mrs. Moffat were called to mourn the death of Mr. Robert Moffat, junior, their eldest son, who left behind him a widow and four children. About this time, too, the venerable missionary sustained a serious loss in his work by the removal of Mr. Ashton, his colleague, to Lekatlong. Mr. Ashton had been of great service to him for many years, being a man able and willing to turn his hand to anything, from binding a book to correcting the sheets of which it was composed; he had also rendered him invaluable help in the important work of translating the Scriptures into the Sechuana language. To complete the list of trials, death removed some of the most honourable converts; the mitigation of this trial being that those who died, died rejoicing in the Lord.

It was Moffat's happiness in 1866 to receive his son John as a substitute in the place of Mr. Ashton. Mr. John Moffat, besides helping his father in the printing-office, gave to a class of young natives instruction in the English language. He also took part in preaching, and he tells how his father, though then seventy years of age, shared with him the labour of riding to distant villages to preach and hold prayer-meetings. On the whole, however, the year was one of discouragement. Bodily sickness was prevalent among the people, with mental and spiritual deadness. The congregations at public worship were as large as ever, but there were few applications for church fellowship, readers were inattentive, knowledge was in a backward state, and the servants of the Lord felt constrained to ask,—"Who hath believed our report, and to whom hath the arm of the Lord been revealed?" Nevertheless, Moffat bore in mind the injunction to sow his seed in the morning, and not to withhold his hand in the evening, and wait for the harvest.

In October 1868 Mr. John Moffat thus described to the Directors of the London Missionary Society the regular mission work at Kuruman, and the general condition of things there :—"The public services are a prayer-meeting at sunrise on Sunday ; preaching in Sechuana, morning, afternoon, and evening; with the Sunday school twice, and a juvenile afternoon service. The early prayer-meeting is left entirely to the natives, the three preaching services to the missionaries, and the Sunday school, with the juvenile service, to my sister. There are also a Wednesday evening service, a monthly missionary prayer-meeting, a church-meeting, and a prayer-meeting on Thursday afternoon. This last is in the hands of the natives. No native takes any part in the preaching on the station, except in extreme cases, when it is regarded as a make-shift. My father and I share the preaching between us. Occasionally one of us rides to two villages to the north-west, holding service at each. My custom at home is to give New Testament reading in the morning, a topical sermon in the afternoon, and Old Testament exposition in the evening. On Monday evening I have a young men's Bible-class, to me the most interesting work, especially as I have much encouragement in it. There is a marked advance on the part of my pupils. For a people so stolid and undemonstrative as the Bechuanas, I have great encouragement, and hope my work will not be in vain. On the Monday evening, also, my sister and I hold a practising class to improve the singing. On Tuesday evening I meet male inquirers; on Wednesday, before the service, I have a Bible-class for women; on Thursday we have our English prayer-meeting; and on Friday evening I meet female inquirers. I need but mention the school conducted by my sister with three native assistants."

He then speaks of the out-stations, the printing-office, and other work :—"There is a circuit of out-stations westward. My father paid them a visit in December 1865, again in February 1867, and I have just returned from them. The printing-office has occupied a large part of my time—three days in every week on an average. There is also an incessant dispensing of medicines, to me most unwelcome, for I have only learned to know how little value there is in the medical practice of any but well qualified men. It is forced upon me by usage, like many other things, and by the persistent desire of human nature, black as well as white, to be doing 'something' for disease, even though it be a mere leap in the dark. I have rarely been able to hold an English service, though very desirous to do so. The benighted Europeans are every year becoming more numerous in this neighbourhood, and do not help on our work, though they are not unwilling to attend an occasional service, which I do not despair of setting on foot."

With regard to the number and social condition of the people, he remarks :—"The population is small and scattered as compared with other parts of the Bechuana field. On

the spot there must be a good many people, and also at two
villages north-west; otherwise the district contains only
villages of from twenty to a hundred huts.   It extends fifty
miles west and north-west, and twenty-five in other
directions. A Christian village, one hundred and seventy
miles north-east, has placed itself under our charge.   The
people are poor, and must remain so.   The country is
essentially dry.   Irrigation is necessary for successful
agriculture, and there are few spots where water flows.
There is no market for cattle, even if they throve, which
they do not.   I despair of much advance in civilisation
where resources are so small, and where the European
trade is on the principle of enormous profits and losses.
Two hundred per cent. on Port Elizabeth prices is not
considered out of the way.   I am obliged to send to
England or the coast for clothing; what is obtained here is
worthless and dear.   I have not yet seen any staple industry
for our Bechuanas.   The ostrich feather trade, like all
hunting, retards civilisation.   The political framework is
disintegrating.   I am not disposed to take alarm at the
encroachments of the Dutch Republics — Transvaal and
Orange Free State.   The country is too poor to be coveted
by Europeans, and the Bechuanas may perhaps be allowed
to exist.   This station is the one spot to tempt the Boers.
If anything could be done to secure it by convention with
the British Government the whole district would then be
left unmolested, for without the spring and the gardens
here there is nothing."

His observations on the religious condition of the natives
are such as to inspire confidence in his good sense and impartial judgment, and impress us with a full belief in the
trustworthiness of the testimony.   " Heathenism," he says,
" is weak; in many places nowhere. Christianity, too, meets
with little opposition.   The people generally are prodigious
Bible-readers, church-goers, and psalm-singers — I fear to a

BEATING SORGO

large extent without knowledge. Religion to them consists
in the above operations and in giving a sum to the auxiliary.
I speak of the generality. Many I cannot but feel to be
Christians but dimly. This can hardly be the result of low
mental power alone. The Bechuanas shew considerable
acuteness where circumstances call it out. The educational
department of the mission has been kept in the background.
On this station the youth on leaving school have sunk back
for want of a continued course open to them. The village
schoolmasters, uneducated themselves and mostly unpaid,
make but a feeble impression. The wonder is they do so
much, and where the readers come from. It is hard to say
that the older missionaries could have done otherwise.
When manual labour and menial duties were accepted as a
share of a missionary's normal occupations, it is not wonderful that he failed to advance his native pupils to a high
standard of attainments."

This subject of education was one that was forced upon
the attention of the missionaries and engaged their most
anxious thoughts. The want of native schoolmasters and
teachers was deeply felt, but the question was how they
were to be obtained. The directors at home shared with
their brethren abroad in these anxieties. The brother missionaries were about to meet in conference at the Kuruman
to discuss this matter and several other matters of importance affecting the interests of the mission, and Moffat wrote
to the directors expressing his views on various new measures
for the better instruction of the people. "Apart," he says,
" from your valuable suggestions, it was resolved by my son
John and myself to bring the subject of a school for superior
training prominently before the brethren. The want is
increasingly felt. But there was no help for it, for here or
elsewhere suitable pupils, or pupils of any kind, were not to
be had. Public feeling is very different now. We have had
to jog on with the material available, and notwithstanding

the lack of theological acquirements, have not been disappointed; but it is time a new order of things were
introduced by having a place with means afforded, and a
period allowed for educating those now anxious to advance
in that kind of knowledge which will make them useful
members of society.   The kind and reasonable proposals
made by the board to supply the wants felt, as well as a
medical missionary, if deemed necessary, will gratify the
brethren."   The promised supplies had reference to the
support of European teachers.   So successful was this effort
at one station that in little more than two years Moffat
received the sum of fifty pounds for books which had been
sold to the natives.

We get a glimpse at this time of the moral influence
which Moffat's name still exerted over the distant tribes.
Eight years had elapsed since he sought and secured for his
brethren an introduction to Moselekatse.   Now this chief,
who had ruled the Matabele tribe as with a rod of iron, was
himself conquered by the King of Terrors.   " He died," wrote
Mr. W. Sykes to the directors, "on Sabbath afternoon, the
6th of September last, at a village about fifty miles south
from Inyate, called Ingama.   For months he had been in a
lingering state, yet sometimes it was hoped he would rally
for another season.   My last visit to him was in June—a
sad and painful one.   I shall never forget how he looked at
me, and how affectionately he said, with a feeble, stammering
voice, 'I am very ill.'   I endeavoured to comfort him, but
the only words that seemed to create any interest in his
mind were those of a message from Moffat, saying that he
was still praying for him and his people.   The moment I
uttered the name his countenance beamed, but he said
nothing.   I told him intelligence had come that the son of
Moffat had been appointed to remain at Kuruman to comfort his father in his old age, and with a mien indicating
inward disappointment and yet approval he signified his

assent by a gentle nod." When Mr. Sykes was leaving the camp a voice was raised above the rest—"Remember me to the son of Moffat!" and, as if by an echo, the whole camp repeated the request, while individual voices, still following him, cried out—"All of us! all of us!" In this we have a prediction of the way in which the names of Africa's two great benefactors, Moffat and Livingstone, will be held on that continent in everlasting remembrance.

Kuruman is now the seat of a Theological Institution for the training of African young men for a native ministry, and is under the care of the Revs. J. Mackenzie and J. Brown. It has long been as a green oasis in the desert, its fountain furnishing unfailing supplies for a large population, and its missionary agencies making it a great centre of life and light. With the large educational establishment now provided there we may confidently hope that it will exert a still greater power in the progress of the country as years go on. Mr. Mackenzie recently writes from there thus :—"I am very much gratified in being able to report that an earnest and anxious spirit has lately prevailed among the people here, and native teachers visiting Kuruman have lately brought inquirers with them, or announce that they have such at their homes. Some time ago I had the pleasure of receiving into church-fellowship a few of the young people belonging to Kuruman and Macoping, and last Sunday I received the wives of two of the students in the Institution and one of the senior boys in Mr. Brown's school, whose earnestness and consistency have been tested for a long time. In my present class of inquirers there are several boys from the boarding-school. Speaking of the church members, I hope I am not mistaken when I report that greater prayerfulness and spirituality of mind obtain among them." He writes again :—"I am writing after the breaking-up of our New Year's gathering for special prayer —the largest I am told which has assembled at Kuruman

for many years. People were present from more than one
village on the distant Molopo River, as well as from the
borders of the Kalahari Desert, Morokweng, Konke, etc. ;
and they not only came in large numbers, but few left until
the week's meetings were over and the services of the secon
Sunday had also been enjoyed. I believe the people were
cheered and strengthened by the succession of spiritual
engagements, and have gone to their various homes thanking God for the past and resolving to trust to Him for the
future. For my own part, I have been much encouraged
by the spirit shewn by the people, as well as by the numbers
who felt called to join in these special services."

CHAPTER XXIV.

RETIREMENT FROM THE MISSION FIELD.

THE period was now near at hand when it seemed desirable that this distinguished servant of God should retire from the scene of his long and arduous labours, to enjoy for the remainder of his life on earth needed and well-earned repose. In a letter dated Kuruman, 9th July 1869, he informs a friend in England that it is more than probable he shall retire from the mission-field, and return home the following year; and he goes on to say :—" My age is over seventy-four years, fifty-two of which have been spent in mission work. It is natural that I should give place to youth and energy. I feel most sensibly that I am getting old. My dear brother, what an animated prospect we have in view ! Our Saviour reigns ; the Lamb is in the midst of the throne. What a stimulus to zeal in all that has a reference to our Redeemer in this world, that we may meet there not only those to whom we have been indebted in this world, but those also to whom God in His great mercy has made us the means of their advancement to the many mansions."

With the beginning of the year 1870 Moffat closed his life's labours on the African continent. The fact that his own health and that of his beloved wife was beginning to fail, together with the affectionate solicitations of the directors of the society whose devoted agent he had been for upwards of half a century, induced him to accept the invitation pressed upon him to return to England. We can well imagine the difficulties which attended his departure. It must have cost him no common effort and pain to tear himself away from the scene of so many years of unwearied and anxious toil, and the people who had long since learned to regard him with reverence and affection. He had, however, the gratification of witnessing the fruits of his patient and prayerful endeavours, and of seeing the fulfilment of that faith and hope which had often cheered him in the early days of his missionary career. The dark heathenism which enveloped the country at the time when he first set foot on its shores had broken and lifted before the light of the glorious Gospel of Jesus Christ. Kuruman, itself the creation of his own hands, had been for many years a standing testimony to the elevating and civilising power of the Christian faith. The regions beyond, which before no individual dare to traverse, were now passed without fear of molestation. European manufactures, to the amount of one hundred thousand pounds, were now annually interchanged with the natives, who previously knew not what commerce was. Above all, among the various tribes of the interior as far as the distant Matabele, a band of brave and earnest missionaries, both men and women, were preaching and living Christianity, setting an example of consistent moral conduct to the savages around, treating them with kindness, teaching them agriculture and useful handicrafts, and imparting to them religious instruction.

The day of departure at length came. It was a day of bitter parting and of affectionate regrets on all hands. On leaving the Kuruman *en route* for England, Mr. and Mrs. Moffat came by a rough yet safe journey of about eight weeks' duration to Port Elizabeth. There, on the 20th of May 1870, they received a hearty welcome from a large number of missionaries and other friends who had come together to meet them. During the overland journey they had been exposed to cold weather and heavy rains, especially in crossing the snow mountains. From Graaf Reinet to Port Elizabeth the roads were fearfully bad. They passed many waggons laden with wool brought to a stand up to their axles in mud. Through the good providence of God, however, they were able to accomplish their journey without accident or loss.

In addressing the company who gathered round him at Port Elizabeth, he thus referred to the accomplishment of his great labours in translation:—"I had hoped that I should be excused as to making a speech, as I am suffering from a cold, but I find it quite impossible to remain silent. I should be a mussel or a cockle, or something of that kind, not to feel impressed with what has been said. I have been reminded of past events, past hours, past days, past years. I have been carried back to past scenes which I can never forget. I still remember distinctly when I first became a missionary—the great undertaking it seemed to be to learn the language of the people among whom I was placed. There were no interpreters to teach us a single word, and great difficulties were thrown in the missionaries' way. However, I laboured on, gathering a few words at a time from one and another until I could string sentences together, and make my wishes known to the natives. I could make you laugh as I laughed when I discovered them, at jokes perpetrated towards us by the natives, and amusing things that occurred to us during our inquiries; but I laboured on. During all this time we had not a friend in the whole nation, not an individual that loved or respected us, or who wished us to remain among them; and although they tried to drive us out, we persevered, and by God's grace and assistance overcame every difficulty. My worthy brother Hamilton was too old to acquire the language, but I in time mastered it. How ardently I desired to see the New Testament in Sechuana, that I might read it to the natives, and that they might learn to read it for themselves. I managed after a time to translate small portions and read them to the people in their own tongue. The mission, I saw, could make no firm footing among them unless the Scriptures were translated. The task of accomplishing this you can scarcely imagine. When I came first out to Africa I had not the slightest intention of ever engaging in such a work. I never aimed at being more than a preacher. I was urged, however, by Dr. Philip (whose letters I have still by me), and by others, to persevere in acquiring the language, and to undertake the translation of the Scriptures; but I thought it altogether beyond my powers. I wrote to the directors that I could not do it, and begged them to send some one out who could. I felt that I had not sat long enough at the feet of any Gamaliel to qualify me. I then heard that my brother-in-law had been ordained to the ministry, and was to join me, and as he had received a liberal education, I prepared materials for him to begin with immediately after his arrival, but his destination was altered; he was sent to the East Indies. I wrote again to the directors, telling them that if they did not send some one to translate the Scriptures I should return home. By-and-by Mr. Robson came out, as I thought, for the work, but he remained in the colony. After this I also visited the colony, and met brother Elliott, now gone to heaven. He, I hoped, might be allowed us, but that was inconvenient. At last I brought myself to the resolution that, if no one else would, I would undertake it myself. I entered heartily upon the work. For many years I had no leisure, every spare moment being devoted to translating, and I became a stranger even in my own family. There was labour every day for back, for hands, for head. This was especially the case during the time Mr. Edwards was there; our condition was almost one of slavery. Still the work advanced, and at length I had the satisfaction of completing the New Testament. Of this six thousand copies were printed by the home society. The whole were soon distributed and found insufficient. When Dr. Livingstone came he urged me to begin at once with the Old Testament. That was a most stupendous work. Before taking it in hand I passed many sleepless nights. Since however it was the wish of all that I should undertake it, I did so, and went on from time to time as I had leisure, daily and nightly. I stuck to it as far as to the end of Kings, when I became completely done up. The directors were themselves afraid that I was killing myself I was advised to go home, to leave the work, but I decided otherwise. I determined, on the contrary, to look up Mo-selekatse, and went off in company with a son of brother Edwards. By the time I had found the chief I was all right again. Coming back, I resumed my work, and have continued it to completion; and now I can look forward to the Word of God being read by thousands of Bechuanas in their own mother tongue."

Having thus spoken of the chief work of his life, he went on to describe the general progress made in the interior. "Christianity," he said, "has already accomplished much. When first I went to the Kuruman scarcely an individual could go beyond. Now they travel in safety as far as the Zambesi. Then we were strangers, and they could not understand us. We were treated with indignity, as the outcasts of society, who, driven from our own race, took refuge with them. But bearing in remembrance what our Saviour underwent, we persevered, and much success has rewarded our efforts. Now it is safe to traverse any part of the country, and traders travel far beyond Kuruman without fear of molestation.   Formerly men of one native tribe could not travel through another's territory, and wars were frequent.   Where one station was scarcely tolerated there are several.   The Moravians have their missionaries, the Berlin Society theirs.   Others, too, are occupied in the good work, besides many native Gospel teachers."

With reference to the difficulties encountered at the outset, the speaker entered more fully into enumeration of the gratifying proofs that many of them had been overcome. "For many years," he added, "we saw not the conversion of a single individual ; for years again we had only one ; but by the blessing of God on great exertion, almost wherever we go we now meet with companies of natives who profess to be members of the Church of Christ.   Not very long since it was considered dangerous to travel into the interior, in fact half-a-dozen miles from the station.   Now I am happy to say the natives can be depended upon, and it is quite common for traders to travel through their midst without the least fear of plunder or interruption.   In former times traders were often basely murdered, or at best not permitted to return.   Now all fears have been dispelled. Once the natives would not buy anything, not even a pocket-handkerchief.   They might now and then be induced to buy a few trinkets or some beads, but nothing of a substantial or useful character.   It is not so now.   No less than sixty thousand pounds' worth of British manufactures pass yearly into the hands of the native tribes round about Kuruman. During my early mission life I often heard of men of one tribe going to trade with another and being murdered.   I was at a native place when a thing of that sort once occurred. A party of men had come two hundred miles to dispose of some articles.   The resident natives, taking a dislike to them, set upon them and killed two of the number.   I asked them why they had done this, and tried to shew them that it was wrong.   They seemed to know that, and from that time I have never heard of anything of the sort. They are now always ready to meet any traders or other persons. Companies of natives can be passed through without fear, and they shew special respect to the missionaries. I assure the gentlemen present that many natives at the Kuruman are well able to discuss and argue upon the doctrines of Christ. I do not mean that they can enter into any lengthy or out-of-the-way points, but this I will say that they can argue with sense upon any general question. They may not always stick to a text, but they will rarely go outside of the Bible. And these are a people who forty years ago were nothing better than savages, but who, by the blessing of God upon the labours of those who have devoted their lives to their work, have been brought to be intelligent disciples of the Gospel of Christ."

After a brief stay at Port Elizabeth Mr. and Mrs. Moffat embarked in the mail steamer *Roman*, and landed at Cape Town on the 2nd of June. The following day they were entertained by the whole Christian community at a public breakfast, and after a few days rest proceeded towards England in the *Norseman*, arriving at Southampton on the 25th of July. On Monday, 1st August, at the board-room of the London Mission House in Bloomfield Street, the veteran missionary was received on his return by the directors of the society. Mr. James Hawkins, late an English judge in India, and chairman of the board, presided, and nearly a hundred directors and friends were present. After devotional exercises the Rev. Dr. Mullens, secretary of the society, performed the pleasing duty of introduction. Mr. Moffat then rose amid enthusiastic applause. "Friends and brethren," he said, "I have been listening with great attention, and occasionally with very deep feeling, to the words which have been spoken, and which have deeply impressed me. I have felt their weight, but, alas! it is not for me on the present occasion to meet the expectations of

14

some with regard to saying a word or two for myself.   I am
unpleasantly situated.   The night before last I had scarcely
any sleep, and last night I had none ; and at the present
time I feel my head like an empty calabash, as we say in
Africa.   It is not very seasonable to give anything like an
address, but a few words I will speak — I cannot help
speaking.   It was not my expectation to be here ; it was
not my intention again to visit England.   When I last left
the board of directors, it was, in thought, for ever.   Never
did it enter my mind that I should set my feet on English
soil again ; but it has been ordered otherwise.   Even on
the first occasion when I came home it was not a matter of
choice.   When I went out I went out for life ; when I gave
myself to the missionary enterprise it was to live and die
in the service.   I always anticipated I should leave my
dust to mingle with those whom I have been instrumental
in gathering from among the heathen, and who are now
participating in the glories of the heavenly world.   When I
came to the Cape, previous to my first visit, I brought a
translation of the New Testament, which I had accomplished
under considerable difficulties, being engaged a portion of
the day in roofing an immense church, and the remainder
in exegetical examinations and consulting concordances.   I
was anxious to get it printed, and I brought it down to the
Cape, but there I could find no printing-office that would
undertake it.   The committee of the Bible Society very
kindly—as they have always been to me ; I say it with
pleasure—forwarded paper and ink to the Cape, expecting
I should get the work done there.   As I said, there was
not a printing-office that would undertake it.   Dining with
Sir George Napier, the Governor, I informed him of the
difficulty.   He said, ' Jump on board a ship with your
translation and get it printed in England, and you will
be back again while they are thinking about it here.
Print a New Testament among a set of Dutch printers !

—why, I can't even get my proclamations printed.' I said, 'I have become too barbarous; I have almost forgotten my own language; I should be frightened to go there.' 'Oh, stuff!' he said. Some time after he met me in the street. 'Well, Moffat, what have you determined upon?' 'I am waiting the return of Dr. Philip.' 'Don't wait for anybody, just jump on board a ship. Think of the importance of getting the New Testament put in print in a new language!' He invited me to dinner again, and said, 'Have you come to a conclusion? I wish I could give you mine. I feel some interest in the extension of the knowledge of the Word of God. Take nobody's advice, but jump on board a ship for England.' He spoke so seriously that I began to feel serious myself. Dr. Philip came, and when all the circumstances were explained, he said, 'Go, by all means!' I was nervous at the thought. I was not a nervous man in Africa; I could sleep and hear a lion roar. There seemed so many great folks to meet with. I came to England, and by-and-by I got over it. I am afraid I have got too old to improve now. On this second occasion there was a necessity. I was a martyr to wakefulness; I was dying by inches. Nothing could induce sleep, no matter what kind of opiates I employed. A week would pass without a moment's sleep; a month, perhaps, with very short intervals. I was a wonder not only to myself but to others. Occasionally I got a little sleep, but that was only the prelude to no sleep at all for a long period. I thought of taking a journey into the interior, but after further consultation I at last came to the conclusion to go home, and saw my path in that direction clear. I was aware I should be received, and verily I have been received, with kindness passing description. I came to Port Elizabeth, and really the people did not seem to know how they could do enough to express their feeling. I thought I was a solitary missionary, and I should just pass by, but they took all out of me they could find in me, and I believe their kind reception had a very salutary influence upon me. I came to Cape Town, and there they had everything prepared before I arrived. I received a hearty welcome from all sections of the church, every one congratulating me and passing encomiums. Some of the speeches were admirable. I only wish they had been taken down. Since coming into this room I could hardly allow myself to think of the last assembly that I witnessed here. There sat Dr. Tidman, and there the other secretary, Mr. Freeman. There, too, were Mr. Coombs, Mr. Philip, Mr. Arundel, Dr. Waugh, and last, not least, Dr. Henderson, to whose own translations I felt so much indebted. These are all gone; it is depressing to think of it; we are following, and others will follow. But, say they are gone. Oh! brethren, the work for which God became man—a man of sorrows and acquainted with grief, the first missionary in the world—what a glorious work in which to be found, whether in life or in death! How is it to go with me I know not. I shall do all that in me lies for the advancement of the missionary cause. I shall not fail, wherever I am, to use all the means within my power, by presence or word, to advance that great cause to which I have devoted my life. It would have been pleasant just to remain with the people among whom I laboured so long, by whom I am beloved, and whom I love. Oh, that parting was a scene hard to witness without emotion! Not only from Christian converts, but from heathen chiefs did I receive tokens of goodwill. Their amanuenses brought letters deploring my departure, and presents to induce me not to quit the country, but to remain, promising to give me so much more if I would but remain. It was gratifying to see these tokens, especially from the heathen and those able to appreciate one's labour among them. One sent an ox, another a kaross, and so on; a lady of quality sent me four feathers. Some of them asked how they were to live—how they were to exist

—if I went out of the country; that is a form of expression among them. It is consolatory to think that the influence of the Gospel in that dark benighted country is spreading and is going into the interior, covering hamlet after hamlet, until its advance, let us be assured, will cover the whole land. It is for us to pray and to labour, and we have the assurance that Ethiopia shall yet stretch out her hands unto God. I feel exceedingly grateful to my friends for the kind way in which I have been received, and in my secret hours I will return thanks to God for all these tokens of friendship of which I have been the recipient this day."

CHAPTER XXV.

SINCE his retirement from the mission-field, Dr. Moffat has continued to render important services from time to time to the cause, and has been honoured by all sections of the Church in many ways. Within a few months after his return to England, he appeared on the platforms of the London Missionary Society, and the British and Foreign Bible Society, in Exeter Hall, speaking at the anniversaries of both these societies in 1871.

His welcome at the annual meeting of the London Missionary Society was most enthusiastic, the whole audience standing up to greet him with repeated cheers when he rose to speak. He spoke of the changes he had witnessed in the character of the people among whom he had laboured, and of the great moral and social elevation which had followed the preaching of the Gospel in Southern Africa. At the British and Foreign Bible Society's meeting he was also most warmly received, and was listened to with the most earnest attention while speaking in tones of endearment of the land which he had left, but where he would fain be labouring still, and recounting his labours in the translation of the Scriptures into the Sechuana tongue, and telling of the longing of the people to possess copies of the Word of God.

The following year the veteran missionary again stood on the platform of the London Missionary Society at its great anniversary, and addressed the crowded audience. He was greeted with the warmest demonstrations of respect, and adverted to the success of the effort which had been made by the juvenile friends of the society for the Moffat Institution, as it was proposed to call the seminary for training native teachers in South Africa, and for which upwards of five thousand pounds had been raised during the previous twelve months. He thanked the little folk for their handsome subscription, with tender pathos expressed a longing to clasp them all to his heart, and invoked the Divine benediction on them and their efforts. He seemed, as he spoke, to combine in himself both the patriarch and the apostle, and neither the matter nor the manner of his address will ever be forgotten by those who heard it. One of the subsequent speakers at that meeting was the Rev. J. Fleming, a clergyman of the Established Church. In adverting to Dr. Moffat, he called him "our Robert Moffat;" the remark called forth thunders of applause. "Yes," repeated the speaker, "our Robert Moffat, for I cannot allow that he is only yours; such a man as Robert Moffat belongs to all the Church of God."

In May 1873 Dr. Moffat received a very substantial recognition of his long, faithful, and valuable services in the mission cause. One morning about three hundred ladies and gentlemen breakfasted together at Cannon Street Hotel, London. The chair was taken by Mr. Samuel Morley, M.P. After breakfast the chairman read a brief sketch of the distinguished South African missionary's career. More than half a century ago, he said, when Dr. Moffat crossed the Orange River into the Bechuana territory, there was nothing but vice, misery, and degradation. Now the Sabbath is a recognised institution, and the people are making rapid progress in Christian civilisation. An address to the reverend gentleman was read by the Rev. Dr. Binney, in which a hope was expressed that the guest of the day might be permitted to see and welcome to his native country his distinguished son-in-law, Dr. Livingstone. The hope, alas! was not fulfilled. Instead of welcoming his living son he was only permitted to receive his dead remains.

Mr. Morley stated that a number of Dr. Moffat's friends had felt it laid upon their hearts to present him with some testimonial which should be an expression of their Christian love and thankfulness, and their high appreciation of his life-long devotion to Jesus Christ and the souls of men, and which at the same time should make some provision for the comfort of his declining years. He stated that the total amount received was £5812, 10s. 6d., that of this amount £5250 had been invested in the names of trustees in East India Guaranteed Railway Stock, yielding a minimum income of £234, 10s. per annum, and that the balance would be paid to Dr. Moffat. The presentation of the trust-deed having been made, it was acknowledged by Dr. Moffat, who said that during the last fifty years he had travelled thousands of miles among savage beasts and still more savage men, and sometimes had been delivered from danger by the skin of his teeth. Though, on looking back upon a long life of missionary labour, he felt that he ought to have done more work, and to have done his work better, his heart overflowed with gratitude to God for the blessings which He had poured on missionary efforts in that part of Africa with which he had been connected. He recalled the days of early missionary labour, when the allowances were, under Dr. Vanderkemp and the Dutch directors at the Cape, eighteen pounds seven shillings for a single missionary, five pounds five shillings for a wife, six pounds three shillings for building a house, and eighteen pounds seven shillings for the purchase of cattle or sheep. It was with such resources that he commenced his career.

Dr. Moffat has not confined his advocacy of Christian missions to the London Missionary Society. His breast is filled with the expansive and all-embracing love which the Gospel inspires; he looks with compassion on all mankind, and with the affection of a Christian brother on all who bear the Saviour's name and image, and he wishes the most complete success to follow every effort for the conversion of men to God. Hence, in 1875, we find him among the speakers in Exeter Hall at the annual missionary meeting of the United Methodist Free Churches. In the course of a most able and attractive address on that occasion, he said that it was now fifty-eight years since he first laid himself on the missionary altar, and during all that period his mind had been undivided in devotion to the work. He had made it his one great business to try to benefit the poor African both for the present life and that which is to come. His motto was that of the Apostle Paul—"This one thing I do."

Some years ago the Archbishops of Canterbury and York, feeling the importance of promoting missionary work throughout the world, and the need of God's blessing to render it successful, instituted a day of intercession for Christian missions, and issued a joint invitation to all to engage in its general observance. The year 1876 was memorable, because Dr. Moffat, at the invitation of Dean Stanley, delivered a lecture on the day set apart for the intercessory services in Westminster Abbey on the theme so near his heart, and his devotion to which has been demonstrated by the labours of a life. It was an impressive manifestation of that Christian unity which ought to exist among the disciples of our common Lord in the great work of the evangelisation of the world, and the proclamation of his grace and mercy in the Gospel. To behold the venerable

Nonconformist missionary standing in one of the oldest ecclesiastical structures devoted to the worship of the English Church, surrounded with accessories so different from those to which he was accustomed when conducting missionary services in Africa, was to every right-minded Christian present in the large assembly a pleasant gratifying sight, and one which will not soon or easily be forgotten.

The occasion suggested an article in the *Times*, in which the writer remarked :—"For a man to have surrendered himself so completely to the interests of the people whom he desired to evangelise, that he has at length to apologise to an assembly of his own countrymen, as Dr. Moffat did, for having ceased to think in his native tongue, is a rare exhibition of the true missionary spirit.   It will certainly be one of the most memorable incidents to be recounted by some future Dean Stanley, when supplementing the already recorded history of Westminster Abbey, that Dr. Moffat, speaking near the grave of Dr. Livingstone, should have described within its walls the principles on which he and his illustrious follower laid the first real foundation of South African Christianity.   Such an occasion was no doubt one to fire with an unusual expansiveness the liberal enthusiasm of the Dean of Westminster, and it would indeed have been impossible for him to say too much on behalf of the claims upon our honour and gratitude asserted by the missionary energy of other Christian communities besides the Church of England."

As one of the fruits of the religious awakening in our land of late years, an unprecedented number of medical students and others have been offering themselves as candidates for medical missionary training.   This gratifying fact, along with the great and increasing demand for medical missionaries, led the Edinburgh Medical Missionary Society, a few years ago, to erect a commodious Medical Mission Dispensary and Training Institution.   The establishment is appropriately associated with the honoured name of David Livingstone, who was himself a medical missionary and a corresponding member of the society. On the 9th of June 1877 Dr. Moffat was honoured to lay the memorial stone of the Livingstone Memorial Medical Institution in Cowgate, Edinburgh, in the presence of a large assemblage of spectators, including Sir John M'Neill, G.C.B., who presided, and many of the leading citizens of Edinburgh. On the occasion he advocated in an earnest and eloquent manner the claims of the institution. Elsewhere he says of it:—"The Livingstone Medical Missionary Memorial will be a living one, diffusing influence and scattering blessings, not to Africa only, but to every quarter of the globe where suffering humanity is crying for the sympathy of human aid. Many a time have I witnessed results of the most gratifying character from medical aid, and that not in reference to the present life only, but what is infinite—eternity. The reports of the labours and successes of medical missionaries are calculated to arouse the deepest sympathy and love of every Christian heart." By this and similar acts of service Moffat has, even in what may be called his retirement, continued to give material assistance to the great cause of Christian missions. His name possesses a charm — the story of his life and labours is one which men never weary in hearing—his appearance and age excite reverence—his association with any good movement, and his advocacy of its claims, must be a source of strength and prosperity.

In October 1878 a General Conference on Foreign Missions was held at the Conference Hall, Mildmay Park, London. A similar conference had been held at Liverpool in 1860, which was pleasant and profitable at the time, and had been productive of much subsequent good. It was considered that the time had arrived when another gathering of the friends of missions might be convened, in order that those who were closely identified with the practical side of missionary life might again compare notes in regard to the character and position of their work, and specially might consult together as to whether they could combine their forces and increase them, so as to secure a larger range of Christian service among the heathen nations of the earth.

The conference lasted four days, and was largely attended. The list of members shewed representatives of the Berlin, the Rhenish, the Basle, and the Paris Missionary Societies; several American gentlemen testified to the work carried on by the missionary agencies which flourish so greatly on the other side of the Atlantic, while the English and Scotch Societies were well represented.

At the first session the subject of mission work in Africa came up for discussion, when Dr. Moffat was one of the chief speakers. After alluding to the hard climate of this country, for which he had had to exchange the sunny skies of interior Africa, he said :—" I came here with no intention of making a speech ; I am quite unprepared to say anything. But whenever Africa comes up, that is a text upon which I can always speak. I am always willing to hear anything about Africa, and am always willing to say something in regard to it. Of course it might be expected that I can say a great deal, for I have spent the most of my life in the interior of that vast continent. From the day I went out in 1816 to this day I have been advocating the claims of Africa. One friend just remarked that if he were a young man he would like to go there again. I would go out to-morrow were it in my power, and I think I am not too old yet. It was an over-taxed brain that brought me home, and brought on wakefulness, which nothing can cure.

" My heart has been warmed by the grand things which I heard this morning respecting Africa. Already great triumphs have been accomplished. When I first landed there, in the year 1816, there was only one missionary beyond the boundaries of the Colony. It was not until our society resolved to send missionaries beyond that the thing was attempted at all. The London Missionary Society has been a pioneer society in this respect. It has been so to the South Sea Islands; it has been the pioneer to China, it has been the pioneer to Madagascar, and it has been the pioneer to the tribes beyond the boundaries of the Cape Colony. Until missionaries were sent to the Kaffirs and Zulus, nothing was attempted. The noble Moravians had established a mission station near the coast—and noble missionaries they are, and ever will be; but they confine their labours exclusively to the people about the coast.

"When I landed on the shores of Africa Joseph Williams had just died in Kaffirland; he was followed by Brownlee. Now what do we see? We see the Zulus from Port Natal to Delagoa Bay, behind the range where the Kaffirs are, and the Bechuanas extending to twenty degrees of south latitude, and all the other tribes—tribes which are merely names in your ears, but which are great tribes and important fields when viewed from the closer eye of missionary labour—we see them all open to the sound of the Gospel; we see the messengers of the church proclaiming that Gospel to thousands and tens of thousands among them who not long ago lived in gross darkness and ignorance.

"In Namaqua land I once laboured for a short time under the noble Africaner—a land which has been occupied by our noble German brethren, who have persevered and have won its people. They have gone even beyond: they have reached the Damara country, and have met the Portuguese on the West Coast. Thus we have a bright prospect in reference to the whole interior of Southern Africa. I expect by-and-by to hear that the boundaries of the colony will be extended to the Kuruman, and ere long the young people of to-day will see those boundaries extending to the Zambesi. And so it will go on and on, until from South Africa we meet those missionaries who are now entering the

East Coast, and are making their way to the shores of the great lakes.

"We have good news to encourage us this day. Think only of the translations of the Scriptures—think only of the Press—by means of which they are now able to read the Word of God in their own country and in their own tongue. In the early years of my labour there was not one person who could read ; yet now, as I say, a multitude of them can read in their own language. For instance, there are the Bechuanas, an extensive tribe. Thousands of men, women, and children among them are now reading the Scriptures and books in their own tongues. I know that for years no one among them could be made to comprehend that a book or a paper could speak ! The Gospel and Christian missions have done it all.

"Look again at the advance that has been made in their social position. I have seen men returned from the battle ; men once glorying in the number they have slain—I have such men now in my mind's eye—standing up, taking the Word of God, giving out a text or reading a portion of Scripture, and proclaiming to their fellow-men, 'Peace on earth and goodwill to man.' I have known the wonderful influence of the Gospel even upon heathen minds.

"Bad as the African mind is represented to be, it is strong to see and apt to appreciate the principles of the Gospel, and to love those principles of peace which are commended in the Gospel. I remember an individual, the chief of a tribe, who was invited to come to us, but he declined to receive the Gospel. That man heard that others were concocting war after years had rolled by, when the chiefs had agreed to bury their spears, and that there should be no more fighting. Well, this chief heard that some of the other chiefs were concocting war in his neighbourhood, and contemplating war upon another chief who thought himself the greatest. Time rolled on ; the reports of impending war increased ; the prospect seemed to grow darker.

"He called them to a feast; and the Bechuanas are always ready for a feast whatever else they dislike. He called them to a parliament, or pitcho, to which they attach great importance. They went to the assembly, which was bristling with spears, for every one at least had a spear, or axe, or shield. He stood in their midst; he stretched out his hand to them: 'Hear! O ye nobles of the people, ye leaders of the nation, I address myself to you. Hearken, for I have something to say—something that is good for you as it is good for me.' They all listened. 'I hear you are going to war.' Now the speaker was an unconverted man, a pure heathen, but he had witnessed the influence of the Gospel among the people, and admired what the Gospel had done. He admired the principles of love that existed there and that were promoted among his people. He said: 'You are going to war; allow me to ask you, What is war? I am a man of war. I have shaken my spear in the face of my enemies; I have driven them away with the sound of my shield. You have done it. But let me hear, What is war?' All were silent. 'Allow me to tell you what war cannot do.'

"'In going to war we attempt to accomplish some end. Now I will tell you what war cannot do, and what war has done, and I will tell you what war will do. Hearken unto me, O ye rulers of the people, ye wise ones that teach knowledge! War cultivates no fields; it plants no gardens. War raises no families and builds no houses. What is war? Will you know what war has done? Go to the fields where the strife of battle has raged, where some of you have shed your blood, and caused the blood of others to be shed. Go; look at the people who have been enslaved, and ask them, What are you doing here? They will reply, War sent us down here. Go to the widows; ask the widow, Why do you yet mourn? The widow will answer, War devoured my husband, and I am alone. Go to the fatherless, and they will tell you, I had a father, but war ate him up. And to go into war—is this the result of all the joy that we have felt during the peace that has been wrought among us by men from far countries? Has it come to this, that we have danced, and our wives and our daughters and our children have danced too—when we fear no evil, and raise our head in the morning without hearing the sound of war or the roar of battle on the plain— is this the result, that now we are going to resume it? Are we going to unearth the spear?' One rose in the middle of the company and said: 'No, no; let spears be burned. Let there be no more war. Let us return to our own homes, and let us rejoice still in the peace that we had enjoyed before.' Alas! my dear friends, at the present moment a dark cloud is passing over these very nations. The demon of war has spread over Kaffirland and into the Bechuana country; the tribes are arrayed in opposition; volunteers have gone out, and they are joined by others; and there is war. The tribes are being scattered, and I mourn. I would that I were there, for I know that there must be much affliction, much sorrow. I do not blame the Government or the nation. Both are to blame in concocting, at least in increasing, the spirit of war. But still, let God be praised, the work is going forward and increasing; this light affliction is for a short time. We shall see brightness in the days to come."

Towards the close of the year 1878 the veteran missionary was presented with the freedom and livery of the Turners' Company of London, at the Mansion House. In acknowledging the compliment, he gave an interesting sketch of his labours among the Bechuanas since 1816, when he laid himself on the missionary altar. When he first set foot in Africa, he said, they had no missionaries beyond the boundaries of the towns, but since then they had not only gone beyond the colony, but were to be found in the whole length and breadth of Africa.   It was no longer true that, as had been written by Swift—

> "Geographers in Afric's maps
> Put savage beasts to fill up gaps,
> And o'er inhabitable downs
> Put elephants for want of towns."

Now their missionaries were pressing forward among the Bechuanas, Zulus, and other tribes, and they had no fewer than forty thousand members of Christian churches.   Their missionaries were now labouring seven hundred miles beyond where the work first commenced among the Bechuanas.

One of the latest public recognitions of the work of this honoured servant of God was of an unusual kind.   Civic banquets are often given in honour of statesmen and warriors, and merchant princes, and men of literature and science, but it is not often that we hear of one being given to a missionary of the Cross.   All honour to the man who had the Christian consistency and courage to make in this matter a new departure.   On Saturday, 7th May 1881, the Lord Mayor of London, the Right Hon. William M'Arthur, M.P., gave a banquet to the distinguished South African missionary, and as might have been expected, a most enthusiastic reception was accorded to him by the company, which included the Archbishop of Canterbury, the Earl of Shaftesbury, and the leading representatives of the Christian churches of the country.

During the earlier years after his return home, Dr. Moffat was a frequent attendant and speaker at public meetings, but latterly his public appearances have been more seldom, and even when present he often takes no part.   His mere presence, however, is always enough to awaken the enthusiasm of the audience.   We must not forget to mention that some years ago the University of Edinburgh conferred upon him the honorary degree of Doctor of Divinity.

In addition to his advocacy of the mission cause in the pulpit and on the platform, Dr. Moffat has written some interesting papers on the subject for the periodical press. Extracts from one or two of these will prove interesting to our readers. In an article in *Sunday at Home*, on his African recollections, he thus writes of Bechuana hymns and music:—"In the early years, when a few began to appreciate instruction and attend Divine service, it was some time before they, especially in the outlying villages, could be taught to sing. It was known that we sang hymns at the chief, and then the only, missionary station, and when I have had occasion to visit these villages for the purpose of introducing the knowledge of the Saviour, nothing would satisfy them but that they too must sing. I shall never forget the jumble of voices. It was in vain to tell them that they must first be exercised before they could join in music which spoke of the God that rules on high, and their condition as sinners, and God's love to them. It required line upon line to make them understand this, but they could understand making a noise with the voice; and they thought, from what they had heard occasionally with their own ears, that there really was something uncommonly sweet in our music. There was no alternative but to yield, and of course I would select the Old Hundredth or some very plain tune—but oh! the jargon of voices. When I rose they sank, and when I was slow they were fast. This would again and again throw the leader off the rail.

"It was in vain to tell them that they could not be taught to sing properly till they were first taught to know the hymns. I have sometimes, after much toil, taught them the verse of a hymn, and kept to one tune in order to prevent perfect confusion, when all the notes of the gamut might be heard at once. When I had a wish to introduce a new tune at our new station, where the same tunes were commonly sung, I found it necessary to drill a few till I got them so far advanced that I could depend on them to aid me in public when a new tune was introduced. I selected six girls, and having tuned up an old violin, of which I knew something, I played and sung, in which they followed till they became familiar. The first tunes taught were 'Ye Banks and Braes,' and 'Auld Lang Syne.'

" Singing is now become very general, so that there are few at our principal mission stations and outlying villages who cannot sing. The people in general began to give a decided preference to sacred music over the hoarse war song, or monotonous repetition of a few notes, accompanied with the females clapping the hands, while the men kept time by striking the ground with their feet, producing a hollow sound like distant thunder. Accustomed to music so utterly wanting in symphony, it required patience to get them into the habit of modulating their voices to sacred song. Now, however small the village may be where the Gospel is preached, there is no difficulty in finding one to lead the singing, and although in many instances it is not so euphonious as it ought to be, it is an improvement on the past.

"In the interior, where there are many scattered villages, it is an important part of the missionary's work to itinerate, paying occasional visits to the more distant portions of his parish. On occasions like these it happens that there are couples who are waiting to be joined in matrimony, and whose names have been 'hung up,' as the natives express the publishing of banns. No one in that country thinks of remaining unmarried. The ceremony is generally performed after a week-day's service, when, instead of the heathen dress, with bodies lubricated with red ochre and grease, and heads anointed with a mixture of a black shining substance with butter, they dress after the European fashion, with their very best, for the occasion; and if they have not enough suitable clothing they borrow from their neighbours. The groomsman and bridesmaid are not wanting.

"The ceremony is performed generally in the public fold in the middle of the village, no house being large enough, as many at that season come from a distance to see and to come in for a share of the feast. The ceremony over, they retire to eat a simple but abundant fare. There is no dancing, whether members or no members, but the time is passed in singing; and they *do* sing, possessing a wonderful facility in taking the different parts. Every hymn-book is in requisition, and not a tune of which they know anything is untried. Nearly the whole range of the hymn-book is gone over, while favourites are sung over and over again. The missionary's waggon, which is his castle and bed-room, stands generally not far from the scene, and not unfrequently repose and sleep are needed after, it may be, miles of walking, visiting the outlying abodes of those who may be unable to attend the services of the day. While wishing that sometimes their music were behind a hill, or at some distance, he cannot find it in his heart to tell them to desist when they seem so happy."

Writing of the beneficial effects of hymns—the strength, and comfort, and joy imparted by them—Moffat goes on to say:—"In many more instances than I can at present call to mind, I have witnessed the importance of hymnology during the introduction of the Gospel among what may justly be called savage races. This has been witnessed not only in public worship, but in places all solitary, where the dolorous howlings of the hyena have mingled with the sacred song of evening praise; aye, and while the voice of praise has been ascending to heaven after the weary day's travel, the lion's roar has been heard at no great distance. Travellers on errands of friendship, or trade, or hunting, very frequently spend their evenings, and often beyond the midnight hour, hymning the love of God to man. Many nights have I passed among such companions far away in the desert, listening to the theme which will be our song in heaven.

"In the evening sacrifice of praise around the family altar sacred song frequently bears a most important part, and I have listened with inexpressible delight to the sweet melody of sacred music poured forth from an enlightened family while worshipping God before retiring to rest. In the solitary home where affliction has entered I have heard the hymns of praise, resignation, and joy coming from the dying lips of those who were wont to revel till past midnight in music all meaningless. Music such as I have heard hundreds of times among the Southern tribes is monotonous in the extreme, but they like it. For instance, on one of my journeys into the interior I halted at a heathen village, the chief of which was very ill. On going to see him, I found a number of young people dancing and singing before the door of their dying chieftain, to whom I remarked that I feared the noise they made would do him harm. 'He likes it,' was the prompt reply. The prostrate dying heathen liked the familiar sounds of his earliest years.

"How different the experience of such a one to that of a sinner I knew of no ordinary character. Notable in her heathenish state for determined hostility to the Gospel and every kind of instruction, possessing an uncommon measure of energy which she exercised as far as she dared in persecuting those over whom she had any authority, in the midst of her violent opposition she was arrested by the Word of God. Her daughter was a believer, as a member of a Christian church is called among the Bechuanas, and not unfrequently came in for a share of the old woman's wrath, who would sometimes drive her out of the house when she would read or pray. She kept a watchful eye over her grand-daughter, whom she ardently loved; but resolved that she should never enter into a school or place of worship. On one Lord's-day morning, during the absence of the grandmother, the mother naturally took the child with her to church. Just after the introductory part of the service was over, and the preacher had selected his text, the furious woman rushed in in search of the child. Observing where she happened to be, near the door, she pounced upon the girl, but while stooping to lay hold of her, the women near seized her and held her down.

"After a short pause the preacher resumed. The woman listened to two or three sentences of the discourse, and then became quite calm. Those that held her loosed their hold, when, escaping from the place of worship into which she had rushed in a rage to drag away her grandchild, she hastened to her home. In the course of an hour she was found on her knees, and with tears streaming down her wrinkled cheeks, imploring Jesus to have mercy on her. She lived for years to testify to the power of the Gospel by a consistent and holy life, ever zealous for all that had a reference to the kingdom of Christ. On her deathbed her attendants wondered over her eloquence, and when she could no longer move her head or hands, she could move her tongue in singing and solacing her dying hours with the hymns she had committed to memory, and which had often been her songs in the night.

"One incident more. There was a young man amongst those engaged to accompany the missionaries from the Kuruman to the Matabele, under the chief Moselekatse. He had for some time been one of the inquirers, and would soon have been received into church-fellowship. He was clever and intelligent. After some months our camp was visited by the well-known African fever. Everything was done that our knowledge and experience could suggest. It was not very long that through the means used most of them were recovering. Marilole, the young man, had a second relapse, arising entirely from want of attending to regimen prescribed. Instead of taking spare and light diet, he eagerly, unknown to me, satiated his growing appetite with beef and boiled millet. Everything tried to reduce fever failed. He became insensible to all around him, and to every entreaty to take something which might again do him good. He lay for two days motionless in a comatose condition, from which no effort could arouse him. On the evening of the second day I was at work repairing my waggon, about thirty yards from the house in which the sick man lay. I heard some one singing with a strong, clear voice. Inquiring who was singing to the sick man : 'It is himself,' was the reply. I hastened to the spot, and found it even so. He was lying as I had left him an hour before, but with a firm voice he was still singing one of our hymns, which embodied some of the striking parts of the eighty-fourth Psalm. When I entered and knelt down beside him he was singing the last verse, to which I listened with inexpressible feelings of gratitude, presuming that there was a change for the best. I addressed him ; he was deaf. I tried to arouse him ; it was in vain. I felt his pulse ; it was performing its last beats ;—and while I was looking at his motionless lips, his spirit departed to that heavenly Zion about which he had just been singing. Thus died the young convert Marilole."

In a very interesting paper contributed to the *Sunday Magazine*, our missionary gives some valuable information as to the civilising effects of his labours among the African race. "Christianity," he says, "brought with it civilisation, for those who embraced the new religion were at once seized 'with the desire to reform their personal habits and social usages. Cleanliness began to be practised, and instead of besmearing themselves with grease they washed themselves with water. Ornaments which were formerly in high repute as adorning, but more frequently disfiguring, their persons, were now turned into bullion to purchase skins of animals, which, being prepared almost as soft as cloth, were made into jackets, trousers, and gowns. For a long period, when a man was seen to make a pair of trousers for himself, or a woman a gown, it was a sure intimation that we might expect additions to our inquirers. Abandoning the custom of painting the body, and beginning to wash with water, was with them what cutting off the hair was among the South Sea Islanders—a public renunciation of heathenism.

"Thus, by the slow but certain progress of Gospel principles, whole families became clothed and in their right mind. In their eagerness for improvement the people sometimes arrayed themselves in grotesque garbs. One would have on a coat of many colours; another would wear a jacket with only one sleeve, because the other was not finished, or cloth was wanting to complete it. The people were now anxious to learn how to use the needle, and to make garments; and at first it was no easy matter for them to do this, as the hands of many were hard and horny from field work, and the tiny needle was scarcely perceptible to their touch. Our congregations became a variegated mass of people of all descriptions, from the lubricated wild man of the desert to the clean, comfortable, and well-dressed believer. It was the work of the men to sew and prepare garments. I never saw a woman with a needle, or rather bodkin, with which the men sew with great neatness and skill.

"Then came the desire for improvement in their households. Formerly they had been contented with sitting on the floors of their huts, eating their food by the light of flickering wood embers, and lying down to sleep wrapped in their mantles which they had worn during the day; but now they wished to have, like ourselves, chairs, tables, chests, candles, and other articles contributing to the comfort of a house. These they came to make under our direction, though of course very clumsily at first. It is singular, however, what rapid progress in the arts of civilised life a people will make when once the desire for reformation has taken thorough possession of them.

"The Bechuanas were like men waking up from a long sleep and anxious to redeem the time they had lost. They began to take great interest in field and garden labour. In place of restricting themselves to their native grain and a few vegetables, such as pumpkins, kidney-beans, and water-melons, they thankfully accepted the seeds and plants of grains and vegetables we had introduced—namely, of maize, wheat, barley, peas, potatoes, carrots, and onions, and planted fruit-trees wherever they could irrigate. There was also a demand for ploughs and spades for the proper tilling of the soil, and also for bullock-waggons. The men were no longer too proud to put their hands to the cultivation of the ground, but set to work with a will, and in a few years the country all around was smiling with fertility.

" A considerable trade has sprung up between these tribes and Europeans from the Cape Colony, and foreign manufactured goods of the value of two hundred and fifty thousand pounds are annually imported into the country and exchanged for native produce. There was no commerce or barter carried on between Europeans and the Bechuana tribes at the commencement of missions among them, nor could they be induced to trade till, through the Divine blessing, converts were made. These were the first to adopt a European dress. During the previous years traders came as far as the Kuruman mission station, bringing all kinds of tempting articles, which they displayed before the natives, who could not be made to see either comfort or beauty in them. These men, who had hoped to realise a profit by ostrich feathers, ivory, cattle, and other things, could only dispose of a few pounds of beads, and returned some hundreds of miles sadly mortified. The example set by our first converts approved itself to others, and it being entirely out of our power to supply them with what was required, having but a scanty supply for our own wants, they were instructed to make dresses from skins prepared for the purpose, and in which they made a very respectable appearance. It was soon found necessary to apply for a merchant to come and settle on the station.

"Now that we can look to the number and extent of missionary stations, and missionaries of other societies as well as of our own, which occupy a vast extent of country, and the number which have been gathered into the fold of the Redeemer, we may well say, What has God wrought? The Scriptures are translated into several languages, and are read by thousands, and institutions are raised for educating a native ministry, some of whom have gone forth and are proclaiming the everlasting Gospel to their own countrymen. Little more than fifty years ago there were only a small mission station in Namaqua land, and another at Griqua Town. These were all beyond the Colony except the Kuruman, still in an embryo state. Now, missionaries from half-a-dozen societies occupy stations from beyond Natal on the east to the Damaras on the west, and among their churches forty thousand church members are the fruits of missionary enterprise. If every one bearing the Christian name, and hoping to be saved through Him who tasted death for every man, were to do what he is expected to do in reference to every creature to whom He commissioned His disciples to go to tell of full and free redemption, we might hope that two-thirds of the world would be reclaimed in fifty years more."

So this noble man continues to labour still in the cause of his Master, bringing forth fruit even in old age, proving that the Lord is faithful. He has known weary wanderings in the desert, when his tongue was so parched with thirst as to be almost deprived of the power of speech; he has been in perils from savage men and ferocious beasts of the wilderness; he has visited and conciliated barbaric kings, whose rude halls were hung with the execrable trophies of cruel and exterminating wars; he has confronted and overcome Herculean difficulties in the spirit of a Christian heroism loftier than that which animated his ancestors on the sanguinary field of Bannockburn ; and he has witnessed transformations of character and social life more wonderful than the most daring poetry has ever imagined.

Looking back from the height of his numerous years on the scenes of protracted and agonising toil and sublime achievement, still glowing with the missionary ardour which, in the beginning of his course, impelled him to dangers and hardships amid the sterilities of Namaqua land, and having before his eyes visions of Africaner and a crowd of glorified converts from Kuruman beckoning him to eternal blessedness, he is worthy of the golden phrase which, in happy parody of Milton, the Rev. W. Arthur applied to him on a great public occasion—"that old man magnificent."

And what more needs to be said? Nothing; save to express the hope that to the aged servant of God there may yet be allotted many years to see fruit growing up from the seed which he himself in long past days cheerfully planted in much faith and hope. Though now quietly closing his days amid the beauties of his Kentish abode, yet he is the centre of the missionary history of South Africa—the connecting link between its various apparently disconnected parts ; and when science and trade shall have carried their lamps through the length and breadth of the vast continent, discovering all its hidden recesses and bringing to light its buried treasures, they will yet be compelled to cast a generous and grateful glance back at Robert Moffat as having done more than any other man to make their many triumphs possible.

CHAPTER XXVI.

ELEMENTS OF CHARACTER.

IN reviewing the life we have sketched in this volume we are struck with its noble character. In attempting to analyse it, its most important and peculiar elements readily appear. It may be observed at the outset that Moffat has been a man of grand physique, noble presence, robust intellect, quick perception, sound judgment, ready and eloquent utterance. His very appearance commanded attention, and his whole bearing shewed that he was a man born to rule men.

One of the most distinguishable features in Moffat's character is *philanthropy*, or the love of man as man, apart from all distinctions of race and nationality. This quality, in combination with the love of God, lies at the foundation of all true and noble effort for the regeneration of the world. Philanthropy in its truest and deepest sense came into the world with Christianity. It was unknown until Jesus of Nazareth taught it as one of the prominent doctrines of His ministry, and illustrated it by His death. The parable of the Good Samaritan, as it was the first, will remain through all time the most famous discourse on true philanthropy. Patriotism was expounded and enforced by the sages of ancient heathenism. Plato lays down the doctrine that we are not born for ourselves alone, but that "our native country, our friends and relations, have a just claim and title to some part of us." Cicero, in one of the most important of all his works, admirably expounds this doctrine of Plato and of the Stoics. He insists that "whatsoever is created on earth was merely designed for the service of man, and men themselves for the service, benefit, and assistance of one another. In this we certainly ought to be followers of Nature, and second her intentions; and by doing all that lies in our power for the general interest, by mutual acts of kindness, by our knowledge, industry, riches, or other means, we should endeavour to keep up that benevolence and friendship which ought to subsist among men. When we have gone over all the relations in the world, and thoroughly considered the nature of each, we shall find none more binding, none more intimate or dear, than that which we all bear to the commonwealth. We have a tender concern and regard for our parents, for our children, our kindred, and acquaintance, but the love which we have for our native country swallows up all other affections whatsoever; for his country no man of honour would refuse to die, if by his death he could do it any needful service. Now, if there should be any conflict or competition between these relations, which of them ought to preponderate? Our first regard is due to our country and our parents, to whom we lie under the most endearing obligation; the next to our children and household, who look up to us alone, and have nobody else they can depend upon; next in order come our kindred and relations, whose fortunes are generally connected with our own."

This patriotism of the heathen is a poor, selfish, and narrow affection as compared with the philanthropy of the Gospel of Christ. Moffat's life has been dominated by that philanthropy. His ruling passion is the love of man, in the largest acceptance of the term, without respect to colour, clime, or language. It comprehends in its embrace all men, with all their temporal and eternal interests. It has not been a mere theory with him, but has received the amplest and most varied illustration by a long life of self-sacrifice and devotion. It was this love for men that moved him to give himself to the mission work; it was this that sustained him for years at his post amid the most discouraging circumstances and conditions—his labours unsolicited, his presence unwelcome, his endeavours to benefit the natives thankless, daily liable to be expelled, and in constant peril of his life. In this unwearied love of man Moffat has furnished one of the best evidences of his love to God. Abou Ben Adhem saw in a vision (so runs the Eastern legend) an angel writing in a book, and asked—

> "'What writest thou?' The vision raised its head,
> And, with a look made of all sweet accord,
> Answered, 'The name of those who love the Lord.'
> 'And is mine one?' said Abou. 'Nay, not so,'
> Replied the angel. Abou spoke more low,
> But cheerily still, and said, 'I pray thee, then,
> Write me as one that loves his fellow-men.'
> The angel wrote, and vanished. The next night
> It came again with a great wakening light,
> And shewed the names whom love of God hath bless'd,
> And, lo! Ben Adhem's name led all the rest."

Courage is another quality of this man. Emerson defines courage as "the perfect will, which no terrors can shake, which is attracted by frowns or threats, or hostile armies; nay, needs these to awake and fan its reserved energies into a pure flame, and is never quite itself until the hazard is extreme; then it is serene and fertile, and all its powers play well." This definition is applicable to both physical and moral courage. "Physical courage," he further remarks, "which despises all danger, will make a man brave in one way; and moral courage, which despises all opinion, will make a man brave in another. The former would seem most necessary for the camp, the latter for council; but to constitute a great man both are necessary." We see both combined in Joshua, who succeeded Moses as the leader of the children of Israel. He shrank from no command of God. With a true heart he took the reins of government. He led the tribes across Jordan, and went before them to the conquest of Canaan. No rumour as to the number or strength of his foes alarmed him. He faithfully administered the laws. He was brave in counsel and brave in fight, and thus he fulfilled the Divine command—'Be strong and of a good courage; be not afraid, neither be thou dismayed.'

In all his missionary career Moffat displayed this courage. He was often placed in circumstances of great danger; his life was often in peril from wild beasts, and sometimes he was threatened with destruction by savage men. In carrying out his Christian commission he went into inhospitable countries, and stood before cruel and despotic monarchs, always fearless of evil, because his trust was in the Lord his God. Fearing God, he felt that there was nothing else he need fear. If he had to encounter a difficulty he never turned aside from it, saying, There is a lion in the path. Having resolved upon mastering it, he never ceased till it was overcome, and every successive triumph inspired him with that confidence in himself and that habit of victory which make all other conquests easy. He was just the man to lead the enterprise which reflects such glory on his career.

One illustration of his courage may be given in his own words. It relates to his visit to Makaba, the chief of the Bauangketsi:—" I resolved on a journey which I had been contemplating for some months. This was to visit Makaba, the chief of the Bauangketsi, a powerful tribe situated upwards of two hundred miles north-east of Lithako. I had various reasons for taking this step. The Batlapis and the neighbouring tribes were living in constant dread of an attack from so powerful an enemy, of whom they could never speak without stigmatising him with the most opprobrious epithets. It was desirable to open up a friendly intercourse to prevent hostilities, and it seemed advisable for me to attend more exclusively to the acquirement of the language by associating for a time with the natives, when at the same time an opportunity was thus afforded for becoming better acquainted with the localities of the tribes ; and in addition to these objects was the ultimate design of introducing the Gospel among that interesting people.

"About this time, receiving an invitation from Makaba, the path of duty was plain, but Mothibi, and indeed all the people, were greatly opposed to my design. Everything injurious to the character of the Bauangketsi was raked up and placed before me. All the imaginary and real murders Makaba had ever committed were set in array, and every one swore by their king and their father that if I went my doom was fixed, for I should never return, and therefore Ma-Mary and the two children might leave and return to our friends in England, for she would never see me again. When the day arrived for my departure, Mothibi, finding he could not prevail by arguments, positively forbade those under his control to accompany me. Feeling no inclination to give up my intention, I started with such men as I had. On reaching Old Lithako, on the third day, I found the reports about the Mantatees somewhat revived, and the natives strongly advised me to proceed no farther than Nokaneng, about twenty miles distant. The reports being such as we had heard before, and knowing that they wished by every means to intimidate me, I proceeded on the following day, after having preached to a great number of the natives. On arriving at Nokaneng I found that rumours had reached that place that the Barolongs at Kunuana, about one hundred miles off, had been also attacked, and the towns were in the hands of the marauders; but as spies had been sent out to ascertain the truth, I remained, employing every opportunity afforded to impart instruction. The spies returning without having heard anything of the reported invaders, I proceeded with my small company towards the Bauangketsi tribes."

It must also be said that to this courage we must add *a spirit of adventure.* Moffat was not a man to go quietly along in a dull beaten track. Some men seem to have no disposition, no power, to forsake the old ruts, but his soul was always reaching forward to the regions beyond. He had no wish quietly to settle down in the midst of other men's labours. This spirit of adventure and enterprise, sanctified by the grace cf God, led him to seek out new fields of toil—to break up the fallow ground, and to plant the Gospel where hitherto it had been totally unknown. The same spirit moved him to adopt all kinds of methods that were likely to be successful in the accomplishment of his sublime purpose, and though sometimes great and trying obstacles encompassed his path and obstructed his progress, yet his undaunted soul bore him through a multitude of difficulties which would have deterred most men.

Moffat's career also illustrates *great readiness and power of adaptation to circumstances.* He was often placed in strange and novel conditions of life. Unexpected demands were frequently made upon his ingenuity and resources, but he was always found sufficient for the occasion. He could travel for weeks in an African waggon; when he had not the opportunity of riding on horseback he would ride on the back of an ox; he could sleep in a native hut or in the open air; he could subsist for months on flesh and milk— sometimes he only had one, sometimes the other, sometimes both. While he always maintained a proper self-respect as a civilised man and a Christian, yet he could associate on the most familiar terms with the rude savages around him, and make himself quite at home in their kraals and villages. Like the great apostle of the Gentiles, whom in so many things he so closely resembled, he became all things to all men, hoping thereby to save some.

He had *a distinct and comprehensive view of his work.* He knew that his great mission in going to Africa was to save souls; yet in all his labours among the African race Moffat cared for the temporal condition of the people— sought to benefit their bodies as well as their souls.   What his illustrious son-in-law, Livingstone, says of *his* work, may fitly describe that of Moffat himself:—"After family worship and breakfast, between six and seven, we kept school —men, women, and children being all invited.   This lasted till eleven o'clock.   The missionary's wife then betook herself to her domestic affairs, and the missionary engaged in some manual labour, as that of a smith, carpenter, or gardener.   If he did jobs for the people, they worked for him in turn, and exchanged their unskilled labour for his skilled.   Dinner and an hour's rest succeeded, when the wife attended her infant-school, which the young liked amazingly, and generally mustered a hundred strong; or she varied it with sewing-classes for the girls, which was equally well relished.   After sunset the husband went into the town to converse, either on general subjects or on religion.   We had a public service on three nights of the week, and on another, instruction in secular subjects, aided by pictures and specimens.   In addition to these duties, we prescribed for the sick and furnished food to the poor.   The smallest acts of friendship, even an obliging word and civil look, are, as St. Xavier thought, no despicable part of the missionary armour."

He never lost sight of the fact that everything he did was to be made subservient to the great object of seeking to save the souls for whom Christ had died.   All other efforts and aims were only valuable in his estimation as they proved helpful to this. He saw the ruin and wretchedness into which sin had plunged the people, and he desired to lift them out of the horrible pit and the miry clay. They were in the prison-house of an awful and degrading bondage, and he would fain bring them out into the large liberty of the sons of God. Hence he preached to them, in all its fulness and power, the Gospel of salvation through Jesus Christ—declared to them the glad tidings that "God so loved the world as to give His only-begotten Son, that whosoever believeth on Him might not perish but have everlasting life."

In making the preaching of the Gospel his chief business, and the salvation of souls his chief end, he knew that he was pursuing the best course for the attainment of all. In this respect there was a most striking agreement between his views and practice and the views and practice of that other celebrated and successful missionary, John Williams of Polynesia. Speaking of his labours in the South Sea Islands, Mr. Williams says:—"While our best energies have been devoted to the instruction of the people in the truths of the Christian religion, and our chief solicitude has been to make them wise unto salvation, we have at the same time been anxious to impart a knowledge of all that was calculated to increase their comforts and elevate their character. And I am convinced that the first step towards the promotion of a nation's temporal and social elevation is to plant amongst them the Tree of Life, when civilisation and commerce will entwine their tendrils around its trunk, and derive support from its strength. Until the people are brought under the influence of religion they have no desire for the arts and usages of civilised life, but that invariably creates it.

"The missionaries were at Tahiti many years, during which they built and furnished a house in European style. The natives saw this, but not an individual imitated their

example. As soon, however, as they were brought under
the influence of Christianity, the chiefs, and even the
common people, began to build neat plastered cottages, and
to manufacture bedsteads, seats, and other articles of
furniture. The females had long observed the dress of the
missionaries' wives, but while heathen they greatly preferred
their own, and there was not a single attempt at imitation.
No sooner, however, were they brought under the influence
of religion, than all of them, even to the lowest, aspired to
the possession of a gown, a bonnet, and a shawl, that they
might appear like Christian women. I could proceed to
enumerate many other changes of the same kind, but these
will be sufficient to establish my assertion. While the
natives are under the influence of their superstitions, they
evince an inanity and torpor from which no stimulus has
proved powerful enough to arouse them but the new ideas
and the new principles imparted by Christianity. And if
it be not already proved, the experience of a few more years
will demonstrate the fact, that the missionary enterprise is
incomparably the most effective machinery that has ever
been brought to operate upon the social, the civil, and the
commercial, as well as the moral and spiritual, interests of
mankind."

Mechanical ingenuity has been a striking feature in
Moffat's character. Highly endowed with the faculty of
invention, he would have attained distinction had he devoted
himself to the improved application of mechanic powers.
The exercise of his genius in this direction was one of the
sources of his amazing success in the missionary field. His
exhibitions in this way spoke to the senses of the savages,
who stood in dumb amazement, and, when regaining speech,
confessed the white man's superiority. Of course in the
planting and training of trees and plants he was quite at
home. He could cultivate and irrigate the ground. But
he soon learnt to make waggons, and tables, and chairs; to

VILLAGE BLACKSMITHS

forge and weld iron, and make implements of labour. The account he gives of one of his attempts in this direction may be quoted as an illustration. He sets about repairing a waggon. "After ruminating," he says, "for a day or two on what I had seen in the smith's shop in Cape Town, I resolved on making a trial, and got a native bellows made of goat's skin, to the neck of which was attached the horn of an elk, and at the other end two parallel sticks were fastened, which were opened by the hand in drawing it back and closed when pressed forward, but making a puffing like something broken-winded. The iron was only red-hot after a good perspiration, when I found I must give it up as a bad job, observing to the chief, if I must accompany him it must be on the back of an ox.

"Reflecting again on the importance of having a waggon for the purpose of carrying food, when game happened to be killed (for our sole dependence was on the success of hunting), and Africaner evidently not liking, on my account, to go without a waggon, I set my brains again to work to try and improve on the bellows, for it was wind I wanted. Though I had never welded a bit of iron in my life, there was nothing like trying. I engaged the chief to have two goats killed, the largest on the station, and their skins prepared entire, in the native way, till they were as soft as cloth. These skins now resembled bags, the open ends of which I nailed to the edge of a circular piece of board, in which was a valve. One end of the machine was connected with the fire, and had a weight on it to force out the wind, when the other end was drawn out to supply more air. This apparatus was no sooner completed than it was put to the test, and the result answered satisfactorily in a steady current of air; and soon I had all the people around me to witness my operations with the newfangled bellows. Here I sat receiving their praises, but heartily wishing their departure, lest they should laugh at my burning the first bit of iron I took in my hands to weld. A blue granite-stone was my anvil, a clumsy pair of tongs, indicative of Vulcan's first efforts, and a hammer never intended for the work of a forge.

"My first essay was with some trepidation, for I did not like so many lookers-on. Success, however, crowned my efforts, to the no small delight of the spectators. Having finished what was necessary for the waggon, I was encouraged to attempt the repair of some gun-locks. In doing this I began with one which I thought I could not spoil should I not succeed, and accomplishing that, I was able to put the others in order; but in doing this I had, for the want of steel, to sacrifice two of my files." And all this was absolutely necessary to success in the circumstances in which he found himself in South Africa. When St. Boniface landed in Britain, he carried with him a Gospel in one hand and a carpenter's rule in the other. So Robert Moffat carried with him to Africa, as part of the religion he had to teach, some knowledge of the useful arts and handicrafts of life.

Marvellous as were the ease and skill with which he executed the various, and some of them difficult and complex, contrivances of art, the moral devices by which he sought to interest and elevate the people around him exhibit features scarcely less remarkable than those of the mechanical. In both there was the same clear apprehension of ends, the same ready suggestion and perfect adaptation of means. Success, whether in framing a plan of Christian beneficence or in constructing a useful machine, was never a happy accident, but always an anticipated result. The movements of his mind and of his hand were not made at random, but were guided by wise forethought and founded upon careful calculation. Hence their favourable termination and valuable fruits.

Perseverance was another element of our missionary's

success. Some persons are continually changing their pursuits and aims. They never accomplish any great results, because they never persevere in the means necessary to their accomplishment. Unstable as water, they never excel. They only serve to illustrate the old proverb—"A rolling stone gathers no moss." When Moffat undertook a work he carried it out. He owed as much to perseverance as to power; to unremitting diligence as to original and excellent plans. Constituted by nature and prepared by grace for a life of labour, he became, in every sense of the words, "a workman that needed not to be ashamed." To each service he undertook he gave himself wholly. Indolence, and procrastination, and vacillation were as contrary to his predominant propensities as they were to his religious principles. He deferred not until the morrow what the duty of every day required. In his exertions there was nothing capricious or fitful. He wrought by rule. As steady, moreover, in the prosecution of a plan as he was careful in its conception, he rarely left his work unfinished. His course was never marked by hesitancy and change. Each day witnessed the progress of what he had taken in hand, and if unavoidably diverted from it for a season, his interest in the occupation did not decline, but as soon as the interruption ceased he returned to it with unrelaxed vigour. With application and determination, such as he brought to bear upon every important design, failure was scarcely possible. Such resolute purpose and unremitting labour could not fail to ensure success.

The translation of the whole Bible into the Sechuana tongue was a stupendous undertaking—one that required the patient and persistent toil of years. Many and great were the difficulties to be overcome. The monotonous character of the work must have made it at times depressing and irksome. But the man who had the boldness to undertake it had the perseverance not to abandon it; he never turned aside till the work was done. So with everything else that he took in hand. He had two mottoes: *Nil desperandum — Perseverantia omnia vincit.* Inspired by these, he applied himself to all the details of his great mission. Whatsoever his hands found to do he did it with his might. He was steadfast, immovable, always abounding in the work of the Lord, knowing that his labour would not be in vain in the Lord.

Moffat gave the fullest proof of *his love for the people among whom he laboured.* He identified himself with them ; sought to guide and influence them by persuasion. He therefore found his way to their hearts, and conquered their prejudices and passions by the omnipotent force of love. He has always been a firm believer in "the law of kindness," and to his uniform observance of this law we must in a great measure trace his success. Many examples of this might be given ; one will suffice.

A chief of the Corannas called Paul, to whom Moffat had once preached, and who had then produced a somewhat favourable impression on the missionary's mind, afterwards became the head of a marauding commando, and pursued a course of murder and rapine. He had robbed the people among whom Moffat laboured of their cattle, and declared his purpose to destroy the station, and the missionary desired an interview with him. Paul had sworn that he would not see Moffat, and for a time kept his oath. At length he consented to an interview, and thus Moffat describes it :—
"I again met my half-way delegates, when, after a long conversation with Jantye and another message to Paul, he made his appearance slowly and sadly, as if following a friend to execution, or going himself to be slain. His face appeared incapable of a smile. Taking his hand as that of an old friend, I expressed my surprise that he who knew me, and who once listened to the message of salvation from my lips, should come with such a force for the express pur-

pose of rooting out the mission. I referred him to the time when more than once I had slept at the door of his hut and partaken of his hospitality. He replied that his purposes were unalterable, because more than a year ago a body of his men, who had passed into the interior to take cattle from the Barolongs, were attacked by Mothibi's people, and that although Mothibi was fled, many of his subjects and the Batlaros were on the station. His eyes glared with fury as he said, 'I shall have their blood and their cattle too !'

" People in this country can scarcely conceive how difficult, not to say how impossible, it is to argue with such characters, for some will not hear. But Paul could argue ; and having once listened to my voice with pleasure, the long time which had elapsed had not effaced the impressions made by the visit and presence of a teacher. Although I was not preaching, I spoke with great solemnity, asking him if the bleached bones on the Barolong and Kalagari plains, the souls his clubs and spears had hurried into eternity since he left home, and the innocent blood with which he had stained the desert but a few days ago, were not sufficient to glut his revenge, or rather to make him tremble for the judgments which such a career would certainly bring upon himself and his people, and which had already begun to be poured out on the blood-guilty tribes of the Orange River?

" After having talked to him for some time in this strain, I begged him to call to mind his first and only visit to me while with Africaner, and his declaration, at a subsequent period, that he and his people were leaving because it was rumoured that Africaner was about to remove from the country in which his presence had been the bond of union, entreating him to compare his state of mind at that time with what it was now. This had scarcely passed my lips when he ordered his men to go and bring the cattle which had been taken from our people, and added that he would not go a step further, but return by the way he came. In the course of a subsequent conversation, I inquired why he was so determined on not seeing me. 'I could not forget your kindness to me in Namaqua land,' was the reply. In this the reflecting reader will observe a fresh instance of the omnipotence of love, even among the most barbarous of the human race."

Then, covering all, there was *his complete devotion to the Lord Jesus Christ.* He considered himself the servant of Christ,—this above everything else. What he did he did unto the Lord, who had ransomed him from sin and all its consequences. He felt that He had redeemed him at the cost of His own blood, and that such a Redeemer deserved his heartiest and best service. The thought that in all things he was serving Christ—living under law to Him, living as in His eye and for His glory, elevated and enlarged his conceptions of the most common work. Indeed no work to him was common. He realised in himself the spirit of George Herbert:—

> "A servant with this clause
>   Makes drudgery divine ;
> Who sweeps a room, as for Thy laws,
>   Makes that and th' action fine.
> This is the famous stone
>   That turneth all to gold ;
> For that which God doth touch and own,
>   Cannot for less be told."

He considered himself as Christ's, and Christ's alone. Tennyson makes King Arthur say—"My knights are sworn to vows of utter hardihood, utter gentleness and loving, utter faithfulness in love, and uttermost obedience to the king." Such were the vows Moffat took upon himself when he went forth to the missionary field. Henceforth he had a single eye in all things to the pleasure and glory of his sovereign Lord. Dr. Judson, the great Burman missionary, formed among other resolutions for the regulation of his life this one—" Resolved not to do anything which does not appear at the time to be well-pleasing to Christ." The spirit of this resolution was the inward principle of Moffat's missionary career.

Taking him altogether, we have in Robert Moffat one of the noblest characters—one of the finest specimens of sanctified humanity the world has ever seen. His name will be remembered in Africa to latest ages with gratitude and honour. When some future historian, rising up from among the people themselves, shall write its history, Moffat and his distinguished son-in-law, Livingstone, will be spoken of as two of its greatest benefactors. Through all ages their memory will be more precious than jewels—more fragrant than the spices of Arabia or the breath of May.

CHAPTER XXVII.

IT may not be inappropriate to devote in closing the last two chapters of this book, one to a brief sketch of missionary work on the African continent, the other to a general survey of missionary operations throughout the world. As Dr. Moffat was an agent of the London Missionary Society, our references have been chiefly to labours in connection with that institution; but several other societies have laboured long, and are labouring still, among the various peoples of the African race. In their ultimate object, and the general means employed for its attainment, these several societies, and all united, stand in close relation to Moffat's life-work.

The Wesleyan Missionary Society began its share in the evangelisation of Southern Africa in the year 1814, when the Rev. J. M‘Kenny was sent out as the first missionary. He arrived in Cape Town in August of that year, but such was the jealousy of the Government authorities that he was not allowed to open his commission, or to preach in the colony, although he produced credentials of the most satisfactory character. He was therefore instructed by his committee to proceed to Ceylon. They were not disposed, however, to relinquish their efforts for the spiritual welfare of the degraded tribes of Southern Africa in consequence of the failure of their first experiment. In 1815 they appointed the Rev. Barnabas Shaw to attempt the commencement of a mission at the Cape. On his arrival he presented his credentials to the Governor, but met with no better success than his predecessor. His Excellency declined to give him permission to preach in Cape Town, on the ground that the English and the Dutch colonists were provided with ministers, whilst the owners of slaves were unwilling to have them religiously instructed. Mr. Shaw naïvely says:—"Having been refused the sanction of the Governor, I was resolved what to do, and commenced without it on the following Sabbath. My congregations at first were chiefly composed of pious soldiers, and it was in a room hired by them that I first preached Christ and Him crucified in South Africa." Although it would appear that the Government authorities took no notice of this infringement of their regulations, yet the spirit of prejudice against missionary efforts prevailed to such an extent among the colonists that Mr. Shaw was much discouraged, and saw little prospect of good in Cape Town. Under these circumstances he longed for an opening to preach the Gospel to the heathen in the interior, where he would not be subject to the annoyances and hindrances experienced in the colony.

At length an opportunity was afforded of engaging in this enterprise. One of the agents of the London Missionary Society came to Cape Town from Great Namaqua land on a visit, and he made such representations of the openings for missionary labour in that country, that on his kind invitation Mr. Shaw and his wife resolved to accompany him back. Leaving Cape Town, the missionary party had pursued their toilsome journey for nearly a month, when, by a remarkable providence, Mr. Shaw found an opening for a suitable sphere of labour. He actually met with the chief of Little Namaqua land on his way to Cape Town to seek for a Christian teacher. Having heard his affecting story, and being deeply impressed with the fact that the finger of God was pointing in the direction in which he ought to go, the missionary agreed to accompany the chief to his mountain home. On reaching the end of their journey, a council was held by the chief and some of his head-men respecting the arrival of the missionary, when they all entreated him to remain with them, and promised to assist him in every possible way. He therefore immediately opened his commission by proclaiming the glad tidings of salvation, and by teaching both old and young the elements of religion and the use of letters. It was trying work, and required much patience, but labour, prayer, faith, perseverance, were eventually rewarded with success. A number of children and young people learned to read with tolerable facility, and a native church was formed of faithful members, who were a credit to their religious profession. At the same time, the civilising influences of Christianity were brought to bear upon the people, and from year to year their temporal condition was materially improved.

Whilst the missionary was thus endeavouring to instruct the people, he had to labour hard at intervals to build a house to live in, and a sanctuary for the worship of God. In the accomplishment of these undertakings many difficulties had to be overcome. The people, although willing to assist, had never been accustomed to continuous labour, and ludicrous scenes were witnessed in the progress of the work. When the buildings were ready for the roofs, no trees fit for timber could be found within a day's journey of the station, but when they arrived at the place the missionary produced for the first time his cross-cut saw, himself working at one end and a Namaqua at the other. Great was the joy of the people on beholding the result, and they could scarcely be restrained from cutting more timber than was required, on account of their delight at witnessing the performance of the instrument as one tree after another fell to the ground. Nor were their delight and surprise the less on seeing the first plough set to work, which the missionary had made chiefly with his own hands. The old chief stood upon a hill for some time in mute astonishment; at length he called to his counsellors at a short distance, saying, "Come and see the strange thing. Look how it tears up the ground with its iron mouth! If it goes on so all the day it will do more work than ten wives!" Hitherto the work of tilling the ground had been left to the women and slaves, but the introduction of the Gospel into the country was destined to mark a new era in agricultural pursuits as well as in the moral condition of the people. Mr. Shaw had taken with him to Africa a few garden seeds, the rapid growth of which amused the natives greatly, but when they saw the use to which the lettuce and other salads were appropriated, they laughed heartily, saying, "If the missionary and his wife can eat grass, they need never starve!"

A brief account of a visit to this station in recent years will give some idea of the progress that has been made. Mr. Moister, speaking of what he saw in 1853, says:— "After a toilsome journey through the wilderness we arrived at Bethel, on Friday the 14th of July, and were glad to find that the resident missionary, the Rev. J. A. Bailie, and the people of the station, had already removed to the Underveldt for the winter months. Saturday was spent in conversing with Mr. Bailie and a few of the head-men on various matters pertaining to the religious and temporal interests of the institution, the result of which was very satisfactory. Towards evening a number of the natives arrived at the station from distant places, some in waggons and others on horseback, to be ready for the services of the Sabbath. At an early hour on Sunday morning we were awoke by the singing of the natives, who had already assembled in the adjoining chapel to hold their usual prayer-meeting. We immediately arose and joined them in their devotions. The prayers were offered partly in Dutch and partly in Namaqua." The same gentleman paid a second visit to this station two or three years after, when he found there a beautiful new chapel, capable of holding six hundred persons, built of stone at a cost of about £1000, erected by the united efforts and contributions of the people, without any foreign aid, except the gift of the pulpit by a few friends in Cape Town. There were abundant evidences also of material progress and improvement in the temporal affairs of the people. About seven hundred acres of land had been brought under cultivation, and the natives belonging to the institution owned about one hundred ploughs, thirty waggons, two thousand five hundred horned cattle, four hundred horses, and seven thousand sheep and goats.

The Rev. W. Threlfall, one of the earliest missionaries, was brutally murdered in 1825. Accompanied by two native teachers he set out for Great Namaqua land on a journey of observation, with a view to the extension of the work. They travelled without molestation till they had got two or three days journey beyond the Orange River. At this point they came in contact with troublesome wandering tribes of Bushmen. Although they had with them a few goods for barter, they suffered much for want of food, the people being unfriendly and unwilling to supply them. They obtained a guide at one of the villages, but he and his companions formed a plot for the destruction of the whole mission party, that they might take possession of their effects. The following night, while Mr. Threlfall and his companions were sleeping under a bush, without the slightest apprehension of danger, their foes came upon them and murdered them in cold blood. Although this circumstance prevented the establishment of a mission to the north of the Orange

River at that time, yet in 1832 the work was begun there, and has continued to the present time. In the Bechuana country something has been done also by Wesleyan missionaries. Remnants of various scattered tribes have from time to time gathered around them, and through their influence have settled down and become a comparatively prosperous and happy people.

The labours of the Wesleyan brethren cover other large districts in Southern Africa. There are about seventy missionaries preaching the Gospel in the vernacular tongues of the people to whom they minister, eleven thousand five hundred and twenty-four church members of different nations and tribes of people, and twelve thousand three hundred and forty-three scholars receiving instruction in the mission schools. It is a noteworthy fact also, that the holy Scriptures and other religious books have been translated into five or six different languages by the missionaries for the use of the natives. Some of these languages never had been written when they undertook the task of reducing them to a grammatical form.

In 1821 two missionaries, Messrs. Thomson and Bourne, went out to South Africa from Glasgow, under the direction of what was then called the Glasgow Missionary Society, with the view of commencing a mission in Caffraria. They were afterwards followed from time to time by other missionaries, and several stations were established. For some years they had to encounter great difficulties, partly from the indifferent and stupid character of the people, and partly from the unhappy disturbances which prevailed between the people and the British Government. The situation of the missionaries was at once difficult and perilous. Flushed with success, or whetted by revenge, the Caffres would not bear to be spoken to, and when the British troops began to scour the country, and burn their kraals, and seize their cattle, and make reprisals, they became excited almost to fury, and charged the missionaries with being their enemies because they did not prevent the devastation of the soldiers. The missionaries stopped in the country as long as they could, but they were at length obliged to escape for their lives. Parties of soldiers were sent to protect them on their way to the English camp, and they afterwards escorted them to Graham's Town. In the latter part of 1835 peace was restored to the country, and they returned to the scenes of their work.

The missionaries after their return set themselves to repair their houses, which had been destroyed by the natives. They supplied the people with food, paid them for their work with goats, spades, picks, seed-corn, and other useful articles, deeming it their duty to make a vigorous effort to convince them that by a little exertion they might save themselves from famine without having recourse, and that in vain, to a rain-maker. The missionaries also resumed their accustomed labours amongst them, and everything by degrees assumed much the same aspect as before the war. Schools were established for general instruction to the youth of both sexes, and also for teaching the girls sewing. Many of the Caffres were baptised, but they had to bear much from the opposition of their countrymen, and often from their nearest relatives, and in their own dwellings. The native teachers especially were frequently hooted and laughed at when endeavouring to set before their countrymen the truths of religion. The teacher of one school was debarred from making his usual visits to the neighbouring kraals, and the children were not allowed a footpath to the school because a child belonging to the head-man of the district had died, and it was said the teacher had killed it with his prayers. Another of the teachers was prevented for a time from visiting some kraals, because he dressed in European clothing, thereby giving proof of his disposition to bewitch the people, and especially the children. The mother of a family was charged with killing her children since she began to pray and serve God. There prevailed throughout Caffraria great dread and mistrust of missionaries. Their stations were regarded by many as branch establishments of the Colonial Government for the wholesale murder of the natives, and for despoiling them of their country.

In 1846, and again in 1850, hostilities broke out between the English and the Caffres, and were attended on each occasion by the breaking up of the mission and the destruction of the stations, including a large amount of property. Subsequently the work was resumed, and has been carried on with comparative success to the present day. It is now under the direction of the Free Church of Scotland.

The Lovedale Institution is an educational establishment in connection with this mission of no mean order. Lovedale lies about seven hundred miles north-east of Cape Town, on a small river which once formed the boundary of Caffraria proper. The aims of Lovedale are very varied, though it has one to which all others are subordinate. It seeks to train as preachers such young men as may be found fit for the work ; to train teachers for native schools ; to train a certain number in various arts of civilised life, such as waggon-making, blacksmithing, carpentering, printing, bookbinding, telegraphy, and general agricultural work ; to give a general education to those whose course in life is not yet decided. There are two main departments in the institute—the male and the female. The buildings are separated by a short distance. In both the work carried on is educational and industrial ; but while each department of work has its own special aim, the institution as a whole is carried on with one primary object—the essential purpose of Lovedale is to Christianise.

The results of the work at Lovedale have been eminently satisfactory. It has given birth to other institutions of a similar character. Blythswood, in the Transkei, is a direct offshoot from it, and was begun at the request of the natives, who wished for an institution similar to Lovedale. Livingstonia, on Lake Nyassa, may be regarded as another offshoot. From the theological class have proceeded native pastors, well-educated and intelligent men; there are also many others in different positions for which they have been qualified by the higher course of education. From the trades departments there are many who went to Lovedale at eight shillings a month now earning five to seven shillings a day as waggon-makers, blacksmiths, and carpenters. The spiritual results have been most satisfactory. Sixty workers are sent out every Sunday to hold evangelistic meetings in the neighbouring kraals. There are three periodicals published monthly—*The Christian Express* in English, *The Isiqidimi* in Caffre, and *The Lovedale News* in English.

Among the favourable opinions which have been expressed concerning the institution by public men, we may note the following. Sir Bartle Frere says: "Nothing would do more to prevent future Caffre wars than a multiplication of such institutions as Lovedale and Blythswood." Mr. Anthony Trollope, in his "South Africa," says: "Lovedale has had, and is having, very great success. It has been established under Presbyterian auspices, but is altogether undenominational in its tuition." Dr. Dale, Superintendent-General of Education in Cape Colony, recently in the *Daily News* expressed his opinion thus: "Undoubtedly the Lovedale Institution is one of the noblest and most successful missionary agencies founded and supported in the Cape Colony by British philanthropy."

The Paris Society for Evangelical Missions was established in 1827. Among the measures which it early adopted was the institution of a college for the education of young men as missionaries. Some of the first brethren sent out from Europe settled in Wagenmaker Valley, about thirty miles from Cape Town, among the descendants of the French refugees and their slaves. Others went into the interior, and settled at a place called Motito, in the Bechuana country. In a few years fresh stations were established, extending over a wide extent of country, and the success of the mission was on the whole highly pleasing. The congregations were considerable, and numbers of natives were baptised and admitted as communicants. Many gave abundant evidence of piety, and were zealous to make known the Gospel to their countrymen. Schools were established, and were attended by considerable numbers, both old and young. The wives of the missionaries rendered valuable service by superintending the schools for females, by inculcating on them habits of order, economy, and propriety, and by giving them the first notions of the management and training of children.

The missionaries translated into the Sechuana language the Book of Psalms and the Gospels of Matthew, Mark, and John. They also printed school-books, a catechism, a collection of hymns and prayers, and short tracts on the chief doctrines and duties of religion. The people made considerable advances in some of the more common and necessary arts of civilised life. Many of them built themselves convenient houses instead of their old smoky and unhealthy huts. In place of the skins of animals, which they used to throw over their bodies, the men adopted in part the European dress, while the women who had learned to sew made decent clothes for themselves and their daughters. They obtained ploughs and other agricultural implements, and extended their husbandry; and many of them occupied themselves in the culture of corn, which they sold to the Dutch farmers for cattle, clothing, salt, and other useful articles. The missionary stations furnished a striking example of the influence of Christian missions in improving the condition of the most savage tribes; sometimes, however, they suffered, in common with other parts of the country, from the depredations which the native tribes carried on against each other, and the people had at such seasons to remove their cattle to distant parts. Of late years the missionaries have been able to pursue their work with great encouragement.

This society has at present a flourishing Basuto mission. At the Mildmay Park Conference in 1878, M. Appia, a representative of the society, thus spoke of its position and influence:—"Our first missionaries, when they went out, thought of the Korannas. Whilst they were ready to go to them, they remained a whole night praying for guidance. The next morning there came a white hunter, and he said, 'Are you not missionaries?' They said they were; whereupon he replied, 'I am sent by a chief in the interior of Africa to seek after teachers; his name is Moshesh, of the Basuto tribe.' And so three of our friends were led by the hunter to that spot. Our mission has saved one part of the Basuto country from drink—the great curse of your country. Your Government sent representatives to Moshesh, holding out to him the prospect of free trade. They came to us, and we asked them, 'What have they sent?' 'Free trade!' 'Yes,' we said, 'it is a right principle;' and they said they must be subject to the Queen. I said, 'That is right; but you must not do one thing—you must not allow the selling of strong drink.' Some Dutch and white merchants once came with casks of brandy and whisky to sell, and the black chief ordered his men to take out the bung, and while the liquor rushed down the streets the white man was taking his hat and catching as much as he could and putting it to his lips, and the black man was standing wondering all the time. Our French missionaries have built a wall against strong drink around Basuto land, and neither whisky nor brandy shall enter into that land. This, let me tell you, is important. I think you can test by this means the influence our missionaries have had upon the country. Now for the numbers. We have in our schools upwards of three thousand scholars and about four thousand communicants. During the last year three hundred and fifty-two children were baptised, and three hundred and forty-eight adults. We have fifteen missionaries, sixty-six out-stations, and ninety evangelists."

The Rhenish Missionary Society was constituted in 1828, by the union of three previous existing associations at Elberfeld, Barmen, and Cologne, and they were soon after joined by other associations in the Rhenish Provinces and in Westphalia. The society derives its support chiefly from the territory between the Rhine and the Maase. The first missionaries sailed from London for the Cape in 1829, but they were afterwards followed by others, and numerous stations have since been formed both within and beyond the colony. The work was carried on long without much fruit, but in later years there have been many tokens of blessings.

In 1833 the Berlin Missionary Society was formed, and commenced its foreign operations by sending four missionaries to South Africa. These were afterwards followed by others, and a number of stations were formed in the Cape Colony, Caffraria, the Bechuana country, and Natal Colony. 'In 1845 the Rev. Mr. Scholtz, who with four other missionaries had lately arrived in South Africa, was murdered by two Caffres when on the way to the scene of their future labours. Addressing the Mildmay Park Conference, to which we have adverted more than once, Dr. Wangemann, the secretary of the Berlin Society, presented the following view of its work :—"The Berlin Missionary Society, which I have the honour to represent before this conference, has, though limiting its labours to South Africa, acquired a very large field for its operations. It has spread out its net of forty-two stations over a country a thousand miles in length, and five hundred in breadth, comprising within its limits seven different nations, among whom the Gospel has to be preached in seven different languages. Besides its fifty-three ordained labourers, four colonist missionaries give instructions to the natives in industrial branches. About eight thousand baptised converts from among the heathen come together in our churches, two thousand children are in our native schools, and there are more than a thousand inquirers in the rooms of the catechists. Our forty-two stations extend over the whole of South Africa. Five of them are in the Old Cape Colony, five in Old Caffre land, six in the Orange Free State, six in Natal, and twenty-two are in the Transvaal. The whole are divided into six superintendencies. I make bold to say that scarcely any missionary work in South Africa exceeds ours in extent.

"One characteristic feature of our society is our poverty. Having only £12,000 a-year to spend on this extensive work, it is evident that our missionaries live according to the apostolic rule ; having food and raiment they are therewith content. Nevertheless, we in Berlin are very zealous in promoting the education and instruction of our missionaries. For five years they receive daily instruction for two hours in Bible knowledge, and for three or four more in the ancient languages, systematic theology, and kindred disciplines. Before being sent out they have to undergo a somewhat hard examination under the presidency of a member of the Ecclesiastical Consistory. A second characteristic of our work is its caution and sobriety. We never baptise anybody in whom we have not before seen visible indications of the working of the holy Spirit ; nor do we ever employ worldly means to swell the number of our members. We exercise strict church discipline. It is very seldom that one of our converts will be found in prison ; and while there is a general complaint against the Christian black servants in Africa, our people are sought in general as good, useful, trustworthy labourers and servants."

The American Board for Foreign Missions sent out six missionaries to the Cape in 1834, half of them to labour in the interior and half on the coast, at Port Natal or its vicinity. On their arrival, three proceeded by way of Griqua Town and Kuruman to Mosika, where the French missionaries had begun a station a few years before; they were soon, however, compelled to leave the country and join their brethren at Natal.

In 1838 James Backhouse and George W. Walker, two members of the Society of Friends, visited South Africa, and prosecuted their pious and benevolent labours among all classes of the population. In the course of their extensive journeyings they visited the stations of most of the societies to which we have referred, although they were scattered over a vast extent of country, and often at a great distance from one another. By the missionaries of the various denominations they were received in the most friendly manner, and every facility was given them, and assistance afforded, in addressing the people under their care. Though their addresses were not free from the peculiarities of Friends, yet their declarations concerning the way of salvation through Jesus Christ were such as to shew the substantial unity of all evangelical Christians.

' The Moravian brethren still carry on their useful work in South Africa; but passing by them, and one or two efforts on a smaller scale, we hasten to furnish this sketch with a notice of the Oxford and Cambridge South Central African Mission. The geographical discoveries of Dr. Livingstone, when told by himself on his visit to this country in 1856, awakened a profound and widespread influence. The unaffected and simple bearing of the great traveller, the evident high principles of the man, the resolute will, and the calm self-possessed power that had carried him through the toils and perils of his sixteen years African research, opened all hearts to his story. Livingstone knew how to turn the position he had gained to the account of the cause for which his geographical researches had been prosecuted. With a mind thoroughly unsectarian he appealed to all sections of the church, and alike to Episcopalians and Nonconformists. His visit to Cambridge, about a year after his return, was the most remarkable event of his home life. His reception was an ovation. His lecture on the occasion closed with words that could not be forgotten in an assembly composed at once of the grave and reflective, and of the impressive, ardent, and enterprising minds of the university. "I'll go back," said he, "to Africa to try and make an open path for commerce and Christianity. Do you carry out the work which I have begun. I leave it with you."

The seed which Livingstone sowed in that lecture ripened slowly. A dead lull succeeded the storm of enthusiasm, and Livingstone and his Africans seemed forgotten. He was not, however, to be altogether disappointed. There was labouring among the Caffres at the time an earnest, devoted man, Charles Frederick Mackenzie by name, who had taken a high place in Cambridge University, and who had gone out some time before to preach among the heathen the unsearchable riches of Christ. The energy and zeal of Mackenzie were apostolic. In his wilderness home at Umhlali, in the Caffre school, or in the midst of the Caffre village and the native infant churches, he found scope for his simple, earnest, Christian faith and work. There, as he rejoiced in the abundance of his congenial labour, and thought of the brief twelve hours of the Sabbath day on which it had mainly to be wrought, he wrote home: "My only regret is that I cannot make more of my Sunday than what I do. I wish I could say, like Joshua, 'Sun, stand thou still.'"

The missionary labours of Mackenzie were abruptly closed by his coming to England in prosecution of arrangements for the appointment of a missionary bishop to the Zulu country. The Oxford and Cambridge Mission received a fresh impulse at the time of his return. The field chosen was South Central Africa, and the object of the mission announced to be the establishment of one or two more stations as centres of Christianity and civilisation. With the Christian instruction of the natives there was to be kept specially in view the promotion of agriculture, lawful commerce, and ultimate extirpation of the slave trade. The mission was cast after the conception of those early mission monasteries to which England and Germany owed their Christianity and first lessons in civilisation, only free from their monastic restraints. It was to be a settlement practically to illustrate Christian life, and from whence, as a centre, to spread Christian truth. The scheme was planned on a scale worthy of the universities, and if the ultimate choice of a location had corresponded with the sagacity of the preliminary arrangements, its brief history would have presented a less discouraging record of failure.

The most anxious of the preliminary steps was the selection of a leader for the enterprise. This difficulty was being keenly felt when Mackenzie, reappearing at Cambridge like one, as it was said, who had dropped from the clouds, was at once recognised as the man to head the mission. He accepted the leadership, and sailed for Africa. At Cape Town he was consecrated "Bishop of the Mission to the tribes dwelling in the neighbourhood of the Lake Nyanza and the River Shire." By arrangements with Dr. Livingstone, the missionary party was conveyed up the Zambesi and Shire in the small steamer which the Government had placed at the command of the traveller. It was not allowed to Bishop Mackenzie to mature the plan of his mission settlement, or, in despair of success, to transfer its operations to another field. His strength was soon prostrated by successive attacks of fever. By an unfortunate accident his canoe had been upset, and his store of quinine and packet of medicine for combating fever swept away. No substitutes were at hand, and nothing could be procured to sustain the strength which the fever was striking down. He consequently fell a victim to its power, and died in the midst of his work. The natural unhealthiness of the settlement quickly drained the strength of the European members; even the natives sank under the fever-air of its low position, fifty having died within the first twelve or eighteen months. When it was at length determined to abandon the station and settle at Chibisa, the heat of the new station was found to be intolerable. The entire mission on the Zambesi and Shire was ultimately broken up.

At present the Universities' Mission is under Bishop Steere, and occupies the country lying between the Lake Nyassa and the East Coast. Stations have been established at Magila and Masasi, and the efforts to afford industrial training to the released slaves and other natives, and to promote education in the schools in Zanzibar, appear to have been highly successful, as is proved by the fact that no expedition to the interior is thoroughly complete without one or more of the lads trained in the schools. It was one of these lads who, with the permission of Mr. Stanley, was left with King Mtesa, and there translated and read the Bible, following up the efforts of Mr. Stanley to unfold the main truths of Christianity before that chief and his court. Whatever the future of the Universities' Mission may be, if it have no other story to tell than the life of its first bishop, its work will not have been in vain. The record of his self-dedication, noble unselfishness, heroism without display, cheerfulness under all trials, and singular union of feminine gentleness with calm energy of will and loving unfaltering submission to duty, will yet summon many a soldier to the mission ranks, prepared to follow in self-sacrificing love the footprints of Charles Frederick Mackenzie.

There are other Christian Missions in Africa. Among

those on the West Coast one of the most interesting is that conducted by the Baptist Missionary Society. Its origin and history are alike remarkable. Soon after the emancipation of the slaves in the West Indies a black man of the name of Keith sold all that he possessed, worked his passage to Africa, and proclaimed on the very spot whence he had been stolen the Gospel of salvation. Many others offered their services. When it was hinted that they might be made slaves again, they answered, "We have been made slaves for men; we can be made slaves for Christ." In 1840 the mission to Western Africa was commenced. The Rev. John Clarke and Dr. Prince were sent to explore the coast, especially on or near the banks of the Niger. Everywhere they met with a cordial reception from the natives, but favourable circumstances led them to select, as the seat of the mission, the island of Fernando Po, immediately opposite the mouth of the Cameroons River. This island presented an encouraging field for missionary enterprise among the aborigines of the interior, as well as in the colony of Clarence, then much frequented by traders on the coast and by Her Majesty's cruisers employed in the suppression of the slave trade. The chiefs on the banks of the Cameroons River also gave them a hearty welcome. Stations were soon formed in Fernando Po and on the coast. The languages of the people were diligently studied and reduced to writing. Vocabularies and school-books in various dialects were prepared, and portions of holy Scripture were translated and put to press. Then disease and death began to invade the homes of the missionaries, and the prospects of the mission became clouded with sorrow and strife.

In 1843, in 1846, and again in 1856, the Government of Spain, in pursuance of its claim to the sovereignty of Fernando Po, sent Jesuit priests to stay the progress of heresy, and to present themselves as the only legitimate teachers of Christianity. In 1858 the Spanish authorities proclaimed the religion of the colony to be that of the Roman Catholic Church, although there was not a single native adherent of that church on the island. All other forms of Christianity were absolutely prohibited. Protests were in vain. Led by the Rev. Alfred Saker, the bulk of the people determined to seek freedom of conscience and liberty of worship elsewhere, and they found a new home on the wild forest-covered shores of Amboises Bay, at the foot of the great mountain of Cameroons. Here the colony of Victoria was established, and amid many privations and hardships a new temple was raised for the worship of the Lord of Hosts.

Since the exclusion of the missionaries from Fernando Po by the Spanish Government the operations of the society have been confined to the Continent. During the time when the slave trade was rife the population was greatly diminished. Entire districts of the country were devastated, and the towns and villages demolished, to supply the accursed traffic. Since the abolition of the trade the tribes have again increased in numbers, and villages have been planted on the desolated spots.

About twenty miles from the mouth of the Cameroons River we come to the mission settlements. "I cannot describe," says Mr. Saker, "the condition in which I found this whole people. A book they had not seen; the commonest implements of husbandry and tools of all kinds were unknown. I brought with me tools to make my own dwelling. These attracted immediate attention, and soon several youths learned to use the saw, the plane, and the adze. Implements of husbandry, the spade, and the hoe were introduced. Then I taught them to cut the large timber-trees, and supplied the cross-cut and the pit-saw, and aided them in sawing till they could do it alone. I taught them better modes of culture, and planted ground as an example. I introduced seeds from other parts of the coast at a considerable charge, until the country was stocked with the sweet potato, and I had the pleasure of seeing a gradual extension of cultivation, with much less suffering from want."

The missionary's first home was a native hut, without windows, built of split bamboo, and thatched with twisted palm leaf. An improved dwelling was required, for health as well as for the conduct of the work itself. Mr. Saker's first attempt at building was a framed timber-house. By-and-by it was found practicable to make bricks, and by slow degrees he succeeded in building a brick dwelling, chapel, and school-house. Strenuous efforts were made to acquire the language. Mr. Saker found no books existing to assist him in the study. He had to acquire a knowledge of the words and of the elementary forms of the native tongue from the lips of the people. Step by step a vocabulary was formed, then came a grammar, then easy school books, and last of all the entire Bible in the Dualla tongue. In the printing Mr. Saker had the assistance of his daughter, and of natives to whom he had taught the art. As the missionaries acquired fluency of speech they used their gift to preach the Gospel, and the preaching was not without fruit—one after another came forward to confess the name of Christ amid much persecution.

It must not be supposed that all this was done without much suffering on the part of the missionaries. Their lives were often threatened, attempts were made to poison them, and the practices of witchcraft were indulged in to remove them from the spot; but God was their shield, and no harm befell them. Then much suffering was endured from insufficient food, from the plundering habits of the natives, from the torrid heat of the climate, from weakening fevers; but through all the missionaries persevered, and it pleased God to crown their labours with success. The effects of the Gospel are not limited to the churches that have been formed or to the education which many have received. They are seen in other ways. Old sanguinary customs have been abolished ; witchcraft hides itself in the recesses of the forests which stretch inland ; the fetish superstition of the people is losing its hold on them ; here and there are springing up well-built brick or timber houses, chiefly the work of men taught in the mission, the chiefs and others of the people availing themselves of their skill ; dress is become an article of necessity among the Christian community ; and many are slowly gathering around them the comforts of civilised life.

Another useful mission in West Africa is that carried forwards on the Gold Coast and at Ashantee by the Basle Evangelical Society. It has been in existence above half a century, and prosecutes four different branches of missionary work. The Accra and Tshi languages have been reduced to writing, and the whole Bible translated into both. The Gospel is preached in nearly every town and village of the eastern district on the Gold Coast. From the beginning education has been regarded as most important, and at all the stations there are elementary schools for male and female children. Industrial work is not neglected. A number of lay missionaries have been sent out, who have opened carpenters', joiners', black and locksmith, and shoe-makers' shops. All Europeans who have been on the Gold Coast acknowledge that the industrial work of this mission has been an eminent blessing to the country and a powerful stimulus to the elevation of the people.

The United Methodist Free Church Mission in East Africa has been in existence for about twenty years. The base of its operations is Wanyikee, and was selected at the suggestion of Dr. Krapf. Its earliest history was charac-terised by a great deal of sorrow and suffering to the mis-sionaries, of disease, and in some instances of death. One devoted man died soon after his arrival, and the nails he had taken out with him for use in his station had to be employed upon his coffin. Charles New, another agent of this mission, was a traveller of some note, and was the first and only man that ever climbed Kilimanjaro, bringing snow from the top to the bottom to prove to the people that he had been to the summit. Here again, in connection with preaching and Christian instruction, industrial operations are carried on. A mechanic has been sent out to teach the natives carpentery and building, and a printer instructs them in the art of printing. A plough is also being used in the cultivation of the land, and some good specimens of cotton have already been sent home as proofs of their success. The work thus begun is being extended as rapidly as possible in the direction of the Wapokomo, among the peoples of the Galla country.

There are Christian missions in Egypt which possess an interest peculiar to themselves, having for their object the spiritual benefit of the natives of the country, and persons from neighbouring countries who reside there. Dr. Watson, who has been labouring there for upwards of twenty years, thus speaks of the American mission with which he is connected :—"The Arabic-speaking population of the country consists of Mohammedans, numbering perhaps four and a quarter millions, Copts about three hundred thousand, and Syrians of various sects to the number of twenty-five thousand, together with a respectable number of Jews in the cities of Alexandria and Cairo. In our efforts to reach these various classes we have acted on the principle to enter in at whatever door the Lord in his providence should open to us, rather than to be influenced by any preconceived opinion as to the most hopeful class or the most interesting sect. It has been all one to us whether we were directed to the door of a Mohammedan or a Copt, or a Roman or Greek Catholic, or a Jew, believing that all souls are equally precious to Him who so loved the world that He gave His only begotten Son, that whosoever believeth in Him should not perish but have everlasting life.

"The methods used for reaching the people are—the public preaching of the Word, evening meetings for its study, visitation from house to house, keeping the doors of our own dwellings open to inquiries after the truth, extensive yearly tours by means of the Nile for book distribution and evangelical work, and instruction in schools of various kinds and grades."

We cannot close this brief and imperfect sketch of Christian work in Africa without observing, that within the last few years several schemes have been organised and initiated to establish important centres in the very interior of the continent. The valley of the Zambesi and the Shire, and the country surrounding Lake Nyassa, have been specially selected by the Free Church Missions, and in connection with them the Established Church and the United Presbyterians. Lake Tanganyika, and the tract of country surrounding it, is designed to be the scene of the labours of the London Missionary Society. If we consider the position of the Victoria Nyanza, its distance from the coast, our ignorance of many of the tribes that inhabit its banks, and the fact that some of them already regard Europeans as their deadliest enemies, the Church Missionary Society, in selecting this sphere of labour, has in some respects shewn itself the most enterprising of all. The Baptist Missionary Society has chosen the Congo as the route for its agents towards the interior, and several brave and devoted men are already engaged there in arduous work. All Christians of every name and denomination must rejoice in these new schemes for Africa. May the day soon come when the entire population of that vast continent shall be won for Christ!

CHAPTER XXVIII.

GENERAL SURVEY OF CHRISTIAN MISSIONS THROUGHOUT
THE WORLD.

BEFORE the Lord Jesus Christ ascended to heaven, He commanded His apostles, and through them all His followers in every age, to go into all the world and preach the Gospel to every creature. The mission of the church is to evangelise the world. This great work committed by Christ to His disciples has been strangely delayed. For the first three centuries it was prosecuted with vigour; the Gospel was carried into Armenia, Iberia, Arabia, Persia, and even India, in the East; into Ethiopia and other parts of Africa; into Gaul and Britain in the West. But this primitive zeal in propagating the Gospel declined as Christianity became corrupted, and as the church was converted into a vast hierarchical organisation, and eventually allied itself with the civil power. Even after its action was encumbered by this alliance, and its spirit vitiated, and its life all but destroyed, its self-propagating power still shewed itself, and from the midst even of the corrupted church light was sent forth whenever a new region was discovered that was without it. The numerical strength and the area of Christendom continued to increase.

The downfall of the Roman Empire brought Christianity and civilisation into contact with the tribes of the North, and several of the German nations became Christian. Even during the dark ages nominal Christianity continued to spread, chiefly in the North of Europe; occasionally, as in Russia in the eleventh century, it was inaugurated as the religion of the State. Here and there the pure Gospel was kept alive; now and then a sincere and devoted missionary would go forth and labour in the spirit of primitive times, but this long period witnessed mainly but the enlargement of the nominal church and the extension of an ecclesiastical corporation, by no means the thorough evangelisation of the world, much less the conversion of mankind to the faith and practice of the Gospel.

The sixteenth century was the age of reformation: its powerful agitations were confined within the pale of Christendom; its work was renovation, not aggression, although the Romish Church, weakened in many parts of Europe, embarked in various projects of hierarchical ambition in pagan lands. Ignatius Loyala stands pre-eminent as a model of missionary zeal. The seventeenth century witnessed occasional incipient missionary movements among the Dutch, the Swiss, the Swedes, the British, and the inhabitants of the North American colonies. The last century gave birth to numerous missionary associations, and reduced to system the work of evangelising the world, then distinctly recognised as a Christian duty. The present century has carried out that system with increased zeal and energy, and on an enlarged scale; has multiplied benevolent associations and the means of prosecuting the work of missions, and has established that work in the hearts of Christians as the great enterprise of the Church. Since apostolic times no age has been so distinguished for evangelistic effort as that in which we live. Not to speak of the home labours of the churches of Christendom, there are now in existence in Great Britain,

America, on the continent of Europe, and in other parts of the world, upwards of seventy missionary societies, having for their special object the conversion of the world to God. These societies occupy upwards of twelve hundred stations, employ about twelve thousand agents of all kinds, and are supported by an income of above one million pounds sterling. Through their instrumentality the Gospel is preached all over the earth—in crowded cities, in the wilderness and desolate places, where population is scant and small, and in the islands far off on the sea.

India has six hundred missionaries, who, with their three hundred native companions, are abundant in labours—preaching in the vernacular, broad systems of education, extensive literatures in many tongues, humane efforts in famines, pestilences, and pain—all are employed, steadily and in faith, to make known the good news of Christ's saving love. Good churches, with no despicable number of converts, have been gathered, are growing, and are proving themselves worthy of all esteem. But the thorough leavening of India with Gospel truth is the principal feature of the great work carried on for the enlightenment of its people, and the effect of it is wonderful and widespread. Special advance has been made in recent years in female education in India. The Ladies' Society for Female Education in the East—the pioneer amongst women—after its long and useful career, still occupies the foremost place in this important branch of Christian work. But the Zenana missions of many American and English societies, and lady missionaries devoted to this service, have greatly multiplied in recent years, while wide and effectual doors into the homes of Hindu society are ever opening in larger numbers.

The growth of the various missions of the principal societies is exceedingly interesting and encouraging. Beginning with the Baptists, who were earliest in the field, we find that from 1850 to the present time their converts in all the missions of the Baptist societies of England and America, in India, Ceylon, and Burmah, have increased from about thirty thousand to upwards of ninety thousand; those of the Basle missions of Germany have multiplied from a thousand to upwards of six thousand; those of the Wesleyan Methodist missions of England and America from seven thousand to upwards of twelve thousand; those of the American Board from three thousand to thirteen thousand; those of the Lutheran Church, belonging to five societies, from four thousand to upwards of forty thousand; those of the Presbyterians of Scotland, England, Ireland, and America, from nine hundred to ten thousand; those of the London Missionary Society from twenty thousand to forty-eight thousand; and those in connection with the Church of England from sixty-one thousand to one hundred and sixty-four thousand.

A steady growth is displayed in all directions. The indirect influence of Christianity in India is as remarkable as the baptism of converts and the formation of Christian communities. The great progress in the enlightenment of the people; the general awakening of thought throughout the entire country; the wonderful transformation native society is undergoing; the yearning after something better than a religion with its myriads of gods can give; the eager desire for a holier and purer faith manifest in many directions—these changes cannot adequately be accounted for except by the spread of Christian principles, which are enlarging the minds, stimulating the conscience, and quickening the religious sense of the people. These are facts which admit of no question or doubt. The steady increase on a high ratio of Christian converts is a matter of statistics, of careful counting, from which there is no appeal. The moral growth of the nation, and the radical changes for the better which are taking place in native society throughout the length and breadth of India, are, as evidences of improvement and progress, verities from which again no appeal is possible.

Fifty years ago not a Protestant missionary was living within the bounds of the Chinese Empire, though a few were training themselves and gaining experience in its out-lying colonies, waiting for the opportunity of entering it, which they were convinced must come. Since then, by various steps, nine provinces of the empire have been occupied by settled missionary stations, and at most important points—the twelve treaty ports—some forty societies have placed bands of missionaries, by whose constant efforts their populations have been brought under careful instruction. As the Chinese themselves maintain schools and desire the education of their children, the direct preaching of the Gospel in the vernacular tongues is the most prominent feature in these evangelistic labours. Under this plan, systematically carried out in fixed places by many workers, English and native, some seventy thousand sermons are preached in China in the course of each single year.

The Scriptures, too, are supplied in ample numbers. No country has so large and so good a supply of sound Christian literature. Itinerancies are numerous, and in recent years the other nine provinces of the empire have been traversed, and in part occupied, by missionaries chiefly of the Inland Mission. Widespread instruction—the leavening of the mass—has been a needful and most important step in these great missions. But God has blessed them also with true converts. Thirteen thousand communicants, in a community of some forty thousand Chinese Christians, are an earnest of the future and a great present gain, and the formation of strong, self-reliant churches, and the increase of native ministers and missionaries, are guarantees that that future will be of the noblest kind. The painful famine in China a few years ago was not without its compensating blessings. The kindness of foreigners produced a profound impression upon high and low, and thousands of Chinese have, as the result, come nearer to Christ's people to ask about the religion from whence such benevolence springs.

The Rev. W. F. Stevenson, who a year or two ago visited China and closely examined the character of mission work in that country, bears the following testimony to the sincerity of the converts and the stability of the native churches. After speaking of the wonderful results of Christian labour in that land, he says :—"It would be a profound mistake to suppose that such results as I have pointed out are transitory, that the impressions made are shallow, or that those who join the Christian Church are of so indifferent a character that Christianity has been little more to them than a bribe. In a country like China it costs too much for a man to become a Christian to make the advantage that the Protestant missionary can offer him worth having, for that at the most is a salary so small that he would be hard pressed indeed if he could not earn more at his own calling, while it is burdened with a social ostracism and contempt that are bitterly felt; and as for the great bulk of the Christians, they continue in their calling— artizans, farmers, tradesmen, whatever it may be—and with a difficulty in making their livelihood that they never had before.

"The native Christians are often men that have not only taken joyfully the spoiling of their goods, but hazarded their lives for the Gospel. 'They could cut off our heads,' some grave men said to me, 'but they cannot behead Christ.' I found in Amoy an elder of a native church, diligent in Christian work, and earning his living by carving olive stones into the exquisite bracelets that ladies wear; that man had been the best carver of idols in the city. I met a theological tutor, a man of the highest education and culture. He had gone into a barber's shop one day, and this barber makes it a point to speak a word to his customers for Christ; so he spoke to him of the Gospel, and dwelt upon the judgment-day, and what he said became the turning-point in that man's life. I have listened to many native sermons, and though there was the serious disadvantage of hearing only through an interpreter, who would kindly whisper sentence by sentence into my ear, yet I have never heard more impressive sermons than some of these were—full of admirable imagery, which was used to illustrate evangelical doctrine; and among the preachers there are men of an originality and eloquence that enables them to sway their audiences as famous preachers sway them here.

"There are noble-minded and nobly-living women there also in all the churches, and I cannot forbear mentioning one whom I met. She came as a patient to a missionary hospital, and as every helper about that hospital is a Christian, it was not long till she heard of Christ, and though she could not bear at first to hear a name that she associated with evil, yet, when after a few months she could leave the institution cured, she was also baptised. For some years her husband closed his house against her, but her unwearied patience and faith prevailed; and first he, and then her son, then other relatives were baptised, until she had led eleven of her kindred to Christ. I have found nowhere in Christian lands men and women of a higher type than I met in China, of a finer spiritual experience, of a higher spiritual tone, or a nobler spiritual life. Where missions shew such fruit they are beyond the impeachment of producing shallow and transitory impressions, and I came away with the conviction that there are in the native churches in China not only the elements of stability, but of that steadfast and irresistible revolution that will carry over the whole empire to the new faith."

The first Protestant missionaries to Japan were commissioned by American societies, and reached the shores of that empire in 1859 and 1860.   At that time there was not one native of Japan residing in the country, so far as can be ascertained, who knew or imagined that "being justified by faith we have peace with God through our Lord Jesus Christ"—not one who believed in Christ as his Saviour. The missionaries found, however, a very different state of society from that which they expected.   They found the people, women as well as men, generally able to read and write.   Everybody, girls and boys of all classes, had received a fair education.   The people were intellectually bright and quick, eager to learn, inquisitive, and readily apprehending new truths and novel facts.   The mass of the people are Buddhists.   Among all classes there is a high regard for the moral teachings of Confucius and Mencius.   There are about fifty missionaries in Japan, representing various societies in this country and in America.   Connected with these missions there are about thirty Christian schools for girls and boys, and these institutions are very popular. The holy Scriptures have been translated into Japanese, and thousands of copies distributed to a large extent by sale.   The Japanese Christians are very active and zealous, and unusually independent and self-reliant.   They accept foreign aid reluctantly, and only because they must.   They do not spare themselves in endeavours to extend the knowledge of the truth.   An unusually large proportion of the male members of the churches engage in preaching the truth as opportunities present themselves.   The amount of Christian literature is as yet limited.

Some tracts have been published, and a monthly newspaper is in circulation.   Defences of Christianity from the pens of native Christians, and from men intellectually favourable to Christianity but not connected with the churches, have also been written.   No one can tell the future, but the indications at present are that the Church of Christ will have a rapid and vigorous growth amongst the people of Japan. We may reasonably expect that, if the churches of Christian lands are faithful, the native membership in a generation will embrace tens of thousands of souls.

Christian missions in Burmah began with the late Dr. Judson. He and those who joined him devoted all their time and labour for many years to the evangelisation of the Burmese. Their labours succeeded to a hopeful and encouraging degree, but the chief enlargement of their work was to be in another direction. It was God's plan to call a race who in times past were not a people. The Karens are scattered over all parts of Burmah, and are also found in Upper Siam and Western China. They are generally regarded as belonging to the Caucasian race, though nothing is certainly known concerning their origin. Their name simply signifies *wild men*. They are distinct from the Burmans, and in physical and mental qualities they are inferior to them. They are a subject people, and for generations have been cruelly oppressed by the Burmans. Like other wild men, they are wandering and migratory in their habits, and they generally build their villages at points remote from large Burman communities, that they may escape the cruel exactions which would be otherwise made upon them. Even when the Burmans do not enslave them, they compel them to till their fields and to perform all kinds of menial service. It may be partly from the desire to escape these oppressions that they have fallen into the nomadic life which they pursue.

It would not be correct to say that this interesting people had no religion, but they presented the remarkable spectacle of a people without a priesthood or any established forms of worship. They possessed the knowledge of many revealed truths, which it is supposed must have been derived from the Hebrew Scriptures, or from the same Divine source. They believed that there is one God ; that man was created in a state of innocence, and fell through transgression at the instigation of a malignant spirit; that the soul is immortal; and that there is a state of future rewards and punishments. Coupled with these fundamental beliefs, there were certain singular national traditions which were carefully transmitted from generation to generation. They were taught that their fathers were the objects of the Divine favour, but that they had forgotten God, and wandered from Him, that they had thus lost the knowledge of His ways, and that all their woes and oppressions were the consequences of the hidings of the Divine face from them. They also had old prophecies of a better day. White teachers were to appear in the fulness of time, who would bring a book which would restore the lost knowledge of God, and through the truth and guidance thus obtained they would again be blessed with His presence and favour.

It was amongst this people that the Gospel was to succeed in a manner almost miraculous. Mr. Boardman baptised at Tavoy a servant of his whom he had redeemed from slavery, and who had given hopeful signs of conversion. He was a Karen, and his name was Ko-Thah-Byu. Though he was not converted till past middle life, and was without culture, he proved one of the most successful preachers of modern times. He knew little more than that Christ Jesus came into the world to save sinners, that He had saved him, and that He will save all that believe in His name. He was the first apostle among his people. He went from village to village and from province to province preaching the Word, the Lord working with him mightily. The people were prepared by the presence of the Spirit as well as by the tendencies of their traditions. Multitudes everywhere turned to the Lord. The American missionaries in connection with the native preachers followed up the work.

The result of all this and of subsequent labours is that hundreds of Christian churches have been formed, and are served by an efficient body of native pastors and teachers. The number of Karen churches on 1st January 1877 was four hundred and seven. Seventy-one of these churches were served by ordained preachers, the others were under the care of missionaries or of unordained preachers. Two-thirds of these churches maintain Christian schools, in which between four and five thousand children and youths are under instruction. The Karen villages now dotting the surface of British Burmah, whether Christian or heathen, may be counted among the natural results of Karen evangelisation; for the security and prosperity of the Christian settlements have not been without their influence on vast numbers who have not yet received the Gospel. Multitudes are sharers in the temporal benefits of Christianity who have not entered into the blessings of the spiritual life.

The present condition of Christian missions in Polynesia is such as to call forth the liveliest gratitude to God. In that part of the world, including Hawaii, the seven great groups of islands best known to Englishmen have become nominally Christian. In these and their attached groups some four hundred thousand converts, including ninety thousand communicants, have been brought into the Church of Christ. These are largely under the instruction of native pastors paid by themselves. Four aggressive missions are now at work in Western Polynesia, one chief element of which is the strong force which they contain of native missionaries. In most of the older missions Christianity has become a power for good over the people generally. Public morality has become benefited by it. The political, social, and domestic life of the people has to a greater or less extent received a more healthy moral tone. It is generally considered to be respectable to conform, at least outwardly, to the observances of religion. The Sabbath is usually strictly observed. Nearly all the people make a practice of attending public worship at least once on the

Lord's day. Family worship is almost universally observed. Nearly all the people are able to read, and indeed they do read God's word, which they possess in their own languages.

A most interesting mission field is Madagascar. The Jesuits had a mission there in the seventeenth century, and have had influence, more or less, over portions of the island for nearly two hundred years past; but their mission has not produced any permanent effect on the country, and this may be easily accounted for by the fact that they never gave the people the Word of God. They gave them the Lord's Prayer, the *Hail Mary*, the Ten Commandments—with the second, of course, left out—and short portions of the Bible, but they never gave them so much as a single book either of the Old or New Testament.

Protestant missions date from 1820, and the work may be divided into three periods—that of planting the Gospel, that of persecution, and that of progress. The first of these lasted sixteen years, the second twenty-five years, and the last now twenty years. The men who began the work laid the foundations upon which present labourers have been building for several years past. They did a noble work: they reduced the language to writing; they gave the people their own tongue in a written form; they translated and printed the whole Word of God; they gave the people an educational system, provided them with a considerable literature, and taught them many of the useful arts of civilised life. Their labours laid that firm foundation which resisted for twenty-five years all that a heathen queen could do to root religion out of the land. The results are patent to any intelligent and honest traveller who may pass through the country. There are undeniable facts to shew that Christianity is now exerting a real influence upon the social life of the people. It is introducing civilisation and opening up commerce in a way unmistakable to those who know what the country was a few years ago, and can contrast it with its position at the present time. In 1863 there was not a single European house of business in the capital. Now there are a number of them, and trade is extending largely along the eastern coast. With regard to the clothing, dwellings, and other matters affecting social life, there has been a wonderful advance during the last twelve years.

The tone of morals, too, is greatly improved. The people were very immoral, and are so still where the Gospel is not known. Chastity and purity were almost unknown things; but now, in the central province of Imerina, polygamy may be said to have disappeared. The merciful influence of the Gospel is seen in the abolition of cruel customs and laws. By the old code of laws in force during the time of the persecuting queen, a great number of offences were punished by death, and the wife and family of a delinquent were reduced to slavery. That has all passed away. The law by which soldiers were burned alive for running away in battle is also now a thing of the past. Thus the loving and beneficent influence of the Gospel is doing away with the old cruel habits of the people. Christianity is spreading through a great portion of the country, and it can only be a matter of time for the whole island to be brought to the knowledge of Jesus Christ.

About a thousand miles north of New Zealand lie the group of islands called the New Hebrides, extending about three hundred miles from south-east to north-west. Here there is an important mission supported by the Free Church of Scotland and the Presbyterian Churches of Canada, New Zealand, and Australia. It has been one of the most difficult mission fields in the South Seas. One great difficulty is the low and degraded state of the natives, all the cruelties and all the abominations of heathenism were found rampant among them; they were ignorant and superstitious in the extreme, with an unwavering faith in the power of witch-craft. Another difficulty arises from the unhealthiness of the climate. Fever and ague prevail on nearly all the islands. White men and natives of other groups are alike subject to it. In every swamp, in every valley, and in every thicket lurks the invisible, mysterious malaria. A third difficulty is the number of languages. There are not fewer than twenty different languages spoken in the group, every one as different from all the rest as English is from Gaelic, or as Latin is from Greek. And a fourth difficulty is the operation of an unsanctified commerce. The islands are now in danger of being deluged with intoxicating drinks. Referring to the way in which these difficulties have been met, one of the missionaries says :—" We have ascertained to a great extent the laws of health, and can thus ward off a great amount of preventible sickness. We have mastered among us, somewhat fully, nine of the languages, and can thus make known to the natives in their own tongues the way of salvation. The sandal-wood trade is over, and the liquor traffic, though not suppressed, is greatly modified ; and to meet the evils of the *foreign* knaves, as the natives call alcoholic drinks, all our twelve missionaries are total abstainers."

The large island of New Guinea is now creating a con-siderable amount of interest in the commercial and scientific worlds; and both from its size and from its proximity to Australia—from which it is only separated by Torres Straits —and from its probable mineral wealth, it must come to occupy an important place in the consideration of all men. To the Christian philanthropist, above all, it is a country of great interest. The population of New Guinea is composed of an immense number of races, among whom the London Missionary Society have within the last ten years begun evangelising labour. Mr. Lawes, one of the leaders in this work, thus describes the field :—" Our mission extends from

Ule Island to the eastern extremity of New Guinea ; and even there we have an immense admixture of races, though all of them I believe, from their appearance, from their customs, and from their condition and languages, belong to the Malayo Polynesian family. We have a great number of sub-divisions among them. When I tell you that I know of twenty-five different languages spoken on the three hundred miles of coast with which I am acquainted, you will form some idea of how New Guinea is split up and divided. We find the people in a primitive state, which we almost fancy in this nineteenth century had become totally extinct. We find there the old lake villages, and there is still the stone age in full operation. I know of no vessel, implement, tool, or weapon made of metal which they employ. It is the stone age yet, and everything else agrees with this.

" Morally, we find what we should expect—viz., the people low and degraded, but by no means so much so as those we have had to do with in some other parts of the world where they are now Christians. Liars, thieves, and murderers they are ; but it is not the existence of these things that causes one so much surprise as the utter absence of anything like what may be called a tone of public opinion by which these vices could be at all stigmatised or the evil-doer be disgraced. They would unblushingly bring back the goods they have stolen from you, and offer them for sale, without even an atom of shame. Religiously, the darkness is darkness which can be felt but cannot be described."

Of the methods the missionaries employ to alter this state of things, Mr. Lawes thus speaks :—" I have had personally sufficient experience during eleven years' residence on Savage Island, in the South Pacific, to know where we ought to begin. Men who never tried the experiment may believe in civilising agencies. But we who have tried them may be pardoned if we decline to try the experiment over again. The very agencies that are depended upon we find to be fruitless. Clothe the natives, and they do not know how to use clothes. I have given them a good Birmingham hatchet, and had it returned rather than they would give up their stone ones. If there is no hope for them without civilisation and civilising agencies, then the salvation of New Guinea I believe to be hopeless. But my experience amongst tribes and races such as these warrants me in believing strongly that with them also the Gospel is the power of God unto salvation to every one that believeth. In the early days of a mission like that of New Guinea, very little dependence can be placed on oral teaching. I believe strongly, more strongly now than ever, in the power of a consistent Christian life."

Let us pass from New Guinea to the West Indies. The population of the twelve following islands and their dependencies — viz., Jamaica, the Bahamas, the Virgin Isles, Antigua, Montserrat, Barbadoes, St. Vincent's, Grenada, Tobago, Trinidad, and Dominica, amounts to something above one million. The first settlers in the chief of these islands were members of the Church of England, and that form of the Christian faith was established in them. Its spiritual labours were, however, mainly confined to the Europeans or planters, and only in rare cases was any attempt made to instruct the slave either in secular knowledge or in Christianity. The Moravians were the first religious body to visit the West Indies in 1734, and in the island of St. Thomas they commenced their self-denying efforts to give the oppressed negro the comfort of the words of eternal life. In 1778 the Wesleyans opened their very successful labours in the West Indies in Antigua, and in 1814 the Baptist Missionary Society sent its first missionary to Jamaica. If much had not been done by the Church of England towards the evangelising of the slaves, it must be remembered that the malign genius of the system of slavery was adverse to the attempt. In fact, whatever Christian agencies existed, they were of the most meagre sort. Only here and there did a planter or a converted free negro put forth any efforts to bring the slaves under Christian instruction.

Utterly neglected, without the opportunity or the means of learning, the negroes for the most part practised the fetishism of their native land, and were sunk in the most degrading lusts and superstitions. Marriage was scarcely known amongst them. The constant sales of the slave-stock of the estates broke up every family tie that had been formed. Concubinage with all its evils became the normal practice of the people, and its mischief invaded the home of their better-instructed masters. Then came the struggle for freedom. It was long and severe, but ended at length in emancipation. The munificent gift of twenty millions sterling by the British Parliament set every slave free. With freedom came the fullest opportunity for the play of moral and Christian agencies, devoted to the social and religious elevation of the emancipated people.

Since emancipation, the West Indian Colonies have experienced great fluctuations; nevertheless there has been great progress. Education has been largely promoted, especially so in Jamaica. This is greatly owing to the hearty co-operation of the missionaries. On this point we may take the remarks of the inspector of schools in Jamaica as generally applicable throughout the British West Indies. He says the Government system "has enlisted the sympathy and hearty co-operation of the most influential men of the community—viz., the ministers of all the religious societies in the island. To their valuable assistance as school-managers must be attributed in a great measure the success that has attended the carrying out of the system." Since emancipation, too, the means of public worship have very largely increased. From reliable sources, it appears that fully one quarter of the population may be regarded as regular frequenters of the means of grace supplied by the various denominations. It is not possible to estimate with accuracy how many of the hearers of the Gospel are actually in full communion with the churches. It may, however, be safely affirmed that at least eighty-five thousand individuals observe the great eucharistic ordinance of the Christian Church.

We must not omit from this sketch the efforts of American Christians in the Ottoman Empire. When the attention of American Christians was first turned to the Ottoman Empire as a field for missionary effort, it included, with its tributary provinces, portions of three continents. It combined the greatest variety of soil and climate; it stretched across the highways of the world's commerce, and embraced in its wide domain the earliest seats of civilisation and the scenes of greatest interest recorded in secular and sacred history. It presented to the world a most remarkable conglomerate of races, languages, and religions, without sympathy one with another, all subject to an unenlightened and often barbarous despotism. It had a population in all estimated at thirty-five millions, of whom about twelve millions were known as Christian descendants for the most part of those who, in the early days of the Church, had accepted the Gospel. Degenerated, degraded, sunk in ignorance and superstition, they were yet holding fast to the Christian name, to which, though with little sense of its spiritual import, they had clung through centuries of oppression. It was to this empire, the head and front of the Mahommedan world, long the deadly and unrelenting foe of the Gospel of Christ, that the American Board sent their first missionaries nearly sixty years ago.

Ever since its first establishment this mission has continued to grow and prosper. It is now represented by one hundred and thirty-two devoted men and women from the churches and best institutions of learning in America; by over five hundred native preachers and teachers in active service ; by ninety-two churches, with a membership of over five thousand ; by twenty higher institutions of learning—colleges, seminaries, and boarding-schools—with an attendance of over eight hundred youth of both sexes ; by three hundred common schools, with an attendance of over eleven thousand ; by two hundred and eighty-five places of worship scattered as so many light-centres through the land, from the Balkans to the Bosphorus, and from the Bosphorus to the Tigris, where Sabbath after Sabbath over twenty-five thousand men and women are gathered to listen to the Gospel message ; by the Scriptures, in the various languages of the people, now distributed by tens of thousands of copies ; and a Christian literature, from Sabbath-school lesson papers up to elaborate volumes on the evidences of religion and the history of the Church—all now confirmed by the living examples of the power of the Gospel. These are the moral forces now brought into the field, the heritage of the patient labours and prayers of American Christians of the past sixty years.

Then there is the Indian Archipelago. There are at present about fifty Dutch missionaries at work belonging to eight different societies, and scattered almost over the whole archipelago—on Sumatra, Java, Bali, Celebes, Almaheira, and some smaller islands. In the Minnahassa, forming a part of the Island of Celebes, of a population of about one hundred and fourteen thousand, upwards of eighty thousand are converts to the Christian faith, or form, as children, parts of Christian families. Heathenism has in consequence lost there its signification and its influence. No less than two hundred congregations are under the care of the mission-aries and of twenty-two native evangelists ; and there are a hundred and twenty-five schools, the teachers of which are at the same time catechists. In consequence, civilisation has reached a comparatively high degree. The schools and churches are regularly visited by children and adults decently dressed; and it is a delight to see how order and prosperity reign everywhere. From an ignorant, superstitious, abject population, divided by hostilities and feuds, they have grown into a nation, feeling that they have the same interest, that they are sons and daughters of the same country, many of them sons and daughters of the Most High God. Family life has a new aspect; husband and wife no longer leaving each other for the slightest reason, live together in harmony and care for their children. Whereas formerly numerous families lived together in large barracks built upon high poles, difficult of access for fear of the attacks of neighbouring tribes, now every family lives in its own cottage, neatly built, open to any visitor, where the missionary is received with decency and delight.

There are many other smaller fields of missionary labour, every one presenting its own peculiar features of interest and importance. Among the Indian tribes of North America, once thought so dull and hopeless, whether on the North-West Coast, scattered over the broad plains of Manitoba, or settled on the Reserves of the United States, many thousands of converts have been gathered, and in some of these tribes there are no heathen left. There are missionaries among the Afghans, in Ceylon, in Greenland, in Patagonia—almost every country of the habitable globe. They are wonderfully and wisely located; they are settled at the most important points in the wider realms open to their efforts. They are exerting a moral influence—are making spiritual impressions, and are breaking down the ancient heathen religions with a power infinitely greater than the churches which maintain them are at all aware. One fact of supreme moment must be stated here, and should be borne in mind, that in connection with all this Christian effort the holy Scriptures are at the present time printed and read in two hundred and twenty-six modern languages, and that from the importance of many of those tongues, such as English and German, French and Russ, Bengali and Chinese, those Scriptures have now became available to three-fourths of the population of the globe.

We see from the foregoing sketch of Christian missions throughout the world that there has been progress—rapid, great, encouraging progress. And yet the evangelising of the world, rightly viewed, is to be looked upon rather as a work which has been and yet is retarded, than as a work progressing rapidly toward completion—as a work which ought long since to have been done, but which has been and yet is unworthily delayed. How strange that after eighteen hundred years, with the known will of Christ that His Gospel should be everywhere proclaimed, and with the facilities afforded in every age for doing that work, it should still be true, that the world—the great preponderating mass of mankind—still lieth in wickedness. To use the words of John Foster: "Christianity, after labouring for eighteen centuries, is at the present hour known, and even nominally acknowledged, by very greatly the minority of the race, the mighty mass remaining prostrate under the infernal dominion of which countless generations of their ancestors have been the slaves and victims—a deplorable majority of the people in the Christian nations strangers to the vital power of Christianity, and a large proportion directly hostile to it, while its progress in the work of conversion, in even the most favoured part of the world, is distanced by the progressive increase of the population."

When we consider the earnestness of Christ's command, the largeness of His promise, the wisdom and munificence of His arrangements, and the intensity of His desires in respect to the conversion of the world, we can find a solution of the painful mystery of its delay only in some hindrance on the part of those who are commissioned to fulfil the mighty plan.

The kingdom of Christ has been retarded in various ways by the social and political condition of the world.　And yet Christianity would have proved itself ere this to be the great reforming power in the political and the social institutions of men, had not its influence been crippled and arrested by some other cause than those institutions themselves.　The full power of Christianity in opposition to all false systems of religion, of government, and of social organisation, has not yet been proved; for the condition of the exercise of that power—namely, a lively Christian faith, imparting vitality and efficiency to the appointed instrument of the work, has not been fulfilled on the part of the Church.

There are several fundamental facts involved in the missionary enterprise in respect to which there is a large amount of scepticism in the Church.　There is scepticism with respect to the actual condition of the heathen world.　That the heathen are for the most part in a state of deep moral and social degradation is beginning to be generally understood.　Their true condition was long hidden from Christian people.　Mere secular travellers gave us entertaining accounts of the manners and customs of different nations, with occasional outlines of their philosophical tenets or their religious belief, and sketches of their sacred places and institutions and modes of worship; but they seldom described the general state of morals, or held up to reprobation their prevailing vices and crimes.　Commercial residents in heathen lands generally visit them for a single object—the purpose of gain; they seldom contemplate a permanent residence; they commonly acquire but a superficial knowledge of the language, the literature, the religion and the morals of the country.　It was not till Christian missionaries went among the heathen that the moral state of the world became truly known.　That state is one not merely of degradation, but also of guilt. Only in proportion as we believe this shall we earnestly seek to save the heathen.　There is scepticism in some minds as to God's purpose to have the world evangelised and converted to Himself. Admitting that the heathen are in a state of guilt and condemnation, and on that account are proper objects for Christian sympathy and effort, it is still questioned by some whether the plan of redemption in its final results comprehends the conversion of the world at large. Scepticism in respect to missionary work is further developed in doubts and queries as to the proper time for attempting to evangelise the world. Some contend that the world must be civilised before we attempt to spread the Gospel, and others that Christ's second advent must precede such an event. Then there is another topic in connection with the missionary enterprise, respecting which there is not a little scepticism in the Church, that is the practicability of evangelising the world at all by any known instrumentalities.

Such scepticism paralyses the arm of the church. If one is in doubt whether the heathen would really be benefited by the Gospel—if he does not feel that they are in perishing need of it—of course he will do little or nothing to send it to them. If one is in doubt whether God really intends to accomplish the conversion of the world to Himself, whether it is His will that the Gospel should be everywhere propagated, of course he will scarcely make an attempt to evangelise the world. If one is in doubt whether this is the time for engaging in this work, he will not engage in it heartily, if at all. If one has little confidence in the present means, he will act with little energy or keep aloof from such impracticable schemes. Thus the work is crippled on every hand by unbelief. Unbelief, besides restraining the energies of the Church, incapacitates those who indulge it for appreciating the work of the Lord, and for rendering Him the glory which is His due. Viewed as a check upon Christian activity, unbelief is without doubt one of the great hindrances to the missionary work.

Such unbelief is unreasonable and wicked. Look at the

course of providence in relation to the missionary enterprise, especially of recent years. In no period of the history
of Christianity has the providence of God been more marked
than of late years in its bearing on the extension of the
Redeemer's kingdom. What facilities we have for communication
with all parts of the world, and with what
security missionaries can now labour in almost any part of
the globe! How has the British Empire, like the Roman
Empire of old, made a highway among the nations and
across the seas for the advance of Christianity! How large
a portion of the globe appears to be placed by Providence
at the disposal of Christendom! God is indicating to His
people their duty, and also His readiness to do mighty
works by their instrumentality. What is needed and what
is warranted, so that the Gospel may be preached "in the
regions beyond," is an increase of faith. And this increase
of faith all Christians should seek to obtain.

One wise and important method for strengthening faith
in missionary operations is to make ourselves familiar with
them. Read the letters and statements of missionaries; the
Reports of missionary societies; the lives of such men as
John Williams, Adoniram Judson, William Burns, Robert
Moffat; or if there be an objection to missionary literature
as one-sided and partial, then we might take the testimony
of competent independent witnesses—such as that given
by Commander Hood in his "Cruise of H.M.S. *Fawn.*"
Speaking of what he saw in the Samoan group of islands,
he says that the "rigid observance of Sunday presents a
rather humiliating contrast with its profanation in more
favoured regions. Our amusements were suddenly suspended by hearing the master of the house commence
singing the evening hymn, in which most of the assembly,
taking their books out of their waistcloths, joined; and we
removing our hats also, added our voices to the best of our
ability, hymn-books being handed to us. The psalm finished,

our host made a long extempore prayer, the Lord's prayer concluding the service. It certainly was a striking scene—half-a-dozen unarmed Englishmen sitting here in the midst of a crowd of half-naked islanders, and receiving a lesson of this kind from people so lately designated 'ferocious savages.'"

Take again the testimony of Mr. Thompson, who, during his eight years' residence at the Cape of Good Hope, travelled much in the interior, and who was neither a missionary nor connected with any missionary society. He says:—"Having now visited the whole of the missionary stations in Southern Africa, it may not be improper to express in a few words the opinion I have formed regarding them. I may safely affirm that, at every missionary station I have visited, instruction in the arts of civilised life, and in the knowledge of pure and practical religion, go hand-in-hand. It is true that among the more savage tribes of Bushmen, Korannas, and Bechuanas the progress of the missions has hitherto been exceedingly slow and circumscribed. But persons who have visited these tribes, and are best qualified to appreciate the difficulties to be surmounted in instructing and civilising them, will, if they are not led away by prejudice, be far more disposed to admire the exemplary fortitude, patience, and perseverance of the missionaries than to speak of them with contempt and contumely.

"These devoted men are found in the remotest deserts, accompanying the wild and wandering savages from place to place, destitute of almost every comfort, and at times without even the necessaries of life. Some of them have, without murmuring, spent their whole lives in such service. Let those who consider missions as idle or unavailing visit Gnadenthal, Bethelsdorp, Theopolis, the Caffre Stations, Griqua Town, Kamiesberg, etc.; let them view what *has* been effected at these institutions for tribes of the nations, oppressed, neglected, or despised by every other class of men of Christian name ; and if they do not find all accomplished which the world had perhaps too sanguinely anticipated, let them fairly weigh the obstacles that have been encountered before they venture to pronounce an unfavourable decision.

"For my own part, utterly unconnected as I am with missionaries or missionary societies of any description, I cannot in candour and justice withhold from them my humble meed of applause for their labours in Southern Africa. They have without question been in this country not only the devoted teachers of our holy religion to the heathen tribes, but also the indefatigable pioneers of discovery and civilisation. Nor is their character unappreciated by the natives. Averse as they still are in many places to receive a religion, the doctrines of which are too pure and benevolent to be congenial to hearts depraved by selfish and vindictive passions, they are yet everywhere friendly to the missionaries, eagerly invite them to reside in their territories, and consult them in all their emergencies. Such is the impression which the disinterestedness, patience, and kindness of the missionaries have, after long years of labour and difficulty, decidedly made even upon the wildest and fiercest of the South African tribes with whom they have come in contact ; and this favourable impression, where more has not been achieved, is of itself a most important step towards full and ultimate success."

Take the testimony of four Governors of India. Lord Napier says :—" The progress of Christianity is slow, but it is undeniable. Every year sees the area and the number slightly increase. The advance of Christianity has at all times been marked by occasional fitful and spasmodic movements in India. The present period is one of moderate progression, but it does not include the expectation of rapid and contagious expansions such as were witnessed in the sixteenth century in Malabar and Madina, in the last century in Tanjore, and more recently among the Shanars of the South. In conclusion, I must express my deep sense of the importance of missions as a general civilising agency in the south of India. Imagine all these establishments suddenly removed, how great would be the vacancy! Would not the Government lose valuable auxiliaries? The weakness of European agency in this country is a frequent matter of wonder and complaint; but how much weaker would this element of good appear if the mission was obliterated from the scene." "In many places," says Sir Donald Macleod, "an impression prevails that the missions have not produced results adequate to the efforts which have been made; but there is no real foundation for this impression, and those who hold such opinions know but little of the reality." This is the testimony of Sir Bartle Frere:—"I speak simply as to matters of experience and observation, and not of opinion—just as a Roman prefect might have reported to Trajan or the Antonines; and I assure you that, whatever you may be told to the contrary, the teaching of Christianity among one hundred and sixty millions of civilised, industrious Hindoos and Mahommedans in India is effecting changes, moral, social, and political, which for extent and rapidity of effect are far more extraordinary than anything you or your fathers have witnessed in modern Europe." Lastly, there is the testimony of Lord Lawrence, Viceroy and Governor-General:—"I believe," he says, "notwithstanding all that the English people have done to benefit India, the missionaries have done more than all agencies combined."

Christian people should make themselves familiar with testimonies such as these, and then when men whose worldly interests, or whose habits of life, cause them to look with an unfriendly eye on the missions of the Church, or men who have never troubled to inform themselves concerning them, seek to shake their faith in their usefulness, or to restrain their efforts in their promotion, that faith will be found firm as an immovable rock.

Faith in Christian missions may be strengthened by considering the universal adaptation of Christianity to the state and needs of mankind. It is suited to man as man in all parts of the world. There is nothing local in its nature or requirements. It is not circumscribed by any geographical limits. Its ideas may be expressed in all languages. It can exist under all forms of government. It will accord with all systems of sound philosophy. Its converts exist in Europe, Asia, Africa, and America. In its entire harmony with the condition, needs, character, instincts, aspirations, and capabilities of our common humanity, who can fail to see that it is God's provision for the world?

Faith in Christian missions is, moreover, to be strengthened by considering the commission of Christ to His church— "Go ye into all the world and preach the Gospel to every creature." This commission remains imperative in all its original force. Whatever may be the result of the proclamation of the Gospel, though not one to whom it is preached should accept it, the command of Christ Jesus binds His followers to make it known. Duty calls, and it is at our peril we neglect the call. He who speaks to us speaks with authority. He has a right to order us to any service He may require, and by our profession of discipleship we are held to implicit obedience. Obedience to Christ's command is rendered dear to us by gratitude. He who speaks is our Redeemer. We are not our own, for He has bought us with a price—even the price of His own blood. Standing by our Lord's side on Olivet as He issues His great commission, we remember Bethlehem and Nazareth—we have Gethsemane and Calvary before our eyes; and while His words come to us as a royal edict, they also come as the last request of our dearest friend. Obedience to Christ's command is in a special manner devolved upon British Christians. Our physical and mental qualities, our national training for centuries past, the immense and ever increasing wealth in our possession, the character of our political and religious institutions, the vast territories we own and the many millions of people over whom we exercise rule, our commercial relationships with all the nations of the earth, and our missionary history and experience for the last hundred years—all are designed by God to fit us to carry out the purposes of His mercy to a perishing world.

Christians should strengthen their faith in missionary work by the recollection of the declared purpose and promise of God. It is His purpose that the Gospel should be preached to all nations. He indicates this purpose by prophecy—by such predictions as declare that the earth shall be filled with the knowledge of the Lord as the waters cover the sea; that it shall come to pass in the last days that the mountain of the Lord's house shall be established in the top of the mountains, and shall be exalted above the hills, and all nations shall flow into it; that the kingdoms of this world are to become the kingdoms of our Lord and of His Christ.

An increase of faith in missionary operations will ensure their more rapid growth and success. It will do this in several ways. There will be deeper compassion for the heathen—a truer sympathy with them in their wretched condition. Spiritual wretchedness—the loss and misery of the soul without God and goodness, under the power and exposed to the penalty of sin, is worse than anything else a man can endure. And if we look at this miserable state of man without Christ—having no hope and without God in the world—if we look at it till the sight becomes clear to us in all its truth and reality, then the salvation of these lost ones will become our heart's great desire.

With an increase of faith there will be a rising up of

men to preach the Gospel to the heathen, sufficient supply of funds to send them forth, and an increase of earnest prayer for the blessing of God to give success to the work. With all this there will be the seeking out of new fields for effort. Many parts of the world, as we have already seen, are occupied. In India, in China, in Japan, on the coasts of Africa, and in the interior, in various parts of America, in Australasia, in the islands of the sea, east and west, north and south, the missionaries of the cross are to be found. But large tracts of the earth remain unvisited. With an increase of faith these will be occupied too. The various sections of the Church will search them out, and divide them among themselves, as waste places of the earth to be reclaimed and cultivated, till they blossom and bear fruits of righteousness like the garden of the Lord; and this will go on till there shall not be a tribe of mankind to whom the Gospel shall be an unknown sound. Then shall God's way be known upon earth, His saving health among all nations.

NOTES

SITUATION, FORM, AND EXTENT OF AFRICA— PHYSICAL FEATURES — CLIMATE — PRODUC- TIONS—ANIMALS—POPULATION—RELIGIONS— FORMS OF GOVERNMENT—COMMERCE, &c.

AFRICA is situated in the eastern hemisphere, to the south of Europe and the south-west of Asia, and lies between lat. 37° 20' N. and 33° 50' S., and long. 17° 30' W. and 51° 30' E. In form it is an irregular triangle, of which the southern extremity forms the blunt apex; having the Mediterranean Sea on the north, the Isthmus of Suez, the Red Sea, and the Indian Ocean on the east, and the Atlantic Ocean on the west. From the Mediterranean, where its breadth is already considerable, it becomes gradually broader, until within a few degrees of the Equator; it then contracts suddenly, and passing southwards, narrows until it terminates at the Cape of Good Hope. It is almost insular; the connecting isthmus being seventy-two miles across, of no great elevation above the sea-level, and in part occupied by salt lakes and marshes. Practically, now, Africa is an island, inasmuch as the canal opened through the Isthmus of Suez a few years ago has separated it from Asia, and connected the Red Sea with the Mediterranean.

The coast-line is marked by few indentations or projections; the most important gulf being that of Guinea on the west; and the extreme points to the north, west, south, and east being respectively Cape Bon, Cape Verde, the Cape of Good Hope, and Cape Guardafui.   The breadth of Africa, at the Equator, is about two thousand four hundred miles, but its *greatest* breadth, from Cape Guardafui to Cape Verde, is upwards of four thousand six hundred miles.   Its greatest length, from Cape Blanco, in the Mediterranean, to Cape das Agulhas, is about five thousand miles; and its entire area, including the adjacent islands, nearly twelve million square miles.

Africa is the most compact of all the great divisions of the globe.   To use the expression of Ritter, it is "like a trunk without limbs."   The other continents have their coasts lengthened by being deeply indented with bays, capes, and long necks of land.   This is not the case with Africa. There are only a few islands near the shores, and with the exception perhaps of Madagascar, none of them seem to be connected in physical structure with the adjacent continent. The Equator cuts Africa into two masses of unequal magnitude.   The northern portion has twice the superficial area of the southern, and may be considered as about equal in extent to South America, while the southern portion is about the size of New Holland.   Its general configuration may be briefly sketched under the following heads:—The triangular region south of Cape Guardafui and the Gulf of Guinea is mostly a high table-land, having fringes of mountains crowning its edges.   Between the coast and the beginning of the elevation runs a belt of lowlands varying from fifty to three hundred miles in breadth.   The Lupata range, seen running parallel with the coast, forms the eastern crest of the table-land, and reaches in the snow-clad Kilimandjaro and Kenia the height of twenty thousand feet. These are believed to be the real Mountains of the Moon.

LOCUST
DRAGON TREE
MUSHROOM SHAPED
HILLS OF THE WHITE ANT
BANANA TREE
AFRICAN BULL FROG

The mountainous country of Abyssinia is the eastern prolongation of the plateau, and its elevated crest, which rises at the northern extremity, in the summit of Abba Yared, to fifteen thousand feet. At the south the hills rise from Table Mount to the summits of Nieuweld and Sneuwberg, in the north of the Cape Colony ; these latter mountains being variously estimated at from seven to ten thousand feet in height. Towards the north-west the border of the table-land rises, in the Cameroons, to the height of thirteen thousand feet. Within this region are the Orange River, the Zambesi, and the source of the Nile, which, flowing from Lake Victoria Nyanza through Nubia and Egypt, empties itself into the Mediterranean. Here, too, in addition to Victoria Nyanza, are the Lakes Albert Nyanza, Tanganyika, N'gami, and Nyassa.

North of the great triangular table-land lies Sudan, or Central Nigritia, under which name may be comprehended the countries watered by the Senegal, the Gambia, and the Niger, along with the coast of Lower Guinea, and Lake Tchad. In the west of this section is a mountainous table-land, in which the above-named rivers take their rise. Eastward of the Niger the country is hilly, alternating with rich, often swampy plains. In the basin of Lake Tchad is a vast alluvial plain, one of the largest on the globe, and of great fertility.

Between Sudan and the cultivated tract which borders the Mediterranean stretches the Sahara or Great Desert. Its average breadth from north to south is about a thousand miles, and its length, from the Atlantic to the western edge of the valley of the Nile, two thousand. Over a great part of this region rain never falls, and everywhere it is rare. Here and there are tracts of fine shifting sand, while the greater part of the surface consists of naked but firm soil, composed of indurated sand, sandstone, granite, and quartz rocks. This general desolation is, however, interrupted at intervals by districts covered with bushes and coarse grass, and often marked by great fertility and beauty.

The Atlas region comprehends the mountainous countries of Morocco, Algeria, and Tunis. The northern slope towards the Mediterranean is similar in aspect, climate, and productions to the opposite coast of Europe; the southern side merges gradually into the Sahara. Some parts of this mountain chain are considerably above the snow-line, and the highest summit is reckoned at fifteen thousand feet. The remaining region is that bordering on the Red Sea, and which consists of Abyssinia, Nubia, and Egypt. Abyssinia, as we have seen, is the mountainous termination of the great southern plateau. Between this and the Mediterranean extends the low valley of the Nile, separated from the Red Sea on the east by a lofty rugged district, and from the Libyan Desert on the west by a low ridge of limestone and sandstone.

The climate of Africa is distinguished by its general want of humidity and its warmth; of this fact the immense extent of arid and burning deserts affords incontrovertible proof. The most northern and the most southern districts are equally without what can be called a winter. In some districts the heat is frequently insupportable. Thus at Ombos and Syene, in Egypt, the sand under a noon-day sun absolutely scorches the feet of the traveller, and eggs may be cooked by burying them in it. There are three great varieties of climate corresponding to the physical structure of the continent. First, that of the plateaus; second, that of the terraces which lead to them; and third, that of the coasts. In the vast desert of the Sahara, extending over an area equal to that of the Mediterranean Sea, the heat of the day is uniformly contrasted with the coldness of the night; while on the terrace-land of Limba, situated behind the Sierra Leone region, we find a temperate and whole-some climate; and the natives of Congo call their terrace-lands, which are well cultivated and thickly peopled, "the Paradise of the World." But the flat coasts, which are often over-flooded in the rainy season, have a very oppressive atmosphere; and from the morasses at the mouths of the rivers a malaria arises which is pestilential to Europeans. The region of pestilential air has been calculated to extend about one hundred miles inland, but only forty miles out to sea, and to rise to a height of four hundred feet above the sea-level.

The climate of Africa is less modified by the ocean than that of any other portion of the globe, not even excepting Central Asia. It is true that a cold current from the Antarctic seas sweeps along the Cape of Good Hope and the Agulhas bank, and immense Antarctic glaciers float on-wards nearer the Equator than they do in the northern hemisphere; yet from the figure of the African continent, these ocean currents only influence the temperature of the coast to a small extent, while the rest of the continent is surrounded by oceans of elevated temperature. It seems requisite that there should be a high central table-land, with numerous snow-capped mountains extending across the greater part of the African tropics, to modify the solar influence, which, were it exerted on such an immense extent of level and low-lying surface, would become excessive. Such an excessive elevation of temperature does, in fact, partially exist in the Great Sahara, forming the north-west corner of the continent. From the greater breadth of Africa to the north, and its vicinity to the neighbouring continents, the temperature of the northern portion is considerably above that of the southern. Egypt and the Cape Colony are in the same parallels of north and south latitude, but the southern colony has a much milder climate than that of Lower Egypt. The rivers of both regions are subject to periodical overflowings, but the flooding of the Nile prevails from June to September, while that of the

Orange River flowing through the Namaqua country, and the Fish River, and others which flow into the Indian Ocean, have their risings and floods in November and December, both being respectively influenced by the summer solstices of the northern and southern hemispheres.

During eight months of the year constant fine weather is prevalent throughout a great part of Africa. The sun rises every morning in a clear atmosphere, and spreads a clear glaring light over the whole country, too brilliant almost for the eye to sustain; no cloud casts a passing shadow over the landscape; and in the evening the orb of day sinks magnificently to rest. But the excessive heat diminishes the pleasure that otherwise would be felt in contemplating the glorious sky, and the first clouds which foretell the approach of rain are hailed with delight by the European resident overwhelmed by the oppressive heat.

African vegetation is less varied than that of Europe or Asia. Along the Mediterranean sea-board it greatly resembles that of Southern Europe. Thus the olive, orange, and citron of Tripoli and Algiers rival in luxuriance the similar productions of Andalusia and Valencia. The date-tree in Tripoli attains the height of one hundred feet, and bears clusters weighing from twenty to thirty pounds. The vegetation of Egypt is highly characterised, and presents many indigenous plants, which, even under the most imperfect developments, readily indicate the country to which they belong. The celebrated and classic lotus grows so abundantly in this country that some of its ancient inhabitants are represented to have made its fruit their principal article of subsistence; and thus they come to be distinguished by the Greeks as *Lotophagi*, or Lotus-eaters. The Nile produces many aquatic plants, which spread their large leaves over its surface, and gracefully rear their flowers above its waters.

The vegetation of Abyssinia appears to differ considerably

from that of the tropics, but it bears some affinity to that of the Mozambique coast, and of the Cape of Good Hope. Coffee grows indigenously on the African coast of the Red Sea, near Babelmandib, and in the interior to the south of Abyssinia. Certain palms are characteristic of different parts of Africa, and are of the greatest importance to the inhabitants. Such are the date-palm and the doom-palm which grow in the arid, sandy regions of the north, and the cocoa-palm and the oil-palm which flourish amid the tropical luxuriance of the west. A large quantity of oil is produced also from a plant of a very different description—the ground-nut, a leguminous, herbaceous plant, which has the remarkable peculiarity of thrusting its pod into the ground to ripen there, and which is now so extensively cultivated that ten millions of bushels of ground-nuts are annually exported from the Gambia. In the hot and humid districts of Senegambia, besides the productions common to the similar climates of Upper Egypt and Arabia, there are plants which have been considered peculiar to the Indian Archipelago, to Madagascar, and South America.

The tropical regions are not so rich in species of plants as those of South America, but still they exhibit many peculiar genera. South Africa presents one of those centres of vegetation which are, in some respects, distinct from other regions of the earth. Leguminous and euphorbiaceous plants abound. Every one is familiar with the splendid Cape heaths, which flourish more particularly in the coast districts, and become rarer in the interior. Numerous species of the cacti suit the aridity of the soil; and here the aloe plant flourishes. As we leave the coasts, and ascend .the terraces towards the interior, we pass gradually from tropical productions to those of the temperate zones, which all flourish well in several parts of Africa. Though the forests cannot rival those of Brazil, yet they are rich in valuable woods, especially the harder kinds—some of them excellent for shipbuilding. Ebony, certain kinds of rose-wood, and the timber called African teak, are among the productions of these forests. The butter-tree is one of the most remarkable productions of the central regions. Extensive level tracts are covered with the gay and graceful acacia, distilling those rich gums which constitute so important an item in African commerce. Here also flourishes the baobab in all its gigantic magnitude.

Gordon Cumming says of this tree:—"It is chiefly remarkable on account of its extraordinary size, resembling a castle or tower more than a forest tree. Throughout the country of Bamadgwato (lat. 22° S.) the average circumference of these trees was from thirty-five to forty feet; but on extending my researches in a north-easterly direction throughout the more fertile forests which clothe the many boundless tracts through which the river Limpopo winds, I daily met with specimens of this extraordinary tree, averaging from sixty to a hundred feet in circumference, and maintaining this thickness to a height from twenty to thirty feet, when they diverge into numerous goodly branches, whose general character is abrupt and horizontal, and which seem to terminate with a peculiar suddenness. The wood is soft and useless; the leaf similar to the sycamore: the fruit is a nut the size of a swan's egg. A remarkable fact in connection with these trees is the manner in which they are disposed throughout the forest. They are found standing singly or in rows, invariably at considerable distances from one another, as if planted by the hand of man; and from their wondrous size and unusual height (for they always tower high above their surrounding compeers), they convey the idea of being strangers or interlopers on the ground they occupy."

On the borders of Lake N'gami Livingstone found the wide-spreading baobab-tree, with trunks from seventy to seventy-six feet in circumference, Palmyra palms, the banyan-tree, and fruit trees, with fruit resembling the orange and plum. In the dry plains of the interior a succulent root is found which is of the utmost importance to the thirsty native. The stem appears above ground from three to four inches high, with small narrow leaves, and is in appearance somewhat like the dandelion. The bulbous root is about the size of a child's head, and is porous throughout, and full of pure limpid water. The bulb grows from eight to nine inches from the surface, and is eagerly searched out and dug up by the natives when, in their hunting expeditions, they are overcome by thirst. Several other succulent plants, with thick juicy leaves, are also found springing up from the dry-baked soil of the desert and a species of water-melon abounds in the Kalahari desert which also affords a cooling food for the natives. Most of these plants and roots form, too, the food of the numerous herds of antelopes; and even the elephant digs them up with his tusks and pliant trunk, and finds in them pleasant sustenance.

The fertile valleys of Africa, both in the tropical and temperate parts, are favourable to the productions of other countries. Maize is now extensively cultivated, as well as rice, wheat, and millet. Coffee grows luxuriantly, and of good quality. Indigo and tobacco are easily cultivated. Cotton has succeeded well where it has been introduced, as in Egypt, where, however, it requires artificial and laborious irrigation; while in the fertile and well-watered soil of Sennaar it flourishes even with a most careless style of cultivation, and might without doubt be produced in enormous quantity. Other regions, as Natal, are also likely to produce it abundantly. The vine is cultivated with success at the Cape of Good Hope, and the sugar-cane in different parts of the continent.

In his admirable survey of the geographical distribution of the mammalia, Wagner, dividing the globe into certain zoological provinces, takes the northern frontier of the

Sahara as a line between two distinct African provinces. This line coincides nearly with the parallel of 30° N. lat. ; all Africa south of it he makes the zoological province of Africa ; but those provinces situated on the north of it, and comprising Barbary and the other coast countries bordering on the Mediterranean, he includes within his European province, on the ground that, although African types still appear there, those of Europe are predominant. In this respect the Mediterranean separates North Africa from South Europe less than does the Sahara from the main part of Africa. Indeed, the entire basin of the Mediterranean, including the European, Asiatic, and African shores, is peculiar in itself, both as to animal and to vegetable life.

The configuration and character of the surface of Africa explains the peculiar fauna of quadrupeds of this country, which on the whole resembles that of the Turanian steppes. The forest-inhabiting deer are completely wanting, except in the transition province of Barbary, and they are replaced by the antelopes, which are more numerous here than anywhere else. Among the many and important varieties of the animal kingdom furnished by Africa the first place must be given to the lion. Then come the leopard, the hyena, the jackal ; a species of elephant, different in some respects from the Asiatic ; several species of the rhinoceros, the hippopotamus, the wart-hog, many kinds of monkeys, particularly within the tropics ; the giraffe, the zebra, and the quagga, and numerous species of the antelope, which, as we have intimated, occupy in African zoology the place of deer in other parts of the world. The gnu is one of the most remarkable of the antelope genus ; some of the species occasionally appear in prodigious numbers, devastating the fields of the colonists. The extraordinary swiftness of many of these animals, which enables them to seek their food at great distances, is peculiarly adapted to the immense plains of the country. The comparative scarcity of forests corresponds with that of the squirrel tribe, those that are found being mostly ground-squirrels. Mice are numerous, as are also hares, which latter prefers steppe-like country to woodland. Camels are said to have been introduced by the Arabs, and are plentiful in the northern regions. Among birds the ostrich is found in almost all parts of Africa; parrots also, flamingoes, guinea-fowls, and other representatives of the feather tribe are numerous. Crocodiles are found in the rivers; and many kinds of lizards and serpents occur, not a few of the latter being poisonous. There are also tortoises and turtles of different species.

Africa is the principal home of the lion, who here reigns undisturbed as king over the animal creation, while in Asia his power is divided with the tiger. He inhabits all parts of this continent, except the north-east portions, the Sahara, and those districts where European civilisation has won its ground. Over the more secluded parts of South Africa he is very generally diffused. He is, however, nowhere met with in great abundance, it being very rare to meet more than three, or even two, families of lions frequenting the same district and drinking at the same fountain, except in times of great drought. It is a common thing to find a full-grown lion and lioness associating with two or three young ones nearly full-grown; at other times full-grown males, to the number of three or four, may be found associating and hunting together in amicable alliance. There is something so noble and imposing in the presence of the lion when seen walking with dignified self-possession, free and undaunted, on his native soil, that no description can convey an adequate idea of his striking appearance. The male lion is adorned with a long, thick, shaggy mane, which in some instances almost sweeps the ground. The colour of these manes varies—some being very dark, and others of a golden yellow; the colour being generally influenced by age. He attains his mane in his third year; at first it is yellowish, in the prime of life it is blackish, and when he has numbered many years, but still is in the full enjoyment of his power, it assumes a yellowish-grey pepper-and-salt sort of colour. When old, lions are cunning and dangerous, and most to be dreaded. The females are entirely destitute of a mane, being covered with a short, thick, glossy coat of tawny hair. The manes and coats of lions frequenting open-lying districts entirely free from trees, such as the borders of the great Kalahari Desert, are more rank and beautiful than those inhabiting forest districts. No one who has once heard the deep-toned thunder of the lion's roar can ever mistake it; it is extremely grand and peculiarly striking. It consists at times of a low deep moaning, often repeated, ending in faintly audible sighs; at other times he strikes the forest with loud deep-toned solemn roars, repeated five or six times in quick succession, each increasing in loudness to the third or fourth, when his voice dies away in low muffled sounds, very much resembling distant thunder. At times, and not unfrequently, a troop may be heard roaring in concert, one assuming the lead, and two or more regularly taking up their parts, like persons singing a catch. They roar loudest in cold frosty nights; but on no occasion are their voices to be heard in such perfection as when two or three strange parties approach a fountain to drink at the same time. As a general rule lions roar during the night, commencing in the evening, and continuing at intervals until the morning. In hazy and rainy weather they are to be heard at every hour in the day, but their roar is subdued. It often happens that when two strange lions meet at a fountain a terrible combat ensues, which sometimes ends in the death of one of them. The habits of the lion are strictly nocturnal; during the day he lies concealed beneath the shade of a low bushy tree or wide-spreading bush, either in the level forest or mountain side. He is also partial to lofty reeds, or fields of long rank yellow grass, such as occur in low-lying valleys. From these haunts he sallies forth when the sun goes down and commences his nightly prowl. When he is successful in his beat, and has secured his prey, he does not roar much that night, only uttering occasionally a few low moans. Unlike other quadrupeds, he seems unwilling to visit the fountains during moonlight; so that when the moon rises early he defers his watering till the morning, and when the moon rises late he drinks at an early hour in the night. Though considerably under four feet in height, he has little difficulty in dashing to the ground and overcoming the lofty and apparently powerful giraffe. The lion is the constant attendant of vast herds of buffaloes; and a full-grown lion, so long as his teeth remain unbroken, generally proves a match for an old bull buffalo, which in size and strength greatly surpasses the most powerful breed of our English cattle. The lion also preys on all the larger varieties of the antelope, and on both varieties of the gnu. The zebra also is a favourite object of his pursuit. The female is more fierce and active than the male; and lionesses which have never had young are much more dangerous than those that have. At no time is the lion so much to be dreaded as when his partner has got small young ones. At that season he knows no fear, and in the coolest and most intrepid manner will face a thousand men.

The African elephant differs from the Asiatic in his rounder head and more convex forehead, his larger ears, and the lozenge-marked surface of his grinders; the tusks are also longer; while the female elephant of Africa is furnished with tusks as well as the male, though smaller. The elephant is widely distributed over the forests of South Africa, but does not attain so large a size there as in the more tropical parts of that continent. The male is much larger than the female, and is furnished with tapering and beautifully-arched tusks from six to eight feet long. Old bull elephants are found singly or in pairs, or sometimes in herds of six to twenty. The younger bulls remain for many years in company with their mothers, and then form large herds of twenty to a hundred. The elephant feeds on the branches, leaves, and roots of trees, and also on various bulbous roots, which he finds out by his exquisite smell and digs up with his tusks. Whole acres of ground may be seen thus ploughed up. He passes the greater part of the day and night in feeding, and consumes an immense quantity of food; roaming over a vast extent of surface, and making choice of the greenest spots of the forest. When a district becomes parched and barren he will forsake it for years, and wander to great distances in search of food and water. In his wild state he entertains a great horror of man, and a single human being, even a child, by passing between them and the wind, will put a hundred to flight. When a single troop has been attacked by the hunter, all the other elephants of the district become aware of the circumstance in a few days, and a general migration takes place to more frequented grounds. They keep themselves more secluded than any other wild quadrupeds, with the exception of some rare species of antelope, choosing the most remote and lonely depths of the forest, generally at a great distance from the rivers and fountains to which they resort at night to drink. In dry, warm weather they make nightly visits to the drinking fountains; in cool and moist weather they drink only once every third or fourth day. They commence their march at sunset, and travel from twelve to twenty miles; they generally reach the water between the hours of nine and midnight, when, having satisfied their thirst, and cooled their bodies by spouting large quantities of water over their backs with their trunks, they resume their way back into the depths of the forest. When in places of perfect security, the old bulls lie down to sleep for a few hours on their sides, generally leaning against the large hill of the white ant. The females rarely lie down, and both males and females, when liable to disturbance, always keep standing beneath some shady tree. Having rested themselves they then proceed to feed. Spreading out from one another in a zigzag course, they smash and destroy all the forest trees which happen to be in their way; and the devastation which a herd of bull elephants will produce in this manner is almost incredible. They are extremely capricious, breaking down whole groups of trees, and perhaps tasting only one or two small branches, leaving the trunks lying prostrate in all directions. During the night they will feed in open plains and thinly-wooded districts; but as day dawns they return to the dense coverts, and here they remain, drawn up in a compact herd, while the heat of the day lasts. The pace of the elephant, when undisturbed, is a bold, free, sweeping step; and from the peculiar spongy formation of his foot, his tread is extremely light and inaudible, and all his movements are attended with a peculiar gentleness and grace. This, however, only applies to the elephant when roaming undisturbed in his jungle, for when roused by the hunter he proves the most dangerous enemy, and far more difficult to conquer than any other beast of chase. The tusk of an elephant weighs from a hundred to a hundred and fifty or seventy pounds; and the price of the ivory in the English market is from £28 to £32 per hundredweight. The native Bechuanas devour the flesh of the elephant with great avidity, regarding the legs, when cooked after a peculiar fashion, a special delicacy; they also make water-bags of its inner skin.

The largest and best known species of the hippopotamus is found in almost all parts of Africa, to which quarter of the globe it is entirely confined. A smaller species has recently been described as an inhabitant of the rivers of Western Africa within the tropics, and is said to differ remarkably from the common species in having only two incisors, instead of four, in the lower jaw. The common hippopotamus is one of the largest of existing quadrupeds, the bulk of its body being little inferior to that of the elephant; although its legs are so short that its belly almost touches the ground, and its height is not much above five feet, it is extremely aquatic in its habits, living mostly in lakes or rivers, often in tidal estuaries, where the saltness of the water compels it to resort to springs for the purpose of drinking, and sometimes even in the sea, although it never proceeds to any considerable distance from the shore. Its skin is very thick—on the back and sides more than two inches; it is dark-brown, destitute of hair, and exudes in great abundance from its numerous pores a thickish oily fluid, by which it is kept constantly lubricated. The neck is short and thick; the head very large, with small ears and small eyes placed high, so that they are easily raised above water without much of the animal being exposed to view. The respiration of the hippopotamus is slow, and thus it is enabled to spend much of its time under water, only coming to the surface at intervals to breathe. It swims and dives with great ease, and often walks along the bottom completely under water. Its food consists chiefly of the plants which grow in shallow waters and about the margins of lakes and rivers. It often, however, leaves the water to feed on the banks, and makes inroads on cultivated fields, cutting grass or corn as if it were done with a scythe, and devouring and trampling the crops. The flesh is highly esteemed; the fat, of which there is a thick layer immediately under the skin, is a favourite African delicacy, and when salted is known at the Cape of Good Hope as *Zee-koe-speck*—that is, Lake-cow-bacon. The tongue and the jelly made from the feet are also much prized. The hide is used for a variety of purposes; and the great canine teeth are particularly valuable as ivory, and form a very considerable article of African commerce.

There are four varieties of the rhinoceros in South Africa, distinguished by the Bechuanas by the names of *borele* or black rhinoceros, the *keitloa* or two-horned black rhinoceros, the *muchocho* or common white rhinoceros, and the *kobaoba* or long-horned white rhinoceros. The latter is in all probability the "reem" or unicorn of Scripture, the forehead being furnished with a long curved horn, which projects in front, with a small rudimentary horn behind. Both varieties of the black rhinoceros are extremely fierce and dangerous, and rush headlong and unprovoked at any object which attracts their attention. They never grow fat, and their flesh is tough and not much esteemed. They feed almost entirely on the thorny branches of an acacia. Their horns are short, seldom exceeding eighteen inches in length; while those of *kobaoba*, or white rhinoceros, often exceed four feet. The horns are merely connected to the skin, not to the bone of the head; they are solid, hard, and capable of receiving a fine polish. During the heat of the day the rhinoceros will be found asleep, or standing indolently in some retired part of the forest; in the evening he commences his nightly rambles, and visits the fountains and waterpools. The black rhinoceros is subject to paroxysms of unprovoked fury, often ploughing up the ground for several yards with his horns and assaulting large bushes in the most violent manner. Both kinds of the white rhinoceros are considerably larger than the black, nearly equalling in size the elephant; they feed solely on grass, and carry much fat; they are less swift, but more gentle in their dispositions than the others, and have longer heads, which they carry low when running. The rhinoceros, as well as the hippopotamus, has a singular parasite, the rhinoceros-bird, of a greyish colour and nearly the size of a thrush, which perches on the backs of these huge animals, and feeds on the ticks or insects attached to the skin. When an enemy approaches, these watchful birds give the alarm by ascending about six feet into the air, and uttering a loud scream, wakening the leviathan from his soundest nap.   Day and night these birds adhere to the back of their patron, and even when pursued and scrambling through brushwood, if a branch of a tree happen to jerk them off, they assiduously fly forwards and regain their position.

If the lion claims the title of the king, the giraffe may well be called the queen of African quadrupeds.   Though gigantic in size, its exquisite beauty, and softness and gentleness of manners, may well entitle it to this feminine pre-eminence.   In the forests not molested by man they are found in herds of from twelve to sixteen, sometimes even thirty and forty, but sixteen is the average number.   These herds are composed of individuals of various sizes, from the young of twelve feet in height to the dark chestnut coloured old bull, whose majestic head towers to the height of twenty feet.   The females are of low stature, and more delicately formed than the males, and average from sixteen to seventeen feet.   Some writers have discovered ugliness and a want of grace in the giraffe; but Mr. Cumming says that it is one of the most strikingly beautiful animals in creation; and that when a herd of them is seen scattered through a grove of the picturesque parasol-topped acacias which adorn the native plains, and on whose uppermost shoots they are enabled to browse by the colossal height with which nature has so admirably endowed them, he must indeed be slow of conception who fails to discover both grace and dignity in their movements.   As is the case with many other defenceless animals, their colour, too, seems to be admirably in unison with the grounds over which they roam; for even the sharp-sighted natives often at some distance fail to discover their spotted chestnut forms amid the decayed trunks of trees and brown herbage.

Africa is the country of antelopes, unquestionably the most lively, graceful, and beautifully-proportioned of the brute creation.   Wherever they are known, they have attracted the attention and admiration of mankind from the earliest ages ; and the beauty of their dark and lustrous eyes affords a frequent theme to the poetical imaginings of the eastern poets.   Their names are of frequent occurrence in the most ancient of the Oriental mythologies, and their figures occur amongst the oldest of the astronomical symbols. One of the largest of the African antelopes is the bubale, equal in size to a stag.   It congregates in troops, among which frequent and sometimes fatal combats take place. This species was well known to the ancients, and it is represented among the hieroglyphical figures of the temples of Upper Egypt.   It inhabits Barbary and the Great Desert of Northern Africa.   The blue antelope formerly met with in the Cape Colony is now so rare in Southern Africa that no specimen has been killed there since the year 1799.   Its history and manners are little known.   Some travellers are disposed to regard it as merely a variety of the roan antelope, which is a very large animal, measuring nearly eight feet in length, and which was found by Mr. Burchell among the mountainous plains in the vicinity of Lattakoo. The Caffrarian oryx or gemsbok is about the most beautiful and remarkable of the antelope tribe.   It inhabits elevated forests and the rocky regions of the south, and is exceedingly fierce during the rutting-season, especially when wounded.   A friend of Major Smith having fired at one of these animals, it immediately turned upon his dogs and transfixed one of them upon the spot.   The oryx affords the best venison, next to that of the eland, found in that part of Africa.   It possesses the erect mane, long sweeping black tail, and general appearance of the horse, with the head and hoofs of the antelope, and long projecting horns.   Its height is about that of the ass, and colour nearly the same.   The beautiful black bands which adorn its head, giving it the appearance of wearing a stall-collar, together with the

manner in which the rump and thighs are painted impart
to it a character peculiar to itself. It thrives in the most
barren regions, and is perfectly independent of water, which,
according to Cumming, it never by any chance tastes. The
eland is the largest and finest species of antelope, being
equal in size to a large ox, and its flesh is tender and
highly palatable. It lives for a long time without water,
and frequents the borders of the Kalahari Desert in herds
varying from ten to a hundred. The springbok inhabits the
plains of Southern and Central Africa, and assembles in
vast flocks during its migratory movements. These migra-
tions, which are said to take place in their most numerous
form only at the intervals of several years, appear to come
from the north-east, and in masses of many thousands,
devouring like locusts every green herb. The lion has been
seen to migrate, and walk in the midst of the compressed
phalanx, with only as much space between him and his
victims as the fears of those immediately around could
procure by pressing outwards. The foremost of these vast
columns are fat, and the rear exceedingly lean, while the
direction continues one way; but with the change of the
monsoon, when they return towards the north, the rear
become the leaders, fattening in their turn, and leaving the
others to starve, and to be devoured by the numerous enemies
who follow their march. At all times, when impelled by
fear either of the hunter or the beast of prey darting among
the flock, but principally when the herds are assembled
in countless multitudes, so that an alarm cannot spread
rapidly and open the means of flight, they are pressed
against each other, and their anxiety to escape impels them
to bound up in the air, shewing at the same time the white
spot on the croup dilated by the effort, and closing again in
their descent, and producing that beautiful effect from which
they have obtained the name of springbok and showybok.
Cumming says: "That the extraordinary manner in which

springboks are capable of springing is best seen when they are chased by a dog. On these occasions away start the herd with a succession of strange perpendicular bounds, rising with curved loins high into the air, and at the same time elevating the showy folds of long white hair on their haunches and along their back, which imparts to them a peculiar fairy-like appearance different from any other animal; they bound to the height of ten or twelve feet with the elasticity of an india-rubber ball, clearing at each spring from twelve to fifteen feet of ground without apparently the slightest exertion. In performing the spring, they appear for an instant as if suspended in the air, when down come all four feet together, and striking the plain, away they soar again as if about to take flight. The herd only adopt this motion for a few hundred yards, when they subside into a light elastic trot, arching their graceful necks and lowering their noses to the ground, as if in sportive mood. Presently pulling up, they face about and reconnoitre the object of their alarm. In passing any plain or waggon-road on which men have lately trod, the springbok invariably clears it by a single surprising bound; and when a herd of perhaps many thousands have to cross a track of the sort it is extremely beautiful to see how each antelope performs this feat—so suspicious are they of the ground on which their enemy, man, has trodden."

The only species of the buffalo peculiar to Africa is the *Bos caffer*, or Cape buffalo, the *qu'araho* of the Hottentots, a fierce and vindictive animal, of great strength. This species is characterised by the dark rufous colour of his horns, which spread horizontally over the summit of his head, with their beams bent laterally and their points turned up. They are from eight to ten inches broad at the base, and divided only by a slight groove, are extremely ponderous, cellular near the root, and five feet long, measured from tip to tip along the curves. The hide is black and almost naked, especially in old animals. This buffalo lives in herds or small families in the brushwood or open forests. According to Sparrman, he is not content with simply killing the person whom he attacks, but he stands over him for some time in order to trample him with his hoofs and heels, crushing him also with his knees, and tearing to pieces and mangling his whole body, and finally stripping off the skin with his tongue. The surest way to escape is, if possible, to ride up a hill, as the great bulk of the buffalo's body, like that of the elephant, is a weight sufficient to prevent his vieing with the slender and fine-limbed horse in swiftness. It is said, however, that in descending this formidable animal gets on much faster than the horse.

The zebra is one of the most fancifully adorned of all known quadrupeds; but the beauty of its external appearance is its chief merit, as its disposition is wayward and capricious in the extreme. The mountain-zebra is scarcely ever seen in the low countries. The zebra of the plains is a better known and more abundant species than the other. It is chiefly distinguished by the want of rings upon the legs. The quagga is more nearly allied to the zebra of the plains than to that of the mountains. It lives in troops in the neighbourhood of the Cape, and in common with the zebra is frequently found in company with ostriches. The wary disposition of these birds, and their great quickness of sight, are supposed to be serviceable to the congregated group in warning them of the approach of their enemies.

The camel, or "ship of the desert," as it is beautifully called in the figurative language of the Arabs, has spread from Arabia all over the northern parts of Africa, and has long been essential to the commerce of those dry and desert regions. It has been well said : "That to the wild Arab of the desert the camel is all that his necessities require. He feeds on the flesh, drinks the milk, makes clothes and tents of the hair ; belts, sandals, saddles, and buckets of the hide ;

he conveys himself and family on his back, makes his pillow on his side, and his shelter of him against the whirlwind of sand. Crouched in a circle around him his camels form a fence, and in battle an entrenchment, behind which his family and property are obstinately, and often successfully, defended." The ancient authors do not seem to take notice of the camel as an inhabitant of Northern Africa. It is however mentioned in Genesis as among the gifts bestowed by Pharaoh on Abram, and must therefore have been well known over the banks of the Nile at an early period.

Vague accounts of apes of great size, and of which very wonderful stories were told, were from time to time brought from Western Africa, but it was not till 1849 that the gorilla became really known to naturalists, when a skull was sent to Dr. Savage of Boston by Dr. Wilson, an American missionary on the Gaboon River. Since that time not only have skeletons and skulls been obtained in sufficient number for scientific examination, but information has also been secured concerning the habits of the animal in its native haunts. The accounts of the gorilla given in Du Chaillu's " Explorations and Adventures in Equatorial Africa," are regarded by the highest scientific authorities, and particularly by Owen, as in the main trustworthy, and there is little doubt that they are in accordance with all that we have learned from other sources. The height of an adult male is commonly about five feet six inches, or five feet eight inches, although there is reason to think that it sometimes exceeds six feet. It has a black skin, covered with short, dark-grey hair, reddish-brown on the head; the hair on the arms longer, that on the arm from the shoulder to the elbow pointing downwards, and that on the fore-arm pointing upwards to the elbow, where a tuft is formed. The face is covered with hair, but the chest is bare. There is scarcely any appearance of neck. The eyes are deeply sunk beneath the projecting ridge of the skull, giving to the countenance a savage scowl, the aspect of ferocity being aggravated by the frequent exhibition of the teeth. The belly is large and prominent; in accordance with which character the gorilla is represented as a most voracious feeder, its food being exclusively vegetable—partly obtained by climbing trees and partly on the ground. It is very fond of fruits and of some leaves, as the fleshy parts of the leaves of the pineapple; and employs its great strength of jaws and teeth in tearing vegetable substances, and cracking nuts which would require a heavy blow of a hammer. It is not gregarious in its habits. It spends most of its time on the ground, although often climbing trees. It is capable of defending itself against almost any beast of prey, and is much dreaded by the people of the countries in which it is found, although by some of the tribes its flesh is sought after for food. It has a kind of barking voice, varying when it is enraged to a terrific roar. It is only found in regions where fresh water is abundant, and inhabits exclusively the densest parts of the forests.

To these brief descriptions of the history and habits of some of the more remarkable quadrupeds of Africa others might have been added, but our space forbids their introduction. The great preponderance of the antelope tribe, the existence of the giraffe, and the hippopotamus, and the gorilla, and the numerous troops of equine animals, such as the zebra and the quagga, may be stated as forming the principal zoological characters of this extensive continent, so far as concerns the mammiferous tribes.

The arid and wide-spread plains which compose so large a portion of the continent of Africa are unfavourable to the existence and multiplication of the feathered race. Yet the more umbrageous banks of the rivers, the extensive forests which here and there impede the drifting of the desert-sand, and those green and grateful oases which towards evening cast their far-stretching shadows across a waterless land, harbour in their cool recesses many a gorgeous form of the winged creation; nor are the mountain summits, and those *sierras* which occasionally interrupt the horizontal view of the bleached wilderness, uninhabited by birds of prey, eagle-eyed and swift of wing, there perched securely amid their rocky fortresses, but ever ready to descend with voracious cry when the blast of the simoon overwhelms the exhausted caravan.

The first place must be given to a species which not only forms the most remarkable character in the ornithology of Africa, to which country it is probably peculiar, but presents in itself the most singular example of the feathered race. This extraordinary creature is the ostrich, the tallest of its class, and probably the swiftest of all running animals. It is distinguished from all other birds by having only two toes on each foot, though the bones or rudiments of a third toe are said to have been perceived beneath the skin. It inhabits the open and sandy plain of a great extent of Africa, from Barbary to the Cape of Good Hope, and being consequently a native of one of the most anciently-peopled countries of the earth, it has excited the attention of mankind from the remotest periods of antiquity. It is frequently mentioned in the Book of Job, and in other portions of the Old Testament. Herodotus, among the early Greek writers, was acquainted with its history and appearance, and in later times it was frequently exhibited by the Romans in their games. Adanson narrates an occurrence as having taken place at Podor, a French factory on the southern bank of the river Niger, which exemplifies the great strength and swiftness of this bird. "Two ostriches," he says, "which had been about two years in the factory, and although young, were nearly of their full size, were so tame that two little blacks mounted, both together, on the back of the largest; no sooner did he feel their weight than he began to run as fast as possible, and carried them several times around the village, as it was impossible to stop him otherwise than by obstructing the passage. This sight pleased me so much that I ordered it to be repeated; and to try their strength, directed a full-grown negro to mount the smallest, and two others the largest. This burden did not seem at all disproportioned to their strength. At first they went at a tolerably sharp trot, but when they became heated a little, they expanded their wings as though to catch the wind, and moved with such fleetness that they scarcely seemed to touch the ground. Most people have, one time or another, seen a partridge run, and consequently must know that there is no man whatever able to keep up with it, and it is easy to imagine that if this bird had a longer step its speed would be considerably augmented. The ostrich moves like the partridge, with this advantage; and I am satisfied that those I am speaking of would have distanced the fleetest racehorses that were ever bred in England. It is true they would not hold out so long as a horse, but they would undoubtedly be able to go over the space in less time. I have frequently beheld this sight, which is capable of giving one an idea of the prodigious strength of the ostrich, of shewing what use it might be of had we but the method of breaking and managing it as we do the horse." In spite of its speed, it is successfully hunted by men on horseback, who take advantage of its habit of running in a curve instead of a straight line, so that the hunters know how to proceed in order to meet it and get within shot. It is often killed in South Africa by men who envelop themselves in ostrich skins, and admirably imitating the manners of the ostrich, approach it near enough for their purpose without exciting its alarm, and sometimes kill one after another with their poisoned arrows. The ostrich feeds exclusively on vegetable substances; its food consists in great part of grasses and their seeds, so that its visits are much dreaded by the cultivators of the soil in the vicinity of its haunts. It swallows large stones, as small birds swallow grains of sand, to aid the gizzard in the trituration of its food. It is patient of thirst, and is capable of subsisting for a long time without water. The eggs of the ostrich are much esteemed as an article of food by the natives of Africa, and are acceptable even to European travellers and colonists. Each egg weighs about three pounds, and is thus equal to about two dozen ordinary hen's eggs. The egg is usually dressed by being set upright on a fire, and stirred about with a forked stick inserted through a hole in the upper end. The long plumes of the ostrich have been highly valued for ornamental purposes from very early times, and continue to be a considerable article of commerce, for the sake of which the bird is pursued in its native wilds.

The gigantic stork is sometimes seen in Africa upwards of six feet in height. It is very common in many of the interior parts of the continent, and is called *marabou* in Senegal. According to Major Denham, it is protected by the inhabitants on account of its services as a scavenger; its appetite being most voracious, and nothing coming amiss to its omnivorous propensities.

Of the numerous hawks, a smaller species of the falcon tribe which inhabit this continent, we shall allude only to the chanting-falcon. It must not be supposed, from the name of this bird, that its notes in any way resemble the harmonious notes of the nightingale, or even those of our less celebrated songsters. Its voice is merely a little clearer than usual, although it seems impressed with a high idea of its own powers. It will sit for half-a-day perched upon the summit of a high tree uttering incessant cries, which the darkness of night is sometimes insufficient to terminate. It builds in the forests of the interior, and commits great havoc among quails and partridges.

Considerable discrepancies have occurred among many naturalists regarding the habits of another African bird—the indicator, moroc, or honey-bird, a species allied to the cuckoo. Sparrman asserts that he frequently watched the habits of the bird, which, with a particular cry, attracts the attention of man and guides him to the nests of bees. La Vaillant doubts this altogether, while Barrow again, an accurate observer, confirms the statement of Sparrman. Cumming says of this bird: "I saw to-day, for the first time, the honey-bird. This extraordinary little bird, which is about the size of a chaffinch, and of a light-grey colour, will invariably lead a person following it to a wild bee's nest. Chattering and twittering in a state of great excitement, it perches on a branch beside the traveller, endeavouring by various wiles to attract his attention; and having succeeded in doing so, it flies lightly forward, in a wavy course, in the direction of the bee's nest, alighting every now and then and looking back to ascertain if the traveller is following it, all the time keeping up an incessant twitter. When at length it arrives at the hollow tree, or deserted white-ants' hill, which contains the honey, it for a moment hovers over the nest, pointing to it with its bill, and then takes up its position on a neighbouring branch anxiously waiting its share of the spoil. When the honey is taken, which is accomplished by first stupefying the bees by burning grass at the entrance of their domicile, the honey-bird will often lead to a second and even a third nest. The person thus following it ought to whistle. The savages in the interior, whilst in pursuit, have several charmed sentences which they use on the occasion."

Bunbury describes another bird called the Cape honey-sucker, not much bigger than a wren, of a brownish colour, with a tail of many fine, long, soft, wavy feathers, three or four times as long as the body, the beak slender and arched. "Many of these birds," he says, "were feeding on the blossoms of an American aloe by the road-side, thrusting their bills into the flowers and sucking the honey. They do not, however, feed on the wing like humming-birds, but while perching; their flight is short, jerking, and unsteady, as if they were embarrassed by the length of their trains."

Of the other birds of Africa—the secretary-bird and the beautiful jacana, with its long claws, darting nimbly over the broad leaves of aquatic plants as if it walked on the water; the weaver-bird, sewing the long leaves together with the threads of the spider's web to form its nest; the several varieties of cranes, herons, spoonbills, fish-hawks, kingfishers, pigeons, turtle-doves, canaries, martins, &c., we can in these notes only mention them, as their variety and species are so numerous.

A brief account must suffice here of a very limited number of African reptiles. The common crocodile, celebrated in the ancient history of Egypt, is spread over a considerable extent of this continent. The Nile, however, is the best known haunt of this terrible creature. The crocodile feeds on fish, floating carrion, and dogs, or other animals, which it is enabled to surprise as they come to drink at the water's edge; but man frequently falls a victim to its voracity. In revenge for this treatment all nations persecuted with this pest have devised various methods of killing it. The negroes of some parts of Africa are sufficiently bold and skilful to attack the crocodile in its own element. They fearlessly plunge into the water, and diving beneath the crocodile, plunge the dagger with which they are armed into the creature's belly, which is not protected by the coat of mail that guards the other parts of its body. The usual plan is to lie in wait near the spot where the crocodile is accustomed to repose. This is usually a sandy bank, and the hunter digs a hole in the sand, and armed with a sharp harpoon, patiently awaits the coming of his expected prey. The crocodile comes to its accustomed spot and is soon asleep, when it is suddenly aroused by the harpoon, which penetrates completely through the scaly covering. The hunter immediately retreats to a canoe, and hauls at the line attached to the harpoon until he drags the crocodile to the surface, when he darts a second harpoon. The struggling animal is soon wearied out, dragged to shore, and despatched by dividing the spinal cord. In order to prevent the infuriated reptile from biting the cord asunder, it is composed of about thirty small lines, not twisted, but only bound together at intervals of two feet. When on land it is not difficult to escape the crocodile, as certain projections on the vertebræ of the neck prevent it from turning its head to any great extent. The eggs of this creature are very small, hardly exceeding those of a goose; numbers are annually destroyed by birds of prey and quadrupeds, especially the ichneumon.

The common chameleon is plentifully found in Northern Africa. It lives in trees, but exhibits none of the activity usually found in arboreal reptiles; on the contrary, its movements are absurdly grave and solemn. The whole activity of the animal seems to be centered in its tongue, by means of which organ it secures flies and other insects with such marvellous rapidity that the ancients may be well pardoned for their assertion that the air formed the only food of the chameleon. Highly exaggerated descriptions have been given of the changes of colour in this animal. The changes are by no means so complete, nor are the colours so bright, as generally supposed. The power of the chameleon to move its eyes in different directions at the same time gives it a most singular aspect. Its enormously long tongue can be withdrawn into the mouth when not in use; but when the creature sees a fly within reach, the tongue is instantly darted forth, and by means of a gummy secretion at the tip secures the fly. The whole movement is so quick as almost to elude the eye.

The puff-adder is an inhabitant of Southern Africa. It is a short, thick, flattish snake, of a most sinister and malignant aspect. The following alarming adventure occurred to Mr. Cole, a resident at the Cape :—"I was going," he says, "quickly to bed one evening, wearied by a long day's hunting, when close to my feet and by my bed-side some glittering substance caught my eye. I stooped to pick it up; but ere my hand quite reached it the truth flashed across me—it was a snake! Had I followed my first natural impulse I should have sprung away, but not being able clearly to see in what position the reptile was lying, or which way his head was pointed, I controlled myself, and remained rooted breathless to the spot. Straining my eyes, but moving not an inch, I at length clearly distinguished a huge puff-adder—the most deadly snake in the colony, whose bite would have sent me to the other world in an hour or two. I watched him in silent horror; his head was from me; so much the worse—for this snake, unlike any other, always rises and strikes back. He did not move—he was asleep. Not daring to shuffle my feet lest he should awake and spring upon me, I took a jump backwards that would have done honour to a gymnastic master, and thus darted outside the door of the room; with a thick stick I returned and settled his worship."

The first, and by far the most considerable object of African export in modern times, is the human species, and to their eternal disgrace, Europeans have been the principal abettors in this most atrocious traffic. In some years as many as upwards of a hundred and twenty thousand slaves have been transported from the shores of Africa across the Atlantic. The victims of the foreign slave trade have been drawn chiefly from the tribes inhabiting the heights of Central Africa, while the slave-marts of the Barbary States, Egypt, and Arabia, have been kept plentifully supplied from Nubia, Abyssinia, and the unexplored districts to the south of these countries. Among the causes which have retarded the progress of the commerce and civilisation in Africa, no doubt slavery has been one of the chief, if not the chiefest of all.

Grievous as are the physical evils endured by Africa, there is yet a more lamentable feature in her condition. Bound in the chains of the grossest ignorance, she is the prey to the most savage superstitions. Christianity has made but feeble inroads on this kingdom of darkness; nor can she exercise much sway so long as the traffic in man pre-occupies the ground. Were this obstacle removed, Africa would present one of the finest fields for the labour of Christian missionaries which the world has yet opened to them. To this noble end Livingstone devoted his heroic life; and this is the object still in view by the best friends of Africa. To raise that great continent from the dust is an object worthy of the efforts of the highest order of ambition. The most patriotic and loyal British subject cannot cherish a loftier wish for our country and our beloved Queen than that her reign, which in its dawn witnessed the deliverance of our colonies from slavery, may be prolonged till, through British agency, Africa shall also be released from a still greater curse.

Printed by WALTER SCOTT, "*The Kenilworth Press,*" *Felling, Newcastl*

www.ingramcontent.com/pod-product-compliance
Lightning Source LLC
Chambersburg PA
CBHW021752110726
47902CB00006B/1499